Erosion

Greg McLaughlin

Dedicated:
To my childhood best friends
Mike, Marc, Benji and Joey,
circa 1978-1984

Also, to Sarah, Consie
and so many others.

Greg McLaughlin sees the world and questions what he sees. He seeks to capture the beauty and meaning of the people and places around him. And he aims to understand and investigate the delicate relationships and bonds between family, friends, lovers and strangers.

He lives in Greenwich, CT with his wife, and he has two adult sons. He graduated in 1991 with a degree in English, Creative Writing and a minor in Film Studies from Rhode Island College, where he also wrote, directed and starred, along with a talented troop of comic actors, in his own original sketch comedy television show called LATEST WITH GREGORY. He later earned his MBA at the University of Connecticut, and has pursued a 25-year career in Journalism, Marketing, Business Operations and Management Consulting.

He's written full-length fictional novels and screenplays for the past twenty years, recently publishing all eight novels as well as a personal memoir on Amazon. His published novels include four social-political thrillers; THE SECOND COMING, THE THIRD PARTY, BROKEN ENGLISH and UNDER THE AURORA, two dramatic romantic comedies; THE CURVE IN THE ROAD, and THE TRIPLE DATE and two family-oriented dramedies; THE B TEAM, MATUNUCK and his latest, EROSION.

His inspirational personal memoir, HEADLOCK, tells the story of his recent mission to lose 80 pounds, rebuild the strength he had in his 20's as an elite NCAA collegiate wrester and battle the ravages of time to return to top athletic shape - all in his late 40's - in a bid to ultimately compete in the USA Wrestling Senior National Championship.

His latest novel, EROSION is a follow-up to his best-selling first installment of a newly emerging series called, MATUNUCK. It continues his most deeply personal and emotional story, inspired by the summers he spent in the quaint Rhode Island beach community throughout the 1970's, 80's and 90's. Related to prominent Matunuck families such as the Galloglys, Terrys, Gambles, Mullaneys, Clarkins and Aherns, he spent his summers at a stretch of beach between Green Hill and Deep Hole called Matunuck with his grandparents, several great aunts and uncles and countless cousins, who all either lived in town year-round, stayed for the summer, or rented.

The story captures the struggle to keep love and beauty alive in the face of pain and difficulty.

Special Thanks:
John McLaughlin, Beta Reader
Sarah Campagnone, Copyeditor
David H Sherman, Cover Photo

Contact:
Greg McLaughlin
E-Mail: gdm126@outlook.com
Facebook: https://www.facebook.com/greg.mclaughlin.501
LinkedIn: https://www.linkedin.com/in/gregmclaughlin/
Twitter: https://twitter.com/GMcLaughlin126
Amazon: https://www.amazon.com/~/e/B08P578YTC

Chapter 1

Shelly Newsome lounged on the wraparound porch of the Matunuck Inn-By-The-Sea. She watched the gentle sloping ripples of the vast Atlantic Ocean wander toward the shore and calmly dissipate into the bright, golden sand. Beyond the break of the unusually small surf of the day, the bright blue fabric of the sea crinkled and stretched like an endless tarp waving listlessly in the morning breeze. It stretched from shore to horizon, meeting the cloudless sky just below the brim of Shelly's floppy hat.

The powerful summer sun radiated the gentle swells as they eased forward in a slow, rhythmic cadence. Cobalt blue against the rich azure sky, the lethargic sea lulled her into a melancholy peace as if Mother Atlantic sleeping late on a quiet summer morning. Shelly had come to expect the loud crash of the typically larger Matunuck waves. But, the lazy surf of her soothing Saturday morning made barely a murmur as they caressed the sand and slid quietly up the slope of the beach.

One of the most serene August days Shelly could recall, the modest rollers ambled toward the shore from the depths of the sea as if in slow motion. The aftermath of each wave raked the sandy pebbles beyond the break, alternating between an eager flow up the incline and a reluctant retreat back to the gravity of the sea.

Shelly watched the seagulls dance and dip through the sky. Children dug holes in the sand while their parents sat in squat folding chairs, surrounded by plastic coolers and tall umbrellas. A spry, young dog chased a tennis ball as it bounced along the hard sand by the break of the waves. The pup clenched the wet, slimy orb and proudly pranced it back to his owner, only to repeat the exercise numerous times as they moved out of sight. Two young boys frolicked in the surf, splashing in the break of each wave, oblivious to the world around them. Two young girls, close in age to the boys, tread water nearby, whispering and giggling.

A pair of teenagers, one in long red shorts, the other in a skimpy floral bikini walked by the porch, hand-in-hand, disappearing around the bend of the dunes.

Shelly sipped her coffee. The gusty wind off Cards Pond next to her property ruffled the brim of her hat. Her wispy blond hair flapped across her cheek and into her eyes.

The ten-room inn behind her rested in the summer breeze. Empty of clients, her guests had all eaten and exited to their adventures for the day. As with most gorgeous summer mornings, the premises of her inn remained largely vacated while the sun continued to shine. The late morning break gave her pause to rest on her porch for the few hours of serenity she afforded herself between tasks to manage the establishment.

She heard the clank of plates as the restaurant staff cleared the breakfast tables. In the distance, a door slammed as her cleaning staff freshened the second story bedrooms. Beyond the few reminders of her thriving business, the busy world behind her all but dissolved as she observed the carefree world in front of her.

In her repose, she forced the upsetting letter from her conniving older sister out of her consciousness. Her grandmother had willed her the property more than a decade earlier. She owned it fair and square. Lindsay was given the option of co-ownership. She refused. She was given the chance to contest the will. She didn't show up. She had no rights to the multi-acre plot of land, nor the three-story inn, mansion and restaurant that Shelly had built with her own blood, sweat and borrowed money. And yet, the letter, sent through certified mail, written by some fancy New York lawyer seemed to indicate otherwise.

Through her telescope, Shelly studied the fifty-foot-tall sand dunes that faced Matunuck beach across the ten-mile water gap between the Rhode Island mainland and Block Island. She could make out the crowded state beach and the row of hotels along New Shoreham harbor.

Rotating to her right and undetectable by the eye without the assistance of her viewer, she traced the tip of Orient Point, the eastern-most bit of Long Island, New York. She roved further along the southwestern horizon, across the mouth of the Long Island Sound. Just over the Connecticut border, she found Watch Hill and the Misquamicut Beaches, two of the state's most celebrated tourist destinations. Even from twenty miles away, she could make out the tapestry of beach towels and umbrella-tops that crowded the popular sandy expanses.

Moving further east, Shelly spotted the breachway at the far end of Charlestown Beach, which ultimately connected to the much smaller, quieter patch of sand adjacent to Matunuck, called Green Hill Beach. With only a few streets and a couple dozen homes, Shelly knew very few Green Hill residents. Even though her property at the westernmost tip of Matunuck represented only a skip of a stone across Cards Pond, the lonely Green Hill Beach always felt like miles away to her.

Immediately adjacent to Shelly's private swatch of sand sat Moonstone Beach. The narrow area between Green Hill and Matunuck gained recent fame as a protected watershed for an endangered species of Piping Plovers. But in past decades, the hundred-yard-long stretch of beach also served as the unofficial sanctuary for local nude sunbathers.

Shelly recalled as a child, seeing pale, naked bodies strewn across the compact area of sand and pebbles. As a young kid, she had vivid memories of men and women lying face down with their bare buns projected into the sun, or sprawling unabashedly up to the sky with all their glory on display for public viewing. They grilled. They threw footballs and frisbees. They sat on chairs drinking and smoking. They hugged and kissed, all naked and glowing in the sun.

Shelly's parents tried to bar her from venturing to Moonstone, directing her to stay on the eastern side of the beach. But the allure to nine-year-old Shelly pulled at her. Despite their relatively strict parenting, they couldn't watch her twenty-four hours a day. That first visit, in which she viewed a fully naked grown man, standing completely upright, scared the wits out of her. She ran home in tears, refusing to explain to her parents what made her so upset. Of course, they knew, but they never let on to her. She didn't return for several years following that traumatic event.

Four years later, she and her friend, Vivian, gathered the courage to revisit the enigmatic beach next door. But by the time she did so as a young teenager, the excitement of the taboo had worn off. Instead of fear or shock, she just perceived the whole nudist experience as strange and disgusting. Despite her newly hormonal interest in teenaged boys, she actually found herself more intrigued by the form of the female body than the ugly, hairy men that outnumbered the opposite gender by at least a three-to-one margin. Not yet blossomed, nor having experienced her period, she wondered when puberty would hit. She imagined herself resembling the voluptuous women that delicately rubbed oil on their chests, stomachs and thighs, attracting the constant attention of the men around them.

As she focused her telescopic viewer, Shelly appreciated the fact that nude sunbathers no longer frequented the beach next to her place of business. As much of a fun novelty in the nineties, the practice just didn't seem to fit the current time period.

Shelly moved her telescope to the east. She observed Roy Carpenter's Beach to her left. Only two years removed from the devastating Hurricane Constance that barreled across the Rhode Island coast like a bandsaw, the dunes at Roy's famous beach took a terrible beating. The community consisted of nearly a hundred tiny two- and three-room shacks. They aligned along a dozen parallel streets wedged between her property to the west, the corn fields by Cards Pond Road to the north, the potato fields to the east and the Matunuck shoreline to the south.

With the hurricane from a couple years back and several subsequent winter storms over the past two years, the entire first row of beach cottages sat slumped over the eroded edge of sand like broken toys in a sad garage sale. With windows boarded and blue tarps covering gaping holes in their roofs, the half-dozen cottages awaited demolition like death row inmates wasting away in their cells.

The old beach club house, where they used to sell hamburgers, hotdogs, sodas and candy, sat abandoned, protruding into the sand of the beach. It lingered precariously close to the lapping of the waves.

Shelly remembered attending teen dances in the little white building that held maybe two dozen people comfortably and close to three dozen on a regular basis. Boys from Warwick, Cranston, Woonsocket and other Providence area suburbs used to show up for a week or two at a time, looking for someone to make out with for a few hot summer evenings before disappearing back to the north for another eleven and a half months.

Shelly traced the edge of the pavement. It sagged, appearing cracked, jagged and broken next to the sand of the beach. Orange containment fencing sought to hold back the ravages of erosion that attacked the hundred-year-old beach club. But, the flimsy, makeshift wall of wooden stakes and plastic mesh bent and lilted under the pressure of a resentful Mother Nature that seemed obsessed with claiming the land for herself and swallowing it into the endless blue-grey Atlantic Ocean.

Further along the coast, Shelly spied the top of the Willow Dell private beach club building. The more exclusive of Matunuck beach clubs, Willow Dell members had enough foresight and investment dollars in the late nineties to move their wooden clubhouse several hundred feet beyond the dunes. They even moved it a second time a decade later as the ocean continued to rise. At the time, it seemed like a silly move. Beach club members criticized the Willow Dell board for ruining the view of the ocean from the open deck. But, years later, with the sandy incline carved to oblivion and the position of the wave breaks encroaching several dozen feet closer to the crest of the dunes, the positioning of the Willow Dell building seemed prescient in hindsight.

Beyond Willow Dell, Shelly spied the little round bathhouse for the town beach. It sat as a replacement to the old Blackberry Beach Club building which had washed out to sea thirty years earlier. The state constructed the little round structure about a decade after the demise of the beloved Blackberry clubhouse. It stood a couple hundred yards up and about as far back as the Willow Dell building.

Shelly had seen pictures in her grandmother's photo album of the iconic Blackberry Beach clubhouse in its heyday. Made of dark, aged pine planks, the wide deck of the original building overlooked the since defunct Blackberry Beach, next to the elevated trailer park, which sat atop a wall of rocks.

The Blackberry boardwalk served as the main congregation area for many local parents and children. Despite rules against using the deck for activities other than sitting and observing the view, the wide space was perfect for ball playing and games of tag. The biggest drawback to the construct of the building was the constant threat of massive splinters from the frayed, salt-worn floorboards.

Unlike its sister club, Willow Dell, the plot of land where the Blackberry Beach Club Association built its bathhouse backed up to a protected salt marsh. As the ocean engaged in its offensive up the plane of the beach, the members of Blackberry Beach Club had no room for retreat as their neighbors at Willow Dell did. Once the envy and crown jewel of the half-dozen Matunuck beach clubs, a massive winter storm eventually scooped the remaining mound of sand out from under its cement pylons and sucked the wooden structure out to sea.

In place of the long-gone Blackberry Beach clubhouse, the state erected a beautiful boardwalk, which extended from the new bathhouse to the top of the dunes. Made from distinctive blue-grey, smooth pressure treated lumber, the structure arched high over the sand and enabled amazing views of Block Island. But like the absconded Blackberry Beach clubhouse building, the state boardwalk had also long since given out to the mad, rising sea. It took about ten years. Every other year another section succumbed to the relentless ocean until Hurricane Constance finished it off for good.

Shelly recalled the remnants of grey, waterlogged timbers landing in front of her plot of land along the westernmost point like a shipwreck of broken, rotted planks.

She could still see the flattened space in the dunes where the Blackberry Beach clubhouse used to stand.

In contrast, the massive rock outcropping that buffered the elevated trailer park, rose above the shadow of the old Blackberry Beach. The ugly seawall defiantly protruded into the relentless Atlantic Ocean. The waves, a little rougher and angrier than the ones in front of Shelly's inn, splashed against the black gnarly rocks, spraying white foam high into the air. Along the top of the rocky plane, several metal trailer homes projected into the sky against the horizon as if taunting Mother Nature to just try and pull apart their igneous protective barrier.

The constant crash of the waves against the immovable seawall of boulders looked like a clash of titans to Shelly. She watched the frustrated ocean continue to hurl its might, seemingly in vain at the thousand-ton man-made pile of rock.

The unsightly outcropping at the trailer park - most Matunuck residents surmised - sat at the epicenter of beach erosion that escalated well before the turn of the twenty-first century. It had already claimed most of Mary Carpenter's Beach from the trailer park wall to Deep Hole at Matunuck Point. The widely-held theory was that as the ocean edged forward, the rocks forced a greater volume of water to scoop to the left, attacking Blackberry Beach, or to the right, eroding the beach owned and managed by Roy Carpenter's sister, Mary.

Once existing as enormous stretches of unabated sand, capable of supporting hundreds of revelers and beachgoers, both Roy and Mary Carpenter's Beaches as well as Willow Dell and the defunct Blackberry Beach all resembled ghosts of their former forms. Dating back to before the forties, fifties and sixties, thousands of families traveled from Connecticut, Massachusetts and New York to enjoy what many considered the east coast's finest places to soak the sun, surf the waves and swim the vast Atlantic.

But, not any more. With the erosion, the shoreline moved north, destroying the dunes, wiping out waterfront property, claiming places like the Blackberry Beach clubhouse and wiping out many of the available areas for parking. The devastation at Roy Carpenter's Beach created hundreds of thousands of dollars' worth of damage, if not millions. But the carnage at Mary's basically shut down the beach altogether. Where there used to be a hundred-foot-wide parking area, protected by massive cement blocks, the ocean dashed the entire space, scattering the withered cement and leaving no clearance between the crash of the waves and the tiny beach road that harbored the community's iconic bar, sole pizza restaurant, famous ice cream shop and numerous hundred-year-old historic homes.

With declining amenities and the hundred-foot-long beach withdrawing to sometimes fifteen or even ten feet wide, only the most devoted Matunuck-lovers continued to visit.

Shelly felt it in her business. The local Tuni Grill, which long-time owner Lenny Bozzutto finally had to sell, felt it. The Ocean Mist pub along the top of Mary Carpenter's Beach felt it.

Unless the town or the state could offer a plan to address the erosion, Matunuck Beach faced the prospect of total destruction and near extinction from the glory years of the past.

Marty Fazzini, owner and head chef at the Seafood-By-the-Sea restaurant at Shelly's inn, walked through the open double doors and handed her a remote telephone.

"Your sister's lawyer," he said, his black buttons contrasting the reflection of the sun on his white chef's coat. "Reminder about the meeting in his office later today. He's pretty pushy."

Chapter 2

Mick Maguire rested his hand under his father's shoulder to steady him as they strode past the Matunuck Inn-By-The-Sea and made their way to the beach.

The rich, cobalt sky stretched from above their heads to the horizon, interrupted only by the bump of Block Island protruding from the straight line across their eye-levels.

As Mick escorted Gordie down the soft, hot sand, he peered through the windows of the inn trying to catch a glimpse of his neighbor, Shelly Newsome, who sold him his adjacent property. Unable to see her, he turned his view to the porch, where he knew she often rocked on her chair and viewed the island through her telescope.

The chair swayed in the wind, but he saw no sign of his good friend, the beautiful owner of the inn.

Gordie stumbled in the shifting sand. Mick had to reach with a second hand to steady him.

"Careful," Mick cautioned his seventy-something father. "Watch where you're stepping."

"Me? Watch where I'm stepping?" Gordie miffed. "You stepped on my foot. Jeez Al Patsy, you Communist. You'd think you were the one with the terminal brain tumor and not me."

Mick wrapped an arm around his father and helped him to the flatter, stiffer sand by the break of the waves.

"I'm fine. I can walk by myself," Gordie exclaimed. "If you want to see her, just go up there and see her."

Mick scoffed and shrugged his shoulders.

"She's been so busy with her business," Mick said. "And between teaching at the elementary school, writing music and playing gigs, I've just been too busy to connect with her. You know how it goes."

"I guess," Gordie replied, pushing his son's hand away from his waist. "If you like her, just tell her. Life's simple that way."

"It's not always as simple as you might think."

"It seems pretty simple to me," Gordie countered. "You know, I'd do anything for five more minutes with your mother. Even sick and dying, I'd trade however much time I have left just to sit right here with her by the sea and listen to the waves crash against the sand."

Mick eyed the spot along the shore where he, his siblings and his father had released her ashes, only a few weeks earlier, into the waters of Matunuck Beach together. The finality of her passing gripped him in a bout of longing that matched the mental anguish in his father's voice.

"I know Dad," he whispered. "I miss her too."

Mick and Gordie walked along the narrow gap between the ebb and flow of the waves and the bludgeoned sand dunes between Roy's and Willow Dell. Racked by the last hurricane to strafe the coastline, and carved by the inordinate high tides of the past winter's storm season, the erosion across the full stretch of Matunuck Beach reached the worst level anyone had ever seen. Where the ocean rose at the extended high tide of the last storm, the sand all pealed from the dark brown clay of the potato patch. Rusty hundred-year-old pipes from beach-front homes long-since claimed by the Atlantic extended from the dirt at eye-level. Chunks of ragged, crumbled cement peeked from beneath the sand along the base of the dunes, the only remnants of beach homes long-ago destroyed by the rising sea.

"It's terrible what's happened to this beach," Gordie mused. "When your mother and I used to come here in our twenties, you could run a hundred strides from the top of these dunes to the break of the waves. We used to be able to play ten-on-ten games of touch football in the hard sand in front of all the people lying on towels and sitting in chairs."

"It was like that even when I was a kid," Mick replied. "I remember the guy who used to ride his horse on the beach from Charlestown, all the way to Deep Hole."

"Yes, but you should have seen this place before you were even born," Gordie continued. "See the top of those dunes up there?"

Gordie pointed to what looked like a ten-foot cliff. The face of the sheer incline showed layers of sand, dirty and clay. Roots from the crab-cherry blossom bushes atop the dunes stuck out, exposed. A broken pipe protruded like a pirate's telescope, staring ahead at Block Island.

"The top of that dune used to be where the flat beach started," Gordie explained. "This whole space where we're standing would've been completely under the top of the beach floor. We'd be literally buried in ten feet of sand."

Mick looked back and forth between the cliff-like dune and the ocean.

"The water was hundreds of feet back," Gordie continued. "That dune would have been even higher and there were a bunch of houses all along the top of it."

Mick picked up a flat skipping stone and hurled it against the placid ocean. He watched it hop eight or ten times before colliding into a small swell.

"They're all gone now," Gordie continued. "There's barely any beach left. And, people just don't come here as much as they used to."

They approached the Willow Dell Beach Club. The dark grey wooden building with its open deck and plush green grass lawn sat fifty feet back from the highest dunes adjacent to the cramped village of two- and three-room cottages at Roy Carpenter's Beach.

"You remember this place?" Gordie asked, as he did many of the other times they walked by.

"Sure do," Mick replied.

"When the Blackberry Beach clubhouse washed out to sea, we had to join this one," Gordie said. "It was nice, and most of our friends from Blackberry came over. But it was never quite the same. Blackberry was a special place. I'll never get over how they converted it to a town beach. You go there now and you just don't know anyone."

"Dana's there with her kids," Mick informed his father. "She's going to come over for dinner tonight."

"How nice," Gordie said. "You could have told me your sister would be here."

"I did," Mick replied. "This morning before we left and again as we walked past the inn."

Gordie stopped walking abruptly and stared across the calm, flat ocean. Mick stepped behind him and placed a hand on his shoulder. They watched the fabric of the sea rise and fall as if in a deep slumber. A seagull wailed in the distance. The remnants of a small, rolling wave lapped their toes.

"This spot always gets me," Gordie said, his face pitching red and bags forming under his eyes. "She's out there, where she always loved to be."

Tears welled in Gordie's eyes. Mick recalled how his father had swum past the waves only a few weeks earlier with the urn containing his mother's ashes and slowly poured them into the agitated water.

Mick studied the ripples of the surf as if he'd see his mother's ashes still congregated just beyond the break of the waves. He pictured her treading water, floating over each swell as it lazily rolled to shore.

As he envisioned her, Gordie cast his shirt up the sandy beach, beyond the high tide mark and waded into the break of the surf.

"Are you wearing your suit?" Gordie asked him.

Mick folded his keys into his own t-shirt and carefully rolled it into his ball cap. He grabbed his father's shirt and moved it higher into the soft, dry sand to ensure the tide wouldn't reach it. Gordie had reached the ditch and flopped his way over a small wave. It looked like he would be knocked off his feet, but he turned his hips and shoulder and barreled through the oncoming gush of water.

Mick approached the break of the waves and shuddered at the cold Rhode Island water temperature. Even during the hottest days of summer, the Matunuck surf rarely broached sixty-five degrees.

By contrast, some of the California beaches he used to take Melodie to visit featured waters in the mid to high seventies.

"Come on ya chicken," Gordie called to him from twenty feet beyond the break of the waves.

His white hair, wet and matted, flopped into his face. His fluffy beard clung to his cheeks and chin. With a burst of energy, Mick tensed his body and threw himself into a sizeable wave that curled over the ditch. The shock of extreme cold lasted a few minutes. But, once he submerged his entire body and swam out to his father, his chest

13

accepted the new temperature and he felt comfortable, despite the frigidity of the Atlantic Ocean.

"I love the big waves," Gordie said. "But sometimes, it's nice to come, swim out beyond the break and just bob along on a nice calm day like today."

They stood just beyond the break of the soft rolling waves and allowed the water to ride up their bellies to their chests at the crest and then back down to their hips in the valleys between the swells. Gordie swayed with the passing current, but stood firmly with his feet planted in the sand. Mick's body acclimated to the temperature of the water and suddenly felt warmer dipping his shoulders below the surface than remaining above it.

Gordie turned to face the shore and without warning, flung his arms forward and lunged his body along the top of a breaking wave. The movement of the tide projected him into the break and he body-surfed the small ripple flawlessly, riding a dozen feet up the sand beyond the ditch.

"Still got it," he called to Mick, who watched and admired the old man. He could barely walk in the sand, but had the muscle memory to ride a Matunuck wave over the ditch and into the foam of its aftermath.

Gordie pushed himself up and trod slowly back into the ocean. A gush of water spilled from his shorts, including a blob of wet sand that coated his legs. He pushed through the oncoming swell and joined Mick a little deeper beyond the break. They tread water together. Their heads bobbed like buoys in the gently rhythm of the ocean.

"Can't you just feel her out here?" Gordie asked.

Mick nodded and put his foot down to test the depth. He couldn't reach the bottom, so he took a gulp of air and flung himself downward. After coasting about three feet, his toes made contact with the soft, smooth sand of the sandbar that covered the ocean floor just beyond the tumultuous break of the Matunuck waves.

"Sand bar?" Gordie asked.

"Nice and soft," Mick agreed.

Gordie followed suit and disappeared under the glass-like surface to dig his feet into the firm, flat plane below. He reemerged a few seconds later, sucking a gulp of air.

"You know how this sand gets out here don't you?"

Mick generally understood the cycles of beach sand depletion and replenishment, but deferred to his father out of respect.

"The late summer hurricanes and winter storms carve the sand from the beach and pull it out here to sea. Then, in the spring, the tides change and the sand gets deposited back on the beach."

"That's why the beach looks so terrible all winter, but then comes back in the summer," Mick contributed to his father's geology lesson.

"The problem is," Gordie continued. "There's more sand going out than there is coming back."

"And that's causing the beach erosion?" Mick asked, knowing the answer, but giving his father the chance to opine.

Mick expected his father to talk about how every winter, some portion of the sand gets pulled too far out into the body of the ocean to make its way back to the shore in the spring. Mick would blame the problem on rising sea-levels due to global warming and Gordie would scoff at him for believing the scientists and journalists.

But none of that happened. Instead, Gordie grew quiet. Mick didn't notice at first, but instead of his father's head and shoulders protruding from the water, only his mouth, nose, eyes and hair broke the surface.

It took a few seconds the register, but Gordie was slowly sinking. By the time Mick recognized the problem, he could only see Gordie's panicked eyes, nearly at the level of the sea.

Mick sprang into action and clutched his father by the underarm. Over his head in nine feet of water, he had little leverage to use in forcing the elderly man to stay above the surface, other than the force of his frantic kicking.

Gordie had some strength in his legs, despite his glazed look. They paddled in unison, with Mick hoisting Gordie onto his chest and flapping backward toward the shallower water.

They reached the ditch and put their feet down into the sand. Mick helped Gordie walk through the undercurrent and extricate himself from the ocean.

They sat in the dry sand next to their shirts and panted for air. A passerby asked if they were okay and Mick nodded in appreciation.

"What the hell happened?" he asked his father.

"It was no big deal," he replied.

"Dad, you sank like a rock," Mick snapped. "Talk to me. What's up?"

A shadow crossed Gordie's eyes. He seemed to wipe the annoyance from his face, and a sad expression overtook him.

"This is where we scattered your mother's ashes," he said.

"I know it is, Dad," Mick replied.

"It would have been fitting for me to go right here with her, don't you think?"

"That's not funny," Mick reprimanded his father, "Seriously? What's going on?"

Gordie shrugged.

"I just got a little dizzy, that's all."

Mick chided himself for even letting Gordie in the water in the first place. He felt like he couldn't win with his father. Every time he exerted extreme caution – like when he refused to allow him to renew his drivers' license – Gordie seemed fine and resented the loss of freedom. And yet, every time he relaxed and let his dad live a little, he suffered the grim reminder that his brain tumor could cause havoc at a moment's notice, like a ticking time bomb waiting to explode.

They sat in silence for a few minutes. Mick formulated the thoughts in his head and rehearsed the sentence a few times.

"Maybe we should go see Doctor Clark again," he said. "There could be new treatments. Maybe it's not too late…"

"I'm not doing that," Gordie interrupted him. "I told you two years ago and many times since. I'm playing with house money here. They gave me a few weeks to live. That was two years ago."

"I know, but if there were a way to get five more years, ten more years. Wouldn't you want to do that?"

"You know the odds," Gordie's voice tightened with resolve. "There's a small chance of success with an upside of a couple more years. And there's a high chance of failure."

"Isn't your life worth taking that chance?"

At that, Gordie's face tensed even more. His cheeks flushed and his ice blue eyes darkened.

"You weren't here all those years your mom suffered in that wheelchair," he snapped. "She couldn't walk. She couldn't move. She couldn't speak or communicate. She was in constant pain. God bless her. She was an angel about it. She never complained. She never felt sorry for herself. She never even questioned God's will. She just fought tooth and nail every single freaking day to get from the morning to the night and live one more damn day."

Mick's stomach tightened at the image of his cancer-stricken mother in her dying twilight, with her rail-thin bald head, her sunken cheeks and boney arms and legs. Guilt at his twenty-year absence from Matunuck and his family, while he pursued his music career in Los Angeles, overtook him. He felt tears form in the base of his eyes.

"They wanted to drill holes in my skull," Gordie continued his rant. "If I'd let them dig around in my noggin and try to cut around this damned tumor and they so much as nicked a nerve, sliced into the wrong brain cells or damaged the wrong tissue in there, I'd have been wheelchair-bound just like her. And, damnit I don't want that."

Mick's mind froze with the assertiveness of his father's conviction.

"I believe God has a plan for me," Gordie concluded. "And I believe it's time to let that plan run its course. Sometimes, the best approach is to do nothing at all and let nature take care of nature."

Mick dusted the sand from his keys and returned them to his pocket. He noticed a text on his phone from his sister, Dana Fonteneaux, that she had arrived at the town beach, only a quarter mile east of their location.

"Drop by and see the girls," she suggested. "And bring Dad."

Mick stood. He flipped his ball cap onto his head. He extended a hand to his father and helped him to his feet.

"Feeling better now?" he asked.

"Yes. I'm fine," Gordie replied. "You understand my position?"

"Yes, Dad," Mick sighed. "I do."

"They're my wishes and intentions for myself," he restated. "I'm not as strong as your mother. And, I don't want to go into a home, surrounded by doctors and nurses with hoses in my veins or machines hooked up to my head or even hopped up on drugs. You understand that? I hope you can respect that and support me."

"I do," Mick repeated. "I get it. I respect your wishes. I'll be there for you, Dad. I promise."

Mick shrugged. A breeze caressed the crest of a wave and spritzed him with pungent salty spray.

"You can't fight Mother Nature and you can't beat Father Time," Gordie said. "Just don't tell your sister about this."

Chapter 3

Mick and his sister, Dana, sat on beach chairs a few feet up from the tide. Dana's two girls built a sand castle by the edge of the waves with Gordie. Dana handed Mick a miniature box of raisins as their mother always had at the beach. Mick covered his legs with a towel. Dana, in shades, rubbed sun screen on her cheeks and forehead. Her reddish freckles glimmered in the mid-day sun.

"Is Shelly coming to dinner tonight?" Dana asked.

"I don't know," Mick replied. "I haven't seen her."

"She's your next-door neighbor," Dana scoffed. "Just knock on her door."

"She's been really busy," Mick replied. "She's been working at the inn every day and night since opening day back in May. I barely see much of her."

Dana rolled her eyes and sipped her soda.

"Fortunately, it's not 1999 anymore," she quipped. "We have these devices called cell phones."

"I know," Mick laughed. "I just don't want to distract her from her work."

Mick took a bottle of water from Dana's cooler and chugged a long sip.

"You did a great job organizing the Tuni-Fest this year," he told her. "It was nice to get everyone together."

"We've got it rented for next year already," she answered him. "Plus, I called it Matunuck-Palooza in the e-mail."

It had been only three weeks since the family congregated along the edge of the ocean and watched Mick, Dana and their brother, Conrad, accompany Gordie in the water as he uncorked the urn and spread their mother's ashes into the ocean. It had taken Gordie two years to gather the strength to let her go. But, by then, it had become a liberating, almost happy moment for Gordie and the adult children.

Soon after the somber moment at the shore, they held a sizeable party at the nearby Community House to celebrate the life of Gordie's amazing spouse and the mother that had always held the family together until her illness robbed her of the ability to do so.

Dana organized the party with help from Mick, Conrad and their cousin, Haley Davies, who lived in town. Dana called it the Matunuck-Palooza. Haley referred to it as Matunapalooza. Whatever the name, they decided to make it an annual event. And as word spread about the epic gathering of old friends and relatives, it grew in size and number of days.

"We're expecting fifty people next year," Dana commented. "We'll probably have a family night on Friday and a friends party on Saturday."

Dana's girls called to her to show off their sand castle. Their chirping voices sounded like the plovers along the dunes at Moonstone. Gordie carefully smoothed the sandy edges of their creation with an old shingle he found on the beach. Using dixie cups, the older daughter constructed a series of towers on top of the ramparts. The younger one used her hand to scoop sand from the bottom of the wall and make a tunnel under the structure.

"It's looking good girls," Dana said, taking out her phone to snap photos. "Thank Grampa Gordie for helping you."

Dana turned to Mick and peered right through his eyes.

"How's Dad doing?" she asked.

"He's up and down," Mick replied.

"More down than up, I hear from Trudy," she said. "Seems like he gets bad headaches almost every day."

"He does," Mick replied. "They pass."

"And he has pills that dull them, but he doesn't always take them?" Dana asked, relaying what she'd heard from their aunt who frequently checked on Gordie during the daytime while Mick worked.

"He takes them when he needs them," Mick answered her. "You know Dad. If he can gut it out, he'd rather fight it naturally."

"Sure, but how much longer can he live there and be on his own, even for an hour here and an hour there?"

"I don't know," Mick lamented. "I don't want to think about it right now."

Dana and Mick watched a large wave ride up the shore and tap the base of the sand castle's wall. Usually striking in groups of three or four, Gordie anticipated the oncoming larger-than typical waves. The second smashed into the front wall of the sandcastle, causing some damage to the beautifully crafted structure. As the third of the three large waves crested and poised to attack, Gordie noticed the horror in the eyes of his two granddaughters and took action. With impressive agility for his age, he slid his body horizontally in front of the sand castle, serving as a hard barrier to stop the water from reaching it. The wave clashed with his pale, freckled chest and splashed fervently into his face. But the maneuver protected the castle, eliciting cheers from the two young girls.

Dana chuckled at the sight of her father sprawled across the sand, his white hair matted into his face and her two girls hugging him across his neck.

Finished with the creation and ready for their next adventure, the two girls took their grandfather by the hand and led him to the water to wash off their fingers and feet.

"The Palooza's getting really big," Dana told Mick as her girls looked for sea glass with Gordie. "Everyone heard about it and wants to come next year. Mary Cuddy's going to come up from DC. Ronnie's brother's coming. Marty's brother'll be there too. Oh, and your friend Lizzy Gingrich heard about it from Carrie Donnelley on Facebook. She says she's going to come too. She's down for a couple weeks at her parent's house. We saw her at the market. She says hi."

Mick recalled Lizzy Gingrich, Carrie's best friend growing up in Matunuck. As much as he and his buddies Marty Fazzini, Kenny Forrester, Ronnie Benjamin, and Jack Valerian dubbed themselves the Kings of the Beach, Lizzy, Carrie and their clique served as the Queens. The group roved the bucolic community together in a pack. They lined the top of Blackberry Beach along the deck of the clubhouse on their towels - often in boy-girl order. They cranked pop music from their radios and giggled loudly, oblivious of the adults and families around them.

Mick hadn't seen Lizzy in twenty years since he left Rhode Island to pursue his music industry career in California. According to Carrie's Facebook page, Lizzy married and had a few kids. As much as Carrie played the flirt with Mick during those teen years, Lizzy, a little older and far curvier, all-out teased his friends, especially Kenny and Jack, who vied for her affection.

"Carrie told a few other people about it too," Dana intruded Mick's reverie. "Everyone's so excited to come back to Matunuck."

Since finishing construction in time for the summer, Mick's modest four-bedroom bachelor pad that he shared with his father had become the official family summer gathering point.

Dana's huge house north of Providence served as the family holiday headquarters for Thanksgiving, Christmas and Easter. But Mick's place remained unlocked all summer for anyone related to him to enter at will, shower as needed, use the kitchen, take a nap or even sleep over if required.

"Sounds good to me," Mick nodded. "We have a year to plan. Just let me know the specific dates when the time comes."

A good distance away, Gordie and his two grandchildren walked the beach together. Mick watched him pass through Willow Dell and cross the narrow strip in front of Roy Carpenter's Beach.

They stopped and spoke with a young woman in a green one-piece bathing suit. Mick recognized her as his daughter, Melodie Maguire. After a brief chat, Gordie pointed his way. Melodie, hand-in-hand with her college boyfriend, Kian Taomessina, trotted past the bathhouse to Dana's encampment.

"Hi Daddy; Aunt Dana," she beamed in the sun. "We just saw Grampa Gordie at the spot on the beach where they released Gramma Jaimee's ashes. He seemed sad. But the girls were comforting him."

"He tears up every time," Mick said, hugging his daughter and shaking hands with her boyfriend. "I didn't know you were coming today."

"I didn't have any homework and we just decided to drop by," she replied.

"You should come to the house for dinner tonight," Dana interjected. "Your father's grilling London Broil."

"It's been marinating in soy sauce and onions all morning," Mick added.

"Oh, sorry," Melodie said, with a subtle shirk. "Kian's dad has a place in Jamestown and we're going up there for dinner. He's taking us out on his boat. Maybe another time?"

"Lunch tomorrow?" Mick asked.

"His mother's having us over her house in Burrillville," Melodie replied. "I'm sorry."

"It's tough with divorced parents," Kian explained. "One usually gets Saturday and the other gets Sunday."

"Of course," Mick nodded. "I can see how that would work."

Melodie spread her towel next to her father and shared it with Kian. They lounged shoulder-to-shoulder with their feet intertwined. Dana offered them grapes and water. Melodie read a quirky romantic comedy while Kian studied an engineering text book. Only in her second year of college, Mick withheld his consternation at the living arrangement where Melodie and her beau shared a two-bedroom off-campus house in Peacedale with another couple.

As much as he worried about her sleeping with some college senior from Burrillville that he barely knew, her mother, back in Los Angeles, seethed at the arrangement. She called in lawyers to contest the lease, and to argue against her daughter's ability to make her own adult decisions. She tried to convince her to transfer out of the University of Rhode Island. She even threatened to extort more money from Mick through the arbitrator if he didn't pull her out of the school.

In the end, Mick largely ignored Danielle, his ex-wife of nearly four years, politely tuning out her ranting and raving about the situation. He hired his own lawyer to handle her lawyers. And the final conclusion of the inane discussions between representatives - aside from an unnecessary loss of thousands of dollars - turned out to support the twenty-year old college student's ability to make her own free-thinking choices about her private social life.

Melodie collapsed her book to her chest and turned to her father.

"Oh, hey, when I parked at the house and walked past the inn, I saw Miss Newsome," she said. "She offered us free lunches and told us to say hi to you."

Dana glared at Mick out of the side of her eyes. Mick thanked his daughter, who returned to her book. Dana waited a few minutes, quietly watching a young boy play in the waves.

"So, are you going to invite Shelly to dinner tonight?" she finally asked.

"It's Saturday night," Mick replied. "I'm sure she's busy."

"I saw you holding hands with her at the beach a couple weeks ago," Dana remarked. "I know it was pretty emotional with us releasing Mom's ashes and all. But she seemed into you. What's the problem?"

Mick recalled the overcast afternoon on the beach near Shelly's inn. Soaking wet from a swim in his clothes with Gordie, Dana and his brother Conrad, they had just watched their father pour the ashen remains into the ocean.

Afterward, Mick played his guitar and the family sat on blankets singing folk songs and Irish lullabies. In support, Shelly slipped her hand into Mick's and held it for several minutes before unclenching her fingers and folding them into her lap.

"I don't know." Mick mumbled. "You know how long it's been since I was single and in the dating world?"

"You've been single for four years," Dana retorted.

"And celibate a lot longer than that," Mick added. "I just have to figure out the right time and way to ask her out."

"It's not hard," Dana quipped. "Wanna go out for dinner? Done."

Mick met Shelly two years earlier around the time that Hurricane Constance struck the Rhode Island coast. As the eye passed right over Matunuck, the category-four winds destroyed her grandmother's mansion that stood a couple hundred feet closer to the sea than the rebuilt version Shelly currently owned. Mick recalled every detail of that evening. It also marked the night his mother succumbed to the ravages of cancer.

Soon after, Mick bought a plot of land that Shelly owned, adjacent to the inn she built. His payment served as her seed money for the

24

construction of the Matunuck Inn-By-The-Sea, which she opened a month before the start of the summer.

Mick had spent a year living with friends and relatives while saving his money and building his own Victorian-style home next to her property. Both Mick and Shelly obsessed on their work. They saw each other often, but for fleeting moments at a time. Shelly spent most of the first year collaborating with the construction crew to oversee their work. Mick had bills to pay, alimony checks to cut and several jobs to maintain. In addition to teaching music at the elementary school, he freelanced as a songwriter, delivering scores to local music groups. He filled his bits of remaining time by providing private piano and guitar lessons to local children out of his home.

The timing of an extended relationship with Shelly never seemed to present itself. Three weeks removed from the emotional release of the ashes, they had yet to follow up on the tiny flare of a spark that emitted from the palms of their hands. Gun shy from eighteen years of marriage followed by four years of divorce and zero experience in the adult dating world, Mick opted not to push any envelopes with his neighbor. He liked her enough not to want a repeat of the animosity between him and his ex-wife Danielle.

"I don't know," Mick mumbled. "I'm not totally sure if she's free or interested or even available tonight."

"Well, there's one way to find out, Dana replied, grabbing Mick's phone and holding it out for him to take. "Text her and ask."

Chapter 4

Mick approached the inn from Roy Carpenter's Beach. As he neared it, the three-story mansion grew against the deep blue afternoon sky. The rocking chair sat empty on the porch. Flowing champagne curtains flapped in the breeze, rustling past the open French doors to the back room of the inn's restaurant.

"...wondering if you'd do me the honor of..." he mumbled to himself, searching for the words to use in asking her out to dinner. "... was hoping you'd be inclined to oblige me..."

Usually, good with words in his song lyrics and lesson plans, his stilted romantic phraseology made him feel like a John Wayne character in an old western, asking for the damsel's hand in marriage.

Mick entered the inn calling for Shelly. He poked his head into the kitchen looking for his friend Marty Fazzini, who co-owned the restaurant with her. The fry cook told him Marty had left to tend to his other restaurant in Coventry.

He asked for Shelly at the front desk. But the clerk hadn't seen her since the lunch crowd dispersed. He crossed the cobblestone circle and parking lot to her tiny guest cottage and lightly knocked on the door. When she didn't answer, he knocked louder.

"... was wondering if you'd like to have dinner with me," Mick fine-tuned the words in his head.

A blur of color caught his attention. He saw the back of Shelly's head across the side yard of the inn, by Cards Pond. He called to her, but she didn't hear him. He crossed the spongy marsh grass and called again, catching her by surprise and causing her to swivel quickly at mention of her name.

"Come quick," she whispered, while gesturing urgently with her hand.

Mick trotted to her side and peered over her shoulder. The sweet smell of lavender and peach wafted from her neck and hair. She crouched, pulling Mick down with her and pointing through the cat-tail grass.

"See the nest?" she whispered.

Mick squinted. He spied a mass of dried grass, twigs and mud, balled into a circle and wedged between the tall stalks. Shelly moved aside, giving Mick a better view. A splash of color came into sight and he spotted several blue orbs nestled into the depths of the nest.

"Plovers," she said. "They don't usually nest on this side of the pond."

Shelly stood and faced Mick. Her blue eyes and blond hair blended with the sandy stalks of cat tail grass and the bluish green pond water behind her.

"I, uh, you know," Mick shuddered.

"Know what?" Shelly asked with a laugh.

"What I was trying to say was that, uh, you know, uh."

In his head, the phrase 'have dinner with me' fought through the muddle of other more insecure filler words as he struggled to piece together his plea.

Shelly flinched and pulled her phone from the wide pockets of her culottes. She looked at the avatar and her face tightened.

"I have to take this," she said, turning her shoulders and answering, before turning back to Mick with her hand over the face of the phone to mute it. "Sorry, it's my lawyer. I have a lot going on today."

Mick took a step back and nodded in understanding.

"I'm so sorry," she continued. "Can you text me?"

Mick gave a thumbs up and turned back toward his house.

"I know you wanted to tell me something," she added, a twinkle forming in her eye. "Or, uh, maybe ask me something?"

Ted Callahan spoke in calming, but measured tones. He assured Shelly that her sister's lawyer had a flawed claim to her property.

A local Matunuck resident her whole life, Shelly had grown up with Mr. Callahan's daughter, Vivian, along the eastern side of town before her parents died and she had to move into the mansion with her grandmother. Shelly spent countless evenings at Vivian's four-room cottage along the top of the dunes by Deep Hole. They ate dinners on the deck. They tried, and usually failed to surf the rolling waves east of Mary Carpenter's Beach. They walked the shore, late in the evenings.

And they flirted with the older boys under the pale light of the Sea View community center that stood next to the pub for fifty years before it finally succumbed to the ravages of the ever-encroaching tide of the Atlantic Ocean.

Ted offered Shelly a generous 'friends and family' discount on his services, charging only a couple hundred dollars to help her and Mick come to terms on the sale of her property. A regular at her restaurant, he promised to face off against her sister's lawyer on a pro bono basis until they understood what Lindsay wanted.

The opposing counsel, Silas Pavinuzzi spoke with a harsh New York accent. In his blunt, abrupt manner, he demanded the meeting take place at four in the afternoon in his North Providence office on a Saturday afternoon. Shelly had hoped to start earlier and return in time for the inn's dinner crowd. But the stubborn New Yorker wouldn't budge.

She had a file in a bin of paperwork from the original transaction where her grandmother deeded her the house. She forwarded to Ted a series of e-mails exchanged with Lindsay at the time. She collected all her building permits and filings with the town and provided them to Ted with a week's notice.

Ted expressed confidence to her that Lindsay had no legitimate claim to the property. He promised to make sure her lawyer couldn't pull any unseemly legal maneuvers to make her life difficult.

As she spoke with him on the phone, she received a text from Mick inviting her to dinner with his father, his sister and her family.

"I'm cooking steak," he wrote in his text. "Stuffed jalapeños, grilled veggies and bacon-wrapped water chestnuts. Should be a good time. Would love to see you there."

A quick read of the text prompted a smile and warm gush down the back of her neck. It had been several weeks since she held his hand on the beach. But since then, he had barely spoken with her. It felt like a deliberate act of ignoring her. She couldn't understand why, other than the feeling that he might have regretted her gesture of affection. She recalled the comfort of his hand, meshed with hers.

The feeling went numb at the words of her attorney.

"I wanted to let you know that there seem to be a few discrepancies in the paperwork," Ted told her by phone, from the car, as he traveled to pick her up.

"What discrepancies?" she asked.

"Well, the hard copies are all signed, which is good," he replied.

"But?" Shelly asked.

"There was an e-signature that your grandmother does not appear to have signed."

"An e-signature?" Shelly repeated.

"Yes," Ted explained. "It's a legally binding means for signing documentation when a physical signature can't be obtained. It serves as a proxy and has the same full legal standing as a hand signature."

"Okay," Shelly said. "What does this mean?"

"Don't worry," Ted calmed his voice and spoke slowly. "All of the most important paperwork is in good order."

"What's missing?" Shelly asked.

"It's an attestation as to your grandmother's state of mind," Ted replied. "Apparently, she'd suffered a stroke during the course of the transaction."

"A minor one," Shelly acknowledged. "A TPA or TIA or whatever those little ones are called."

"Yes, a Transient Ischemic Attack, or mini-stoke as it's commonly called." Ted responded. "I see where she physically signed off on her initial Mental Health Attestation. That should be good enough. It looks like one of the estate lawyers requested a second signature after the stroke event."

"The doctor signed off on that one as well," Shelly said. "I was there for the signing. I remember my grandmother's lawyer protesting that it wasn't necessary because the stroke was a physical ailment. The doctor vouched for her mental health. I remember it all."

"But your grandmother couldn't make it to that meeting?" Ted asked, even though he knew the answer from the paper trail.

"No, of course not, she'd just had a stroke," Shelly raised her voice in frustration. "Her lawyer signed on her behalf."

"It looks like the lawyer agreed to an e-signature that never took place," Ted said.

"My grandmother didn't even have a computer."

"This is the one hang-up that we could face," Ted conceded. "Your grandmother's attorney is now deceased, but we have the initial hand-signed attestation, only a few weeks before the TIA event. We have the follow-up letter from the mental health professional after the stroke. I think we have a tight case."

"I sure hope so," Shelly said.

Mick boiled hot water and poured it over a terry cloth towel. He heard Gordie grimace in the television room.

"I'll be right in," he called to his father. "I just have to let the towel cool for a minute."

He trotted to Gordie, leaned him back on the leather couch and wrapped the towel around his head.

"Does that feel better?" Mick asked.

Gordie didn't respond, instead, sighing and leaning even further into the seams of the couch.

"Did you sip your herbal tea?" Mick asked.

Gordie still didn't answer. His breathing grew deeper. He inhaled the steam from the hot towel that soothed his searing headache.

"I think it's better," Gordie moaned from beneath the fluffy beach towel. "It's not pounding as bad."

Mick brought the empty tea mug to the kitchen and marked the tally on the refrigerator notepad to track the medicine his father had taken. He heard the leather ruffle, followed by the jostling of the coffee table and a thud on the ground. His senses pictured the scene even before he arrived. Gordie had fallen.

Mick found him on the ground in somewhat of a pushup position.

"Jesus, Dad," Mick yelped. "Are you..."

"I'm fine," he snapped, hoisting himself up on the coffee table. "I knocked my shin against this damn hunk of glass in your television room."

Mick rattled through his punch-list of first aid questions.

"Did you hit your head?"

"Are you dizzy?"

"Can you move your arms and legs?"

"Is your breathing impaired?"

"Are you bleeding?"

In his usual caustic manner, Gordie scoffed and shrugged off each question with combinations of his trademark phrases.

"Come on now."

"Relax, will you?"

"I'm fine."

"Get off my back."

Mick worried privately. The incidents were happening more frequently. At first, he and his siblings braced for the worst, when they initially learned of his diagnosis two years earlier. At the time, they had their ailing mother in her final days of her life to worry about. But, time in Matunuck sometimes felt like a time warp. It passed so slowly, marked explicitly by each summer season, until one entire year slipped by unnoticed. During that time, as Mick built his house, Gordie lived relatively peacefully in his assisted living facility. He had attendants and nurses checking on him several times a day. If he experienced headaches or dizziness, he didn't share it with his family, or possibly even with the staff at the facility.

He simply soldiered through it and moved on.

Mick painted a cheerful expression and aided his father to his feet. Gordie wobbled at first, but seemed to regain ample balance with relative ease.

"Why don't you just use your cane?" Mick asked.

Gordie scoffed and shuffled toward the staircase.

"I was planning to take a nap before dinner," he said. "If you want to help me up the stairs to my bedroom, I'd appreciate it."

"Actually," Mick explained. "Dana suggested I move you to the first floor."

Gordie waved his hand dismissively, calling the change unnecessary.

"You think I can't climb a set of stairs?"

"I think you can't stand up from the couch without tumbling over the coffee table," Mick teased his father. "Come on, I swapped my office for your bedroom. I gave you the nice octagon room in front by the porch. You can watch over the potato fields. If you look out the bay window, you can see the ocean."

Gordie latched to Mick's suggestion as a free point of concession.

"The other bedroom only had a pond view," he said. "So, I guess this one's an upgrade."

"Sure, Dad."

"Fine," he said, pulling his arm away from his son. "I'll take it. But I can walk there myself."

Gordie swayed for a step, but straightened himself and made his way around the corner.

"Good," Mick called to him. "Because, I already moved your bedding and all your clothes."

Mick sat on the couch. He turned on the television but set the volume low to avoid disturbing his father's sleep. He checked his phone for a response from Shelly. Not seeing a reply, he stuffed the device into his pocket and scrolled through the movies for something to catch his interest. Gordie poked his head around the corner.

"What time's the party again?" he asked.

"Like sixish," Mick replied.

"I'll set my phone for five."

"Sounds good, Dad."

"How do I do that again?"

Mick took his father's phone and showed him how to set an alarm for himself.

"Dana's coming with Miguel and the girls?"

"Yup," Mick answered him.

"Conrad?"

"He's got a big housing development his company is excavating," said Mick.

"Trudy and Bethanne?"

"Yup."

"Haley, Miles and her two little ones?"

"They'll be here too."

"What about your girlfriend?"

"I don't have a girlfriend," Mick reminded him, flipping to the climactic scene of a Rocky movie.

"Sure, you do," Gordie smiled. "Uh. What's her name?"

"Shelly," Mick filled in the blank for him.

"She must be the one," Gordie laughed. "I never said her name, but you knew exactly who I meant."

"I haven't heard from her," Mick spoke flatly. "I think she's busy."

Shelly spent the hour-long car-ride to Providence in Ted Callahan's passenger seat, peppering him with 'what if' scenarios.

"Could Lindsay win partial ownership?"

"Would I have to buy her out?"

"How would they assess the value of the property?"

"Would she be responsible for the debt as well as the assets?"

Ted patiently responded to each concern with a generally satisfactory answer as to how he would avoid each potential challenge. As they exited Route 95, Shelly recalled the text from Mick, inviting her to dinner. She accessed her messages and scrolled to Mick's.

"Sorry," she typed. "Busy."

She intended to elaborate. But upon pulling into the parking lot, she saw her sister emerge from her lawyer's car and walk toward the door to the office.

"What the hell's she doing here?" Shelly asked.

"It's not unusual for the client to appear with the attorney," Ted explained. "You're here with me."

"I live here," Shelly exclaimed. "She's from Vancouver."

Ted pulled into a spot. Lindsay, not having seen Shelly, disappeared into the building.

"But why's she here?" Shelly repeated.

"I guess we'll find out when we get in there."

With a quick gesture, Shelly sent her text to Mick, stashed the phone and hustled into the law office of Attorney Silas Pavinuzzi.

33

Chapter 5

After watching the last ten minutes of his favorite Rocky film, Mick heard Gordie's loud snoring. He flipped to the Weather Channel and caught an update on a series of storms climbing the east coast. They appeared on target to ruin the upcoming Labor Day weekend.

Mick turned off the television and strummed a few bars of a song he was writing on his guitar. He took out a notepad and jotted ideas for lyrics. Gordie's snoring intensified as if in reaction to his playing.

Since his divorce and layoff from his high-paying corporate music industry job in Los Angeles, his career had taken an unexpected turn. At the end of the summer, in just under a week, he would start his second year of teaching music at the Matunuck Elementary School. The facility sat a mile down the street from his house. He didn't even need a car, which worked well, since he didn't have one. Gordie's old Mustang sat in the garage, but hadn't seen the road since their blow-out fight over Mick's refusal to let Gordie renew his license. The argument caused a rift between them for days after Gordie hid the keys in the inner pocket of his guitar case and refused to reveal their whereabouts.

As it turned out, neither of them had a reason to drive anywhere, anyway, and Mick sold the vehicle to help with the costs of hosting his father.

Mick's teaching job was a brisk one-mile walk. The center of Matunuck offered just enough amenities to subsist peacefully. They could walk to the market for groceries. The church sat only a block from the market. The ice cream shop was another couple hundred yards away. And the pizza restaurant and pub remained no further than a quarter mile further east on the Matunuck Beach Road.

As great a toll as the conversation about Gordie's loss of driving privileges weighed on him, the upcoming stand he'd have to take about barring his father from swimming in the ocean felt like it could derail their relationship indefinitely. Mick shuddered at the thought of the looming battle and resigned to procrastinate it for a few more weeks. He just hoped Gordie wouldn't someday swim out to sea and not return.

Mick strummed his guitar during the closing credits of his Rocky movie.

Between classes and throughout the summer, he played gigs at the inn for tips. Unlike the steady paycheck he received as a music industry executive, he found himself scrambling to cover his alimony, his daughter's college payments, his living expenses and the debt from building his house.

The money from his various jobs trickled slowly into his bank account. But he welcomed the escape from office politics and cut-throat corporate business behavior. With such diversity and variety in his work activity, the days flew by. In contrast to his old office job, for the first time since his teens, he looked forward to playing his music every day. And after long hours of teaching, writing, tutoring and performing, he went to bed feeling productive each night.

Around the time he started as a music teacher, Mick called through his contacts from the music industry for songwriting commissions. For a year, he spent evenings in his third-story music studio dabbling in original songs and churning commercial jingles for advertisements.

But, over the past six months, he started writing more commercially viable pieces for successful rock and pop bands. He slowly worked from local to regional musicians and groups, elevating his payout as he climbed the ladder.

His most recent client excited him, but made him nervous as well. Through a connection at his former job as Chief Operating Officer at Golden Records in LA, he hooked up with a rising country music star out of Nashville. While he had little background in country music, Mick understood the rhythms and southern rockabilly roots pretty well. He'd studied all forms of regional and historic music in college. His former business associate arranged a meet and greet session with country recording artist Bo Rutledge over Zoom. After ten years as an entrenched country star, Bo's debut, 'cross-over' country-rock-pop-blended album hit all three charts with great success. With his newly expanded audience, the expectations of his follow-up left him right at that precarious edge between crazed superstardom and overhyped, unrealistic expectations.

In one of those unexplained moments of kismet, in which they both admired the same obscure singer-songwriters, the unlikely pair hit it off. Mick twanged up some of his own original pieces and played them over the jumpy Zoom transmission. To his surprise, Bo liked them and asked him to develop three of the tunes for him to consider adding to his next album.

Only a few weeks removed from the call Mick spent every free moment developing his three melodies and fleshing out the harmonies. During that time, he barely left the house, except for a quick run to the market, a burger at the pub and his daily walks with Gordie.

His aunt Trudy and cousin Bethanne took turns visiting Gordie while Mick worked at the school. Bethanne grilled bacon, cheese and tomato sandwiches for her great uncle while he and Trudy reminisced about the old days before so many of the elder Maguires and Gallaghers passed on.

Gordie's snoring echoed through the first floor of the house. Mick jotted some notes and practiced a line of melody on his guitar until he felt secure enough to try it out in front of an audience. He decided to walk a couple hundred yards to the inn and play for any early birds that might be there. He preferred a later evening gig for the more generous tips, but reminded himself that he had half his family coming for dinner in two hours.

He slung his guitar over his back, grabbed a small amp and power cord and set out into the late afternoon sun. He had an open invitation from Shelly to set up and play in the lobby or the restaurant stage any time he wanted. He took her up on the suggestion once or twice a week, performing partially for the extra cash, and partially for the ego boost of the smattered applause he usually earned. He also leveraged the exposure to the community as a way to connect with parents in the neighborhood who might recognize him from the elementary school and offer to hire him as a music coach or tutor for their children. A couple hours of private lessons brought in as much money as his weekly

36

teacher's salary. And the licensing of his original pieces, albeit sporadic, served as cash infusions to help with the major expenses that depleted his checking account nearly as fast as his paychecks filled it.

Marty Fazzini, his childhood friend and head chef at Shelly's restaurant, greeted him by the side of the stage.

"I haven't seen you here in a couple weeks," Marty commented.

"I've been busy cranking out songs for a big client," Mick replied. "I thought I'd set up on the stage and try one out."

"There's nobody here yet," he said. "We're not even open for dinner."

"I just wanted to get out of the house and play in a different setting. I like to hear the ocean while I play."

"How's your father?" Marty asked.

"Clumsy as a two-year-old, and about as stubborn," Mick laughed.

Marty directed one of the kitchen staff to stock the salad bar with fresh dinner rolls, while Mick plugged his amp and strummed a few notes to check the tuning of his instrument.

"She's not here," Marty said with an amused grin.

"What's that?" Mick feigned misunderstanding. "Who's not here?"

"My sister's kid," Marty snapped. "Mother Theresa. Who do you think I mean?"

Mick strummed an original tune on his six-string and hummed along with the melody.

"I just came to play, dude." Mick interrupted his tune to reply to Marty. "Say 'hi' to her for me when you see her."

Marty watched through the bay window as the clouds rolled in from Connecticut and Long Island.

"It's going to be a big one tonight and an even bigger one next weekend," Marty changed the subject. "It's the remnants of the tropical depression down in South Carolina."

"Who doesn't love a good Matunuck storm?" Mick asked between bars of his song.

"Let's see," Marty counted on his fingers. "The homeowners at Roy's; the trailers by the Vanilla Bean; the cottage-owners along Deep

Hole; oh, and Kyle and Joycie Dolman can't be feeling too good about how their pub is hanging by a thread with the waves literally crashing right under their front porch."

"How that place hasn't joined Blackberry at the bottom of the ocean's a miracle." Mick said, finishing his song and unplugging his amp. "I don't know how the Dolmans can afford to keep sandbagging that place."

"There's a lot of talk about that big metal wall the town plans to build," Marty commented. "They're going to tuck it right under the porch of the pub and hug the road to protect it from the waves."

"I thought they were going to build a nice sandy berm?" Mick asked.

"After they sink the metal beams and plates, they're going to angle the rocks and cap it off with cement blocks."

"It's just going to become a seawall with no beach in front of it," Mick shook his head in disgust. "Just like in front of the trailer park."

"But, if they don't build the seawall, the Matunuck Beach Road is totally exposed to the tide." Marty countered him. "It washes out, and you've got two hundred houses stuck with no way in or out. It'd be a catastrophe."

Marty directed the staff to set the tables in the restaurant. A sous chef asked him a question about the specials. Mick tuned his guitar, adjusted the settings on his amp and grabbed a warm dinner roll from the salad bar.

"I didn't come here to get depressed by talk of beach erosion," he mumbled as he looked at his fingers to start a new song.

"Of course not," Marty teased his friend. "You came here to see her."

"Like I said," Mick replied. "I just came here to play."

"You came to play two songs to an empty house?"

"What do you want?" Mick joked. "I'm an artist. We're weird."

Marty trotted across the floor to check on the kitchen staff's progress in preparing for the evening dinner rush. His chef's hat wiggled back and forth as he moved. He brought Mick a chunk of the house swordfish with gorgonzola and capers. Mick dropped a caper on his guitar face and flicked the little green ball away with his finger.

"Listen," Marty said, quietly, shielding his voice from his staff. "I don't know where you are with her."

"We're good friends."

"Fine, but you dig her and I can tell you she likes you," Marty interrupted him. "Don't let this become a Carrie Donnelley unrequited crush situation all over again."

"Unrequited crush?" Mick asked. "On her part or mine?"

"Have some balls," Marty pressed. "She talks about you. I think she's open to a move. I think you should go for it."

Mick paused, thinking. He looked at his old friend and considered his dating advice. A mental image of Marty kissing one of the Blackberry Hill girls behind a bush in his yard during a game of Hide and Seek rushed to his consciousness. The impulse to ask about it overtook his concentration.

"Hey, who was that girl you made out with in my back yard?" Mick asked him. "Behind that bush."

"What girl?" Marty asked. "What're you talking about?"

"Remember?" Mick pressed, suddenly obsessed with the memory. "We were playing Hide and Seek or that crazy Chase game we used to play."

"What about it?" Marty asked.

"I was trying to capture everyone," Mick explained. "I found you and one of the girls from Blackberry Hill. You had your arm around her."

"That was the girl who lived next door to Jack Valerian," Marty replied. "I had more than an arm around her. And you come around the corner all 'found you'. You ruined the whole night."

Mick laughed. His guitar tipped as he leaned back.

"What does that have to do with anything?" Marty scowled. "Don't change the subject. Seriously, you should ask her out. I think she'd be interested."

Mick walked back to his house under the rapidly deteriorating Matunuck sky. A light mist coated his face. As he reached the covered front porch, the rain started to fall. He had hoped to spread the family out on the back deck as he grilled the steaks. But, with the rain, he'd have to cram them into the television and living rooms.

Gordie stirred in his new first floor bedroom. Dana pulled up to the side of the garage. She, Miguel and their two daughters ran from the car, across the patch of grass to the porch.

"More flooding expected," Dana remarked. "Could be a tough drive back north."

The Fonteneaux family filtered in. The girls darted to Gordie and each hugged him around his waist. They nearly knocked him to the ground. Dana bee-lined for the kitchen to make her salad and heat the appetizers she brought. The girls helped cut the vegetables and decorate the top of the salad. Miguel flipped on the television to catch a baseball game.

"Need help grilling those steaks?" Gordie asked, stretching his arms and shaking off the afternoon slumber.

"I'm good," Mick replied, suddenly changing his mind. "Then again, as long as you don't mind the rain, let's do it together."

Gordie threw on his oversized rain poncho and a pair of rubber rain boots. His giant hood shaded his white hair. Mick grabbed his thick rain jacket, a recent Christmas present from his daughter, and withdrew the marinated meat from the fridge.

"Is Dana coming with Miguel and the girls?"

"They're already here," Mick answered him. "You saw them already."

"Oh, right," Gordie said. "What about Conrad?"

"He's excavating a big construction site," said Mick.

"Trudy and Bethanne?"

"Yup."

"Haley, Miles and her two little ones?"

"Yes, Dad."

"What about your girlfriend?"

Mick sighed and didn't answer. The rain intensified. Droplets sizzled as they careened off the arc of the grill top. Gordie flipped the mass of beef and rolled the baked potatoes. Mick could hear Dana greet Aunt

Trudy and Cousin Bethanne. Soon after, the energy-level in the room exploded as his cousin, Haley, showed up with her two toddlers.

Mick could see Dana's girls crawling around the floor with Haley's boys as Haley lounged on the couch with a large glass of bright, purple wine. She held the glass in the air, toasting him from afar, through the plate glass of the sliding doors.

Gordie tried to remove the slab of meat at ultra-rare. But Mick forced him to cook it more thoroughly. Miguel joined them at the grill with a tall glass of beer and a derogatory comment about his woeful Red Sox.

The wind kicked up quickly. The rain slashed through the air and pelted them with increased forcefulness. In the distance, claps of thunder echoed across the salt ponds. Flashes of faint lightning grew in intensity as the blazing sirloin steak heated from rare to medium rare to medium.

Mick felt the buzz in his pants pocket. He took out his phone and recognized a text from Shelly. He felt his stomach flutter as he opened the message.

The hastily written two-word text dashed any nerves he experienced in his gut.

"Sorry. Busy."

Chapter 6

Melodie Maguire strode through the front door of Mick's two-year-old dream house. He built the three-story Victorian a year earlier with severance he earned at the entertainment conglomerate he left behind when he moved to Rhode Island.

Now, in her sophomore year as a Marine Biology major at the University of Rhode Island, Melodie finally lived only a quick, five-mile, ten-minute drive from her father. Prior to his move to the Ocean State, Mick lived in a motel in El Segundo, California. With moderate traffic, the twenty-mile drive to the home Melodie shared with his ex-wife, Danielle, in Pasadena, could take him more than an hour. And, during rush hour, that sixty-minute commute could easily double. Nonetheless, he made the drive several times a week throughout her high school years. He routinely took her out to dinner on his designated nights of Tuesdays and Thursdays. On the weekends he returned to watch her play on her high school's varsity volleyball team.

Once she attended college just up the road from him at the University of Rhode Island, he expected to see even more of her. But he found the exact opposite with the new arrangement.

Instead of connecting two to three times a week, the almost twenty-year-old, young woman found herself regularly caught up in her classes, occupied with her studies and engaged in learning excursions to investigate the Rhode Island shoreline with her classmates. Beyond the academic reasons for her scarcity, she also dedicated her weekend time to her sorority and spent every other free moment with the budding love of her life, Kian Taomessina.

Kian hailed from Burrillville, Rhode Island, about the woodsiest, most northern and remote section of the state. Between her studies, her parties and the time she spent with Kian's mother in Burrillville and his father's new family in Jamestown, she had little time left for her dad and his side of the family in Matunuck.

"Kian's mother's having us over for Sunday dinner," she often told Mick over the phone. "We're heading out on the boat. We're staying on Block Island for the weekend. We're going to Boston for a game."

She broke his heart the most when she and Kian spent weekends at beaches other than Matunuck.

"It's a cool state," she told him. "There's so much more to do in Newport. The beach at Misquamicut is so much nicer. Watch Hill is such a cuter town. Narragansett has better bars and restaurants."

Anyone from Rhode Island could attest to her observations. But, any lifelong Matunuck resident would vehemently disagree. To Mick, who'd grown up spending every summer in town, Matunuck offered all the entertainment a person could need. It had one of everything; a market, a pizza restaurant, a pub, a surf store and an ice cream shop. The beach, while more quirky, rocky and narrow, had way more unique charm than any other in the state. And the bar and restaurant scene, while limited, rivaled any other entertainment venue as well. Mick would debate anyone who disagreed.

"We've got the Ocean Mist," Mick pushed back on Melodie over the phone. "It's one of the most beloved bars in the state. You can listen to great music, sit out on the porch at the pub and get an awesome meal all with the ocean crashing right under the deck."

With all her varied interests, activities and commitments, Melodie made it to see Mick about every fourth weekend. He'd learned to accept her busy schedule and her freedom as a young woman to follow her own path. Secretly he hoped she'd fall in love with the sleepy beach community and settle in town along with so many of his aunts, uncles and cousins that still owned Matunuck property.

"I don't know a lot about wine," Kian said as he strode into Mick's foyer next to Melodie with his hand glued to hers. "But the man at the shop recommended this one."

Kian shook Mick's hand and commented on the well-constructed house he had built.

"I love the wrap-around porch," he said, as if having prepared a compliment to gain alignment and favor. Mick smiled to himself at the young man's effort and gave his daughter a kiss on the cheek.

Haley's two boys sprung loose from the television room with their father, Miles, in hot pursuit. The boys clutched either of Melodie's legs and hugged her affectionately. Haley, with her wine glass flailing through the air followed behind her husband and the two children. She hugged Melodie aggressively before letting go and doing the same to Kian.

"I'm so glad to have you joining our family," she said to him. "It's the last weekend of the summer. You'll be back in school and we won't see as much of you."

"Actually, you'll see a lot of me," Kian replied. "I'm starting a work-study program with a landscape engineering firm that's been commissioned by the state to study the Rhode Island shoreline. I'll be on a team tasked with making recommendations on how to solve the state-wide erosion problem and account for the environmental concerns of the conservation groups that have gotten involved in the project."

"Serious," Haley shrieked. "Because it's so important we do something to protect Matunuck. The beach erosion has been so bad. It's just heartbreaking to watch."

Haley slung her arm around the young man and walked him into the living room where Trudy and Bethanne sat with Haley's father, Denny. In the kitchen, Dana washed plates and dishes with Miguel while Gordie sliced the steak.

"I'm actually going to be spending a lot of time here," Kian said as he took a seat on the couch next to Melodie. "Much of our research will be done right here between Green Hill and Deep Hole."

"You have to do something about the road near Mary's," Haley blurted with her usual impassioned enthusiasm and zeal. "Hurricane Constance went right up to it and nearly took it out."

"Yes, and the winter storms have been eating away at the sand around those rocks," Trudy added. "That wall has always been makeshift at best. They need to build a much bigger, stronger one to protect all those cottages across the street."

Gordie called the family into the kitchen to get their food. Mick placed several slices of sirloin on paper plates and each family member added salad, a baked potato and zucchini.

Haley cut the steak into tiny pieces and mashed the flaky potato for her two boys. Dana's girls emerged from the basement, grabbed their plates and disappeared back down the stairs to their television show.

After loading their plates and refilling their wine glasses, Trudy and Bethanne parked next to Melodie and Kian on the couch.

"Is the company you'll be working with going to build the seawall?" Bethanne asked Kian between bites of her steak.

"I've been studying this for three years now and building a seawall actually contributes to beach deterioration. The Johnstown Company is an oceanographic landscape management firm that advocates for natural containment and paced retreat."

"What the hell is that?" Gordie asked as he settled into the recliner chair across the room.

"It's a mixed use of supplementary artificial and man-made berm enhancements," he replied.

"Ah, got it," Gordie said with a sip of his wine. "But what the hell is all that?"

"They've been doing that at the pub down by Mary Carpenter's beach for years," Haley interjected. "They pile up a small mound of rocks and pebbles. They build some sort of tiered structure. Then they put down these mesh sandbags and cover them with dirt and clay. Then they bring in fine sand and plant bushes and shrubs to hold it all together. Sometimes they add those slatted fences. It's supposed to stop the waves from going too far up the beach."

"The Dolmans spend hundreds of thousands of dollars a year on erosion mitigation," Trudy added. "Every spring they pile it all up under the deck of the pub."

"And every winter, the ocean scoops it all back out to sea," her daughter Bethanne finished her thought. "There are no easy answers."

"We went on a field trip to Massachusetts last semester," Kian said. "We spent time on the north shore by Revere and then along the ocean-facing side of Cape Cod. Like Matunuck, some of those beaches are losing two and three feet a year."

Trudy and Bethanne leaned in, rapt at Kian's experience at other beaches. Miguel and Mick pulled wooden chairs from the kitchen. Haley stood with one eye on her kids and both ears attached to the conversation.

"In Revere, there's a lot more build-up along the dunes," Kian continued. "They have hotels, restaurants, apartment complexes. It's more like a Jersey beach."

At mention of New Jersey, Gordie sipped his wine and scoffed.

"The city discussed the possibility of erecting a seawall to protect the businesses along the top of the dunes. But, just like Matunuck, the beach kept shrinking."

"What'd they do?" Haley asked. "Because I read that it's better to use sand bags and natural materials."

"That's right," Kian replied. "In Revere, they brought in almost a million cubic tons of sand. The next year, they had a hundred-year storm and the natural berms protected dozens of roads and hundreds of structures."

"Of course, they can't do that in Matunuck," Trudy scoffed. "It would cost millions of dollars that the state can't afford."

"I know," Haley added. "It's just so sad. They didn't do anything years ago when they could have and now the Matunuck Beach Road is at such risk there's no choice but to build a wall, at least to protect the pub."

"What about all the houses next to the pub?" Trudy asked. "They have to build it all the way across. If they build it just to the pub, it'll push the tide further east and wreck the beachfront all the way around the corner to Deep Hole."

At that point, several people jumped in and the conversation fractured.

"A wall would cost even more than bringing in sand," Mick argued.

"You only have to build a wall once," Bethanne countered him. "You'd have to pay for more sand every year."

"They've been trying that for years," Dana interjected. "It hasn't worked."

"Neither has the wall," Mick shouted above the growing din of voices. "Look what the trailer park wall did to Blackberry Beach Club."

"I just don't think there's any choice," Haley said. "We have to protect people's homes."

Haley's father, Denny, as if awakening from a nap, jumped forward from his recliner chair.

"Buses," he shouted.

Haley smiled and pat her father on the shoulder.

"I don't know if buses will help," she said.

"You fill them with cement," Denny continued. "You bring them out a couple hundred yards from the shore and you sink them to the bottom of the ocean."

The group looked at him, perplexed.

"We looked into this thirty years ago," Gordie explained. "I was the President of the Blackberry Beach Association and we were worried about the ocean taking out the beach club, which is exactly what happened later that year. The idea was that these sunken buses would collect sand and seaweed and become a sort of natural barrier, almost like a reef. That way, when the winter storms come and scoop away the sand, the elevated row of old buses would stop it from transferring too far out to sea. This way, in the spring, when the weather calmed down, the tides would bring the sand back to the shore."

The debate paused as the younger family members evaluated the logic of Denny's and Gordie's plans.

"Technically," Kian whispered to Melodie. "Something like that could..."

But Trudy, still irritated from the family debate spoke up and drowned him out.

"That's all very speculative and has yet to be proven effective," she raised her voice in frustration. "The only way to protect the road and all those houses is to build a big wall – whether out of sand or rocks, I don't know. But it's got to extend from the end of the trailers, across the porch to the pub and all along the end of those properties between Mary's and Deep Hole. Unfortunately, there's no other way to save Matunuck."

Kian remained quiet. Trudy's outburst caused a lull as the group pondered her words. The phrase 'save Matunuck' seemed to echo off the walls.

"Unfortunately," Kian spoke up. "The ocean always wins. If you don't build any wall at all, eventually, you'll lose the pub and the road and all those houses."

Haley gulped her wine. Miguel finished his beer. Mick wiped his dinner roll in the juices from his steak. Haley's two boys raced through the room with Miles following closely behind.

"And if you do build the wall," Kian continued. "You may have to keep reinforcing it and hardening it with rocks through the years. Do that, and eventually, you'll lose the beach forever."

Chapter 7

Shelly returned to Ted Callahan's car. The rain drenched her hair. Water droplets fell from her cheeks and doused her jacket. Streams of blond hair hung across her cheek, directing rivers of rain down her chest. The waterfalls cascaded to her long floral skirt.

Ted attempted to cover her with his umbrella, but she walked too swiftly and catatonically across the parking lot. Her reunion with her sister had played out like a horror show. They stared across the table at each other like strangers while the lawyers spoke some otherworldly language to each other.

"It didn't have to be this way," Lindsay said to her by the water fountain during a break in the meeting. "You could have just considered my first letter."

"Where you asked me for a quarter million dollars?" Shelly snapped. "I don't have a quarter of a hundred dollars. I'm up to my neck in debt. I've had this place for like eight years. You never cared about it until Grandma's place got destroyed and I put in my own money and time; not to mention tons of debt. Now, you show up and want half the assets? I don't think so."

The lawyers agreed to disagree on a number of points. The next step would be to hold a hearing at a probate court. Attorney Pavinuzzi had one of those pit bull personalities that would jump on every phrase with a combative retort, even before the salient point makes it to the table. Ted kept his cool, but Shelly could see bits of tension, an eye roll, a loud sigh, even a whispered swear under his breath.

"The guy's a jerk, isn't he?" Shelly asked as they pulled up to the highway on-ramp by the Providence Place Mall.

"He's going to be a handful," Ted conceded. "He's the worst kind of lawyer. Worse than the ambulance chasers. He knows he has no case. He doesn't even expect to win. He just plans to pick at every loose scab and stretch the procedings as long as he can to milk his hours and cost everyone big bucks to see this through."

Shelly tucked a few strands of hair behind her ear and sighed loudly. The rain battered the top of the car, sounding like drumbeats. The wipers struggled to keep up with the barrage of water on the windshield. The traffic slowed and puddles formed in the breakdown lane.

"This can't be good for the beach," Ted changed the subject.

"No," Shelly agreed. "They had to move the beach road a couple feet to the north last winter because the ocean carved out all the dirt and stone right up to it and it was at risk of collapsing."

"They're going to have to build that seawall along the top of Mary Carpenter's beach sooner than later."

"It's been stuck in town committees and lawsuits for ten years," Shelly said. "The environmental groups won't give in."

"I know," Ted replied. "I've had some insight into those discussions and they've been extremely heated."

Shelly pictured the stretch of the Matunuck Beach Road, just past the Vanilla Bean, where it curved east and hugged the top of what used to be the large parking lot in front of Mary Carpenter's beach.

The construction of the trailer park sea wall between Blackberry and Mary's not only caused the destruction of the Blackberry Beach clubhouse, but it also decimated the size and attractiveness of the beachfront at Mary's as well. As Mary Carpenter lost frontage, due to the shifting force of the water repelling off the trailer park wall, she erected large cement blocks to save her parking area. When the ocean rose to engulf the sand and crash directly against the blocks, she engaged in a retreat strategy, moving the blocks backward to keep exposing more sand and beach.

But, the unstoppable ocean, pushed aside by the massive boulders buttressing the trailers, just kept pursuing the blocks and squeezing the sliver of beach left for tourists to enjoy. Eventually, Mary ran out of room to retreat. The ocean overtook her blocks and the erosion reached all the way to the cusp of the beach road which provided the sole access and egress to dozens of homes along the shore and several secondary roads in and out of the salt ponds just a quarter mile north of the strip of beach. In all, more than one hundred homes would be cut off from society if the Matunuck Beach Road were to give out or become overrun by the ocean.

Shelly had read about all the engineering options available to rectify beach erosion. But none of them sounded overly effective. One article talked about using fencing and bamboo mesh sand bags to naturally retain the shape of the dunes. Another called for the planting of American Beachgrass and Saltmeadow Cordgrass with hearty Rosa Rugosa bushes to firm up the berms at the top of the beach. In California, huge dump trucks dropped millions of cubic feet of sand as bulldozers constructed artificial man-made hills.

She read a case study about a formerly wide, open, beautiful beach in South Carolina that used a hard basalt seawall to protect the properties at the tops of the dunes, only to see accelerated erosion and eventual loss of the entire shoreline. In the before photo, a mild incline of golden sand rose from the edge of the water to the elevated grassy dunes in front of the beachfront properties. To her horror, the after photos revealed a row of houses atop a giant wall with nothing but ocean visible against the dark, wet rocks.

"I hope they don't build the steel wall," Shelly said to Ted as he piloted the car from the highway to the Post Road. "I'd rather they keep retreating and filling in with fencing and sandbags to try and build up natural resistance to the erosion."

"Unfortunately," Ted debated her. "The erosion has already reached the main artery through town. There's no room for a natural berm to grow."

"Then they should move the road."

"All the properties south of the road on the other side of the pub, including my own, would be even more vulnerable," Ted explained. "And we'd have to buy out the properties to the north of the road. Plus, it's all wetlands along the salt ponds and the environmental groups are fighting that tooth and nail."

"It's either the properties or the beach," said Shelly. "We build a wall; we protect the homes but lose the beach. We retreat; we have to sacrifice some homes that will get destroyed at some point anyway, but maybe we keep the beach for another couple decades. Maybe longer."

Ted argued with Shelly in calm tones, sticking to factual information and being careful not to take on a combative tone.

"How long do you think we could keep retreating before we backed up into the salt ponds?" he asked her.

"I don't know."

"We're losing between three and four feet each year," he answered his own question. "Where Blackberry used to be, we've lost more like five or six feet a year. We've only got about three hundred feet to Potter's Pond. A retreat strategy might work for as many as twenty or thirty years. But the cost would be astronomical. Every year, we'd have to bring in another million tons of sand and re-plant all the vegetation. As we back up, we'd have to build upward. Let's say we move the road by forty feet. We'd have to move it again every ten years or so. We'd never be able to allow people to build on that land. There are at least a hundred plots on either side of the road from the trailer park to Deep Hole. They're collectively worth a good twenty to thirty million dollars. Maybe California has money like that. Rhode Island certainly does not."

Shelly hugged her knees to her chest. Ted curled through the curved ramp to the northbound side of the Post Road and turned up the Matunuck Beach Road.

"The biggest problems are on the Mary's side to the east of the trailers," Ted said. "You're on the Roy's side, west of the trailers. You were smart to rebuild your grandmother's house so far back. You've got plenty of runway to retreat. The town's been building retaining walls and natural sand berms to protect the endangered birds near you for years. And they can just keep backing up into the potato field behind Willow Dell and Roy's for several more centuries. There'll be lost cabins at Roy's but it's a much easier problem to solve and considerably less costly than the Mary's side."

"I know," Shelly replied. "But I'm not just worried about my own property. I care about the whole town. I want all of Matunuck Beach to stay pristine and beautiful from the Green Hill side all the way down to Deep Hole and everywhere in between."

Ted chuckled as he pulled into her driveway. The rain continued to teem. They could see the whitecaps of the ocean assaulting the dunes.

As they passed Mick's house, she peered through the lighted bay window. She saw Mick and his father hugging Dana in the foyer. Miguel and their two daughters sprinted under umbrellas to their car in the driveway. Shelly tried to figure out if Mick caught sight of her. But with the darkness, the sheets of rain and his focus on his houseguest, she assumed he didn't notice her.

"Before my parents died and Lindsay and I went to stay with my grandmother in the mansion, we lived in one of the O'Hannon cottages next to the pub," Shelly said. "They had just winterized them, and we were one of the few families there after Labor Day. But in the summer, the place was hopping. I had so many summer friends in that cramped row of houses between there and Deep Hole."

"I remember where your house was," Ted said. "You were right next to the pub. You and your sister used to walk on the beach together in morning."

"I had just met Viv when my parents died and I moved to my grandmother's place."

"I remember," Ted spoke softly. "I didn't know your parents well. We had just bought our place and were still getting to know the neighbors. But I actually did meet them briefly. It was such a shame they died so young."

"Thank you," Shelly paused as if in a moment of reflection. "I loved that side of Matunuck. There's so much life there. So much to do. I used to wander through the little village of cottages across the street. There were always kids my age to hang out with. We played kickball and baseball in that little field by the road."

"I remember the boys you and Viv hung out with," Ted muttered with a comical mix of sarcasm and playfulness.

"Everyone sat outside, blasting music," Shelly continued, lost in her recollection. "The parents drank Narragansett Beer, while the kids ran around like they owned the world. We used to stay out from after dinner time until midnight, totally on our own."

"Viv was supposed to be home by ten," Ted interjected. "But your grandmother was a little more relaxed than I was."

"I know," Shelly giggled. "We just wandered the streets, hung out on the beach and danced in the old Sea View club before the ocean destroyed that awesome building."

Ted laughed.

"I danced there with June, probably before you were even born."

"The point is," Shelly stiffened. "I'd hate to see that whole neighborhood get wiped out like those beachfront rows of houses at Roy's."

"The two big concerns are the corner of the beach road closest to the seawall, which could give out at any point," Ted replied. "And what they're calling the Blackberry Beach Gap, where the beach club used to stand. That dune is very flat and low. Behind it, the elevation dips to only a few feet above sea level."

"You mean by that little marshy pond next to the Vanilla Bean ice cream shop?" Shelly asked.

"That's right," Ted replied, as he cut the wheel through the circle and parked under the awning to the front door of the Matunuck Inn-By-The-Sea. "Half the village at Mary's is in danger of a catastrophic flood. If the ocean tops that point and rushes over the beach road into those low-lying areas, they might never be able to fix it from becoming a permanent breachway."

"Oh my God," Shelly yelped. "There are hundreds of trailers and cabins along that side of the road."

"I know," Ted replied. "We've identified about forty-seven high risk properties."

The rain intensified. Shelly watched it fall like sheets on either side of the overhang.

"What can we do about this?" she asked.

"Well, I'm representing a homeowner's group from the Mary Carpenter's Community Association," Ted replied. "We're engaging in a class action lawsuit to force the state to construct a hardened protective emergency barrier across the Blackberry Beach Gap. We're also demanding that it stretch from the side of the trailer park, all the way to Deep Hole in front of all those houses on Matunuck Beach Road. There are environmental groups suing to leave the shore alone and unprotected. We have to fight them in court to save Matunuck from what could be, and most likely will be, a total catastrophe if we don't take action as soon as possible."

"What can I do?" Shelly asked.

"If you want to opt in, I can include you as a plaintiff," he replied. "If you'd like to offer testimony, I'd love to have a resident appear at our upcoming hearing next month. It's a challenge that most of the residents are only here for a few months at a time. Most of the cottages are owned by older folks that don't always live nearby. Most of them are occupied all summer by renters. The owners sometimes take only a few weeks in July or August. So, I need someone to serve as the face of the community in both our legal proceedings and our PR push."

"Count me in," Shelly said, glancing into the inn to gauge how busy it might be. "I'll do whatever it takes."

"I admire your spirit," Ted told her, as she pushed open the passenger-side door. "Nobody loves Matunuck like you do."

"You're wrong," Shelly rebutted him as she opened her door and leaned in to give her closing argument. "Everyone does."

Chapter 8

The low, thick clouds of the Matunuck sky snuffed any trace of the near full moon or the billions of stars that usually danced above the Atlantic Ocean. Rain battered the top of Kian's Subaru as he drove Melodie down Mick's driveway and out toward Cards Pond Road.

Melodie turned up the radio to compensate for the din of rainfall against the thin, glass sunroof. As they reached the turn to Matunuck Beach Road, Kian switched on his left turn signal to head north toward their cozy apartment in Peacedale. But a mild glow to the right caught Melodie's eye.

"Maybe just one?" she purred. "I mean, I love my dad, but hanging out with him, talking about beach erosion all night, is not exactly what I'd call a rocking time. Let's have a little fun before the night ends."

With a smile, Kian turned right and head toward the only discernible light in town, the Ocean Mist bar and pub.

"I actually had a good time with your family," Kian said as they passed the closed and darkened Vanilla Bean ice cream shop.

"I'm glad I'm here and I get to see him more," she continued. "But I moved here because I was too close to my suffocating mom. And now, my dad wants me to have dinner with him every weekend. And he's all disapproving when we go to other beaches instead of this one. I'm almost twenty years old. I've never been out here. I want to see more than just this one dumpy place."

"I kinda like it here," Kian said.

"Me too," Melodie conceded. "But I need my freedom. My dad asked me to text him when I got back to the apartment tonight. What's that all about? He never asks me any other random night. I could have been dead by the side of the road last weekend and he never would have known. But tonight, I have to text him?"

"I think he just cares about you."

"Right," Melodie scoffed. "Too much."

As they neared, the orange illumination of the streetlights revealed the sideways stream of rain. It splashed against the vinyl awning to the front door of the famous Ocean Mist bar. Red and blue neon signs for various brands of beer blazed against the dark night. In their feet, even within Kian's car, they could feel the pounding of music emanating from within the energetic haven of libation.

Kian pulled up to the entrance, one of only a few cars. Melodie held her coat over her head as she dashed under the awning. The cold rain slapped her cheek and chilled her spine. She reached for Kian as he rounded the car to join her, and they entered the warm, stuffy bar together.

A live band played to an audience of a half dozen. A string of yellowy blinking lights brightened the otherwise gloomy dark wood bar area. While nearly empty on such a blustery evening, the crowd in the building made up for their numbers with their spirit and volume. They shouted over the band, laughing and toasting each other. Two women sat with arms around each other, swaying to the music while two men stood behind them singing along to the tune.

A tall, husky, red-haired man from behind the bar greeted them nearly immediately, with an exuberant smile and his arms in the air as if he would hug them.

"Welcome to the Ocean Mist," he shouted above the sound of the acoustic guitar and pounding snare drum. "I haven't seen you here before. Come on in. Sit at the bar. Tell me where you're coming from and the first drink's on me."

Kian asked for a Coke. Melodie pointed at the tap for a draft beer.

"Kyle Dolman," the bartender said, shaking both hands. "Welcome to the best bar in the state."

Kian introduced himself and Melodie, identifying themselves as graduate students at URI. Melodie flashed her fake ID, which had yet to fail her.

"What brings you down here on such a crappy night?"

"My dad lives in town," she explained. "He built the house right behind the inn."

"Ah, the nice Victorian," Kyle said, smacking the bar. "Well done. It's a beautiful house. Adds to the charm of that side of town. Much nicer than these big modern homes they're building along the other side of Cards Pond Road."

Melodie shook her head, not understanding the reference. But Kyle continued, almost speaking to himself.

"They're totally ruining the charm of this place," he muttered, tossing a thin rag over his shoulder. "Next you know we'll have townhouses and condos in Matunuck."

The band took a break between songs and Kyle introduced Melodie and Kian to the regulars. Kian sipped his soda while Melodie took a gulp of beer. Once the crowd learned that Kian had an internship in Matunuck, studying the erosion problem, he morphed into somewhat of a local hero.

"Are you going to fix the beach," one slurry-speeched patron asked.

"We need to build a wall to protect this place," said another, swinging her beer like a baton.

"If this place is going down, we're all going down with it," a third proclaimed. "When Hurricane Sandy hit, we stayed on that deck all night, wobbling and swaying in the wind and the rain and the crazy waves. They had to bring in the State Police and the National Guard to physically yank us outta here."

"The Ocean Mist isn't going anywhere," Kyle shouted over the hum of the crowd. "My pylons go all the way down to hell and the devil's holding on for dear life."

The crowd cheered and exchanged toasts with Melodie and Kian. The band smacked the snare drum and jumped into a rendition of Jimmy Buffett's iconic bar-song "Why Don't We Get Drunk". The energy in the building erupted as every voice, including Kian's and Melodie's joined in. With arms around each other, the eight of them swayed to the lilt of the tune and vocalized until their throats ran hoarse.

Dana stood on the covered porch in front of Mick's house. She had bid goodbye to Melodie and Kian, hugged Trudy and Bethanne and helped Haley collect her two wild-man boys and constrain them to their strollers.

Mick joined her on the porch to thank her for the appetizers and salad she brought to the dinner. Dana glanced over her shoulder at the car. She watched Miguel secure their two daughters in the back seat of her minivan. The blue lights from the girl's iPads cast a silvery haze. Miguel gave her a thumbs up from the driver's seat.

"They're watching Frozen for the hundredth time," she said with a shrug.

"Great," Mick replied, turning to return to his house. "Well, thanks for coming."

Dana paused. She inhaled. The moment of silence grew almost awkward. The pounding rain played a drumroll on the roof of the porch.

"I've been meaning to ask you something," she said. "Is Dad doing alright? I mean really. Be honest."

Mick closed the door behind him and faced his sister.

"He's up and down," Mick replied. "He's had headaches. He loses his balance. He said his vision was blurry a couple times. But he's hanging in there."

"It just doesn't sound like hanging in there," Dana whispered, conscious of the nearby open windows.

"They gave him three to six weeks to live," Mick said. "That was two years ago."

"I know," Dana cut him off. "But he's only going to get worse. It's just a matter of time. You know this."

"And when he does," Mick replied, a wave of sorrow crossing his eyes. "We'll cross that bridge when we come to it."

Dana looked past Mick's shoulder. She saw Gordie head move toward the downstairs bathroom. She saw him carrying a toothbrush and comb.

"I know the doctor at Providence Hospital said he missed the window for surgery," Dana started.

"It's not just that," Mick interjected. "He wants to let nature run its course."

"You keep saying that. It's annoying," Dana's voice tightened. "There are new treatments. Safer options. We should look into them."

"It's not what he wants."

"He doesn't have to be in so much pain,"

"The guy's tough as nails," said Mick.

"I'm going to text you a website," Dana pressed, glancing at her husband in the car with his headphones on and nodding his head to his music. "They have new techniques. They don't have to try and remove the tumor, which is where you get the greatest chance of impact to the brain."

"I don't know Sis," Mick stepped back toward the door.

"Listen to me," Dana pressed as the rain started to subside. "They can drill small holes into the tumor and insert these little pegs."

"Pegs?"

"They're made of the membrane of like pig intestines or something," Dana replied. "They fill them with a spongy substance that dissolves over time and releases the chemo directly into the cancerous mass."

Mick looked at his sister, trying to comprehend the procedure she described.

"It's much safer than what they used to do to remove tumors, which was much less precise and impacted the good cells almost as much as the bad ones." Dana continued. "And the injections last up to six months at a time, reducing the number of visits and invasive treatments he'd have to endure."

"He won't do it," Mick said. "You know how he feels about doctors and medicine."

"I know," Dana laughed. "He thinks they're all Communists."

Mick and Dana chuckled. The sound of their laughter muffled against the pouring rain.

"Just look at the websites," Dana urged. "It's not too late at this stage. The window for this treatment is still open for him. He should think about it."

The pace of the falling rain subsided. In the distance, a sliver between the clouds revealed a hint of moonlight.

"He'll never agree to see the doctor," Mick whispered as Gordie passed the window toward his bedroom and called "goodnight" through the opening. "Plus, I've done some reading too. At his age, the anesthesia alone can cause a decline in his cognitive functions. Put an old person out, there's always a chance they don't come back. And, if they do, they may not come back quite the same."

Mick and Dana moved to the far corner of the porch, out of earshot. The rain dripped off the railings and spritzed them.

"You have to convince him," Dana whispered. "Some risks are worth trying."

"He won't go."

Dana gave her husband a finger to indicate she'd be there in one minute.

"There's a way," she whispered even more quietly as the moon peaked from between the parting clouds.

"What way?" Mick asked, leaning in to hear her.

"It won't be easy," she concluded. "You could force him into it."

"I doubt that."

"No, you absolutely could." Dana leaned in to him. "You can pull rank. Don't forget you're his legal Health Proxy. You can force his hand. You have the Power of Attorney over him."

As soon as the rain stopped gushing from the sky, the patrons at the Ocean Mist spilled onto the bar's long, wooden deck to gaze at the moon. Several others joined them. Kian pointed out the unique contours of the Matunuck shoreline and described the geological factors that contributed to the formation of the surfer waves, the infamous ditch at the break of the shoreline and the unique angle of the beach that led to much of the decline of the dunes.

Melodie rolled her eyes at yet another diatribe about beach erosion. She finished her second beer and urged Kian to leave. But, enjoying the conversation, he asked for a few more minutes. As she started a third beer, Melodie formed an idea to steal Kian's attention from his adoring crowd.

She maneuvered to a corner of the bar where only her boyfriend could see her. With two fingers, she teased the top of her shirt downward to reveal her cleavage and stared straight through his eyes. She lightly caressed herself along the ridge of her collar bone and nodded her head sideways.

Within seconds, Kian gulped his last sip of soda, settled his tab and high-fived each patron before working his way to the door and escorting Melodie back to the car.

Kian piloted the Subaru into a u-turn and sped up the Matunuck Beach Road. As they neared the trailer park. They noticed the bright moon emerging fully from behind the clouds. The silvery light twinkled against the churning sea and gave the sand a heavenly glow.

Already feeling amorous from the alcohol and turned on by Kian's quick response to her teasing gesture, she formed a romantic image of making out with him in the dunes under the light of the moon.

"Pull into the back of the trailer park," she urged him.

Kian parked in the sandy area behind the elevated rock embankment and flush against some rosa bushes. Melodie grabbed two beach towels from the back seat and giggled as she exited the car.

Loud aggressive crickets chirped from the protected pond. The cat-tail grasses swayed in the breeze. Melodie took Kian by the hand and guided him past the seawall into the open space where the Blackberry Beach clubhouse used to stand. She dropped the towels and reached for his face. Caressing his cheek, she arched her calves to elevate on her toes to reach his face. As their salty lips meshed together, a car zipped by. The headlights momentarily beamed through the gap, illuminating them in bright white halogen light.

"Let's walk the beach a little bit," Kian suggested. "There's a nice spot on top of the dunes by Roy Carpenter's Beach that would give us a really nice view of Block Island."

Melodie picked up the blankets and allowed Kian to lead her along the shore toward the western side of Matunuck Beach.

Gordie had long since retired to his bedroom. Dana, Miguel and their two girls had disappeared down his driveway. Mick stashed all the dirty paper plates in his recycling bin and wrapped the extra food in plastic before stuffing it into his refrigerator. He heard Gordie stir. A soft moan emanated from his room. Mick opened the door, but Gordie seemed asleep in peace.

Mick climbed the stairs to his bedroom to change into sweatpants and then spiraled up the staircase to his third story music studio to don his head set and write his second song for Bo Rutledge. He had the music mostly worked out, but had yet to figure out any lyrics to go with it.

He thought of Shelly and decided to text her. He pondered what to say and gazed out his window for inspiration. Looking over the dunes through his high perch, he watched the fog from the humid air lift toward the sky. In the distance, he saw the blaze of the Ocean Mist against the trailer park seawall. Three lines came to mind for his second song.

"The Song of the Ocean Mist."

"The Cry of the Ocean Mist."

"The Ghost of the Ocean Mist."

He decided to make them the three separate refrains. From there, the lyrics flooded his mind and leapt through his fingers onto his scratch pad.

As Mick played his melody into his headphones and refined his lyrics, Gordie continued to stir, two stories below him. He moaned at first. He whimpered. His head pounded. His eyes ached. He rolled left and then right. The covers flopped to the ground. He spoke to himself and rubbed his head.

And then, his eyes flew open.

Chapter 9

Dinner receipts at the Matunuck Inn-By-The-Sea lagged behind the typical average. Whenever storms ravaged the beach, guests avoided the restaurant. Matunuck residents loved a good squall. But they preferred to watch from their outdoor porches and decks in jeans and windbreakers over sitting indoors in wet linens.

"Another dozen cancellations," Marty informed Shelly as she returned from her long evening with her lawyer. "We'll take a bath on the swordfish."

"Take it to the shelter in Coventry," she suggested.

"We mostly just served the hotel guests," Marty replied, glancing across the deserted restaurant floor. "I'll whip up a couple big batches of fish stew and bring it to the Monsignor."

Shelly checked with the hotel night manager before returning to her detached cottage across the circle. She noticed the downstairs light to what she believed was Mick's office and studio - which had recently become Gordie's bedroom. When the window went dark, she assumed her neighbor went to sleep for the night. She washed her hands and face and slipped out of her skirt and blouse. She replaced them with grey sweatpants, a sky blue 'MATUNUCK' t-shirt and a pair of fluffy slippers. She picked up the remote and pointed it at the television, but changed her mind.

Instead, she scrolled to the last text she sent to Mick. She noted the brevity and abruptness of her response to his dinner invitation. She realized that he likely perceived it as an uncaring blow-off. They'd spoken only sparingly in the few weeks since she briefly held his hand on the beach. In the emotion of the moment, she wasn't sure he even noticed. He barely reacted to her touch. And his subsequent standoffishness made her self-conscious about her ongoing interactions with him.

He had definitely clasped her fingers as she slipped her hand into his. Not only did the warmth from his palm radiate her hand, but she could feel the tingle of excitement run up her arm and into the rest of her body. But then, just as quickly as it happened, they let go. She still couldn't figure out whether he detangled his fingers from hers or vice versa. Nonetheless, within a few short minutes, the touch of their hands and the warmth of his body dissipated, leaving her with a chill and a new set of unanswered questions.

Did she come on too strong? Was the timing off?

"Don't make it out to be more than it is," she told herself. "A friendly gesture."

He had just watched his father pour the ashes of his deceased mother into the ocean. He was surrounded by his grieving family. She chided herself, wondering how she could think of her presence with his family at that moment as a romantic overture.

She decided that the brief bout of hand-holding was likely more a sign of support in his time of grief than any further indication of a budding romantic beginning.

"Friends," she said to herself. "He's a great guy. He's my neighbor. I'd hate to ruin what we've got. I can live with friends."

She looked at the text she sent to him five hours earlier.

"Sorry. Busy," she read out loud to herself. "How awful. He must think I hate him."

She pondered what to write that could dampen the harshness of her message.

"Come clean," she told herself. "Just be honest. I was tied up with the lawyers. I meant to fill him in. I appreciate the invite. I'm sorry I missed it. I really wanted to be there. I'm crazy about you and want to..."

She laughed at her own runaway thoughts. As she did, she noticed three blinking balls next to his name that indicated he was typing a text to her. She watched them fade from dark grey to light in a rhythmic pattern like the rippling waves of a lazy summer beach day. The blinking continued for some time. Shelly grew impatient. Then they stopped.

She hesitated, waiting to see if he'd start typing again. The text window remained empty and the blinking balls didn't reappear. She formulated thoughts of her own message to him in her head, but paused.

"If I start typing," she said to herself. "He'll know I'm sending a message to him. Then I'll never find out what he wanted to say to me."

She turned on the television and watched a late-night comedian comment on the day's slate of political nonsense. Still, Mick didn't text her. She grew sleepy and scooped herself a bowl of coffee ice cream to stay awake. She doubled down, squirting a generous coating of Autocrat coffee syrup across the top of her two scoops.

But Mick still withheld his message. Finally, frustrated and annoyed, she stashed her phone on the nightstand, brushed her teeth and climbed into bed.

She set the alarm on her phone for five o'clock and clicked the text icon one more time to see if Mick had sent her anything. She placed the phone upside down and rolled over in her creaky double bed. After a few seconds, she checked the phone again. And again, the text message was blank.

She propped her pillow, pressed her thumb against the glass of the phone and typed rapidly to match her thoughts.

"I'm sorry if my text seemed abrupt tonight," she wrote. "I was with Mr. Callahan facing off with my sister's donkey lawyer. Don't ask. Anyway, I wished I could have had dinner with your family."

She erased the phrase; 'with your family' and rekeyed it as 'with you and your family'.

"Storm looks really bad," she continued. "I have to work the breakfast crowd at six. I'll be free around nine if you'd like to walk and see how the beach held up against the weather."

She hovered her thumb over the send button while rereading and proofing her prose. She knew he might see the grey balls on his end and realize she was writing him a message, but she decided she didn't care. Satisfied, she pressed the Send icon.

"Friends," she repeated to herself.

Within seconds, the blinking grey balls indicated he was typing a reply.

"No problem," his first text said.

"Saw you drive by," said the second.

"Wondered whose car that was," he continued.

Shelly read the texts twice. Short, but cheerful, she decided he harbored no ill will at her curt response from earlier, before his dinner party.

"Tomorrow morning," Mick continued. "See you then."

She watched as the grey balls reappeared. His next text offered a smiley face emoji, followed by a single word.

"G'night."

Gordie Maguire squeezed his eyes closed as tightly as he could. The flexing of his face muscles helped alleviate the searing pain that burned like a dumpster fire behind his eyes. He squirmed in his bed and rubbed the sides of his temples.

He flung his eyes open again and spoke to himself aloud.

"It's not pain," he said to himself. "It's simply a series of electrical impulses between the nerves and synapses in my brain. If I can understand that it's just a chemical reaction and nothing more, I can filter out the sensation of pain and ignore the feeling."

Gordie slowed his breathing and expanded his chest to relax his heart rate. He found a particular shadow on the ceiling of his octagonal bedroom and fixated on it.

A deeply religious man, he prayed to God for relief and thoroughly believed to his core that his Lord would hear him and grant his wish. True or not, the act of believing actually settled him. In the dark of his room, he spoke to his dead wife, asking her for strength.

"No pain," he said to himself. "It's only an illusion."

Gordie focused on his big toe. He attempted to tune out all feeling in his body and instead, think only of his left big toe, as if it were the only body part he had. Slowly, he tried to pretend that the toe was no longer part of his body; that it disappeared into thin air. Using the same relaxation technique, he moved across each toe on each foot and focused his mind to isolate each part, eventually pretending they didn't exist either. He worked his way up his ankle, to his calf, his knees and his thighs.

Eventually, Gordie settled into a warm, coma-like state where his body felt weightless. The exercise soothed his head and allowed him to close his eyes in peace. But, as he drifted to sleep, a new, familiar pain gripped him.

He felt himself dreaming. The image of his adoring wife, Jaime, came to mind. He pictured her smile, which stretched her thin cheeks and widened her green eyes. He recalled her in her mother's wedding dress at their reception, the pearls in her necklace knocking gently against each other. He felt her body against his as they danced to the music of Frank Sinatra, the Beatles, Karen Carpenter and a whole host of Irish folk songs.

He held her hand in his. The sensation felt as real as any. He watched her struggle to give birth three times, to three beautiful babies. He heard her half-drugged voice cry in joy as she held her newborns for the first time.

His dream fast-forwarded to a specific moment in time. He and Jaimee decided to surprise Mickey, Conrad and Dana and take them on an adventure to Manhattan to see the tall buildings. They visited the giant Macy's department store. They stayed in a hotel on the tenth floor along Madison Avenue. They took the subway. They visited Saint Patrick's Cathedral and Central Park.

He could picture Jaimee and the kids walking ahead of him, pointing at the Empire State Building. His heart ached to return to that simple time.

He moved further ahead in time to the amazing trip to Ireland he and Jaimee enjoyed. A sort of second honeymoon, they toured the countryside. They visited tiny pubs in remote villages and sang folk songs with the locals. He recalled how Jaimee had researched the location of the Gallagher homestead at the local library back in Connecticut where they lived with the kids during the winters. After circling several villages in County Leitrim, they finally found the plot of land formerly owned by her parents' parents.

Gordie recalled the triumphant joy in her eyes at her accomplishment.

The happiness of that moment scattered from his mind with the sudden memory of her illness, only a few months after their return. The cancer struck her swiftly and mercilessly. In a matter of weeks, she transformed from a lively angel on earth to a gaunt and ghastly ghost of her former self. Her hair thinned and slowly pulled free from her scalp. The medicine weakened her almost as violently as the disease that attacked her.

Her bones softened. Eventually her leg snapped like a twig and she found herself confined to a wheel chair. Gordie recalled holding her hand on the final day of her life on the deck of the old Matunuck home they shared.

The thought that he had allowed Mick to sell that unique and special house; that he'd part with Jaime; that he'd have to continue on without her; generated a pain in his head far greater than any tumor-induced headache. It filled the numbness he had achieved in his spine, his arms and his legs through his relaxation technique.

In the dark of the bedroom, he cast his feet to the floor and hoisted himself from his prone position.

"I'll never be that happy again," he muttered to himself as he slipped his feet into his docksiders and flung his flimsy bathrobe over his shoulders.

Kian tugged Melodie gently by the hand to a secluded spot in the dunes adjacent to the crop of cottages at Roy Carpenter's Beach. They spread their two blankets next to each other in the cool flat sand and sunk below the beachgrass atop the dunes, out of sight from passersby.

Melodie rolled under her beau and kissed his face and neck. With her arms, she pulled him over her and maneuvered her hips against his. Fully clothed, they made out passionately as the evening breeze teased their hair and tickled their skin.

Melodie felt Kian's roving touch along the bottom of her stomach and slide its way past her belly button toward the base of her bra. In turn, she reached under the back of his t-shirt and caressed the muscles that ran down either side of his spine. They wiggled and squirmed in unison as their shirts slid over their heads and landed in the sand next to their blankets.

Melodie felt the gush of warmth in her face as Kian kissed her neck and worked down toward her collar bone and the top of her cleavage.

She played with his hair and arched her back in enjoyment. As she did, Mick's three-story home came into her view. The image snapped her from the pleasure of Kian's fingers against her sensitive skin. The light from Mick's music studio distracted her. She could see a tiny figure in the window, bobbing back and forth to music she couldn't hear, but could clearly imagine.

"Wait," she jolted and sat upright, self-consciously looking for her shirt. "I can't. I'm sorry. Not here."

Kian, confused, rolled to his back and gazed at the stars.

"Why not?" he asked, before catching himself and putting on his gentleman face. "It's fine. We don't have to do anything. It's just nice to be here together."

"I'm sorry," Melodie said, sitting in a ball with her knees pressed to her chest. "I was really into it. Really. I mean, seriously. But I could see my dad in the window and it just killed the mood."

"I get that," Kian smiled, noticing the light in Mick's window.

"See why I can't be here all the time?" she asked. "I just can't always be so connected to my parents. I need my freedom."

Kian kissed his girlfriend on the cheek and rubbed her back lightly.

"It's fine," he said. "But, can we get back to the apartment … quickly?"

Melodie laughed heartily. The echo from her glee probably made it all the way to Mick's yard. Using the same teasing motion as before, Melodie, played with the v-neck of her shirt.

"Definitely."

Kian stood and slung the two towels over his shoulder. He slid his hand into Melodie's. They stood for a minute admiring the calm of the ocean and the dance of the moonlight in the dimples of the waves.

A strange sight caught both their attention. An elderly man, in boat shoes and a thin bathrobe walked into the moonlight a couple hundred feet away. He moved in their direction, staggering like a drunkard and holding his head. He stopped at the spot near where the Maguire family had scattered Jaime's ashes and appeared to call out to the sea.

Melodie recognized the white hair and beard. She'd seen the ratty bathrobe in her father's house. She took a double take to make sure she wasn't seeing a ghost and gave Kian a concerned look before calling out to him from the dunes.

"Grandpa Gordie?"

Chapter 10

Gordie faced the vast Atlantic Ocean. The black, swirling waves reflected the twinkle of the moon. He toed the spot where only a month earlier he had released his beloved wife's ashes into the dark water and given her last remains the freedom to commune with the place she loved the most during her life.

The clouds parted and the rain subsided. Streaks of lightning danced across the horizon. They illuminated Block Island in the distance.

Gordie looked to the sky. The salt air dampened the ringing in his ears and the sting between his eyes. He felt goosebumps burst from the exposed skin of his legs in the cold of the evening. He stepped toward the high tide mark and felt the soft, cool sand against the bottom of his flimsy shoes. Another few steps further and the reach of the waves would wash his feet in chilly Matunuck water. He shuffled forward, almost trance-like.

"Am I delusional?" he thought. "Sleepwalking? Out of my mind?"

He asked Jaimee what to do. And he spoke to God.

"I could just swim right out into the water as deep as possible," he said to himself. "Just keep paddling out there until the current sweeps me too deep to get back."

He recalled earlier in the day, when he grew dizzy and started to slip under the surface of the water. As much as the sensation scared him, it also engendered in him a curious sense of peace.

"I could join you, Jaimes," he said to the sky. "Right here at the same place where your earthly remains found their eternal home. I could swim into the oblivion and cross right over to you in Heaven."

He shifted his attention from the spirit of his deceased wife to the God he had loved with all his heart for his entire existence.

"What about you?" he asked. "What do you say I should do? You've tested me so much and I've tried so hard not to complain or be bitter. You struck her down. You made her suffer. You took her from me. And now this."

Gordie swallowed the rising anger in his throat and calmed his nerves.

"I don't need to know why," he prayed. "I'm an old man now. I don't need all the answers. I know I'll learn them soon. But, I'm ready. I don't want to do it myself. I won't swim out there tonight. But, if you could just strike me down with one of those streaks of lightning, I'm ready to come be with you... and her."

In the back of his mind, Gordie heard a sound. It resembled the squawk of a seagull in the wind. He interpreted the barely audible noise as some sort of sign, maybe an answer from God giving him direction and answers to the suffering he'd experienced for so many years throughout his seventies.

He heard it again, but this time, he thought he heard words. He heard his name.

"Grandpa Gordie," he heard his granddaughter Melodie calling to him. "What are you doing?"

Gordie swung from the water's edge and eyed the young woman with her boyfriend running down the dunes toward him.

"Why are you out here so late?" she asked. "You'll catch a cold. It's freezing."

Images of swimming to a watery death or awaiting a dramatic thunderbolt to sap him of his human form flew from his consciousness. A wave of realization hit him that despite the loss of his wife, he still had a whole family of loving people around him in Matunuck to celebrate and enjoy. He shifted his mind to formulate an explanation for his late-night appearance on the beach.

"You kidding," he flapped his frigid lips. "It's a beautiful evening."

Melodie reached Gordie and wrapped an arm around his back. Kian stood a few feet away. Gordie eyed them with confusion as if ghosts who materialized out of thin air. Had they been perfect strangers, he would have convinced himself they were agents of the Holy Spirit sent to give him guidance.

"Where did you come from?" Gordie asked with the rosy innocence of an older person. "Hiding out in the dunes?"

The reality dawned on even him and he cleared his throat to clarify.

"I mean, what are you doing out walking on the beach so late?" he rephrased his question. "Catching the beautiful stars like me?"

"Uh, right," Melodie answered him. "I guess we both just wanted to enjoy the beautiful evening."

"I guess," Gordie replied.

Melodie walked her grandfather back toward the gap in the dunes by the inn and the path to Mick's house. Kian wrapped a blanket over the older man's shoulders.

"You looked sad out there by the shore," Melodie said.

"I get sad sometimes," he replied. "I miss my wife; your grandmother. You were young when you lived with us and you only met her a few times since you were a baby, but she loved you so much."

They approached Mick's house. Melodie observed the silhouette of her father in the upstairs window. She could see him texting on his phone, with his noise-cancelling headset still over his ears.

"I regret having lived in California all those years and not having come to visit more," Melodie said, sitting next to him on the swinging wooden bench that hung from two chains affixed to the ceiling of the porch.

Kian stood, awkwardly by the steps to the porch, giving Melodie and her grandfather space, but lurking close enough to take part in the conversation if called upon.

"It wasn't you," Gordie counselled Melodie. "Mick left. He needed to find himself. He needed to be with your mom for those years and be your dad. He did what he had to do. There are no regrets and we all understand his choices. To be honest, we all could have visited you more too."

Melodie rested her head on Gordie's shoulder. Kian leaned against the support beam that held the railing in place.

"Tell me," Gordie started. "How do you like Matunuck?"

Melodie paused.

"I like it here," she said. "The family's here. The beach is nice. There's a lot to do."

"But, you're not sure you want to live here like your dad?"

Melodie paused again and gathered her thoughts. She cast a quick glance at Kian, who seemed amused by the question. Unlike with her father she felt comfortable sharing her inner thoughts with her softer, less judgmental grandfather.

"I don't know," she started her response. "It's nice here and all."

"But there's other places you'd rather be?"

"It's not that," she replied. "It's just that I'm young. I was in California so long and we never really went anywhere. My parents didn't get along that great. We weren't really a family like the Maguires and the Gallaghers. We rarely went on vacation together. I spent all my time with my mom. I just feel like I need to get away and experience some new places on my own."

Gordie smiled softly and stoked Melodie's hair.

"I felt the same way at your age you know."

"You did?"

"Sure," he replied. "Did you know I joined the Navy?"

Kian leaned forward to hear Gordie's story. Melodie perked her head from her grandfather's shoulder.

"For about five years, I was a Naval officer on a ship," he continued. "I spent months in the Mediterranean. On my shore leaves, I went to Paris, Munich, Marseille, Rome. You name it, I've seen it."

"I had no idea," Melodie beamed.

"I did Beerfest in Germany. I practiced my French in Paris. I even ran with the bulls in Pamplona."

Kian stepped closer and leaned his back against the railing.

"I backpacked across Europe with my buddy, working a week here and there for cash and then spending it every night in the bars and pubs."

Melodie flashed her eyes at Kian and playfully smacked her grandfather in the arm.

"That sounds amazing," she said.

"And, I bet you inherited my wanderlust didn't you?"

Melodie gave his statement a thought and agreed.

"I think I have," she opened up to him. "I love my dad and you and all the relatives we have here. It's been great to be part of a cohesive family that really loves each other."

"But..." Gordie interjected.

"But I also want to travel," she continued. "I want to see Boston and New York City and Philadelphia. I want to go to the Caribbean and maybe even Europe. Don't get me wrong."

"Believe me, I get it," Gordie laughed.

"I love my Dad. He's been great."

"But you can't live in the same town as him."

"Right?" Melodie exclaimed.

Gordie stared at Melodie's dark hair and bright eyes. Her cheek reflected the overhead light and illuminated her smile.

"You know you're the spitting image of your grandmother?" Gordie observed. "You have her spirit."

Melodie swung her hips, causing the bench to sway.

"My Dad tells me that all the time."

"Listen," Gordie counselled her, his face softening at the view of his granddaughter by the light of the porch lamp. "You only get one life; one chance to make the most of the time God gives you."

Gordie swayed with Melodie, causing the bench to move from left to right in front of the living room bay window.

"I haven't lived the best life I could since she died," Gordie said, quietly. "But seeing you tonight reminds me that it's up to you to live your own life your own way with no regrets. Go on adventures. Do what you want to do; what you need to do. Being alive is the greatest gift God gives us. He wants us to make the most of it and find what makes us happy. If that's traveling and experiencing the world, then that's what you should do. If eventually, you want to come back and be with the family, like I did, then that's fine too. You'll always be welcome here."

Melodie gazed lovingly into Gordie's eyes. The warmth of her dark brown irises and the authenticity of her huge smile melted him. She hugged him and for a moment, he had a sharp memory of his wife. He could see her exuberance in Melodie's round face. The hug lasted a second or two, but he could still feel the radiance of her body even after she pulled away.

"I haven't lived my life the way I should since my wife passed away," Gordie said.

"And what about you," Gordie turned his attention to Kian. Have a seat and tell me what you want to do with yourself now that you're graduating.

Kian stepped forward and took a seat on the hanging bench. As he opened his mouth to speak, a bit of plaster dust fell into his hair. Three pairs of eyes looked up at the ceiling in just enough time to watch the chain pull loose and crash to the ground.

Tumbling a foot and a half to the floor of the porch, the immediate shock gave way to amusement. They all looked at each other and fell into a fit of laughter. They sat on the floor, with the crumpled remains of the bench at their backs, roaring uncontrollably. Melodie buried her head into Gordie's chest and Gordie slapped Kian's back.

The ensuing pounding of footsteps preceded the smack of the screen door. The surprised look on Mick's face contrasted with the red-faced laughter of the trio of the floor of the porch as Mick shouted in panic.

"What the hell's going on?"

Chapter 11

Mick awoke around eight after getting Gordie back to sleep following his late-night excursion with Melodie and Kian. He stood on a step ladder on the porch and reviewed the damage to his ceiling.

"Shouldn't have done it yourself," Gordie called through the open window. "Your Grampa Shamus woulda done it right. You should try Kenny Forrester. He's pretty handy. I bet he could fix it."

"I'm perfectly capable of installing a hanging swing," Mick called back, annoyed, but scrolling through his contact list on his phone for Kenny's number all the same.

The smell of sizzling bacon wafted up the stairs, around the corner and across the hallway to his master bedroom on the far side of the house. In cotton shorts and a white t-shirt, he ambled into the kitchen, and watched his father whip up one of his famous over-the-top breakfasts.

"I've got spaghetti and eggs," he listed his offerings. "I added the leftover sirloin steak to them. I mushed the baked potatoes, added cream and flour and made potato pancakes. I've got bacon on the griddle and toast about to pop."

As if on cue, two slices of golden white bread jumped into the air. Mick rubbed his stomach. The late dinner and ice cream soda float desserts with Dana's girls still sat in his stomach.

"Sounds great Dad," he said, more out of deference to his father's efforts than a desire to stuff more food into his belly. "Load me up."

With an overfilled gut, Mick showered and dressed in a pair of cargo shorts and a Boston Red Sox t-shirt. The sun shined across the potato field. He could see the ocean, almost as calm as a lake. Gulls flew overhead. Umbrellas extended above the line of the dunes. The dim murmur of the waves only faintly echoed off the south-facing window panes of his house.

Mick had a half hour free before his appointment to walk the beach with Shelly. He logged into his bank account and checked his balances before paying his most critical bills and chipping away at some credit card debt.

He scrolled through several junk e-mails hoping to stumble across a parent or two requesting personalized music lessons. He needed the eighty dollars an hour he could command from his private tutoring sessions to pay down debt and ensure his ability to keep Danielle at bay. She never failed to sick her lawyer on him every time he missed a payment deadline.

He spied an e-mail directly from Bo Rutledge and eagerly clicked it. Typically, Bo's manager interacted with Mick and served as an intermediary between them. So, a message directly from his client caught him as a pleasant surprise.

"Love the song about the beach," Bo wrote. "Figured we'd e-mail direct. I fired Fred. I'm going to take control of my own career for a while."

Nerves lapped Mick's stomach. He'd hoped Bo would include at least one of the three songs on the album. But he recognized the likelihood that none of them would make it. Inclusion of even one piece would rake in enough money to at least zero out his credit cards.

Mick brought up the Word document where he'd written scraps of lyrics to the first song Bo liked.

"*Bottles of beer in the black of the night,*" he read his words and hummed the accompanying tune. "*Fireworks bursting as a bonfire burns. And I'm laying with my baby on a blanket at the beach.*"

He imagined an up-tempo guitar riff kicking in at the end of the refrain and repeating the stanza; "*Laying with my baby on a blanket at the beach.*"

His goal was to paint various scenes of beach life and close each vignette with the image of "*Laying with my baby on a blanket at the beach.*"

He pictured a lyric about his main characters swimming in the sea, cold and wet, and another one about them getting drunk in the dunes. He created a back story for himself about a couple in their early twenties - close to Melodie's age - spending all their time at some beautiful beach. In his mind, the entire song took place in Matunuck. But, given

Bo's status as a country music star, he added bits of lyrics to imply a southern setting of one of the Carolinas or Florida.

Mick checked the clock and realized he had five minutes to trot over to Shelly's and walk the beach with her.

"Where're you off to?" Gordie asked, as Mick bound down the stairs, nearly out of breath.

"Going to walk on the beach," he replied. "Check out the erosion from the storm."

"There's another one coming next week you know," Gordie said.

"I know," Mick replied. "I hear it's going to be a bad hurricane season."

Gordie slid the last few slices of bacon onto a paper plate and handed it to Mick.

"Sorry," he said. "I'm so full."

Gordie persisted, but Mick held firm, prompting Gordie to eat the crispy pork fat himself.

"You never really know when today could be your last day," Gordie grinned as he chomped away. "You want some company on your walk?"

"Oh, uh, well," Mick stammered for a second before composing himself. "Of course."

But Gordie laughed.

"Sure, you want your dear old dad tagging along with you?"

"Why not?" Mick asked, assuming Shelly would be delighted to add his father to their walkabout.

Gordie laughed again.

"I wouldn't want to be a third wheel."

"What made you think I was walking with Shelly?" Mick asked.

"I didn't," Gordie replied. "But I do now."

Mick grabbed a fluffy rainbow-patterned beach towel. He opened his wallet to check to make sure he had cash. He tied his sneakers and slung the towel around his neck.

"Seriously," he said to his father in earnest. "Shelly loves you. You're welcome to join us."

"I would," Gordie said. "But I have a date."

Mick stood in the foyer and gazed at his father, perplexed.

"A date?" he repeated.

"Well, not exactly a date," Gordie explained. "Your Aunt Trudy has been trying to get me to be more social and take part in these programs they offer in the city. I called her this morning and agreed to some silly old-person excursion. She's taking me to the Wakefield Senior Center for a dancing class. I understand it will be me and a dozen eligible ladies."

The image of having released his mother's ashes into the ocean only a few weeks earlier as well as the emotional trauma his father experienced every time he walked past that section of the beach flashed before his mind.

"Uh, okay," Mick said, not sure how to respond to his father's curious new activity. "Have fun then, I guess."

"I plan to, because - you know Mickey - you just don't know how many days you have left," Gordie said with a pat on the shoulder. "You only really know that you have today. So, you just have to move forward as if you've got a whole lifetime ahead of you."

The sun burned bright for nine o'clock on an early September morning. The moisture in the air from the evening's storm held the salt from the ocean and filled Mick's lungs with heaviness. With each deep breath, he felt a tickle as if he had to cough the salt out of his chest.

Shelly stood on the porch of the inn. She wore a flowing cream sundress and wide, floppy hat. The blue-green of the ocean framed her blond hair as it flittered in the wind behind her head like the tail of a kite. Her matching azure eyes fixed on his and the corners of her lips parted.

"The dunes are in bad shape," she said to him, the carefree smile edging downward in reflection of her concern.

With the destruction of the original mansion on Shelly's property during Hurricane Constance, the beach in front of her newly constructed inn - which she moved several hundred feet away from the shore - had the widest patch of sand in town. A little flatter than the cliff-like structures further to the east, the gentler curve of the beach afforded her inn a near perfect view of the shoreline.

But, as they walked eastward toward neighboring Roy Carpenter's Beach, the sandy berms bordering the extreme high tide mark of the previous night's storm appeared to have been carved with a giant cosmic shovel. They looked like one of those tall wedding cakes with a combination of chocolate and vanilla between layers of frosting. And like a wedding cake, the freshly sliced dunes exposed similar brown, grey and yellow alternating layers of earth. There was a ribbon of dark brown clay-like dirt from the potato field. Beneath the dirt lay a vein of hard, grey waterlogged bedrock. Wedged between the dirt and clay, several strips of fine sand, washed in and out through the years with each storm season, gave the embankment it's artistic array of color.

Two of the eight houses at the edge of the waterline lay dashed into disorganized piles of cracked and broken boards. Scraps of metal and broken glass littered the sand around where the houses use to proudly stand. The others sagged even more precariously. Members of the community stood around, looking at the carnage, shaking their heads and hugging each other.

Between Roy's and Willow Dell just further to the east, the height of the sand and dirt cliffs exceeded the top of Shelly's head. All the way past the town beach and the Blackberry Beach Gap, the dunes reflected the aftermath of the storm's greedy scraping claws that tore at the landscape throughout the night.

Mick and Shelly strode the beach shoulder-to-shoulder. Mick held his sneakers by the back of the heels. They swung at his side as his gate alternated from left to right. His bare feet dug into the firm wet sand at the edge of the foamy waves. The two-inch-deep remnants of the rippling saltwater licked their toes like shy, wet puppies.

"Do you think the pub survived?" she asked, of the famous Ocean Mist that perched high above the remains of the old Mary Carpenter's Beach.

"That place'll be the last building to fall," he replied. "It's like the Fort Knox of Matunuck Beach."

They navigated as far as they could before arriving at the corner of what used to be Blackberry Beach. The massive trailer park seawall blocked their passage from walking any further eastward along the edge of the ocean.

Since the onslaught and rise of the Atlantic sea-level had long-since overtaken the beach and lapped directedly against the rocks, passage in front of them to Mary's beach had grown impossible. A sandy path led behind the elevated property. It connected to the Matunuck Beach Road about a quarter mile south of the Vanilla Bean ice cream shop and only a couple hundred yards from the entrance to what used to be the biggest, most popular beach in town.

Ahead of them, rose the salt-worn wooden structure of the Ocean Mist, where owner Kyle Dolman served comfort food, held bingo and movie nights, promoted music concerts and ran a popular annual beer-fest. The building stood like a cranky old warrior refusing to yield to a clearly overwhelming force of powerful oceanic invaders.

The building propped on stilts, half suspended in the air, above the play of the surf. The deck to the adjacent restaurant wrapped along the top of the beach like a rickety train bridge over a dangerous ravine. Long wooden planks supported the reddish-grey, worn balcony from tumbling into the sand and salt water below.

A Matunuck landmark, the building might have long since been condemned had they not built up such a beloved reputation throughout Rhode Island. Nearly all the state's politicians, lawyers, judges and even the Governor herself, harbored cherished memories of partying by the sea at the infamous hot-spot atop Mary Carpenter's declining patch of sand.

Mick stood on the rocks that lay askew along the side of the Matunuck Beach Road. The erosion of the sand behind the rock pile encroached to within a foot or two of the street. Bits of asphalt cracked free and tumbled down the cliff-like structure of sand and dirt.

Next to Mary Carpenter's crumbled pile of granite, limestone, basalt and concrete, the vertical beams beneath the floor joists of the pub sat on tall cement pylons. The Atlantic Ocean crashed against the shaded sand and splashed through the round cement columns. It looked like the high tide mark extended beneath the entire floorplan of the building.

They walked under the dampened rafters. The waves rushed up their calves. The bottom of Shelly's sundress clung to her shins. Mick felt the trim of his shorts soak through to his thighs.

"I wonder how the houses along the point are doing?" Shelly asked. "Mr. Callahan said they were in danger too."

"They're screwed," Mick agreed.

Next to the pub sat a row of two dozen houses. Shelly pointed out the cottage her parents rented when she was in elementary school and the Callahan home a few blocks further to the east.

"In the summer, my dad was a bartender at the pub. My mom made the clam cakes." she explained. "In the winter, my dad worked for the town as a janitor at the school. Some of the kids made fun of me for it. He knew I got teased. He hated that job."

They walked high along the top of the beach past the tiny cottages crammed along the top of the dunes. The tight row of rickety buildings looked like spectators at a sporting event with front row seats to the rolling waves at the eastern tip of Matunuck.

Unlike the western side of town where Mick grew up, the eastern shore featured more traditional waves that broke a couple hundred feet out and rolled along the stones to the sand. It served as a popular surfing spot for Rhode Islanders from Pawtucket to Quonochontaug to Pawcatuck. On any given day, a good dozen wet-suited adventure-seekers waded a couple hundred feet out from the shore seeking just the right curls to ride.

Across the street from the pub, the Dolmans opened the surf shack and pizza shop. They offered boards, wax jobs, wet suits and apparel. The store gained a modest following across the state and always had impressive foot traffic. The pub served a unique blend of home cooked comfort food and classic Rhode Island fried seafood that attracted sizeable crowds on any given night. Mick had developed a taste for brothy Rhode Island clam chowder at the pub, which rivaled his mother's famous recipe. But beside the table service at the pub, the pizza place was the only quick food in town.

East of the pub, the beach widened enough for them to walk along the sliver of dry sand between the break of the waves and the hundred-year-old cottages wedged between the Matunuck Beach Road and the ocean.

"I don't come this way too often anymore," Shelly commented. "Mr. Callahan's right. These houses are in just as much danger as the pub."

"Someday, the ocean's going to wipe them all out," Mick agreed.

"That would be awful."

"I know. But it's inevitable."

Mick walked around the bend. Shelly lingered, looking across the half-mile stretch of squat homes.

"I know what it's like to see your family home crushed by the sea monster," she called to Mick as he waded onto the rock bar at Deep Hole.

Shelly hoisted the bottom of her sundress in her hands and followed Mick into the quiet rippling water.

At Deep Hole, the far easternmost tip of Matunuck Beach, the waves flattened. A sort of misnomer, Deep Hole actually featured one of the shallower places to wade into the water. The infamous Matunuck ditch where the waves broke and violently churned sand and stone disappeared and an entire ecosystem of sea life danced happily under the tapestry of smooth sand, pebbles and time-worn weathered rocks.

Beyond Deep Hole, further east, a massive sea wall stretched nearly a mile and reached as high as twenty feet tall. It curved and tailed with the contour of the shore, buttressing the dead-end street, Ocean Avenue, with its tall houses and beautiful views.

Mick found an abandoned plastic bucket floating aimlessly in the waves and scooped it out of the foam. Shelly slowly worked her way toward him, still trying unsuccessfully to protect the bottom of her sundress.

"Look," Mick held the pail. "Ever catch crabs here?"

Sick of daintily padding across the stones, Shelly dropped the trim of her dress into the water and strode out to him.

"I haven't been here in a long time," she said. "When I lived at this side of town, my sister and I used to come out here all the time. Viv and I were usually too busy being social. Once I moved to the mansion, it was too much of a hike to walk all the way over here."

Mick crouched low to the clear, shallow water and lifted a round rock, like a baseball.

"When you pick up a rock, you have to look carefully," he told her. "All the little sand particles scatter and you can barely see through the dust."

Shelly squat next to him and rested a hand on his shoulder to steady herself.

"The baby crabs scatter as soon as you lift the rock," Mick continued, raising another stone and peering through the sandy dust. "Sometimes you have to look for movement. And sometimes you just reach into the hole where the rock was and try to grab whatever you can?"

"Do the crabs bite?" Shelly asked. "You, know, I mean, with their claws?"

"They're so small," Mick said, catching one as he spoke. "Even if they did, you wouldn't feel it."

Mick filled the bucket with water, some sand and a few pebbles. He dropped the tiny crab, about the size of a quarter, into the little green plastic container. Shelly watched it scurry sideways across the sandy bottom and burrow under one of the pebbles.

"He's so cute," she beamed.

Mick lifted another rock and fished around with his hand, but came up empty. Shelly moved a smaller stone, but also failed to find a baby crab.

"The bigger the rock, the better chance you have of finding one," Mick told her, as he pulled out another crab and dropped it in the bucket with the first one.

"Aww," Shelly smiled. "Now he has a friend."

Mick chuckled and turned over more rocks.

"Or a girlfriend," Shelly added with a subtle raise of her eyebrow, which Mick missed as he obsessed with finding just the right rock to overturn.

They waded deeper. The water changed from ankle high to knee high. Shelly's dress floated in the ripples like a jellyfish surrounding her thighs. Mick found another crab and added it to the bucket. Shelly found several as well. After fifteen minutes in the water, they assembled a community of a dozen crabs. The tiny shellfish darted back and forth across the bottom of the bucket, indiscriminately climbing over each other as they circled their plastic ecosystem. Shelly lifted a large rock with two hands and yelped.

"I got one," she said. "And it's a big one."

She held it up to show him, but it jumped out of her hand back into the water. As if it might bite her toes, Shelly leapt backwards and nearly lost her balance. Mick caught her under the elbow and straightened her onto her feet.

They made their way back to shore. Shelly had a small cut on the bottom of her foot from grazing a barnacle along the side of one of the rocks. A trickle of blood dripped from her big toe. It mingled with the sand as she reached the shore.

"Are you alright?" Mick asked her, noticing a slight limp.

"I'm okay," she replied. "But maybe we could go to the surf shop and see if they have a bandage?"

Shelly twirled her finger into the top of the water in the bucket and said goodbye to their crustaceous pets. Mick dumped the bucket back into the rock bar area, and they watched the crabs scatter like cockroaches under new rocks.

Mick put an arm around Shelly and asked if she needed help. She thanked him, but opted to walk unassisted.

"I'm fine," she said, her face shading in embarrassment. "It's nothing, really."

They walked back to the pub, staying close to the break of the waves where the water could continuously wash over her toes and keep the cut from taking on too much dry sand.

The Matunuck Surf Shop sat in a non-descript square building across the street from the pub. Long-time Matunuck residents, Kyle and Joycie Dolman, owned both the shop, the attached pizza restaurant, the pub and the Ocean Mist bar.

Shelly sat on a bench outside the store, while Mick went inside to seek a package of bandages. He looked up and down each aisle, but the store only offered surfing apparel, water shoes, wet suits and other, very specific merchandise that didn't help. He asked the clerk, who confirmed that they didn't have what he needed. As Mick turned to leave, the teenager suggested the pub might have a first aid kit.

"We can say hi to Kyle," Shelly said, her face lighting up as she spoke. "We went to high school together."

Mick grabbed a handful of napkins from the pizza restaurant and asked the kid at the register to dampen them in the sink. Shelly used them to wipe away the dried blood and put pressure on her cut.

"I just hope his wife isn't there today," Shelly added.

Mick looked at her curiously.

"Another boyfriend?" he asked her.

"It was a long time ago," Shelly replied, her face blushing again. "He was my prom date, and, well, I guess you could say, like, sort of, my first serious relationship."

Chapter 12

Kyle Dolman greeted Shelly with an exuberant hug.

"Hey there Shells," he said, with a kiss on the cheek.

Shelly introduced Mick. They shook hands. Kyle's vicelike grip squeezed the blood from his fingers. He watched them shade from pink to white and then slowly back to pink after letting go.

Kyle wore a t-shirt with the Matunuck Surf Shop logo. His red beard framed his rugged face and bald head. His classic Nordic and Celtic look matched his tall, stout physique. He spoke quickly in a raspy voice and laughed often. He retrieved a bandage from the kitchen and invited them to stay for lunch.

"On me," he proclaimed.

"Where's Joycie?" Shelly asked.

"Her mother needed her at the house in Wakefield," he replied. "Some sort of leaky pipe situation or something like that. I don't know. You know how her mother can be."

Shelly and Kyle laughed as Mick took his seat on the deck overlooking the water. The waves rumbled right up to, and past the pylons that held the deck from crashing twenty feet into the swirling water. Mick watched the foamy tide wash by the railing and out of sight under his feet.

"I've seen you here before," Kyle nodded at Mick, as Shelly took her seat across from him. "You built that sweet Victorian-style house out past Roy's."

"That's right," Mick replied. "I've been there almost a half a year now."

"I met your daughter here the other night," Kyle said.

"Did you?" Mick asked, arching an eyebrow, but keeping her actual age to himself.

"You're the music executive," Kyle continued. "I heard you play at the inn a couple weeks ago. Are those your own original songs?"

"I write them," Mick replied, "I usually try them out there. If people seem to like them, I sell them to local bands."

"You're really good," Kyle complimented him. "You should play here."

Shelly asked about Kyle's five-year-old and two-year-old twins. He boasted of his eldest's reading abilities and railed about the struggle of handling twin babies. He gushed about Joycie's ability to manage their household, care for the children and still oversee their businesses in town.

"She does all the hard work," Kyle laughed. "I just run the bar and entertain the guests."

"You do a lot more than that," Shelly said. "You line up the musical acts. You create all the advertising and promotional events. And, you're doing a great job working with the town."

Shelly turned to Mick to explain further.

"He goes to all the town council meetings and fights for them to spend money to fix the beach."

"We used to fight," Kyle said. "We've become partners, and they've done a good job listening to our concerns lately."

"Of course," Shelly replied. "But you're also spending millions of dollars out of your own pocket to pay for the wall."

"I haven't spent quite that much yet," Kyle stammered, almost embarrassed at Shelly's praise. "The town's approved my plan, but we're tied up in legal challenges on two fronts. I've got the environmental groups saying the plan will destroy the beach and the homeowners complaining that the natural dune construction won't go far enough to protect the community."

"Last year, he got hundreds of people to pack the town hall during the budget hearings when they wanted to half-ass it and just fix the part of the wall next to the trailer park," Shelly gushed. "Are you part of the lawsuit?"

"Which one?" Kyle laughed.

He waved to the kitchen staff and pointed to the fryolator for a basket of fries.

"Too early for beers?" he asked them.

90

"Coffee milk for me," Mick requested.

"You still love egg creams?" Kyle asked Shelly.

"You know it," she replied with a wide grin. "I'll take a chocolate."

As the waitstaff slid the thick-cut fries across the table, Kyle grabbed a bottle of malt vinegar from a nearby shelf. Shelly slathered the fries in the pungent amber coating and Mick shook salt over them.

"We've got an agreement between the town and the state to use emergency funds to firm up and extend the wall," Kyle explained. "It'll be much better constructed with steel girders buried deep into the ground, cement casings and huge, two-ton boulders fitted together by tongue and groove slats and cables. It'll run along the road from the trailers, right under this deck and out another fifty feet past the pub. We're going to buffer it with natural materials to keep the aesthetics and hopefully preserve at least a little bit of beach."

"Seems safer to have all that rock under the deck than letting the ocean eat away at the support beams." Shelly added. "They're just pressure-treated wood. They can't hold out forever."

"We'd have built it already," Kyle concluded. "But this 'Protect the Beach' watchdog group and the Matunuck Point Homeowners Association and a couple other fringe groups are giving us a hard time about it."

"Are you involved with Mr. Callahan?" Shelly asked.

"I heard he's been talking to people in the village," Kyle replied. "I'm not sure what his involvement is. But everyone's suing someone over this mess. So, I wouldn't be surprised."

"I've read about this," Mick spoke up. "A lot of controversy around hardening the shore."

"Protect the Beach doesn't want any wall or barrier at all," Kyle said. "They'd just as soon let everyone get flooded out. The Homeowners want an all or nothing strategy. Either we harden the entire shore and build from here all the way past Deep Hole to the point, or we scrap the wall altogether. They're afraid the current plan only protects the immediately vulnerable area where the road is exposed and will ultimately push the currents their way."

"It reminds me of what they did in Narragansett by the Coast Guard House," Mick said, referring to an area ten miles away. "They built that massive seawall in the fifties for a mile-long section to protect the row of multimillion dollar homes. It eliminated any trace of beach along that stretch of waterfront.

"It's not exactly the same," Kyle hedged. "But they did have to build a pretty hard seawall to protect Ocean Road down there. So, I guess it's a fair comparison."

"So, that'll mean the end of the beach here?" Mick asked. "Like it did in Narragansett?"

Kyle's face tightened. Shelly's eyes flared.

"Look down," Kyle snapped. "You see a beach?"

"What about all those houses on the other side of the pub," Mick retorted. "Won't your wall just push the ocean further east and wipe them out?"

Kyle glanced quickly at Shelly before replying in a softer, more restrained voice.

"For one, studies about that are inconclusive," he started. "And for two, part of my personal investment in preserving the Matunuck beachfront includes paying for sand fences, sandbags, and a couple hundred grand in new sand deposits."

"We do have to protect those houses too," Shelly added. "Mr. Callahan is definitely talking to people about that as well."

Mick noticed Shelly's dark expression and backed off the discussion point. Kyle took their orders and excused himself. The waves filled the silence with their rhythmic scraping across the pebbles by the ditch. Mick could feel the salty spray under his feet through the narrow gaps between the floorboards as each wave lapped the pylons and spritzed the joists.

"You know," Shelly finally broke the mildly tense silence. "He's a local hero around here. He's the only one willing to risk everything he has to save the beach."

"He's saving his business," Mick countered her.

"He loves this town," she raised her voice. "He's lived here his whole life."

Her face reddened. The glow of the orange lights overhead shaded her eyes and cast a rouge glimmer across her cheeks.

"It's not like he took off for twenty years," Shelly continued. "And then just showed up at the last minute all of a sudden thinking someone made him the king of the beach."

"Okay, okay," Mick held out his arms in surrender. "I'm sorry. I didn't mean to be argumentative."

"He's buying us lunch and you insulted him."

"I'll apologize," Mick offered.

Shelly looked out over the ocean. A gentle breeze played with her blond hair. A kitchen staff member brought them their plates of food.

"I just have a strong perspective about what happens when you harden the shoreline," Mick said. "I've read up on it. When you give the ocean resistance, the force of the water doesn't go away. It displaces further down the coast and makes it worse for the areas beyond the wall."

Shelly ate a fried clam and didn't respond.

"I loved Blackberry Beach more than any spot on this earth," Mick continued. "And now it's gone because of that damned wall they put up to protect those stupid trailers. That's why I'm against building walls in Matunuck."

"It's just a club house," Shelly's face went red. "There's plenty of beach for you to enjoy."

"If they never built that seawall, I'm convinced that Blackberry Beach Club would still exist and Mary Carpenter's Beach would still be a beach."

"It's all easy for you to say," Shelly debated him. "Your place is way back from the water. I know what it's like to watch your family's home go down into the ocean. It sucks. You'd do anything to protect it. Mr. Callahan says they should build a wall across the whole beach from here to Deep Hole. And I agree with him."

A slender, dark-haired woman in a bikini with a mesh coverup approached the table. Shelly pretended not to notice her, but she beelined straight for them.

"I hope I'm not interrupting some lover's quarrel," she said, with a sly smile. "How are you, Michelle?"

Mick saw Shelly's eyes roll out of sight from Joycie Dolman.

"Who's your special someone?" she asked with dripping sarcasm.

"He's just a... this is Mick," Shelly muttered. "He's my..."

"Oh, don't be shy, babe," Mick interrupted her, while reaching across the table for her hand. "We've been together almost a year now."

Shelly turned red, but her smile belied appreciation and enjoyment of the ruse.

"We fight with about as much passion as we do everything else together," Mick continued. "Michael Maguire. She calls me Mick, but you can go with Michael. I'm in the music industry."

"You're the music teacher at the elementary school?" Joycie asked, despite knowing the answer.

"That's the day job," Mick replied. "I also write music for rock and pop bands."

"Do you now?" Joycie asked. "Anyone I might have heard of?"

"He's writing music for Bo Rutledge," Shelly jumped in. "Aren't you, uh, babycakes?"

Joycie stood silent for a moment. Mick could see her passive aggressive insult engine churning through her options.

"That's right," Mick replied, still clutching Shelly's hand. "He's one of my more well-known clients."

"How's the inn doing?" Joycie asked, changing the subject.

"Can't complain," Shelly started to reply before Mick interrupted her again.

"Excuse me, sorry to interrupt," he said. "Would you mind bringing me some more tartar sauce for my fish and chips. I don't like it too dried out."

Joycie pivoted and disappeared into the kitchen, eventually sending a member of the staff with the container of tartar sauce.

"Went to high school with her too?" Mick asked.

"Just because she's from Wakefield, she thinks she's all city-girl sophisticated," Shelly said. "And I'm the hick from Matunuck. She wanted him the whole time I was going out with him. She applied to all the same colleges and while they were together at Stonehill, she moved right in on him. I never had a chance."

Mick watched her snap at the waitstaff through the cut-out window. Kyle flipped a burger and dumped a new set of fries into the fryolator. She scolded him for spilling a few on the floor.

"Thanks for all that," Shelly said, realizing their hands were still clasped across the table and flinching in nervousness. "She's always giving me grief for living alone in the cottage."

Mick nodded and nervously twitched a finger that interwove with one of hers.

"If I have to look at her kids one more time, I think I'm going to puke," Shelly made a face as if having eaten a lemon. "They're cute and all, but I don't need them shoved into my face."

Joycie brought them the check. The lunch had been voided, but she charged them for the coffee milk and egg cream beverage.

Mick dropped a ten on the table, draped his arm around Shelly and dramatically walked her through the restaurant. They waved to Kyle. Mick called into the kitchen saying something about "no hard feelings."

Kyle waved a spatula in acknowledgement. Joycie deliberately looked away as if not having noticed their departure.

As the screen door to the pub slapped the wood doorframe behind them, Shelly gasped in excitement, laughing heartily as they walked away from the pub.

"Did you see her?" Shelly asked. "She looked as jealous as she did at the prom. That was really sweet of you. Thanks again."

Mick suggested ice cream at the Vanilla Bean, but Shelley had to get back to her inn.

"Maybe later tonight?" Mick asked.

"I'd like that," she replied, with a smile like the sun.

They walked back along the beach road to the gap behind the trailer park. The path took them to the open space where the Blackberry Beach clubhouse used to be. In front of them, the ocean waves had picked up with the increased afternoon wind, but still resembled a giant flag rippling in the breeze.

Behind them, the dunes sloped down toward the road. The roof of the Vanilla Bean ice cream shop protruded from behind a row of cat-tail grass. The tall green leafy stalks featured long, round cottony masses that looked like hotdogs on sticks.

Mick pointed at the parking lot to the public beach next to the Vanilla Bean.

"We used to go up there at night," he told Shelly, "Back before they turned it into a parking lot. It used to be just acres and acres of potatoes."

"I remember," she reminded him. "I grew up here."

"Right," Mick caught himself. "I used hang out in the field with Kenny Forrester, Ronnie, Marty and Jack Valerian. We'd dig up a dozen potatoes each and throw them onto the roof of the Bean."

Mick made a series of explosion sounds to demonstrate the effect of the potatoes splattering on the roof.

"Scared the crap out of the customers and staff," Mick chuckled. "Until the farmer that owned the field chased us away with his shotgun."

"That was my uncle Jeremy Browning," Shelly laughed. "He only shot rock salt out of that old two-barrel."

"Jack got it right in the butt cheek one night," Mick finished his story. "That was my last night in Matunuck before I left for California to marry Danielle."

A pall fell over them. Shelly put her hand on his shoulder.

"You did what you had to do," she spoke quietly to him, followed by a silent pause and a second thought. "I'm sorry about what I said back at the pub."

"It's alright," he replied to her. "A lot has changed in those twenty years. When I left, this beach was enormous."

"A lot can happen in that time," Shelly agreed.

"You could walk in front of the trailer park. There was a whole pond back here between the beach and the Vanilla Bean."

"It breaks my heart," she agreed. "They call this the Blackberry Beach Gap."

"Now, my God," Mick continued. "The next big storm could break right through here, destroy the Bean and wash out that entire village of cottages across the street."

"That's why we need a wall here," Shelly said, immediately regretting the comment.

"I'm all for natural creation of dunes," Mick debated her as they made their way back down the beach toward the inn and his home. "But a concrete wall will spell the end of Matunuck as we know it."

"Maybe you know this town as a nice little strip of sand," Shelly argued. "But, to me it's more than that. It's also about the houses and the people."

"How many people from your childhood are even still here?" Mick challenged her. "As the cottages get wiped out, people who have been here for fifty, sixty, seventy years end up leaving, while people from Massachusetts and New York buy up all the land in the hills and build big mansions. It's the natural way of life. Matunuck's going to change and we have to change with it."

"Even if it means all those houses down there get flooded and crushed?"

"They knew the risks when they bought here."

"No, they didn't," Shelly snapped. "Some of the people down there bought those places so many years ago when there was no risk at all."

"I'm just saying," Mick defended his position. "Like my Dad always says; you can't fight Mother Nature or Father Time. You do your best. But, building walls, only pisses her off."

As they approached Roy Carpenter's beach, only a few feet from the frontage to Shelly's inn, a woman in crisp beige khaki shorts and a white button-down shirt approached them. She held a clipboard that flapped in the wind. She had just finished accosting another couple.

"Are you willing to sign a petition to help save our beautiful beach community?" she asked them.

Mick and Shelly glanced sideways at each other.

"How?" Shelly asked.

"I'm with the Roy Carpenters Beach Conservation Association," she rattled her pitch. "Working closely with 'Save the Beach', we vehemently oppose the construct of any seawall that hardens the coast and accelerates the already devastating erosion that has claimed more than ten houses here at Roy Carpenter's Beach this year alone."

Shelly rolled her eyes and walked past the woman.

"Oh, you're Mr. Maguire," the woman observed. "You signed the petition the other day. I remember speaking with you."

"Of course, you did," Shelly called to him over her shoulder.

Shelly kept walking swiftly toward the inn, extending the distance between her and Mick. Mick trotted up the incline to the edge of her property as she made her way toward the porch.

"Hey," he called to her. "Are we still on for ice cream tonight?"

"We'll see," she replied as she climbed the stairs to the porch. "It might be a busy night at the inn."

Chapter 13

Shelly texted Mick during the late afternoon that she had too big of a dinner crowd at the inn to see him for ice cream. He considered apologizing to her, but couldn't figure out what he'd done wrong. He had opinions about how to deal with beach erosion. He hadn't committed any offence. He just shared his thoughts with her. He decided to give her the benefit of the doubt.

"Bummer," he texted her. "Maybe another time. Good luck with the dinner crowd."

Mick looked at the calendar. He had another week to finish his demo cuts for Bo Rutledge. He also had his first day of school the next morning. He checked his e-mail for any further messages from Bo. But he'd only received an update from his sister about next year's Matunuck-Palooza and an advertisement for his friend Kenny's landscaping business. Already a client, he considered clicking the "unsubscribe" link, but chose to delete the e-mail instead.

His cell phone jingled, informing him of the arrival of a text.

"Hey buddy," said the message from a number he didn't recognize. "Got your cell phone number from someone at Golden records."

Mick looked at the phone and tried to figure out who was pinging him. He Googled the area code and determined it to be from the Albany, New York area.

"It's me, Bo," a second text clarified. "Loving the 'Blanket on a Beach' song. Want to hear it live."

Mick stared at the message, not completely comprehending at first.

"Will be in New York on Thursday and Friday," a third text added. "Can you make it to the city? Would like to meet IRL."

Mick's body went numb. He pictured himself strolling into some New York record executive's office with his guitar over his shoulder and a folder of sheet music.

Reality set in. He had a day job. He'd have to get a substitute teacher for his class. It was bad form to give the school so little notice and even worse to miss two out of the first five days of the year. As a new, junior teacher, he was only entitled to four personal days a semester.

Mick started to type a response that he couldn't get to New York during the week, but erased the message.

"Even better," he typed. "You should come here."

Mick sent the text and immediately decided to elaborate.

"You could see the beach that inspired the song," he wrote. "We have a hopping pub on the water that serves great beers and amazing food. You could stay at the inn."

"Same pub and inn from the song?" Bo returned the text within seconds.

"That's right," Mick replied. "I think it would help for you to see them."

Mick waited for Bo's response. Nerves raced behind his eyes and gave him a sensation of lightheadedness. He decided to text him a few pictures of the beach he had taken over the summer. He included one of the inn against a fiery sunset. He sent a shot of the pub set against the angry sea. He sent another of the beach on a perfectly sunny day.

"Looks amazing," Bo replied. "Let me pull some strings and make the arrangements. See you this weekend, bud."

During Mick's first year as an elementary school teacher, he felt confined in the drab twenty-square-foot room. He tried to decorate it with posters of his favorite rock bands. He emulated the hip School of Rock teaching style. He even opened the windows to let in the salt air, until the principal made him close them to avoid disrupting the other nearby classrooms.

As his second year commenced, he sat at his desk, planning his agenda for the day. It had been a couple weeks since Gordie's last major health scare in the water, but Mick coordinated with his Aunt Trudy and her daughter, Bethanne, to make sure they'd check on him in regular intervals. He balanced the stress that coursed through his mind, between the start of year two at Matunuck Elementary and his ongoing battle to uphold his father's rapidly declining - and ultimately doomed - quality of life. The words 'Convalescent Home', 'Wheelchair' and

'Confinement' swirled across his consciousness. But he pushed them aside to a dark purgatory in the corner of his mind for consideration in some undefined future time period. Additionally, his more recent concern revolved around the songs he struggled to write for Bo Rutledge.

The bell rang and his nerves raced at the thought of having to teach basic rhythm to a bunch of tone-deaf eight and nine-year-olds. He heard the lockers slam. Tiny footsteps approached. The pitched voices outside his door grew in volume.

"Hi Mr. Maguire," a young girl squeaked as she flopped in her seat. Several others greeted him with similar cheer.

"How was your summer, Mr. M?" one of the boys asked.

A young girl who took piano lessons from him entered the room and handed him a 'Welcome Back' card.

Mick took a moment to collect his reaction to the outpouring of appreciation he felt as the students filled the room. A few of the younger faces looked new to him, but for the most part, he recognized every kid in the class.

"My mom and dad wanted me to say hi to you," said a tall, stocky boy that Mick didn't recognize. "They own the Ocean Mist and said you were going to sing there some nights this fall."

"Awesome," called out a boy in the back that took guitar lessons from him. "Can we go and watch?"

"No dummy," said the Dolman boy. "It's at a bar. Kids can't go there until they're in double digits. Except I can, cause we own it."

"Let's speak nicely to each other, uh, Ricky," Mick said, glancing at his roster of students. "I promise, I'll play just for you guys a couple times during the semester."

Mick's claustrophobia faded as the class cheered. The door to the room rattled and clanked. As it opened, a small, shy boy entered the room. His wild, scraggly mass of bright, blond hair waved into his face as he clamored to his seat. Behind him, Mick's good friend, Kenny Forrester, appeared. Kenny's bald head shined in the reflection of the overhead fluorescent lights. It contrasted with the dark grey beard along his cheeks and below his chin.

"Hey, Mick, sorry," Kenny tried to speak softly - although quiet for Kenny wasn't really a setting within his internal amplifier. "Penny's sick. I didn't know where the kid's socks were. He didn't have any clean underwear. I had to figure out how to use the dryer. Not a good start to the new school year."

"No problem," Mick said, clutching his friend by the shoulder. "I can't believe I'll be teaching your kid."

"Me neither," Kenny quipped. "Easy A. Am I right? Huh? Easy A?"

Acutely aware of the classroom full of kids, Mick put his hand on Kenny's shoulder to shuffle him out, but Kenny looked across the rows of students.

"Hey Ricky," he said, pointing at the beefy Dolman kid. "Say hi to your parents for me."

"Ok," Mick muttered, holding the door to close it on his friend.

"Hey Willow," Kenny continued to point and address the students. "Say hi to your mom for me."

With a twinkle, Kenny leaned toward Mick and whispered in his ear.

"Dated her in college," he said. "So hot."

Mick managed to close the door on Kenny, asking the class to say goodbye.

"Bye Mr. Forrester," they shouted in unison as Kenny eventually withdrew from the room and skulked away down the hall.

Unlike the previous school year, when Mick spent countless hours creating his curriculum and deciding how to fill each block of learning time, he found he could reuse the previous year's lesson plans and repeat the same exercises. He spent the first class talking about how ancient human beings learned to make music by banging ordinary items together, such as rocks and sticks. He invited everyone in class to pick one moveable object and bang it against one immovable object.

"Just nothing dangerous," he cautioned the class as Ricky Dolman grabbed a pair of scissors from his desk. "And, I'm the judge."

Some kids tapped their pencils against their books. One girl clanked maracas against her desk. Kenny's son, Petey, found a pair of drumsticks and smacked them against the wall. Thwarted from using the scissors, due to Mick's safety concerns, Ricky Dolman clapped the back of a stapler against a pipe running up the corner of the room.

"All together," Mick urged them. "Tah, Tah, Tee-Tee, Tah."

Every few seconds, he mixed the rhythms to other well-known beats. On his phone, he underpinned the exercise with rock music such as 'We Will Rock You' and 'The Eye of the Tiger'. The class flew by. The kids all laughed and thanked him. By the end of the day, Mick reminded himself that he actually loved his job as a teacher. Even, when the Principal reprimanded him for the racket, he walked home along the Matunuck Beach Road in a cheerful mood.

And then, he walked into his house.

The first sign he noticed was the extremely loud volume of the television. He spied two empty wine glasses on the coffee table before his roving eyes spotted Gordie on the loveseat. The reflection of the television danced in his glasses. The laugh track that echoed through his living room seemed to mock him as he absorbed the sight.

Wedged next to Gordie, with her hand on his forearm, was a woman. Close to his age, they sat shoulder-to-shoulder, engrossed in an old episode of The Carol Burnett Show as advertised on one of those Pubic Television programs that gives five-minute clips, followed by ten-minute pleas for donations.

Neither Gordie, nor his guest noticed Mick as he slowly approached. Mick opened his mouth to clear his throat. Tim Conway conducted some pratfall, tripping over an end table and pulling down half the set with him. Gordie and the mystery woman next to him erupted in laughter. Gordie removed his glasses and wiped tears from hie eyes.

"Uh, hello there," Mick spoke after their laughter died down.

"Oh, hi, hey," Gordie jolted to attention. "What time is it? I didn't realize. Well, it doesn't matter. How was school?"

Mick didn't react at first, glancing at the woman, who squirmed in discomfort at meeting Gordie's son for the first time.

"Oh, right, uh, Mick, uh, this is Larraine," he stammered. "Larraine, uh..."

"Lang," Larraine stood from the couch with her arm extended. "Larraine Lang, from Green Hill. Just across that little pond. You can actually see my house from your deck."

Mick shook Larraine's hand and mustered a smile.

"We met at the dance class," Gordie explained. "She was my cha-cha partner."

"No Gordo," Larraine corrected him. "That was that other lady, with the white hair. I was your polka partner."

Mick shook his head to wipe the image of his father dancing either a polka or a cha-cha. Mick picked up the empty wine glasses and brought them to the kitchen.

"How have you felt today?" Mick asked his father through the cutout between the kitchen and the television room. "Did Trudy take care of you? Any headaches? Dizziness? All good?"

"I've been fine," he replied. "Turns out, I don't need hot towels or medicine if I just drink enough wine."

Larraine giggled at the comment and then laughed heartily at the television. Mick watched his father chortle with Larraine, completely transfixed by the show. With Mick nearby, Larraine kept her hands in her lap, but they still occupied the loveseat with their bodies pressed closely together.

"I got pizza dough and some really nice pepperoni from the market," Mick said. "I was going to make a homemade pizza."

Mick hesitated, confused and conflicted at the sight of his father canoodling with another woman. After all, just one month earlier the family assembled to set his mother's ashes free in the ocean. Mick wondered how his father could move on so quickly.

Then again, Mick reasoned, while their memorial ceremony took place only four weeks earlier, her passing actually occurred more than two years ago. And, even before that, she suffered for several additional years from a debilitating stroke and ravaging bout of cancer. It's not like his father had moved from a normal, everyday marriage to this television-watching date in the four weeks since that afternoon on the beach. It had been several years since his parents had the joy of operating as a cohesive unit.

Images of his parents hosting family parties and holidays flooded his memory. He recalled the surprise fortieth birthday party his mother threw for Gordie at the Community House. She flew in his siblings. She contacted his fraternity brothers. She brought back his old college hockey teammates. She even found one of his old elementary school teachers.

As visions of his mother in her prime flooded his head, he couldn't help feeling resentful toward a new person occupying his father's affection. He heard additional chuckling from the other room and took a peek at the expression on his father's face. Completely carefree, the blue light from the screen flicked in his eyes as he and Larraine enjoyed each other's company.

"Feel free to stay for dinner," he said, pushing his mother's half-moon smile from his mind.

Gordie turned off the television and stood. He helped Larraine out of the love seat.

"Sorry Mickey," Gordie said. "Larraine and I are headed out to the beach for our din-din."

"The beach?"

"Do you know where the big green blanket is?"

"The one we used to have family picnics on?" Mick asked. "It's in the basement."

"We made cheese sandwiches," Larraine said.

Mick retrieved the blanket from the basement. As he climbed the stairs, he recalled bright summer afternoons on the expansive Blackberry Beach. He pictured his mother sitting with Mrs. Callahan, Mrs. Valarian and Mrs. Donnelley in front of the boardwalk of the Blackberry Beach club house. The green blanket stretched in front of his mother's toes where Dana and Conrad would sit eating saltines and celery sticks while sharing a can of Coke.

The blanket had endured spills, rogue waves, rampant damp, salty air and decades of overexposure to the sun. Paler and thinner than during his childhood, the best feature of the triple wide blanket was its softness. The eight-square-foot piece of fabric had underpinned so many family moments such as the first time Gordie and Jaimee brought baby

Mick to Matunuck beach or the first time they watched the fireworks at Roy Carpenter's Beach as a family. Mick recalled the intrigue of staying up late at night combined with the sheer thrill of watching the bursts of red and blue light so close over the ocean. He could still hear little three-year-old Dana scream in terror at the ear-splitting finale.

Mick recalled the time, ten years later, when Dana's bathing suit ripped and Jaimee had to cover her from embarrassment with the family blanket, or the time he fell asleep face down, and his brother, Conrad, wrote the words; 'Kick Me' in sunscreen across the center of his back.

He'd proposed to Danielle on that blanket. And, just four weeks earlier, the family huddled together on it to sing songs and commune with the beach, in celebration of dispersing Jaimee's ashes into the sea.

The wave of resentment that Gordie would move on with some strange woman washed over Mick's mind again. He considered hiding the blanket and claiming he couldn't find it.

"Is it down there?" Gordie called to him.

Mick reached the top of the stairs and handed it to Gordie. He watched Larraine pack two skimpy white bread sandwiches - with no more than three thin slices of cheese on each one - into plastic baggies.

"Is that all you've got?" Mick asked.

"No, we've got broccoli too," Larraine answered.

"How are you going to cook it?" Mick asked.

"We'll eat it raw," Larraine answered, as Gordie grabbed two water bottles from the fridge.

"Apparently, it's good for brain health," Gordie said, as he loaded the cheese sandwiches and a plastic container of raw, cut broccoli into a brown paper grocery bag.

"Where will you be?" Mick asked as they opened the door to leave.

"Somewhere between Moonstone and Green Hill," Larraine replied.

"Have a great night," Gordie winked at his son. "I hope your pizza comes out okay."

Mick nodded, still in shock to see his father cavorting with another woman. As Larraine exited the house, Gordie leaned in to Mick.

"Don't wait up," he said.

Chapter 14

Counting renters, the summer population in Matunuck dwarfed the number of year-long residents by a wide margin.

On weekdays during the summer, Matunuck had the frenetic buzz of a modest tourist destination – even despite recent troubles with beach erosion. The roads hummed with the sound of cars, trucks motorcycles and bikes. People crowded the streets in ball caps and flip flops with beach towels around their necks and wide floppy bags over their shoulders.

But during the autumn and winter months, the community emptied like a ghost town. The Vanilla Bean boarded its windows. The town beach closed. Renters at both Mary's and Roy's villages vacated in droves. And the air settled into the crisp silence of inactivity.

Mick walked along the dusty Matunuck Beach Road from the elementary school building at the north end of town toward the center of Matunuck. A week past Labor Day, he didn't see a single car for the entire half-mile walk to the intersection with Cards Pond Road.

The Oceanside Market occupied the corner between the Matunuck Beach Road and Atlantic Avenue. A right turn went east, past the entrances to Willow Dell and Roy's along the way to Mick's house and Shelly's inn before continuing past Cards Pond toward Green Hill. Straight ahead, the road bent past the town beach and the Vanilla Bean, eventually hugging the contour of the ocean and passing the pub and surf shop on the way to Deep Hole.

The walk to the Oceanside Market took Mick about ten minutes from his classroom. He rolled up the sleeves of his button-down shirt and trudged along the shoulder of the road in his docksider shoes.

In decades passed, Matunuck residency dropped by more than ninety percent between the summer and the fall. But, more recently, with many new winterized permanent homes built into Blackberry Hill, a modest population stuck around past Labor Day. Regardless, Mick could still feel the loneliness of the trees that lined the beach road, the complacency of the rock walls along the surrounding farmland and the distinct lack of energy in the salty ocean air.

Mick nodded to the local teenager who worked the register at the market. He'd decided to pick up a package of hot dogs to grill for Gordie. He wandered the four-aisle grocery store and grabbed some Lucky Charms, a half-gallon of whole milk, a couple of fresh vegetables for a salad and a package of Gordie's favorite marinated beets.

As he approached the check-out stand, Haley entered with her infant on her hip and her toddler yanking her hand forward as he eagerly darted into the store.

"Hey Mr. Maguire," she playfully called him by his name from their common workplace at the school. "How's the first week of school year number two treating you?"

Mick nodded and gave her a kiss on the cheek. Her toddler took off down the cereal aisle. The baby laughed and reached for Mick.

"I think he wants to be with you," she said.

Mick took the baby from her arms while paying for his groceries.

"Hey thanks," Haley said, patting him on the shoulder. "I'll only be a minute."

Twenty minutes later, Mick stood by the doorway with a squirming baby in one arm and a heavy bag of groceries straining his other. Haley put a finger into the air from across the checkout line and mouthed the words "thank you" to him.

"So, have you seen your neighbor recently?" she asked as she took her baby from Mick and set him into a stroller just outside the door to the store.

"You had a stroller that whole time?" Mick asked.

"Have you asked her out?" Haley ignored him. "What's the hot gossip?"

"Nothing," Mick replied. "We're just friends."

"No? Why?" Haley whined. "She's your girl. She's like Matunuck if Matunuck were a pretty girl. And you love Matunuck, so you must love her too."

"I don't think she's too happy with me," Mick said.

"Oh, no," Haley gave him a disappointed look. "You screwed up already? What did you do?"

"I didn't do anything," Mick defended himself.

"You must've done something."

"Nothing," Mick replied. "I just signed that petition and told her I was more in favor of letting the beach run its course than building a big, ugly wall."

Haley's older son wandered down Atlantic Avenue, prompting Haley to follow him and clasp his hand. They engaged in a mild struggle, with the boy eventually giving in to the superior strength of the mother.

"Take this stuffed animal and play with your brother in the stroller," Haley said. "He needs to be entertained. That's your job as the big brother."

Haley turned her glare back to her older cousin. Her face shaded dark and her eyes beaded.

"What petition did you sign?" she asked. "Not the Roy Carpenter's Beach Association one?"

"I guess," Mick answered. "I don't know. The one that opposes the construction of a big metal and concrete wall along the shoreline."

"Oh Mick," Haley shook her head in disgust. "You did screw up."

"I happen to be against big seawalls," Mick replied. "There's nothing wrong with that opinion. It matches the statewide policy against hardening the shoreline throughout our hundreds of miles of ocean frontage."

Haley sighed loudly. It sounded like forced hot air streaming through an old radiator.

"What about the Matunuck Beach Road down by the pub?" she asked. "It's about to crumble into the sea. What about the Ocean Mist or all those houses down there? You should talk to Kyle Dolman about that. He's got a whole plan and he's willing to put up his own money to help build a tasteful wall with some cement and rock and a whole lot of natural materials."

Mick shrugged his shoulders, causing Haley to roll her eyes.

"There's a meeting at the town hall next week," she told him. "It's hard for me to pull away with these two munchkins keeping me busy. But you should go."

Visions of wasting a night at a town government function instead of putting in the hours to refining his songs swirled in his mind.

"I've got so much to do," Mick hedged.

"Like what?" Haley challenged him.

"Well, there's my dad."

"He's fine on his own for a couple hours," Haley retorted. "Plus, he falls asleep on the couch in front of the television every night. What else have you got?"

Mick shrugged and conjured another excuse to avoid his cousin's conscription to the meeting.

"My dad's going," she beamed. "Kenny Forrester offered him a ride in his pick-up."

"Big night out for old Denny Gallagher," Mick said.

"That's right," Haley agreed. "And if he can make it at his age, you sure can too."

"Well, I haven't really shared this with too many people yet," Mick brought out his heavy artillery. "But I'm busy cranking out three songs for Bo Rutledge."

"Who?" Haley asked. "The country music singer? Wait, he's famous. That's a big deal. I didn't know you did country music."

"I don't really," Mick replied. "But I went to Julliard. So, I actually studied it some in college. You learn to be pretty adaptable."

Haley's face exploded. Her mouth flung open wide. The edge in her voice caught her son by surprise. Both boys stopped playing with their stuffed animals and looked at her startled.

"Oh my God," Haley exclaimed. "You should get him to invest in fixing the beach. You know how celebrities are always looking for causes. He's an uber-rich, mega-famous superstar. You think you could get him to be our spokesperson? Maybe he could throw in a couple million to help us build the wall we need to protect the point?"

Mick stepped back from his exuberant cousin. He tensed his body at the thought of trying to fleece his celebrity client for an investment.

"Just ask him," Haley pressed. "And, see if he'll sign autographs for the boys."

Haley turned toward the stroller.

"You guys want autographs from a famous country singer?" she asked in a pitchy song-like voice to blank stares from the two boys, each under three years old.

Mick spotted Kenny and Ronnie approaching from along the Matunuck Beach Road.

"They're very excited," Haley said as she strolled her children down Atlantic Avenue toward her house on the next street over. "I'm not kidding. Get him to invest in saving Matunuck."

On any given day, Matunuck residents could hear Kenny Forrester's distinctive voice, strong Rhode Island accent and loud cackle from all corners of town.

"Mickey Mouse," he called from a hundred yards away. "How's it going, teach?"

Mick waved and met them at the corner of Atlantic and the beach road.

"Mick, tell Ronnie he's crazy to sell his place," Kenny beseeched him.

"It's not up for debate," Ronnie pled. "I haven't decided for sure. But the property values of these little houses are going down as the beach declines and everyone wants those big houses on Blackberry Hill."

"Dude," Kenny interjected. "It's not about the property value. It's about being here in Matunuck. Once you sell, you can never come back."

"Mick did," Ronnie retorted.

"We're not all big music executives that can afford to buy a prime lot and build a big, ugly house with ocean views," Kenny teased his friend. "No offence."

"None taken," Mick laughed.

"If that big wall comes in, my taxes will go through the roof," Ronnie said. "And, if they don't build it and there's a disaster, I'm still screwed financially. I can't win."

Kenny rolled his eyes and flapped his fingers against his thumb like a hand puppet to mimic Ronnie's moving mouth.

111

"I've had a good run here," Ronnie continued. "But I might have to move up to a condo in West Warwick soon. For what I'm paying down here, I could get such a better place."

"Well, they gotta build the wall," Kenny snapped. "How much you think it'll cost if half of Mary's gets flooded out and the beach road gets washed away? Am I right Mick?"

The tension in Mick's shoulders from his conversation with Haley tightened and sent a sharp pain down his spine.

"I'm not on team seawall," Mick said. "Build it in one place, you may as well stretch it all the way down to the breachway in Charlestown."

"Serious?" Kenny glared at Mick. "You're just gonna let the ocean come in and wipe out all them homes?"

"Maybe they don't belong there?" Mick replied.

"That ain't right," Kenny shook his head at his two friends. "I got a half-a-mind to try fix it myself with my bulldozer."

Mick smiled to himself at Kenny's extreme local pronunciation of the piece of heavy landscaping machinery, which sounded like "bulldozah."

"I'm sure the town wouldn't appreciate that," Mick laughed. "I'm sure it breaks a whole host of town ordinances, not to mention state and federal laws."

"Wanna come to the inn with us?" Kenny changed the subject. "I caught a couple dozen lobsters. Marty's frying up some lobster rolls."

"We could eat them on the beach," Ronnie added. "It's nice out. You should grab your guitar and play tonight."

"We could get old man Maguire to join us," Kenny added.

They walked along Cards Pond Road to the paved driveway to the inn. Mick's house sat on its own lot just before the road bent and circled in front of the ten-room three-story building.

The three of them crossed the covered front porch of Mick's Victorian home and entered the foyer next to Gordie's first floor bedroom. The sound of gunfire and screaming echoed off the walls and filled the modest house.

"What cha watching this time?" Mick called into the television room."

"Gunsmoke," Gordie answered. "We found a channel that plays all old shows from the sixties and seventies."

Ronnie and Kenny looked curiously at each other as Kenny mouthed the word "we?"

"Hi Larraine," Mick forced a smile as he greeted his father and his friend in the love seat glued to the television. "These are my friends Kenny and Ronnie."

"Lovely to meet you," Larraine smiled. "And who are you again?"

"That's my son Michael," Gordie answered her. "You met him the other day."

"Ah, yes," Larraine's head nodded like a bobblehead doll. "Michael, Bobbie and Robbie. Nice to meet you all."

"You want to come to the inn with us for dinner?" Mick asked.

Gordie didn't answer at first, fixating on an action scene on the television show.

"What, oh, no," he answered. "Thank you. Larraine's niece, Theresa, is making lasagna for us."

Mick heard a clank in his kitchen and looked through the hole in the wall.

"Hi," said a cute brown-haired girl in a Roger Williams University sweatshirt and stylish black-rimmed glasses. "I'm Theresa. I hope you don't mind. Gordie said I could use your oven to heat it up."

Mick stared at her blankly. In the background, he could sense Kenny's amused smile. Ronnie stepped forward, his eyes fixed on the woman in the kitchen.

"Why don't we eat here?" he asked. "How much lasagna are you cooking?"

"Sure," Theresa blinked. "There's plenty."

Kenny shifted his weight from side to side. Mick climbed the stairs to retrieve his guitar. Upon returning, he leaned it against the front door and moved to the kitchen.

"Time for your afternoon pills Dad," he said as he poured a glass of water and delivered the medicine to Gordie in the love seat.

"I came for lobsters," Kenny announced to the room, his distinctive accent echoing phonetically as 'lobstah's'. "I'm going to the inn."

Mick returned from the office with an amp in hand and placed it next to the guitar by the door. He gave Ronnie a look and his friend finally stepped back from his vantage point through the opening to the kitchen.

"Another time," Ronnie said to Theresa.

"Sure," she replied with a warm smile.

"Have fun boys," Gordie called to them as they left the house.

They exited back to the covered porch. The door slammed behind them.

"What a dirty dog," Kenny teased Mick with an elbow to the ribs. "Mr. M's getting some, right under your roof."

Mick rolled his eyes and walked by as Ronnie pretended to gag in the back of his throat.

Marty Fazzini met Kenny and Ronnie at the inn. He seated them on the porch and gave them an overfilled basket of hot, homecooked dinner rolls. They slathered them with butter and watched the long, soft rollers ease across the tapestry of the Atlantic Ocean and dash against the shore.

"Where's your girl?" Kenny asked Mick.

"She's in Providence tonight at some rap concert or something," Mick replied. "I can't keep track of her."

"No dumbass," Kenny laughed, with a nudge to Ronnie. "Your girlfriend."

"I don't know," Mick said. "I think that's a dead end."

"She's cute," Kenny chided Mick. "If I wasn't married, I'd be on her like ..."

Kenny clammed his voice when he spotted Shelly through the restaurant by the front desk of the inn.

"I'd be on that like butter on a lobster tail," he completed his thought. "If you know what I mean."

Ronnie put down his roll and squinted at the image.

"We always know what you mean, Ken," Ronnie said.

"What like you weren't all soft and melty at that chick in Mick's kitchen?" Kenny rolled his eyes at Ronnie. "Who woulda thought I'd be the married one between us. What a waste."

Mick glanced at Shelly, but hid his interest. Kenny picked up on the looks, but held his typically hyperactive tongue for once.

"Dude," he whispered. "I know you like her. Just go talk to her."

"I don't think it's going to work out," Mick withdrew. "I've known her for two years and nothing's happened yet. It probably won't."

"I tell you what," Kenny said. "After we eat our lobster rolls, you set up and play. I'll take care of the rest."

Marty arrived as if on cue with three overflowing lobster sandwiches along with coleslaw and thick-cut fries. Ronnie lathered his fries with malt vinegar and passed the bottle around the table. The sun cast an orange glow on the far side of the inn as the sky darkened over Block Island.

"What are you going to say to Shelly?" Mick asked as he finished his sandwich. "I like being friends with her and don't want you to screw that up."

"Dude," Kenny said. "You got friends. We're your friends. What you need is to get..."

"Alright," Mick cut him off. "I'll play."

The restaurant filled for the night. Mick took a spot at the back of the inside dining room. Ronnie watched through the opened doors to the porch. Mick could see through the restaurant into the foyer of the inn. He watched Shelly's blond hair sway from behind as she spoke with one of her guests at the front desk.

Mick tuned his instrument and tested the sound level. He saw Shelly glance over her shoulder toward his vicinity. Her eyes roved away before locking with his. He strummed the first few bars of one of his new songs and observed as Kenny approached Shelly at the desk.

Mick concentrated on remembering the chords and words to his song, while simultaneously eyeing Kenny at the desk engrossed in conversation with Shelly. Another guest waited in line behind Kenny, who moved aside and feverously typed into his smart phone.

Mick wrapped the first tune as Kenny motioned for him to check his text.

"Told her the next one was dedicated to her," he texted. "Make it a good one."

Mick's stomach fluttered. He thought of an original tune that he could sing that would not be too forward, but still express some sentiment of romance.

"Play the one you wrote for Bo," Kenny wrote. "About making out in the dunes on the blanket."

Mick shut off the ringer to his phone. He scrolled through the playlist in his mind. But Kenny's suggestion rattled in his brain and choked out any other choices. He decided to strip the song of its southern rhythm and sing it more like a soulful, beachy folk song.

As Mick strummed the opening chords, Kenny gave him a thumbs up. He noticed a few patrons pause from their meals to pay attention to the soft, comforting sound of the tune.

Mick felt a groove, like a runner's high. The music ebbed from his fingers, he opened his mouth and crooned the opening line.

"*Bottles of beer in the black of the night,*" he sang in a soft, sultry voice. "*Fireworks bursting as a bonfire burns. And I'm laying with my baby on a blanket at the beach.*"

Mick engaged the audience, noticing more heads turning to listen. He kept one eye on the back of Shelly's head at the front desk, wondering when her guest would finish talking to her. By the second verse, the guest walked away, and Mick could sense Shelly turning to listen to his performance. He practiced in his mind, smiling and giving her an up-nod once she turned and made eye contact with him.

He could see her hips pivot. The side of her cheek rotated toward him. She stopped. Her shoulders tensed. Instead, she darted out the front door of the inn, beyond Mick's line of sight. Kenny shrugged and threw his hands outward, perplexed at her curious reaction.

"Maybe she didn't like that one?" he texted. "Try a different one?"

Chapter 15

At hearing from Kenny that Mick's next song was about her, Shelly's heart fluttered. She heard the sweet melody fill the restaurant and waft into the lobby of the inn like a pleasant aroma.

As her client droned on about how much she enjoyed the room and appreciated the service, Shelly's mind beckoned the elderly woman to *"shut up and move on."*

As she wrapped her conversation with the guest, she started toward the restaurant to listen to Mick's tune when a familiar flash of black leather caught her eye. Her sister, Lindsay, pulled up to one of the guest spots in the circle and emerged from her rented BMW.

She wore a gaudy black, shiny jacket over a silk white blouse and tight denim skirt. A gold necklace hung from her neck. Her many charms swayed across the base of her cleavage like little canyon jumpers as she moved. Several gold bracelets clanked together, piled up her arm like a traffic accident under her sleeve. Her skinny chicken-legs looked the same as they had twenty years earlier. She shuffled her way across the parking lot with a duffel bag in hand.

Sensing the onset of a boisterous exchange of voices between them brewing on the horizon, Shelly cast aside thoughts of relaxing in the dining room and bolted into the parking lot to head off her sister before she could disrupt her business.

"What are you doing here?" she asked, standing in the doorway like a linebacker.

"I made a reservation," she replied. "I'd like to see what you've done with the place."

Lindsay took a step forward. Shelly flinched but held her ground.

"I didn't see a reservation for Williams or Newsome," Shelly said.

"I went with Guillermos," she replied. "It's Spanish for Williams."

Shelly could hear Mick finish his song. She expected another, but silence lingered in the air like the tense standoff between her and her older sister. She glanced back toward the dining room, but couldn't see through to the restaurant's many partitions, given her position in the doorway by the overhang.

"Where're your kids?" Shelly asked.

"They're in the car," Lindsay replied. "I told them I wasn't sure if their aunt would let us stay in grandma's house."

Shelly closed her eyes and exhaled. She tightened her stomach to exert control over the anger that welled in her stomach. A guest snaked by her, causing her to move out of the doorway, a step closer to her sister in the parking lot.

"Why do you have to do this here?" she whispered. "We've got the lawyers working it out. I don't think we're supposed to come into contact with each other. "

"You're my sister for God's sake," Lindsay shot back. "This is the house we grew up in."

"That house is out there at the bottom of the ocean," Shelly corrected her. "This is my house."

"On our plot of land," Lindsay retorted. "Our family's land anyway."

Shelly reached for her phone. She weighed calling Ted Callahan, or Pat O'Hannon, the local Matunuck police officer. An image crossed her mind in which red and blue lights flashed across her place of business as patrons tried to enjoy their meal. A domestic dispute would hardly paint her business in a positive light. She envisioned the dramatic scene Lindsay could cause and chose to handle her with diplomacy rather than force.

"Are you going to lead me to the room I reserved?" Lindsay asked. "I have a confirmation number."

Shelly didn't react. Her mind cycled through her options. Her instincts told her not to let her sister into the building, but her intellect understood what a fuss she could make. Movement in the back of Lindsay's rented luxury car caught her eye.

"Should I tell the girls you won't let us in?" Lindsay pressured her younger sister. "We don't have anywhere else to stay."

"There's the Hampton Inn in Wakefield," Shelly listed. "They just built a new Fairfield Inn along Route 1. There's the General Stanton in

Charlestown, the Wind Swept, the Surfside, Willows. They're all along the Post Road and most of them are much cheaper than me."

"I want to come home," Lindsay dripped with sarcasm. "I'm taking the girls back to where we belong."

"What about the Admiral Dewey?" Shelly asked. "We always wanted to stay there as kids. Now's your chance."

"It's only open in the summer," Lindsay responded. "It's after Labor Day. You're the only game in town."

Shelly stood her ground. Her mind screamed at her to find a way to decline entry. She thought about using Marty as a bouncer. Lindsay softened her demeanor and stepped forward.

"Listen, I know we got off on the wrong foot," she used her sweet voice from their childhood. "I have nowhere to stay. You don't know the hellhole in Cranston we stayed at last week. I've got the two girls and no family but them. Lord knows Jeremy's not their family anymore. He doesn't even make an effort to see them with his new little twinkie. I just wanted to come back, maybe reconnect with you; give them some semblance of belonging. You gotta help me out. I gotta get them into school."

Shelly tightened her lips and glared at her older sister.

"Come on Shells. Forget all this legal business," she continued. "Just let us keep our reservation. We'll stay here for a bit while I figure out where to take the girls next."

"Fine," Shelly relented. "But I have to charge you full price."

"Please do," she replied.

Lindsay returned to her car to get her two elementary-aged children. They ran from the vehicle with two miniature roller-board suitcases behind them. They both dropped their mini-luggage and flung their arms in the air, calling Shelly 'Aunty' and hugging her around her hips.

Lindsay pulled a large suitcase from the trunk and slammed it shut. Shelly guided the two girls, whom she hadn't seen since they were an infant and a toddler, into the lobby. She watched the back of Mick's head follow Kenny and Ronnie away from the inn and down the beach. Mick's guitar shifted back and forth over his shoulder as he carried the small amp in his left hand.

Lindsay approached the front desk. Shelley climbed behind it and called up the reservation system on the computer.

"Guillermos," she scoffed to herself. "I should have known a two-week rental of the suite was too good to be true."

"I reserved our old bedroom," Lindsay beamed. "I'm interested to see if it's as nice as I remember from Gramma's old house."

"I have your credit card on file," Shelly stiffened her voice, handing her sister a plastic key card. "I'll be holding the full two weeks at the regular rate. That's going to be expensive."

"Charge me double, I don't care," Lindsay smirked. "It's my soon-to-be ex-husband's credit card."

Lindsay and the two girls made their way to the staircase.

"Come on girls, I'll show you where I grew up," Lindsay said to them before turning back to Shelly. "I assume the layout is still about the same?"

"There's a small elevator now," Shelly nodded.

"We'll just take the stairs like when we were kids," Lindsay smiled as the two girls struggled to hoist their bags from step to step. "Oh, and, uh, I'm using Jeremey's card while I still can. He may dispute the charges."

Shelly nodded again as Lindsay disappeared up the stairs with the two girls close behind her.

Kenny walked ahead of Ronnie and Mick toward the old Moonstone Beach. Every ten feet, he bent to find another flat rock and hurl it across the rolling waves of the ocean.

"Screw her," Kenny complained about Shelly. "I told her you wrote that song for her and she just walks away like she don't care."

They reached a section of the beach where Cards Pond nearly met the ocean with a narrow strip of sand between the rippling sea and the dark, flat pond. Sometimes at a particular full moon high tide, the sand parted allowing the cool ocean water to circulate and refresh the stale, still water of the pond. On either side of the narrow gap, engineers had built tiered wooden structures that resembled the stepped pyramids of the Incas. Each step contained an opening where sand collected. Grasses and small shrubs grew from the top tiers. A retaining fence in front contained a warning sign about the federally protected sanctuary beyond the dunes.

Ronnie found a long, thin flat rock, and with his back to the ocean, skipped it across the perfectly glass-like surface of Cards Pond. Kenny tugged at the wood structure. He kicked the base of it, causing sand to spill forward. Mick looked over his shoulder at the inn.

"Careful throwing them rocks," Kenny said to Ronnie as he bounced a second stone across the murky surface. "You might hit one of them Plovers."

Mick smiled again at Kenny's pronunciation of 'Plovahs.'

They sat in the hard sand. Mick strummed his guitar. Kenny tossed pebbles into the waves.

"Hey," he stopped to reflect. "Remember when we were like fourteen, and we came here?"

"Kenny put his beach towel down right next to some naked woman," Ronnie recalled.

"And you guys stayed way back, afraid to get too close." Kenny laughed. "That was right about here. Before they closed it off for these stupid endangered birds."

Mick improvised a song about naked birds running across the beach. Kenny chuckled and tugged more fervently at the protective barrier built by the federal conservationists.

"They put more effort into saving the damn birds than they do to protect the actual community of people," Ronnie observed.

"I studied this in college," Kenny remarked. "Them birds need a very specific habitat. See the cat-tail plants?"

Ronnie put his hand to his forehead to shield the last rays of the setting sun. Mick stopped strumming and looked with him.

"They nest in the base of them reeds," Kenny said. "This is one of the only places where they have so many of them cat-tails. That's why they had to kick out all the nude sunbathers. That's how they get the feds to come in and build these natural barriers. They get special funding to protect the damned birds. It's like a blank freakin' check. As these plants grow in to the top of the manmade dunes and the sand collects, they'll

121

become good, hard natural barriers. They protect the plovers and don't look half bad from the beach."

Mick returned his guitar into his case and dusted some sand off the grill of his amp.

"Kinda gives me an idea," Kenny said, half to himself.

"What's that?" Ronnie asked.

"Huh, oh nothing," Kenny answered. "Ain't nothing, really."

"Sure?" Ronnie asked.

"I was just thinking we should walk on down to the pub," Kenny's demeanor changed as he glanced eastward toward the Ocean Mist on the other side of the trailer park seawall. "I'll talk to my buddy Kyle Dolman. I'm sure he could squeeze Mick in to play some tunes for an audience that'll actually appreciate him."

Shelly slumped in a booth at the back of the restaurant. Marty brought her a mug of hot tea as he often did at the end of a busy night. As his staff cleaned the tables and cleared the last few plates, Marty sat in the booth next to her.

"He wrote a song about me," Shelly said. "I wanted to hear it, but Lindsay showed up and totally distracted me."

"I saw," said Marty.

"She has this way of getting under my skin."

"I could see that," Marty said. "So, kick her out."

"I don't want to cause a scene," Shelly replied. "Plus, after all, she is my sister. We used to get along before my parents died. We helped each other when they got really drunk and couldn't even take care of us. That's back when she used to be a good big sister. There are debts of gratitude I still owe her from back then."

Marty remained quiet, offering a friendly ear as Shelly expressed her frustrations.

"From what I gathered," she continued. "Her husband dumped her for a younger woman. He took less and less interest in being a dad to the girls. I could see it happening when I visited her five years ago and they were just little babies. I'm surprised it took this long."

"And, now she's after the inn?" Marty asked.

"I don't know what she's trying to do," Shelly replied. "She always wanted out of Matunuck. After my grandmother died, the will offered her half the property. She said she didn't want it. At the time, the house was uninsurable, uninhabitable and condemned. We settled the estate and she declined her ownership stake."

"So, why's she back?" Marty asked.

"And what's her angle?" Shelly added. "What does she want?"

Shelly gave Marty an affectionate pat on the arm and moved to the deck. The dark water of the Atlantic Ocean rumbled. She could barely make out the white foam from the crashing waves. She dialed her lawyer.

"Well, don't let her in," Ted cautioned her.

"Too late," Shelly said.

Ted let out a subtle expression of air from his lungs.

"Was that a mistake?" Shelly asked. "I kind of knew it might be a bad idea, but she put me on the spot. I had a full restaurant. I didn't want to call Pat or have an altercation."

"No, of course not," Ted replied. "I understand she put you in a bind."

"She had her daughters with her," Shelly continued. "She had a reservation. And, she would have put on a big show too. I know her. It's a wonder she stayed married as long as she did."

"Ok," Ted continued. "She'll probably stay a day or two, get a sense of whether she really wants to pursue these legal options and then move on."

"Her reservation is paid for the next two weeks," Shelly said. "I knew I shouldn't honor it, but my reservation person didn't know better. To be honest. I missed it too. I should have recognized that damn Canadian phone number."

"I recommend you keep a daily journal of your interactions with her," Ted said.

"Why?" Shelly asked.

"To protect yourself."

"From what?"

"An attempt to extend her stay beyond the two weeks."

"You mean she could claim some sort of squatters rights?" Shelly asked, panic setting into her chest and shortening her breathing.

"Not exactly squatters rights," Ted replied. "In Rhode Island, that would take ten years."

"Can't I just change the key code and lock her out?" Shelly asked. "I could call Pat. After the way she dumped him in high school, he'd be happy to escort her out for me."

"You have to be careful now," Ted said. "Once she's in, any attempt to force her out could be considered a 'bailment situation'."

"What's that?"

"She could claim you've illegally seized her possessions."

"She can have them," Shelly snapped. "I'll throw them into the parking lot."

"She could file for damages," Ted continued. "She could claim hardship, get a court order and force you to let her back in until you complete a lengthy eviction process."

"So, I'm screwed," Shelly choked back her tears. "I never should have let her in at all."

"We'll get through this," Ted tried to comfort her. "Let's just hope it doesn't come to that."

After closing the restaurant for the evening, Marty trotted along the beach and joined Kenny and Ronnie at the Ocean Mist. Mick rotated between cover tunes by the Beach Boys, the Eagles and Jimmy Buffett. Between sets, he opened and closed with his own original songs. The crowd drank and cheered. A few tipsy patrons danced. He collected double the tips he usually earned at Shelly's restaurant.

Above the din of the crowd, Mick could hear Kenny's bellowing cheers and ear-splitting whistling louder than anyone else in the building.

"Thank you for all your support tonight," Mick monotoned into the mic from his lighted stool on the small stage. "I'm going to close with an original tune that I hope to sell to a major recording artist very soon."

The crowd cheered. Mick decided to amp up the tone of the song. He brought it up-temp and strummed the intro chords almost violently as a rock anthem.

The crowd responded better to his own song than any of the other well-known beach tunes.

"*Bottles of beer in the black of the night,*" he sang in a husky Bruce Springsteen voice. "*Fireworks bursting as a bonfire burns. And I'm laying with my baby on a blanket at the beach.*"

He experimented with a quick jazzy, bluesy guitar riff to bookend the refrain.

The crowd cheered at; "*Laying with my baby on a blanket at the beach.*"

He repeated it a few extra times, wailing the best he could on his guitar. As he progressed, he sensed the soaring energy in the room, especially at the chorus. By the end of the song, the familiar melody resonated and he heard many people in the crowd sing along to the line "*...Laying with my baby on a blanket at the beach.*"

At the end of the night, the remaining patrons pat him on the back and thanked him for entertaining them. Kyle paid him for his appearance and asked him to drop by at a regular time each week.

He, Kenny, Ronnie and Marty walked along the dark Matunuck Beach Road. The sober ones, Marty and Mick, each slung arms around the toasty ones, Kenny and Ronnie, and guided them home. After returning Kenny to his wife in their Park Avenue house and walking Ronnie back to his place on Washington, Marty and Mick strode back along the beach road. Mick worried about being away from his father for so long.

"You know Shelly wanted to hear your song tonight," Marty told him as they passed under the streetlight by the Oceanside Market.

"I guess so," Mick replied. "She's really busy. I get it."

"No, man," Marty said. "Her evil sister showed up. She had a situation to deal with."

"If you say so."

"Serious, she digs you," Marty urged him.

"Everyone says that," Mick replied. "But, we're both just too busy for each other. Plus, I think she's annoyed that I signed that petition."

As they wandered through the dark night, they noticed the low, full moon. It brightened the night with an orange glow. They could see the twinkling carpet of light dance with the ripples of the ocean.

"High tide was about noon today," Marty said. "So, it must have swung back around by now. I've got time. Let's check out how high it is at Blackberry tonight."

They ambled toward the Vanilla Bean, which had closed a few hours earlier. Around back, by the marshy area across from the Blackberry Beach Gap, they stacked a series of milk crates into a stepladder pattern. Mick rested his guitar and amp against a garbage bin and climbed first. He hoisted himself onto the roof and clasped Marty by the wrist to help him up as well. Laying against roof of the small ice cream shack, under the bright late-night sky, they could see the level of the ocean water high on the trailer park seawall.

"Jesus," Marty commented. "Thank God we're not having a storm tonight. The full moon high tide mark is pretty close to the top of those dunes."

"They're saying there's a tropical storm forming down by the equator near Africa," Mick recounted from watching the Weather Channel with Gordie. "It's supposed to be a nasty hurricane season."

"I hope the old Blackberry Beach Gap holds up," Marty said. "Or that little pond will become a pretty damned big lake and all those houses across the street'll be fish food."

Mick surveyed the high sea level and the height of the dunes. He watched the cat-tail grass along the edge of the pond sway in the late-night breeze. He wondered how a breach, as catastrophic for the Mary Carpenter's community, would alleviate the tension of the water against the rock wall and possibly allow the rest of the beach to avoid further erosion.

He pictured a channel running through the old Blackberry parking lot, swamping the pond, destroying the cat-tails, washing out the pavement and flooding half the village.

"They'd have to elevate the road and build a bridge," he thought.

"The Vanilla Bean would be toast," Mick responded to Marty's comment. "Or at least waterfront property. It would suck to lose it."

"Well aside from missing out on the occasional mocha cabinet," Marty snarked. "There'd be a lot of pretty pissed off property-owners too."

"Of course," Mick said. "That would be the biggest tragedy."

They climbed down from the roof, passed through a gap in the bamboo into the town beach parking lot and walked the shore toward the inn. The big dipper hung low in the sky. Mick traced the three distinctive stars of Orion's belt. They twinkled brightly against the black sky, even with the reflection of the giant full moon against the vast ocean. They walked in the quiet comfort of old friendship that neither required conversation, nor the incessant sound of a voice to fill the silence.

They reached the parking lot. Marty slung a leg over the seat of his massive Harley Davidson motorcycle. With a flick of his wrist, he cranked the key and revved the engine. The roar of the powerful engine split the calm of the evening sky.

"Dude," Marty reiterated. "I think she's into you. I know you had the rough divorce and all, but that was four years ago. It's time to let go of it and move forward."

Mick gave his friend a fist bump, which escalated to a hand shake and ended with a half-shoulder hug. Mick thanked Marty and watched him roll down the driveway past his house.

As he traced Marty's Honda with his eyes, he noticed a familiar red truck in his driveway.

"Conrad?" he mused to himself.

Fear washed over him as the second thought crossed his mind.

"Dad!"

Chapter 16

The screen door clacked against the jamb. Mick sprinted into the house. The glow of the television illuminated his younger brother's face against the dark of the living room. The blue and grey shadows danced across his stern expression. Mick darted his eyes nervously across the room.

"He's asleep now," said Conrad, lounged in the loveseat facing the entryway. "No thanks to you."

"What happened?" Mick asked, still out of breath from bolting into the house.

"Where the hell were you all night?" Conrad asked.

Mick flopped his guitar from his back to the couch and sat across from his brother.

"I was playing a gig."

"They didn't have your phone number," Conrad continued. "They found my number somehow and I tried calling and texting you. It went right to voicemail. You never replied."

"Ok, fine Rad," Mick snapped. "What happened?"

"And who are these people Dad's hanging out with?" Conrad laid into Mick. "The old one's a total dingbat. Can't remember anything. And her caregiver, had no clue how to reach you."

"Radley," Mick raised his voice. "Is Dad okay?"

"He's fine, now," Conrad replied. "I thought you were taking care of him."

"I am," Mick snapped. "Damnit, what happened?"

"He had a seizure," Conrad said. "Felicia or Theresa, whatever her name, stabilized him and called 911. Apparently, she's a visiting nurse and knew what to do. After she stabilized him, she tried to find a number for you, but didn't even know your name. She found my number on Dad's bulletin board and called me. I was driving home from the job site in New London. Stroke of luck I was working late."

Mick exhaled. He pulled out the phone that he had silenced just before his first abbreviated performance at Shelly's restaurant.

"I turned it off before I played and never turned it back on."

"Yah you did," Conrad sassed him.

"Is he okay? Did the paramedics come?"

"It passed before they arrived," Conrad explained. "The girl was giving him water. The old lady was freaking out."

"Connie, I'm sorry you had to drive all the way out here," Mick said. "I'm usually all over him. I don't usually leave him alone for more than an hour or two. When I'm at school, Trudy or Bethanne come check on him."

Conrad turned off the television and flicked the lamp next to the love seat.

"Who were those two women you left him with?"

"Larraine and Theresa, I think her name was."

"You don't even know them?"

Mick squirmed in his seat. His guitar slumped and made a twang sound that echoed from the lower bout to the upper bout and out the sound hole.

"Does Dad have some sort of girlfriend or something?" Conrad asked.

"I don't know," Mick replied. "I think he might."

Conrad stood and paced across the room.

"Jesus," he bellowed. "What's he doing with a girlfriend. Does she sleep over?"

Mick stood. His guitar almost slid off the leather couch to the floor, but he caught it just in time.

"God no," Mick said. "He just met her. They sit on the love seat and watch reruns of old shows."

"How do you know they're not ripping him off?" Conrad continued to pace as he spoke agitatedly. "The old biddy pretends to dig the gullible old man while the young one loots the place."

"They seemed..."

"You're even worse," Conrad interrupted him. "Look, you want to teach all day, play gigs all evening and write music all night, that's your prerogative. It's your life. Nobody would begrudge you. I admire you for giving it a shot. But if Dad's not going to get the operation to remove his brain tumor, then, he's only going to get worse; a lot worse. The paramedics said he should get another scan and probably start taking anti-seizure meds. Are you keeping track of..."

"You're damn right I am," Mick could feel the heat rise in his neck as his face shaded red. "I give him his first set of pills as soon as he wakes up. We walk to the seawall and back every morning for exercise. I run home from school – literally run – at lunchtime to give him his second set. And I do the third set in the afternoon after school. I interrupt my private lessons to get him what he needs. I rush home from the inn between sets to check on him. The one freaking night I stay out a little longer..."

Conrad eased the tension in his face. He sat in the love seat and grabbed a deck of cards from the coffee table.

"Fine," he interrupted Mick's soliloquy. "Cribbage?"

The brothers settled into a quiet peace. They played cards, commenting occasionally at good hands or surprising draws. Mick asked Conrad about the housing development his excavation company was working on in New London. Conrad asked about Mick's music and praised him for his potential deal with the country music star, Bo Rutledge.

Mick baked a tray of nachos, melting cheddar and pepper jack cheese over them in the broiler and dabbing the concoction with droplets of salsa. They munched on snacks and watched sports highlights on ESPN.

"What do you think of this special new procedure Dana found?" Conrad asked.

"I don't know," Mick replied. "I read up on it. It sounds interesting. I just don't think he'll go for it."

Conrad didn't react, instead chomping on a handful of cheesy nachos. The sportscasters recapped the Red Sox loss to the Angels.

"Doesn't hurt to call the doctor?" he threw out the suggestion casually. "Just a quick call. Why not?"

"I suppose," Mick replied.

Well past midnight, Mick retired to his bedroom and Conrad curled up in the guest room for the night.

In the morning, Gordie made no mention of his harrowing evening. Instead, he offered to whip up some classic Rhode Island corn meal pancakes, called Johnny Cakes, for his boys and spend quality time together at the kitchen table over crossword and sudoku puzzles.

Conrad decided he could spare an hour before he had to return to his job site. He had a crew working all weekend that generally managed themselves. But, when he made his people work through a Saturday, he preferred to be there with them to show his willingness to roll up his sleeves with them. With a quick check of his watch, he settled into the kitchen table with his brother and father. After a hearty breakfast, he took out Mick's step ladder to look at the damaged ceiling where the hanging bench fell.

"You can't just drill into the joists," he called through the window from his perch on the porch. You have to drill all the way through and use a bolt."

"Can you fix it?" Mick asked.

"I'll have to get in under the roof," he replied. "I'll come back next week."

A silver truck much like Conrad's, older and more dented, ambled up the driveway and skid to a stop in the sand by the base of the mailbox. A massive tool box rattled around the flatbed, bumping against a host of landscaping tools, rakes, shovels and other power equipment. The bright bald head of Kenny Forrester appeared above the far side of the vehicle. His greyish beard wagged in the sun. He shook hands with Conrad, calling him "Con-Con" and fist pumped him with a half shoulder hug.

"Looks like you better lay off them doughnuts in the morning," Kenny quipped at the sight of the broken swing, and climbing up the step ladder to check out the holes in the ceiling. "You can't just drill into the beam."

"I know," Mick tried to interrupt him.

"You gotta drill a hole all the way through and use a bolt with a good strong nut on the end," said Kenny. "Better yet, we could use a clamp bracket and avoid taking apart the roof."

The smell of Gordie's Johnny Cakes with warmed maple syrup and home fries caught his attention. He climbed down, looking like a prairie dog sensing a predator.

"Is that Kenny?" Gordie called through the screen. "Come on in here for some breakfast, will you?"

"Hot damn," Kenny flashed his unending smile and pushed aside the screen door to the house. "I thought he'd never ask."

Conrad called "goodbye" to Kenny through the open window. With mouth full, Kenny told him to "take it easy". Mick gave his brother a fist pump and half hug. Conrad thanked him for a fun night of cards and snacks.

"Think about calling the doctor," he reminded Mick. "At the very least, you're going to need to know what you're up against."

Mick glanced over his shoulder at his father. He watched him clean the pots and pans that he used to make the breakfast.

"It was lucky those two were here last night," Conrad continued. "And that they found my number. And that I wasn't too far away to get here pretty quickly. I mean, it's nice that Aunt Trudy and Bethanne can come by to pitch in. But someday, something's going to happen when nobody's around."

"I missed out on helping Mom," Mick said in a soft, resigned voice. "I hate that. But I'm going to make it up to her and him by taking care of Dad."

"Look, Dude, that's admirable," Conrad said. "But you can't put your life on hold for him. You've got, what, three jobs? And a girl next door, who you really like, that you've totally neglected."

"We're just friends," Mick squirmed.

"Whatever, Dude," Conrad smirked. "Point is, you're going to need someone who knows what they're doing, who has the time to spend with him. You're probably going to need a medical professional on hand to be with him when you can't be."

Mick pinched his mouth in contemplation of his brother's suggestion.

"Dana and I'll help pay for it," Conrad continued. "But, while you're at school, you might want to think about bringing someone in who can really care for him."

Mick nodded in agreement.

"And call the doctor," Conrad nagged his older brother.

A car pulled into the driveway. Mick and Conrad watched it curve into the space next to the red truck that took up half the available space. A curly white head emerged from the passenger side and barely exceeded the height of the car. Conrad exhaled sharply. Larraine's nurse, Theresa, exited the driver's side and held her hand to her face to shield the sun.

"We dropped by to see how your father's doing," Theresa announced. "My aunt was very anxious."

"Hello again, Mark," Larraine said as she hobbled up the porch steps. "John, dear. Nice to see you again."

Theresa gave a funny look and a shrug.

"She's not great with names," Theresa whispered to them as she helped her older aunt up the stairs. "She makes me earn my degree."

"Where's my Gordo?" Larraine called through the open door as she entered the foyer.

"It's Mick, right?" Theresa asked. "And Conrad?"

They exchanged pleasantries. Theresa respectfully checked to make sure Mick didn't mind their visit before entering the house.

Conrad rolled his eyes at the sight of his father hugging the strange, forgetful woman.

"I'm outta here," he said. "I can't watch this."

Distracted, Mick ignored his brother as he wriggled his keys from his jeans and strode toward his truck. Another car, a giant black Chevy Silverado with gold trim and numerous decorative accessories dwarfed Kenny's Ford. It pulled into the sand and angled partly askew across the lawn in front of Kenny's run down ten-year old vehicle.

A medium height man in dusty jeans, a black, satin shirt with big silver buttons and bushy goatee mustache slammed the driver's door shut and took a deep breath.

Conrad stopped to observe the man in his large black cowboy hat and equally oversized silver belt buckle.

"You Mick?" the man asked, striding toward Conrad with his hand extended.

"I'm Conrad," he replied, pointing at his brother on the porch. "That's Mick."

The man shook hands with Conrad fervently before trotting across the walkway to greet Mick at the foot of the porch.

"Mick Maguire? Bo," the man said, his rich baritone voice echoing off the angled roof of the porch. "Bo Rutledge. Great to make your acquaintance."

Chapter 17

Mick led Bo Rutledge into his kitchen. Conrad tucked his keys back into his pocket and flanked behind them as they broached the entrance to the foyer.

Gordie looked up from wiping the counter with a dish rag. Theresa and Larraine each whirled to take in the sight of the man in the black hat and shirt. Kenny leaned against the wall and finished his last gulp of orange juice.

"Hello everyone," Mick announced. "This is Bo Rutledge, the country music singer."

Four pairs of eyes gazed at Bo without any knowledge of him. He took a step into the kitchen, removed his hat and slowly said, "howdy" with a fervent nod of his head.

The sound of his voice prompted Theresa first, who propped from her chair in dawning recognition.

"Do you sing that song about the girl and the flatbed, riding in the truck?"

As she butchered the words to his song, she also warbled the melody for a bar or two before trailing off in embarrassment at her lack of musical talent.

"My Girl and her Flatbed," Bo acknowledged with a nod.

"Sounds pretty," Larraine said.

"Never heard of it," Kenny added.

"Well, sure is lovely to meet y'all," Bo beamed. "I'm real glad to work with Mick, here on some kickin' songs for my next album."

Gordie invited Bo to sit at the last available spot at the table for some hash browns and corn meal pancakes.

"So, this is Matunuck?" he observed, gazing out the window at the corn fields and the sandy, grassy dunes along the ridge of the blue ocean. "Ain't much here."

"It's a lot more than it looks," Kenny said.

The sound of another car arriving echoed through the foyer. Mick whirled just in time to see his buddy Aaron "Ronnie" Benjamin fly out of his car as if in an emergency. In a single motion, he bound up the three stairs of the porch and blasted through the screen door.

"The blues are running," he announced, out of breath.

Kenny sprung to action and bolted through the living room out the house toward his truck. Mick and Conrad exchanged excited glances.

"I got a rod in my truck," said Conrad as he joined Kenny outside.

"I've got a couple in the basement," Mick answered.

Larraine and Theresa shrugged and finished their breakfasts as Mick nearly tumbled down the stairs to his basement.

"Where are they?" Kenny asked Ronnie as he pulled two fishing rods and a white ten-gallon bucket from his trunk.

"Anyone got any lures?" Conrad asked as he pulled his rod from then flatbed of his Ford.

"What's going on?" Bo asked Gordie as he scraped the grease from his pan into an empty tin can.

"The blues," Gordie chuckled. "It happens only once a year for about an hour. And when it does, it's, well, it's, uh. It's pretty indescribable."

"The bluefish," Mick added, thrusting a fishing rod into Bo's hands. "Come on. I'll explain while we run to the beach."

"They were just rounding the point at Deep Hole about fifteen minutes ago," Ronnie reported. "Kyle posted it on Facebook Live. I just happened to catch it at the right time."

Bo followed Mick, his brother and his friends out the house and trotted behind them as they ran past the inn to the beach.

"I figure they're out by the public beach about now," Ronnie estimated. "They should be here in five, maybe ten."

Kenny lugged his tackle box and bucket in one hand and two rods in the other. Exceptionally athletic, Conrad ran ahead of both Kenny and Ronnie, while Mick slowed to give Bo a little better explanation of the urgency.

"Every year," he started, pausing to catch his breath, "A massive school of bluefish run from East Matunuck to Charlestown."

"Blue fish?" Bo repeated.

"That's right," Mick continued. "It's the most amazing sight you'll ever see. There's got to be thousands of them. Tens of thousands. Maybe hundreds. I don't know."

"I love to fish," Bo perked with the added understanding of the situation. "Ain't never had bluefish, but there's always a first for everything. Let's haul us in some fishies."

They caught up with the group, who stood by the aftermath of the wave breaks. Aaron held his hand over his eyes and looked east to try and spot the school. Conrad baited his hook while Kenny filled the white bucket with salt water.

From the inn, Marty, still dressed in his chef's uniform and hat, bounded down the steps of the back porch and kicked off his shoes. Two additional white buckets bobbed at either side as he sprinted to meet his friends by the waterside.

Kenny handed him a rod and filled the two additional buckets with water from the break of a small wave.

Ronnie yelped and pointed.

"Here they come."

All six of them cast their lines as deep as they could throw them. The ocean darkened. Thousands of tiny ripples made a deafening sound as the first throng of passing blues filled the area just beyond the break of the waves.

The sound spooked the few swimmers in the area, who quickly exited the sea. It looked and sounded like the ocean was boiling as an area the size of a football field approached. The noticeably dark-shaded water splashed and churned with thousands of quick, darting fish just below the surface. As fast as they could cast their lines and reel them back in, they plunked eighteen-to-thirty-six-inch-long blues out of the ocean with ease. The desperate sea-creatures flapped in the buckets, thrusting their gills upward and spilling water all about. Marty ran back to the inn and brought out two long red coolers to store more of the captured fish.

Bo hooted as he reeled in one of the larger catches of the day.

"Dayamn" he shouted. "This is seriously like shooting fish in a barrel."

"But without the need for a gun," Ronnie quipped.

"I got one in the truck, if ya'll need it."

Within ten minutes, the dark patch of water passed. The bubbling sea settled and the lines returned empty. Each of them had caught five or six fish, aside from Marty, who sacrificed some prime reeling time to fetch the additional containers.

With nearly forty fish flopping around in three ten-gallon buckets and two thirty-gallon oversized coolers, they opted to donate half of them to the inn. Kenny decided to sell the rest to the little fish market in East Matunuck and split the profits on a couple rounds of beers for the crew at the Ocean Mist.

"I've got an even better idea," Marty said. "Come back later tonight. We'll set up a good old fashioned clam bake, right here outside the inn. I'll get Shelly to advertise it on Facebook. It'll be like old times."

"Alright," Kenny agreed. "But we save a hundred bucks for one round at the bar."

"Hell, boys," Bo shouted. "This was one dang hoot of a good time. Spend that money on some first-rate seafood for this shindig tonight. Drinks at the bar on me tonight."

The group cheered and high fived each other.

Kenny hauled his half of the fish to his truck. Conrad checked his watch and bolted to his truck to get to work. Ronnie gave Bo a quick chest hug and left for his car as well. Mick and Bo helped Marty drag the coolers up the sand to the hatch to the basement.

As Ronnie and Kenny walked away, Mick barely heard his buddy Ronnie ask Kenny the question.

"Who's the dude in the black shirt?"

Shelly noticed the giant midnight blue splotch of darkened water beyond the break of the waves. She saw it coming from the moment it crossed Mary Carpenter's Beach, past the trailer park by the old Blackberry Beach Gap. The enormous blob of darkness looked like a rapidly moving oil spill with violently churning whitecaps as the bluefish flapped and kicked just inches beneath the surface of the ocean. She watched Mick, Kenny, Conrad and his crew of friends sprint across the sand, hastily set up shop and haul in as many of them as they could in the mere fifteen minute window they had to tap into the swarm.

She tried to concentrate on her business call, but the constant hoots and cheers completely distracted her until the monstrous school of fish passed the inn and migrated further west toward Green Hill.

Mick and Marty dragged an oversized cooler up the sand to the basement hatch of the inn, which led to the freezer room. She tried to wave from her second story window, but, engrossed in his activity, Mick failed to notice her.

The voice on the other end of the line repeated a thought to make sure Shelly heard it.

"Are you still there Ms. Newsome?" the voice asked.

"Yes," Shelly replied, clearing her throat and looking away from her window to concentrate more thoroughly on the call. "I told Mr. Callahan I was completely supportive of the plan to build the seawall and I signed his petition the other day."

"Yes, Ms. Newsome," the voice asked, "What Mr. Callahan is asking you do is to give testimony at the town hearing tomorrow night."

Shelly realized that Mr. Callahan's assistant had already asked her to give testimony a few minutes earlier, but she was caught not listening, watching Mick and his friends instead.

"As a successful local business-woman and a life-long resident," the assistant continued. "Your commentary would be very powerful in the fight to save Matunuck from the terrible erosion problem it's facing."

"I'm not sure I'd know what to say," said Shelly.

"We'll e-mail you some possible talking points," the assistant replied. "We want your testimony to be authentic and from your heart. But we'd like to also help you to be factual and well-informed as to the issues and our position. A half-mile seawall from the easternmost point of the trailer park, across the top of the Matunuck Beach Road, underpinning the pub and protecting all fifty homes in front of Deep Hole is the only solution to this problem."

"Right," Shelly agreed. "All those families in those houses. It would be such a shame for anything to happen to them."

"That's right, Ms. Newsome," Ted Callahan's assistant responded. "Go ahead and share your passion for this wonderful community, your love of the people and your concern for the safety of those homes. This is the emotion and the angst we need to convince the town council and the lawyers for the state to take the action and commit the funds we need."

"Ok," Shelly said, caught up in the conversation and failing to notice Mick and Bo Rutledge as they exited the inn's basement and ambled down the beach toward the pub. "I guess I can do this."

"We know you can," Ms. Newsome. "In fact, Mr. Callahan thinks of you as his secret weapon."

"I know I can do this," Shelly added, her confidence growing as she envisioned herself addressing the board.

"Mr. Callahan will call before the meeting to further prep you and get you fired up," she concluded her pitch. "He's good at that."

Shelly's stomach twirled at the image of speaking in front of an audience. But she felt motivated to represent the cause of protecting the Matunuck community.

She cast her gaze across the beach and noticed the recognizable frame of Mick Maguire, treading down along the water's edge next to the man from his fishing crew she didn't recognize.

"Who's the guy in the cowboy hat?" she asked herself.

Chapter 18

Bo Rutledge rolled up the sleeves of his black silk shirt and unbuttoned it to the midpoint of his chest. From a distance, the sweat stains remained undetectable, but Mick could see the darkened round spot in the back and shaded fabric under the armpit. Bo removed his hat and attached it to a hook on his belt, revealing his wet, matted dirty-blond hair.

"That was one hell of a blast," Bo said as they passed Roy Carpenter's Beach toward Willow Dell. "Them fish run like that only once a year?"

"That's it," Mick replied.

"Serious? Just once?"

Mick nodded.

"Dayam then," Bo hooted. "I came just in time."

Mick pointed out the Willow Dell private clubhouse. He showed his guest the pavilion for the public beach. They approached the trailer park seawall and stood in the flattened dune where the Blackberry Beach clubhouse used to stand.

"This is it," said Mick. "This is the spot that inspired that first song."

"The one about laying on the blanket with your baby?" Bo asked.

"That's right," Mick replied. "It's my favorite part of the beach. All my friends and I used to lay right here every day of every summer for more than ten years."

Bo observed the scenery. The dunes opened and parted, giving the beach much greater width. To his right, the beach grasses swayed in the wind. Behind him, the marshy pond by the Vanilla Bean rested still with the occasional cat-tail stubs waving in the wind. To his left, the trailer park seawall rose twenty feet high.

The scraping of the waves filled the air with a peaceful rhythm. The cry of the gulls added timbre as did the occasional yelp of a nearby group of children playing in the sand.

"I can see it," Bo exclaimed, inhaling a gulp of air, holding it and letting it out. "I love it. I listened to your demo a buncha times. We got a lotta beaches down south. Hell, Florida alone's a huge market and everyone down there'll relate to your lyrics."

"Well, if you like that, you'll love the next place I'm going to show you," Mick said.

They passed the back of the trailer park to the Matunuck Beach Road. Mick led him along the gap where the beach threatened to wash out the street to the Ocean Mist bar and pub. Bo pointed at the painted logo on the side of the building and nudged Mick in the ribs.

"Pretty transparent where you get your inspiration for lyrics," Bo laughed.

Mick held the screen door to the pub for Bo. Kyle Dolman recognized the celebrity immediately and catapulted the bar to greet him.

"You're Bo Rutledge," he shouted above the piped music emanating from the overhead speaker. "Right here in my bar. '*Busted, Rusted and Broke*'. I love that song, man. What are you doing here?"

Mick formally introduced his guest. Kyle brought them a plate of clam cakes and steamers, which Bo eyed suspiciously but reluctantly tried. Joycie sat with them, fawning over Bo as he regaled her with stories of cutting his albums and playing concerts across arenas in Nashville, Memphis, Tampa, New Orleans and Texas. Had she harbored any disdain for Mick, she didn't show it in her excitement at meeting the country music celebrity. Mick assumed she must have already forgotten who he was, given her complete absence of attitude toward him.

Bo slid his completed plate of seafood to the side and pointed at the menu, written in chalk above the bar.

"Let me try them hot wings you got," he exclaimed. "Partner, where I come from, you ain't never experienced hot like I have."

"The real hot wings come from upstate New York," said Mick. "Not really a southern food."

"Some'll say the Anchor Bar in Buffalo," Bo spoke heartily, as if performing for the entire bar. "But, give me downtown Ithaca right at the tip of Cayuga Lake, you know, the Fingers?"

Mick, Kyle and Joycie stared at him, unfamiliar with his reference.

"You know, the Finger Lakes," he continued. "The little valley between Ithaca College and Cornell. Give me Mama Teresas, Uncle Joe's,

142

Pudgies, Kelly's Dockside. I'll show you good ole' upstate New York hot wings."

Kyle brought out two dozen wings, rolled in their hottest sauce and ate with him, Mick and Joycie. Bo scoffed at the spiciness, but complimented him on the flavor.

"I'll tell you the secret ingredient, my buddy Pudgie puts in his sauce," Bo said, with his arm around the bar owner. "Port wine. Just pour it right in there. It'll make your forehead break out in a sweat."

Kyle guided Mick and his boisterous guest to the deck and pointed out the surfers coasting along the sizeable waves next to Deep Hole.

"I'll get you a board and a wet suit if you'd like to give it a try," he said.

Bo declined, but stood against the railing, rapt at the dancing, darting surfers and the blush of warm salty air against his face.

"It's nice here," Bo commented. "But dayamn, the water comes right up under the bar. You're gonna get washed out to sea soon, son."

Mick shrugged. Kyle's eyes twinkled.

"We're trying to fix that," he said. "We hope to get the town and the state to pony up the money to protect the community."

"I would think," Bo said, turning his back to lean against the railing. "Them houses available to rent? It's so calm and quiet here. Ain't nothing like L.A. where I've been the last couple months after my tour. I hate it there. Maybe I'll stay here for a couple a weeks."

Kyle suggested he contact officer Pat O'Hannon, whose family owned a set of cottages near Deep Hole.

"It would be great to have you here for a while," Kyle added. "We could use a spokesperson to help with our cause."

"Too bad you got all them houses over there, next to the bar," Bo mused, either mishearing Kyle's plea or adeptly ignoring it and changing the subject. "Take them out. Bring in a couple truckloads of new sand. You'd have a nice big beach like they got down south in Florida and the Carolinas. Big money-makers down there."

Mick gazed across the twenty-five houses next to the bar that crowded the south side of the Matunuck Beach Road between the pavement and the sand of the beach. He tried to imagine another

Hurricane Constance blowing through and wiping out that whole development of homes - like the 1938 and 1954 catastrophes - leaving the sort of long, unencumbered length of open sand like he enjoyed as a kid at Blackberry Beach.

"Imagine that?" Mick responded to Bo's suggestion.

"That would be horrible," Kyle retorted. "Those cottages have been there for fifty, sixty years, maybe seventy. They're some of my most loyal customers. My friends. Those houses are not under as much threat as the bar. The first priority is to protect the road by the end of the trailer park and then the bar."

Bo thanked Kyle and Joycie for the lunch. Joycie asked him to come back for dinner. Kyle invited him to play a set. Bo said he'd think about it.

"Actually, we're having a clam bake at the inn," Mick said. "Twenty-eight bucks, all you can eat bluefish, shrimp, steamers and whatever else Kenny catches today. You guys should come by."

"Mick and I'll play some tunes together," Bo added. "I'd love you to hear 'em."

"We'll be there," Joycie bat her eyes.

"Wouldn't miss it," Kyle agreed. "We'll get the staff to cover the bar."

Bo and Mick walked along the Matunuck Beach Road further east toward deep Hole. To their left, Prospect Road veered north off of the one road in town that cut between the ocean and the adjacent salt ponds. Next to Prospect Road, stood a distinctive mansion, built at the turn of the century with a huge wrap-around porch and three-story tower with panoramic windows facing the ocean and the ponds. It belonged to the family of his old friend Lizzy Gingrich, whose older sister Wendy still owned it.

"Shame they built all them ugly little houses on the beach side of the road," Bo observed. "Imagine how nice this big old house would be with nothing but beach in front of it?"

"I'm sure that was what it was like in the twenties and thirties before they built them," Mick replied. "I've seen pictures of the Hurricane of 1938, where there was nothing but this big house here. The road didn't even come this far. It was just a dirt path."

"I'd love to buy up a bunch them cabins," Bo mused. "Wipe 'em all out; just bulldoze 'em into the sand; flatten 'em and then convert this old baby to a resort with its own beachfront."

Mick tried to picture Bo's vision. He regarded the tiny four- and five-hundred-square-foot, two-room shacks. Many of them featured weather-worn shingled siding, dilapidated roofs, hanging gutters and rotted eaves. He'd never looked at them through the lens that Bo presented, but in light of his observations, they didn't look ugly to him. But he could see Bo's logic.

He ran some quick math in his head. Figure at a half million each for the twenty houses wedged between the beach road and the shore, with an investment of about ten million, Bo could create a sizably attractive private beach. The prospect of a place like the old Blackberry Beach immediately enticed Mick with the vision of past glory from his childhood.

Of course, he thought, they'd all have to go up for sale at the same time.

"Owners would hold out for big money," Bo observed, as if synching his thoughts with Mick's. "I'm sure there'd be hold outs, especially as their neighbors started cashing in."

"Well, wait long enough," Mick replied. "Mother Nature's going to wipe them out eventually."

"How'd y'all figure that?" Bo asked.

"It's the big debate in town," Mick explained. "It's like Kyle was saying. Half the people, mostly the ones from this side of town, want to build a big wall all the way across the beach to block the erosion problem."

"Oh, that's what he wants to do?" Bo quipped. "Nobody likes a big wall at a beach."

"That's what I say," Mick agreed. "The people down my way don't want big, ugly rocks. We'd rather keep the beach natural, like God intended, even if it means a couple houses along the shore have to come down or move further back."

"Or someone just buys them up and takes them out," Bo winked.

"Or that," Mick agreed. "Although they'll never sell."

"Oh, I don't now about that," Bo winked. "Money talks. And I got too much of it that I gotta hide before the government comes and takes it from me. Buying up a buncha properties at a loss would help me out with a little problem I have by earning too much on my last album."

They reached Deep Hole. Mick watched, with amusement as Bo tried to maneuver in the soft sand in his shiny, bedazzled leather cowboy boots. They followed the coastline with their eyes to the large seawall between Matunuck and East Matunuck where the tall homes protruded above Ocean Ave. Waves crashed against the massive outcropping. Bright white foam flailed into the air.

"That's what happens to the beach when you build a seawall," Mick pointed out to Bo. "The beach disappears."

Mick's phone buzzed. A number he didn't recognize popped onto the screen.

"Hello," he said as Bo sat on a log and let the sand out of his boots. "Yes, this is Mick. ... Yes, I'm aware of the meeting... Yes, I signed the petition. ... I hadn't planned to. ... Yes, I do feel strongly about it. ... I hadn't considered that. ... I could do that. ... I wouldn't know quite what to say. ... Uh, sure, you could text me the talking points. ... Ok, I'll be there. Thank you."

Mick stashed the phone in his pocket. Bo put his cowboy hat back onto his head to shield his face from the hot sun.

"Who's that," Bo asked. "Little lady friend?"

"No," Mick replied, lost in thought.

The breeze kicked up some dust from the dirt parking lot in front of Deep Hole Beach.

"Hey," Mick asked Bo, in a sudden burst of inspiration. "Any chance you'll still be here by Tuesday night?"

"Don't know," Bo replied. "I'm liking it here. I could check if the inn's got room for me. We sure could use the time refining your songs."

Mick gazed at the seawall by Ocean Avenue. He watched the Atlantic heave its might at the massive beige and grey monstrosity.

"I have to say," Bo continued. "I'm all in on the '*Blanket by the Beach*' song."

Mick largely ignored Bo's commentary, lost in the thought of the call he just received.

"And, I can appreciate where you got the inspiration for the Ocean Mist song," Bo continued, oblivious to Mick's sudden change of attention span. "But my audience is pretty diverse. And by that, I mean some of them, like in Florida and the Carolina's, are near the beach and the ocean and all. But, there's a huge chunk a real estate in the south that don't know nothing about the beach or the ocean."

Mick nodded in agreement as if listening to Bo.

"I ain't no Jimmy Buffett," he said. "I got fans in Arkansas, Kansas, West Virginia. I'm thinking the Ocean Mist song's gonna have to change. What if we made it about a river or a creek? Maybe we swap the 'Ocean Mist' lyric for 'River Mist'. The rest of the song can be pretty much the same."

Mick repeated the phrase 'River Mist' without registering Bo's words. He clicked the text on his phone and occupied his mind with the message sent to him by the President of the 'Save Matunuck Beach' organization.

"The guy's lost his girl," Bo continued his brainstorm about Mick's lyrics. "He's staring out into the early morning river mist, thinking about her. He thinks he hears her in the sound of the rambling river. He thinks he sees her in the ripples of the water. The lyrics still work. We just adjust it to the audience. What do you think?"

"So, you'll stay longer than just the weekend?" Mick asked.

"I'd sure like to," Bo answered.

"Good. I was hoping you'd come to a meeting with me," Mick said. "You'd be a hell of a surprise guest and a pretty influential secret weapon."

Chapter 19

Kenny showed up at the inn around four o'clock in the afternoon with a flatbed full of ice and chilled seafood. He had fresh crab, oysters, lobsters and quahogs.

Ronnie and Marty used a high-speed circular saw to slice through two fifty-gallon metal barrels. They dug out holes in the sand and buried the half-drums up to their edges. They collected dried grass, kindling and sticks from the top of the dunes and crumbled newspapers on top of them. After washing the pile in lighter fluid, they lit the flammable material and formed a small bonfire. They added larger pieces of wood to fan the flames and amp the heat.

After the height of the fire subsided and the wood burned consistently, they covered the searing logs with medium-sized, nicely-rounded stones. They ranged between the size of a baseball and a softball. They then placed a wide metal grate across the smoldering mass to create a flat cooking surface. The stones retained and conducted the heat through the slats of the grate, creating a wave of scorching hot air. Marty directed his staff to cover the metal with long, wet stands of seaweed. Dark grey aromatic smoke extended into the sky, which also served to ward off the bugs.

Shelly set the tables along the deck. Her staff moved seating to the sand along the top of the beach.

Kenny unloaded his haul onto the top of the seaweed-covered grill while Marty lugged the containers of Atlantic Bluefish up the stairs from the inn's basement. He sat at a table by the pit and gutted each fish, slicing them in half, descaling and deboning them and searing them on the grill.

Customers filtered in, resulting from Shelly's e-mail advertisement blast and Facebook posts. Mick and Bo approached from the Roy Carpenter's side of the beach as the customers took their seats.

The sunset gave them the perfect light. The weather cooperated with a warm, temperate evening. The porch filled, spilling to the runover seating on the beach.

"Not too bad for a post-Labor Day weekend," Shelly mused to Marty. "Seems like everyone in town turned up."

Bo retrieved his luggage from the back of his truck and slung his guitar over his shoulder. As the celebrity ambled across the parking lot to the inn to check in, Mick looked in on his father. He entered a quiet house. Unlike the typical routine, the television was off.

"Dad?" Mick called through the house. "Where are you?"

Without an answer, Mick's nerves raced. He replayed the schedule for the day. Trudy brought him to the dance class. Bethanne made him lunch. Haley stopped by with her two boys in the afternoon. By Mick's calculation, Gordie should have been down for his nap by now. But his bed sat undisturbed.

Mick grabbed his cell phone and called Dana.

"We're just pulling off the Post Road," she said. "We're coming down for the clam bake. Radley can't make it. But I got Miguel and the girls with me."

Mick paused. Dana picked up the red flag in his unusual silence.

"Everything alright?" she asked with an edge of tension in her voice. "Is Dad okay?"

Just before sounding the alarm bells, Mick spied a note on the kitchen table, written in Gordie's loopy, scratchy cursive handwriting.

"Ah, he's fine," Mick said, reading the note to himself. "Apparently he went to Larraine's house for dinner."

"The dingbat lady he met at his dance class?" Dana asked.

"I guess so," Mick replied.

"The girls will be so disappointed. They love when Grampa Gordie cracks open their lobsters for them."

Mick grabbed his guitar. As he walked out to the porch, he noticed that Kenny had already fixed his swing. Mick nudged it back and forth and watched it sway effortlessly from its two connection points in the ceiling. He sat down and felt it support his weight without budging. He noticed a more detailed follow-up text from the 'Save Matunuck Beach' organization that had recruited him to speak at the upcoming town hall meeting. As he waited for Dana, he read through the talking points and clicked the links to the research they provided which validated their naturalist positions. Mick emersed himself in the reading material and found himself vehemently agreeing with the tenets of the grass roots environmentalist group.

Dana arrived in her SUV. Her front tires made a crackling sound against his new pavement driveway as she cut the wheel to park. Her family piled out, and they all walked to the inn together.

As they arrived in the circular driveway, Kyle and Joycie Dolman pulled up in their topless Mercedes, followed by Haley, her husband Miles and their two boys.

They all spilled out and walked around to the back of the inn where several dozen patrons sat at wooden tables on the beach. The smoke from the homemade grill wafted into the air. The two young Fonteneaux girls took Haley's boys to the edge of the water to look for sea glass and pretty stones while the adults occupied a large, round table in the sand. A waiter filled their water glasses and left a printed paper menu in the table.

"It's all you can eat," he explained. "The menu just gives you the choices. There's salad inside and the seafood selections are spread out on a table on the porch. All caught today, within the past few hours. Can I interest you in a bottle of wine for the table?"

"Sure can," Haley blurted, turning to her husband. "Can you make sure the boys don't get their nice shorts wet."

Dana raised an eyebrow at Mick, which Haley noticed.

"I was with them all day at a baby birthday with fifteen other little boys running wild," she explained. "I'm ready for _me_ time."

Joycie spotted Bo at a table with Ronnie Benjamin, Kenny Forrester and several of Kenny's aunts and cousins. Like a jack-o-lantern, her wide smile arched across her face at Bo in his pale, linen half-buttoned shirt and oversized cowboy hat. She craned her neck to spot an empty seat at his table, whispering in her husband's ear, and quietly excusing herself to fill the last available seat.

Shelly emerged from the inn and stood on the porch. The breeze blew her sundress against the front of her legs, giving them shape and definition. She proudly overlooked her successful event.

Mick swung around to catch her eye. Dana gave him a nudge. As she did, Kyle stood from the table and walked right over to her, giving her a hug and a kiss on the cheek. Mick observed them take a seat at a two-person table and engage in an in-depth conversation.

Dana watched Joycie flirt openly with Bo while Kyle and Shelly attended each other with seemingly great interest.

"What do they have?" Dana asked. "Like an open relationship or something?"

Mick shrugged and dipped his bread in a dish of olive oil. Trudy and Bethanne joined them at their table in the spots vacated by Kyle and Joycie.

"Beach looks good today," Trudy observed.

"Nice and wide," Bethanne added. "Of course, it's low tide and the moon is waning now."

The waiter brought dinner and salad plates, placing one in front of each adult. The children continued to play in the sand. The adults joined the line for the seafood table. Mick avoided eye-contact with Shelly as she seemed engrossed with Kyle's company. He could hear Joycie's shrill laugh above the rumble of the crowd. She placed a hand on Bo's forearm as she occupied his attention.

From the west, Mick spotted two figures against the light of the setting sun. As they wobbled toward the inn, Mick made out the silhouette of his father. He walked hand-in-hand with Larraine toward the beach behind Shelly's porch. Mick raised a hand and caught his attention.

They greeted him as he emerged from the porch with a plate full of lobster and crab.

"I thought you were eating at Larraine's house," Mick said.

"We did," Gordie replied. "Four-thirty sharp. Just as it should be. Tomato soup and toast."

"Oh, hey Dad," Dana said. "Is this your, uh, friend?"

"Yes, it is," he replied, introducing Larraine to his daughter. "We came to check out this shindig and to break the lobster claws for my two favorite granddaughters. Where are they? I knew they'd be disappointed if I weren't here to take care of them."

"That's sweet, Dad," Dana said, pointing at her two girls sitting at a small table with Haley's boys, adjacent to the bigger round table.

As he turned toward the kids' table, they heard Larraine speak louder than she probably intended into Gordie's ear.

"Did you say 'Farrah'?" she asked. "And the other one was 'Rick'?"

Dana rolled her eyes and laughed. Bo approached them, and Mick introduced his sister to his celebrity client.

"All everyone talks about is the beach erosion around here," he quipped. "It's like how we all complain about the Democrats down south. Ain't much you can do about it, but everyone hates it all the same."

"You have to understand how beautiful this beach used to be," Mick said.

"If you ask me," Bo replied. "It's pretty dayumn nice right now, long as you don't go comparing it to what it used to be. Let me tell you something. My first guitar; gorgeous when I got it. I was fifteen years old. Played it every day for the past twenty years. Wait 'til you see it now. Piece of crap. It's old and dirty. It's frayed, chipped and cracked. But it still sounds sweet and makes great music."

Mick nodded in appreciation of Bo's perspective.

"You know," he continued. "I looked you up. I heard a buncha your songs. And, of course, I been practicing the ones we're gonna produce together. You spend an awful lot of time and energy lookin' back at how good you had it in the past. I'd like to see you write a song about how amazing the future looks to you."

As Bo walked away to fix himself a salad, a wave of dawning washed over him about his tendency to dwell on the past. He watched Gordie hack at the lobsters for his granddaughters. He watched Kenny, Marty and Ronnie stand around the clam bake pit shooting the breeze. He watched Dana and Haley sip their wine glasses while their husbands tended to their kids. And, for the first time in a long time, the warmth of his childhood filled him with that indescribable feeling of being home; not just physically, but emotionally.

His heart felt whole, or at least nearly whole. He scanned the crowd for the two missing pieces to the puzzle. The one piece, his mother Jaime, was gone forever. He could never fill that hole in his heart. But he also wished his own daughter had chosen to join them. He pictured her at the table with his nieces and nephews, helping Gordie crack the lobster tails. He watched his father, with Larraine by his side. They laughed with the girls. He picked up the littlest of Haley's children and wiggled him gently. He tickled Haley's other boy.

Mick's eye wandered to the porch where Ted Callahan joined Shelly and Kyle. The attorney pulled up a chair and sat at their two-person table, forming a triangle. The conversation continued to engross them, and they seemed oblivious to the rest of the event around them.

Mick started toward the porch to interject himself into the conversation when he was suddenly surprised by a set of hands covering his eyes from behind.

"Surprise," he heard Melodie's soft voice from behind his back.

"You made it," Mick chirped. "I'm so happy."

"I dragged Kian here," Melodie boasted. "I wouldn't miss a clam fry for the world."

Mick shook hands with Kian and hugged his daughter.

"You can take my seat at the table next your aunt," he said. "I think those two boys are going to keep Miles on his toes. So, you can probably take his seat too."

As Mick made his way to the porch, he heard Kian chide his girlfriend.

"It's a clam _bake_," Kian whispered. "And _you_ dragged _me_ here?"

Mick sliced the crowd and headed straight for the porch. Kyle noticed him coming and looked up to greet him. Shelly seemed almost flush. Ted quickly stood to shake his hand.

"Great to see you again," Ted said. "My compliments on a gorgeous house you've built."

Ted offered his seat and walked away to serve himself a meal. Kyle stood from his chair and shook Mick's hand. Shelly looked up and said simply; "hi Mick."

"You guys seem pretty locked in," Mick observed, taking Ted's seat. "What are we discussing so intently here?"

Mick noticed the subtle look between them.

"Well, you know," Kyle started. "The usual. The bar. The inn. Life."

"The beach erosion," Shelly added. "It's just so bad. I can't bear to imagine what's going to happen here in the next five or ten years."

Mick looked over his shoulder at the tall, cliff-like dunes at Roy Carpenter's Beach.

"It'll work itself out," he said.

"Well, it may," Kyle replied. "But I just think we have to help it out a little bit."

"You really think you can stop it?" Mick asked, feeling argumentative at the sight of Kyle occupying so much of Shelly's attention.

"Yes, I do," Kyle said, standing up and facing the crowd of people and then turning back to Shelly. "Is it okay now?"

Shelly nodded. Mick crinkled his brow as if wordlessly asking Shelly what was happening. Kyle's voice interrupted their eye lock.

"Excuse me everyone," Kyle projected from the elevated deck over the sand. "Thank you for your attention and especially to Shelly Newsome and the Matunuck Inn-By-The-Sea for putting on a classic Rhode Island clam bake. Let's hear it for the owner and staff of this amazing Matunuck establishment."

The crowd clapped and cheered. Shelly raised her hand in humble thanks and pointed at Marty and his kitchen staff to transfer the credit.

"Marty's been great," she whispered to Mick. "He pulled all this off even with one of the waiters quitting this morning."

"I asked Ms. Newsome, tonight," Kyle continued addressing the crowd. "If I could use this time to speak to you all for a few minutes about the town hall meeting coming up where the state will be presenting their plan to shore up the Matunuck Beach Road down by the trailer park."

Mick and Shelly traded glances, smiling faintly, but neither giving away their inner thoughts.

"We need as many of you to turn out as possible in support of the walls across both the Blackberry Beach Gap and the commercial zone where the Matunuck Beach Road is about to give out any day now. Many of you live down that way and won't be able to get to your homes if the ocean blows through the dunes or over the existing barriers on the Mary Carpenter's side. There's only one road in and out. And it's in big trouble. We need you all to sign the petition at the inn's front desk and we need you to stand up and speak your mind at the meeting. Can I count on you for that?"

The crowd cheered. Several people shouted supportive comments about how they would be there. Mick nodded to Shelly and stood to find his guitar.

"I think it's time for some music", he said to Bo, in earshot of Shelly. "Let's test out our new songs."

Mick and Bo took out their guitars, pulled chairs to the top stair of the porch and tuned their instruments together. Shelly gave an approving nod as he and Bo synchronized their adjustments. They launched into a southern, twangy, upbeat version of Mick's song about laying on the blanket in the dunes. The song gained a strong reception and some of the patrons danced and sang along in the front row.

As they performed, they could feel the crowd draw near. Dana's girls squirmed into the front row with Haley's boys and danced exuberantly as the people in the back tables stood to catch a better view. Throughout the night, whispers had made their way through the crowd about the celebrity who might perform. So, by the time they wrapped the first song, the crowd acknowledged the sense of uniqueness and significance of the quaint, intimate performance.

As Mick wrapped the final chorus of the first song and Bo kicked into an elaborate guitar solo to close out the track, he watched Kyle return to his wife. They swayed to the music with his arm around her shoulder. He watched Gordie wrap his arm around Larraine and move to the rhythm with her. He noticed Shelly on the porch reengaged in conversation with Ted Callahan. A woman with two young girls emerged onto the porch from inside the inn. She wore a tight skirt with a gaudy black leather jacket and bracelets up her arm.

She recognized Bo right away and danced provocatively in front of the crowd. As she did, Mick watched Shelly scowl and Ted attempt to comfort her.

The song ended and the crowd cheered. Shelly watched her sister garner attention from some of the males in the crowd including Ronnie Benjamin and her own business partner, Marty Fazzini.

Still stinging at the image of Shelly and Kyle locked in connective conversation all night, Mick strummed the opening chords to his wistful song about the Ocean Mist.

"You know," he spoke over the low melody emanating from his fingertips. "One way to deal with the beach erosion problem is to build a wall."

Bo played the baseline repeating it with Mick's cues. He watched Mick speak into his microphone with a perplexed look on his face.

"We can build lots of walls," Mick continued dripping sarcasm. "We can shut out all our problems with walls. Big, ugly walls, like the one down the end of this beach by the trailer park."

Mick watched Kyle's happy face droop with the realization of Mick's message. Shelly stood at the railing and peered at him, trying to understand his angle.

"We can build a wall to shut out immigrants from coming to our country," Mick continued, setting the tone of his voice to the rhythm and cadence of his tune. "But I don't know about you. I hate walls. They're ugly. And they don't solve problems. They just shut those problems out. They help us avoid dealing with them, head on and facing the reality of them. They push our problems of today off until tomorrow for someone else to worry about. We build a big wall down here in Matunuck and that'll be the end of Matunuck Beach."

Mick watched Kyle flash eyes to Shelly and then Ted Callahan. Shelly gave a helpless shrug before turning and walking into the inn.

"So, just remember, when you go to this town hall meeting and voice your opinion," Mick wrapped his monolog. "Maybe we don't need walls. Maybe we need to let nature run its course and take that money we'd spend on a wall and use it to help out the people most affected by this erosion problem we have."

As he finished his speech, some in the crowd cheered. Some stared blankly. He heard a distinct 'Boo'. Bo gave him a look and they kicked into the song.

"This one's called 'The Ghost of the Ocean Mist'," Mick announced.

"_River_ mist," Bo clarified just before Mick starting singing the first verse. "Ghost of the _River_ Mist."

Chapter 20

Mick awoke to the sound of birds chirping outside his window. The sun beamed through the gap between the bottom of his shade and the window sill, reflecting into his eyes. The ocean hummed and the breeze whistled. The gulls wailed and the flag outside Shelly's front porch snapped. Mick imagined a symphony of natural sounds outside his window.

Haley texted him asking if he needed a ride to school and he declined, looking forward to a brisk walk with the melody of the beach serenading him along the way.

With his backpack over his shoulder and his thermos in hand, he rounded the corner at the end of his long, shared driveway with the inn and made his way down Cards Pond Road toward the market.

The grey clouds closed around the sunlight with rapid urgency. And a new instrument joined the timbre of nature's musical score – the distant rumble of thunder.

Mick ran toward the market, trying to beat the rain. But a light, damp mist followed the first distant flash of lightning. Mick withdrew a portable umbrella from his backpack and scurried along the Matunuck Beach Road toward the school. He could feel his socks dampen under his flimsy boat shoes. He called Haley, but her phone rolled to voicemail. She was in the teacher's lounge, he imagined, no doubt regaling her co-workers with stories of her two mischievous young boys, who constantly kept her on her toes.

Mick felt his stomach heave as he quickened his pace. He'd tried to beat the intensifying moisture that floated all around him and wet his nose and cheeks.

A black BMW pulled in front of him. He watched the brake lights shine as it veered into the sand embankment by Lake Avenue.

"Get in," shouted a female voice from inside the vehicle, holding the door partially ajar for him.

Mick trotted to the half-opened passenger door and peered into the dark interior with a mix of curiosity and caution.

"I'm Shelly's sister, Lindsay," she said. "I heard you teach at the school. We just happen to be going there ourselves. Jump in before you get soaked."

Mick glanced at the two young girls in the back seat.

"Come on," Lindsay snapped. "We have to get there early to meet with the principal. I don't bite."

Mick refurled his umbrella and entered the car. As he settled into the seat next to Lindsay, she cocked the vehicle into gear and jolted down the road.

"Thanks for the ride," Mick said. "And nice to meet you."

"I don't know why my sister didn't introduce us at the clam bake the other night."

"It was a busy night," Mick replied.

"It was for her," Lindsay said. "She basically flirted with her ex-boyfriend all night."

Mick shrugged, reluctant to engage Lindsay in a personal conversation about Shelly.

"Your girls are going to Matunuck Elementary?"

"I don't have a permanent residence right now," Lindsay replied. "We're staying at the inn, but I'm going to need to do something for the next month or two I I want them to stay in school."

Mick raised an eyebrow at the prospect of Lindsay keeping her room for the next two months.

"There's a big tropical storm out by the Bahamas," Mick made small talk. "They say it could get here in about a week and a half.

"Anyway," Lindsay returned to her previous line of conversation, disinterested in Mick's talk of the weather. "She's still hung up on him, you know?"

"Who is?" Mick asked, already having forgotten the previous discussion thread.

"Shells," Lindsay replied. "They were hot and heavy in high school. Then he went to college and she didn't, and that was it."

Mick pictured Shelly and Kyle on the deck of her inn, enraptured in conversation, while Kyle's wife, Joycie, practically threw herself at Bo Rutledge.

"What's the deal with him and his wife?" Mick asked.

"She was a bitch in high school," Lindsay replied. "Probably still is." Lindsay lowered her voice with a glance into the back seat.

"Take it from me," she whispered. "Raising a couple a kid's'll take the zip right out of your love life, if you know what I mean."

Mick shrugged, suddenly uncomfortable with the loose-lipped woman he barely knew. They arrived at the school. The mist continued to fill the air like a hazy fog. The two girls exited the vehicle and fell in line behind Lindsay like a pair of baby geese.

"So, you're here for the next two months?" Mick asked.

"I have to establish residency to get them into the school," Lindsay said. "I have to demonstrate to the principal that I have a plan. I'm hoping to stay in the inn."

"For the next couple months?" said Mick. "That's gotta cost you a pretty penny."

"My ex is paying for it now through an emergency court order that my attorney filed," Lindsay cackled, almost like a witch. "He's contesting it. But I have to use his card for as long I can until the divorce gets finalized. I don't have a card of my own. Once the divorce goes through and the pre-nup kicks in, I'll be scrambling."

They reached the door to the school. Mick held it open for Lindsay and the two girls. They stood in the hallway, with Lindsay turning left toward the office and Mick heading right to his classroom. He waved goodbye to the girls, wished Lindsay luck with the principal and thanked her for the ride.

"Do me a favor," Lindsay laughed as she leaned toward Mick out the office door. "Can you keep my financial situation just between you and me? I can tell you kinda like my sister. It's kind of embarrassing to be in this predicament."

At that, Lindsay's smiling face disappeared beyond the glass door leaving Mick to wonder what she meant by her last comment.

One of Lindsay's daughters joined Mick's second period music class. The other attended his last class of the day. They both smiled warmly at him and participated enthusiastically in the class activities. The older one thanked him at the end of the class and politely wished him a good afternoon.

The thought of Lindsay giving him some sort of inside information about Shelly's inner thoughts intrigued him. He also pondered her characterization that she still harbored feelings for her old high school flame. As the last bell of the day rang and the students bolted out the doors, he had to shake the image of an adolescent Shelly in the back of a station wagon with the tall, bearded red-headed man that ran the Ocean Mist.

Outside the school, with the mist cleared and the hot sun evaporating the moisture on the ground, Mick caught the sight of Lindsay's black BMW driving the wrong way in a one-way lane and threading between two buses to pick up her daughters.

He waved to her, hoping to cash in on the intelligence she promised him. He was sure she'd seen him. But as haphazardly as she'd zipped into the buses-only lane to pick up her cargo, she sped toward the Matunuck Beach Road with her engine revving and the sand spitting from the back of her tires.

As Mick walked along the road back toward his house, he pulled out his phone and reviewed his talking points for the town hall meeting later that night. He read the e-mail carefully and repeated the key messages to himself.

A Honda Civic veered off the road and stopped in front of him. He immediately recognized the Matunuck Surf Shack bumper sticker and distinctive; "GAL 1" vanity license plate of his cousin, Haley Davies.

"Ride?" she asked out her opened passenger window.

Mick jumped into the passenger seat and instantly noticed her giant 32-ounce iced coffee wrapped in a plain brown napkin.

"Where'd you get that?" he asked.

"I had an open block last period," she replied. "The kids are at kiddie Camp Fuller until five, so I ran up to the city."

"Starbucks or Dunkies?" Mick asked.

"Neither," Haley replied. "I go to the Wakefield Java Shack, across the street from where Benny's used to be."

Haley proceeded to share every detail of her day with Mick for the duration of the ride to his house. As they rounded the corner from the beach road to Cards Pond Road, Haley gasped as if suddenly remembering something she wanted to ask him.

"You're going to the meeting tonight?" she asked.

"Yup, I'll be there," he replied.

"Make sure you put in a good word for Matunuck," she pleaded. "They have to agree to spend some money on fixing the beach road. It's going to give out any day now."

Mick hesitated to reply. But decided to share with his cousin that he'd be one of the featured speakers.

"Actually, I'm going to give a featured testimony," Mick boasted.

Haley's face lit up. Her smile beamed.

"Really?" she asked. "That's so great. Make sure you support Kyle's plan to protect the road and all the houses on the other side."

"Actually," Mick interrupted her. "I believe in protecting the road, but I'm against any extension of stone or rock beyond the fifty-foot area adjacent to where the road bends next to the shore."

Haley looked at him, trying to understand his angle.

"I don't understand," she said. "We have to build a wall to protect the town. Don't we?"

"Actually, no," Mick replied. "We can build a short revetment along the exposed section of the Matunuck Beach Road to protect it. But beyond that, we should be removing rocks from the beach, not adding them."

"But wouldn't that leave a lot of houses unprotected?"

"It will actually protect the houses more, by alleviating the force of the ocean against the hardened seawall."

Haley looked out her windshield and spied the ocean from across the potato fields. The waves had grown since the calm weekend. They could see the occasional splash of foam above the ridge of the dunes next to the inn.

"I keep hearing about how they need to shore up the Blackberry Beach Gap," she said. "Are you against that?"

"Sort of," Mick replied. "Do you know what that means?"

"Not really," Haley said. "I hear all different stories from different people. I'm not really sure what the best plans are."

Mick took the liberty of practicing his speech on his cousin.

"It means they're going to drain the pond next to the Vanilla Bean, fill it in with dirt and rubble -maybe even cement or asphalt - and dig a big drainage hole. Then they're going to drive a big crane right through that little marshy area, once they've paved it with hard clay and stone and drive two-foot-round iron stakes into the sand."

Haley gasped at Mick's description.

"They're going to erect a big metal wall and drop massive boulders on either side of it, like they did with the trailer park next to the old Blackberry Beach clubhouse."

Haley held her hand to her mouth, expressing concern about how it would look.

"Put it this way," Mick closed. "You know how, when you're driving down the Matunuck Beach Road, you can see the ocean from like five miles away."

"Yes," Haley perked from her seat. "And Block Island looks like it's so close you could swim to it."

"Imagine, instead of a view of the water and Block Island," Mick finished his speech. "All you saw was a big, ugly, black and grey metal wall?"

Haley shook her head in disgust. She turned into the long, shared driveway to Mick's house.

"You have to fight that," she protested. "That would be awful. You can't let them do that."

Mick nodded and started to speak. The wail of a siren not far behind them filled the air and echoed throughout the interior of Haley's Honda.

"Don't worry," Mick assured his cousin, raising his voice over the noise. "I won't."

Haley jolted the breaks to her four-cylinder sedan and veered to the shoulder of the driveway to make room for a speeding ambulance barreling its way from behind them on Cards Pond Road. Haley pulled into the driveway. To her surprise the ambulance turned behind her and honked. The red and blue lights blinded them as the horn and siren filled the car with a temporarily debilitating wail.

The massive vehicle slowed temporarily at the mouth of the driveway before veering around Haley's car and continuing up the driveway toward Mick's house.

Mick and Haley looked at each other with a wave of panic as the ambulance stopped next to his mailbox and the EMT's hopped out of the cab to sprint across the law.

"Uncle Gordie," Haley yelped as Mick uttered "Dad".

Chapter 21

When Mick and Haley entered the house, the EMTs had Gordie propped in his recliner chair. One attendant squeezed air into a ball attached to a blood pressure sleeve while the other shined a pen light into his eyes. Larraine stood behind Gordie rubbing his head and muttering encouragement to him.

Gordie, alert and cranky scoffed and complained at the attention.

"Take each other's temperature instead," he quipped. "I'm fine. I just got a little dizzy, that's all."

Mick's phone rang. A Rhode Island number appeared. He answered and heard the voice of Larraine's caregiver, Theresa, both through the receiver as well as from the kitchen.

"I'm right here," he called to her through the square hole in the wall, causing her to smile briefly and hang up the phone.

"One minute, he was fine," Theresa said as she approached Mick. "They were playing War with two decks of cards. They were at it all afternoon. My aunt got up to make him tea. I was reading a book."

"He looks okay to me," Mick interrupted her.

"And you are...?" Haley asked, an edge of confused sarcasm in her voice.

"Theresa," the woman replied. "I assist Larraine's during the day."

"Right," Haley replied, eying Larraine as she draped her arms around the back of Gordie's neck while the paramedics asked him questions.

"Larraine is the, uh,"

"Friend," Mick answered, as Theresa simultaneously called her "Girlfriend."

"We met at the clam bake," Theresa said, the gentility of the conversation in contradiction with the deliberate movements of the paramedics.

"He seemed fine," Theresa continued her story, ignoring Haley's commentary. "We just heard a thud. When we looked, he was face down on the table."

"He passed out?" Mick asked.

"I was just a little dehydrated," Gordie called to the hallway from his recliner. "Will someone tell these two I'm fine already?"

The lead paramedic stood from his squat next to Gordie and approached Mick. Covered from head to toe in a black uniform with a utility belt around his waist and radio fixed to his shoulder, the burly medical professional took up nearly the entire entryway from the foyer to the living room.

"You're the homeowner?" asked the attendant, whose nametag, reading 'Melvin', seemed like a possible misprint.

Mick nodded.

"I'm not leaving," Gordie shouted from his chair.

"You're the son as well?" the head medic asked, already knowing the answer from having spoken to Theresa upon arriving. "Your father has a history of headaches and blackouts due to his medical condition?"

"Yes," Mick replied. "An inoperable brain tumor. They thought he had six weeks to live, but it's been two years."

"How often does he get these headaches?"

"Every now and then," Mick replied, wondering if 'Melvin' represented a first name or last name.

"More like every day," Theresa spoke up from behind the paramedic. "I'm here most days with him and my aunt. We give him hot compresses and either caffeinated coffee or tea. We dim the lights, play soft music."

"You do all that?" Mick asked.

Theresa nodded, but the Paramedic cut her off before she could respond.

"We should take him to hospital for observation," said Melvin, the medic.

"No," Gordie growled. "I'm fine. I don't need meds. I don't need a doc. I just need a good drink. That usually does it."

"He needs my special peach tea," Larraine added.

"Yes, please sweet-stuff," Gordie replied with an eager grin.

The assistant medic packed his kits and gave Melvin a look of resignation. The older, bigger one bore down on Mick with his eyes.

"He needs medical attention," he said. "We're going to get the stretcher from the ambulance. Let us know what you want to do here."

Mick, Theresa and Haley moved to the kitchen. Larraine filled the teapot and placed it on the gas stovetop. She flicked the knob to strike the flame and heat the pot.

"You've got to make your dad go to the hospital," Haley whispered. "You heard them. He needs medical attention."

Mick hedged, shrugging his shoulders and looking through the opening to the television room where Gordie flipped the channel to a boxing match and eased back with his hands behind his head. Larraine sat next to him tousling his hair and whispering supportively to him.

"You're not seriously going to listen to him are you?" Haley asked. "He needs to see a doctor. He's not in charge. You've got to make the right decisions for him."

The teapot whistled and Larraine yelped that she needed to make the peach tea for her husband.

"Does she think they're married?" Mick asked Theresa.

"No, she just likes to say it," she replied.

Larraine took out a Brown University mug, filled it with steaming water and dunked two black tea bags from the counter. Mick observed her process as she lightly moved the teabag up and down in the mug.

"You know those are just plain black tea bags," Mick said. "I don't have peach tea here."

"I know," Larraine mused, reaching to the highest shelf in the cupboard. She moved a box of pasta to reveal a bottle of peach schnapps.

"Like I said," Larraine smiled. "He likes his tea strong."

The tall, muscular paramedic returned to the house. The younger one wheeled a wheelchair to the door of the porch.

"What's it going to be?" he peered at Mick.

"I'm fine," Gordie called from the other room. "You promised, Mick. You promised."

Haley sneered at him. Theresa retreated to the other room, grabbed her keys from the end table and ushered her aunt into the kitchen to retrieve her purse.

Mick shrugged and dropped his eyes.

"I think he's okay for now," he replied to the medical professional. "I can handle him from here, thank you."

Larraine kissed Gordie on the forehead and promised to check on him the next day. Theresa ushered her out. Haley gave Gordie a hug and told him to feel better. Mick stood awkwardly in the hallway watching his cousin embrace his father.

"Now come on," Mick could hear Haley order his father to move. "Time to get up and get your shoes on."

"I'm not going to the doctor's office," Gordie protested.

"You're coming with me," Haley projected her mommy voice. "We're going to pick up my boys at Camp Fuller day care. Then you're going to join me, Miles and my dad for dinner. I'm making breakfast for dinner; pancakes, bacon, fresh fruit and cinnamon toast."

The chair creaked as Gordie elevated and sought his sneakers.

"Mick has a meeting to get to," Haley continued. "And we don't want to leave you alone tonight."

"Even though I'm fine," Gordie scoffed.

"Sure you are, Uncle Gordie," Haley said.

"You had me at 'bacon'." Gordie replied, grabbing a sweater and slowly standing.

As Haley helped Gordie scuffle into his shoes and search for his wallet, Mick trotted out to his driveway to catch Theresa's attention.

"What's your daily availability?" he asked her. "And what would it cost to hire you?"

"No cost necessary," she said, with a laugh. "I'm already with her all day, and they're together every day. So, save your money and count on me to watch over them both. I've already got a whole schedule worked out with your aunt and cousin."

Haley loaded Gordie into her car and dashed to commence her evening. Theresa drove away with Larraine. In the sudden quiet of his empty nest, Mick checked the Weather Channel for an update on the tropical storm along the Florida coast. He had a meeting with his attorney to review the proposed contract between him and Bo. Mr. Callahan would arrive in ten minutes. They had an hour before they both had to leave for the town zoning hearing.

On the television, a weather reporter stood on a cement wall by a wide, sandy beach. He wore a yellow rain jacket and leaned into the wind as it pelted him from the east. A map showed three possible trajectories; one with the storm veering out to sea and missing the balance of the east coast, one with it darting westward and dissipating into the bowels of the deep south and one with it skirting the mid-Atlantic and marching up the Chesapeake Bay.

"Too early to tell," he concluded, as the rain intensified and the waves churned in the wind. "It could be a weather event. It could be a false alarm. We just won't know for another few days."

Mick heard three knocks on his door and elevated to answer it. A well-dressed Ted Callahan stomped his sandy boots on the welcome mat before entering Mick's foyer.

"Love the house," he remarked. "Beautiful wraparound porch. I like the hanging swing in front of the bay window. Nice touch."

Mick thanked him and escorted him to the kitchen table where he had printed the contract that Bo e-mailed him.

"Where's your father," Ted asked, looking around as if a critical piece of furniture was missing from the home.

"Long night," Mick rolled his eyes. "He's with my cousin."

Ted settled into one of Mick's wooden kitchen chairs. Mick offered him a beer or soda, but Ted settled for a glass of water.

"I read the contract you forwarded to me," Ted said, softening his voice and speaking more formally. "I don't understand this situation. Mr. Rutledge had an agent that was also his attorney, and now he no longer has that representation?"

"He fired his agent a couple weeks ago," Mick acknowledged.

Ted went on to describe the contract as a fairly standard co-publishing agreement. He read each paragraph as written and then translated it to plain speak that Mick could understand. Mick stood to make about a dime for every airing of the song across all platforms. He could take an advance on expected earnings, which would later be deducted from future royalties and he could specify a number of years for which Bo would own the copyright, and therefore control the use of the music and lyrics.

Ted stopped and reread a paragraph toward the end.

"He's got an option to terminate the agreement at any point for any reason," he said. "But you don't. I think you should. You don't want him to be able to screw you. I suggest we redline this section and propose new language that gives you the same options for termination as him. That way, if he misuses your song and you want to stop him, you have an avenue for doing so."

Mick stared blankly at his attorney who clarified his remarks with tangible examples.

"For instance, let's say he licensed the song to a company you found morally objectionable; a gun manufacturer, some sort of on-line gambling company or an adult entertainment film. You'd be able to exercise your termination option," Ted explained. "It's pretty standard in the music industry, especially for artists who might be scandal-plagued or prone to legal troubles. You wouldn't be able to block the song from the album once it's produced. But you could exert more control over who's allowed to license it. Of course, the more you license it, the more dimes you make."

Mick nodded in understanding.

"Plus, it covers you prior to production of the album," Ted continued. "Let's say you don't agree with the creative direction or just change your mind, you've got protection there as well."

"What if he doesn't agree to the redline?" Mick asked.

"He's in a precarious position without an attorney representing him," Ted replied. "Oldest trick in the book. I'm going to redline a bunch of clauses and minor, inconsequential changes. Without a lawyer, I think I'll be able to lull him into agreeing to some, pushing back on others. And, in the process, this is the one clause I'll really fight for. Having won several small battles, which I'll point out to him in grand amazement of his business-savvy, I'll tell him I really just need this one piece and play a light hardball with him. An attorney would pick up on the tactic. I'm not sure he will. I'll let you know how it goes."

Ted finished his glass of water and tucked the contract into his folder. With a glance at the clock, he stood and tucked the manilla folder into his leather satchel.

"I am going to run this back home and then I have to come right back to pick up Ms. Newsome for the big town meeting," Ted explained. "You going too?"

"Yes," Mick replied. "I'm speaking as a resident witness."

Ted raised an eyebrow and gave him an impressed look.

"Really," he said. "I hadn't heard about that. I would have thought they'd have told me that."

Mick smiled and nodded in confusion, feigning to understand Ted's comment.

"Did you coordinate with Shelly?" he asked.

"Shelly? No."

"Oh," Ted's smile drooped and his inherent confusion shined through to his crinkled lips and furrowed brow. "Shouldn't you?"

"I don't know why I would," Mick replied. "Is she speaking too?"

Ted exhaled and turned his head slightly to the side in thought.

"Maybe we should ride together to sort out who's giving which part of our message."

Mick looked at Ted with the same scrunched face.

"So, Shelly's a resident speaker too?" Mick asked, talking over Ted as he interjected at the same time.

"Against the wall?"

"In favor of the wall," Ted's eyes flared in realization of the misunderstanding.

They stared at each other in silence before Ted started toward the door.

"I'll finish up the work on your contract with Mr. Rutledge," he said sternly with an imperceptible clear of his throat. "But we should avoid discussing the beach erosion case."

"Of course," Mick nodded.

"That could be a conflict of interest," Ted continued, clutching the doorknob with his leather briefcase over his shoulder. "It makes you and Ms. Newsome adversaries."

Mick shuddered at the thought that he and Shelly would serve two sides of a legal proceeding. It made him flash back to the arbitration hearings with his ex-wife, Danielle, and the venom that permeated each subsequent conversation.

"As opponents in this," Ted finished his thought before leaving the house. "I'd hate to see it come between you."

Chapter 22

Growing up as a child in Matunuck, before he met Marty Fazzini, Aaron Benjamin or even Kenny Forrester, Mick had a best friend named Jack Valerian.

Mick and Jack spent nearly every summer day together for a decade from age seven to seventeen. Their shared love of sports, candy and dramatically playing in the dangerous Matunuck surf bound them. Like Kenny, Jack lived in Matunuck year-round. And, as classmates, Kenny and Jack knew each other well. But, unlike Kenny, who worked most summer days, mowing lawns, trimming hedges and fishing on his father's boat, Jack had a more carefree life. He and Mick formed the Kings of Matunuck, their informal clique's name. They organized the official Matunuck whiffle ball league and initiated raging games of chase with the local girls that served as their queens. They ate breakfast and dinner at each other's' houses and had weekly sleepovers.

Along with Mick's brother, Conrad, and his cousin, Tripp, Mick and Jack hacked their way through the hundred acres of wild thorny blackberry bushes that used to exist on Blackberry Hill to pick wild blackberries. Two or three times a summer, they'd collected enough plastic gallon jugs of the little purple berries for all the neighborhood moms to bake pies, muffins and jars of jam. At a payment rate of a dollar a quart, they made enough cash for their daily supply of replacement whiffle balls and afternoon candy.

The typical day started at the Maguire kitchen with a Johnny Cake breakfast and a quick couple games of morning whiffle ball, followed by the requisite trip to the market or the grill for candy and then all day at Blackberry Beach. They'd crowd together on blankets listening to the 'Top Forty' countdown on the radio, between hour-long swims in the Matunuck surf. On weekends, the parents would run cook-outs, serving flimsy burgers and shriveled hot dogs with Ocean State Job Lot bargain brand sodas.

At least once a week, they'd journey east, along the base of the trailer park wall to the pub where they'd grab a bag of clam cakes and play a few games of volleyball on the sand court atop Mary Carpenters' expansive beach.

The more dashing and socially mature of the pair, Jack hit it off with the local girls well before Mick even contemplated liking members of the opposite gender. By age fourteen, Jack elevated his status to the true King of the Beach, considered the most eligible teenager in the group. Mick, smaller, less developed and more physically immature, found himself relegated to a Prince or Duke with the others serving as Earls, Barons and other lesser titles of nobility.

Jack also displayed the wildest streak, sneaking into the pub to listen to bands at night, stealing beers and cigarettes from the bar and eventually obtaining a forged license so he could enjoy the annual Mary Carpenter's Summer Beerfest with the older teenagers and twenty-year-old college kids.

Mick could feel his best friend pulling away from the group during his later teens, attracted to the bar scene and the curvy older girls. Games of Whiffle ball and blackberry picking gave way to long car rides to the bars and clubs in Providence and Newport. The joy of candy and pop music gave way to alcohol and rock concerts. Flirty games of 'Hide and Chase' and 'Spin the Bottle' gave way to drunken romps tucked in the dunes and the back of family station wagons.

Not ready for such adultish behavior, Mick withdrew from the group and avoided Jack's more advanced endeavors, preferring time with his parents, siblings and cousins at family parties and gatherings. He spent long afternoons on Blackberry Beach, sometimes on his own without the Kings.

Unlike their common friend, Kenny, who also lived and worked in town, Jack had his sights set elsewhere. He visited friends in Worcester, Nashua and Boston. He had cousins in Portsmouth and along the frigid beaches of southern Maine. He disappeared for weeks at a time, eventually abdicating the Matunuck social throne and dashing the cohesiveness of their childhood bubble with his increasing absence from the kingdom.

Like the encroachment of the Atlantic Ocean up the coast, along the base of the trailer park wall and eventually under the pylons of the Blackberry Beach clubhouse, the delicate social structure of Mick's childhood eventually eroded like the billions of lost grains of sand from the receding beach and the hundreds of splintered pine planks of the long-since destroyed boardwalk.

By the time Mick left for college, the group had moved on to different corners of the state. Marty attended cooking school in Providence. Ronnie moved back to the Bronx. Kenny stayed local, studying Ornithology and Landscape Management at the University of Rhode Island, while Jack disappeared from town for good.

And even Mick, despite how tightly he clung to the joys of a Matunuck childhood, eventually succumbed to the ravages of his unavoidable adult life. Soon after his nineteenth birthday, he met Danielle at an off-campus party while studying music at Julliard. On a rowdy night he could barely remember, he mistakenly got her pregnant. That bombshell event in his life resulted in the birth of his daughter, Melodie, and his nearly twenty-year exile from the east coast, after following his baby-mama and eventual wife to California to live with her for the next two decades.

Mick took his seat at the town hall meeting beside the team of environmentalists that recruited him to speak on their behalf. He didn't know any of them too well. None of them grew up or spent time in Matunuck. Most of his interactions with them had taken place either in passing on the beach as they canvassed for support or by phone. They all greeted him with appreciation. They eagerly repeated their key points around the need to preserve the ecosystem, the wildlife and the natural contours of the beach. They espoused the dangers of 'hardening' the shore. Every other word out of their mouths revolved around the word 'hardening', which they spat with disdain as if the foulest of swear words. As he and Bo sought a seat in the meeting room, they pulled him aside to prep him on his talking points. They thanked him profusely for bringing Bo Rutledge as a celebrity supporter.

175

"I ain't here to make no speech," the barrel-chested country music star reiterated. "I just want to hear what all the fuss is about and decide for myself which way to throw my weight."

As they entered the walnut-paneled town hall meeting room, some residents gasped at the sight of the celebrity, but most either didn't recognize him or looked at him with ambivalence.

The meeting commenced and the First Selectman cued the topic to a full room with residents standing along the back and squeezing to peer through the two open doors at the back of the chamber.

A lawyer for the state addressed the court and laid out a plan to dig a massive trench from the edge of the town beach, across the Blackberry Beach gap to the trailer park wall. He cited federal statutes, state laws and town ordinances to justify the actions proposed by the federal government. He spoke of a public-private partnership with a regional environmental construction firm to conduct the work. He laid out the budget for the program, which came to several million dollars. He gave a rundown of the tax implications, the municipal bonds and the financial benefit to the local real estate interests and businesses of ensuring the ocean does not break through the thin set of dunes where the old Blackberry Beach clubhouse used to stand.

He concluded by informing the town that they'd petitioned the Federal Environmental Protection agency to delist the swampy marsh behind the Blackberry Beach Gap as a protected watershed. Their proposal also required an easement from the town to close off the path behind the trailer park as a protected beach access point.

Ted Callahan stood and directed the board to view a detailed twenty-page spreadsheet. The numbers also projected on a large computer screen above the curved set of board member seats for the audience to review. Ted spoke of the financial risk of not fixing the dunes. He listed the real estate value of the forty-seven at-risk homes and the cost of fixing the road. He listed the businesses dependent on the 'at-risk' Matunuck Beach Road, such as the Vanilla Bean, the Ocean Mist and the Matunuck Surf Shop.

He then introduced the CEO of a regional firm called Enviromark. The well-dressed, grey-suited executive brought up aerial pictures of the

Matunuck shoreline prior to the devastating hurricanes of 1938, 1954, Superstorm Sandy and Hurricane Constance from two years earlier. He played an animation of the receding beachfront from the 1950s to the 1990s, which he referred to as Phase 1. He played the NBC Nightly News broadcast from thirty years earlier when the Blackberry Beach clubhouse went down in a furious late-fall storm. The Phase 2 video started in 2000 and took the viewer through the present day. To Mick, watching the blue of the water close in on the seawall and wash out the beaches to its immediate east and west provided a stark reminder of the power of the vast ocean.

Mick could only see the back of the Enviromark CEO's head. His dark, wavy brown hair swayed behind him as he addressed the town board. His voice sounded familiar, evoking old memories of running around his back yard or swimming in the Matunuck surf.

The Enviromark video splashed a dramatic title page on the video monitor, referencing "Matunuck Beach Erosion: Phase 3". The video, clearly animated by a graphic artist, but rendered to look as close to real surveillance footage as the Phase 1 and 2 videos, played overhead. In it, the ocean continued to creep forward. The video zoomed into the space between the trailer park and the town beach pavilion, showing the dunes split open like a cut lip and widening to resemble a cracked dam. Water poured through the slit, flushing the swampy pond, dashing the Vanilla Bean, destroying the beach road and completely flooding the section of Mary Carpenter's village closest to the marshy pond.

The perspective of the video shifted upward and zoomed into the section of eastern Matunuck between the trailer park and the turn of Deep Hole. Like the previous sequence, the video showed the ocean lapping the homes and dashing the pub, eventually overwhelming all the structures between the Blackberry Beach Road and the shore.

"This, ladies and gentlemen," the CEO of the environmental construction firm stated. "Is why we need to build a firm, but aesthetically pleasing revetment, that can protect the community. We've proposed both a natural option and a more hardened approach. The bottom line is that the town and the state need to invest in protection to avoid millions of dollars in potential losses. With the steel-reinforced stone and concrete structure, we can provide a new form of recreational activity to the area as well as a pleasant and safe way to walk along the beach and enjoy the view. With the natural option, we can protect the endangered homes and preserve the aesthetic quality of the natural habitat. I'd say to the public that it will be different no matter what decision the board makes. It will be a change. But not all change is bad. And some change is inevitable. Changing how the public interacts with the beach can be a positive. And, the alternative of not making this change is both catastrophic and irreversible. Matunuck is changing. We have an opportunity to change it for the better, before it's destroyed forever. Thank you."

The man with the familiar voice sat. Mick could trace the profile of his nose, but could not place him from the limited view of his cheek and jawline.

Shelly stood and delivered her impassioned plea to help the residents of eastern Matunuck by extending the wall all the way across the old Mary Carpenter's beachfront to the far side of Deep hole.

"I've lived here all my life. I own a successful business here. I love this community with all my heart," she concluded. "I ask, on behalf of my neighbors and friends in town that you vote for the necessary ordinances and zoning allowances to save our amazing little village. We're also counting on you to pass the local emergency budget needed to fund immediately critical construction along the most vulnerable areas. And, please partner with state and federal agencies to protect our beautiful Matunuck community."

In his contrarian response, the lead environmentalist cleared his throat as he stood to make his speech. As he did, he pulled up PowerPoint slides depicting before and after images of beaches along the east coast that had seawalls erected. In each case, the beach completely disappeared in less than ten years.

"Make no mistake," the lawyer said. "When they say 'revetment', they mean 'wall'. When they say 'firm', they mean 'hard'. When they say 'aesthetically pleasing' they mean this."

The speaker dramatically flipped his slide to a photo of the dilapidated Matunuck trailer park seawall with the agitated ocean splashing against it.

"A vote for this half mile of iron, cement and sheet metal," the lawyer continued. "Is a vote against the natural evolution of the coastline."

The lawyer clicked his remote control gadget and the screen went black.

"We have a little video as well," he said.

A similar animation to the one shown by the lawyer for the other side of the argument appeared.

"In five years, the ocean reaches the wall by the pub and eradicates any trace of beach."

The animated video showed the proposed wall across the top of the beach with a sliding bar indicating years moving out into the future.

"In ten years," the slim bearded man continued. "Deep Hole shrinks from a fifty-foot stretch to an average of five to ten feet wide. In fifteen years, the wall by the pub is breached and must be extended in thickness and height. It rises to ten feet above the Matunuck Beach Road. By twenty years, the wall at the Blackberry Beach Gap must also be extended and repaired from constant barrage of the ocean, which rises to meet it. Even the elevated trailer park reaches 'at risk' status. The rising sea level moves further west and the beaches at Willow Dell and Roy Carpenter's lose viability for public use."

The murmur in the room ascended to a crescendo and the First Selectman called for order.

"Lastly," the environmental lawyer concluded. "The state failed to adequately highlight the destruction of federally protected marshland just north of the Blackberry Beach Gap next to the Vanilla Bean ice cream shop."

At that, one of the Selectmen interrupted the presentation to ask a question.

"According to the proposal, the federal Government has agreed to suspend the designation of this area," he said. "And, the study before us shows no cases of endangered species observed in that parcel."

179

"There are rare cat-tail grasses and the potential for endangered species to nest in this space that the Federal Government has overlooked," he replied. "We've filed an injunction, citing a URI research report, which we hope will be reviewed at the end of this month by this board."

At that, the Selectmen looked back and forth at each other. The volume escalated with tension in the room breaking out again on both sides. One resident shouted 'who cares' in response to the environmental concern. Another shouted something about not wanting 'some damn ugly wall' blocking the view. The lawyer for the state stood and held his report in the air, defending his position.

"It's federally protected wetland that will be destroyed throughout the construction process."

The First Selectman had to bang his gavel on the table to quell the uproar.

"We'll hear the resident testimony from the opposition," he said. "And, we'll take thirty days to review the proposals, take the feedback into consideration and monitor the injunction to determine our next course of action."

At that, all the eyes in the room turned to Mick. He stood with his notes in hand. He paused to sip a mouthful of water. As Mick prepared to launch into his speech, the CEO of Enviromark turned. Their eyes locked. Recognition crossed both faces.

A slew of memories flooded Mick's mind temporarily flustering him and obscuring his grasp on his talking points. He squinted to confirm the identify.

"Jack?" he asked. "Jack Valerian?"

Chapter 23

Mick gathered his composure. He'd spoken to numerous audiences, between his corporate career as a music executive, as a performer and as a teacher. The lawyers for the town and the state conferred while Jack Valerian removed his charts and diagrams from the easels at the front of the room.

As Mick scuffled his hips across the walnut bench, he heard a familiar voice fill the room. The microphone at the front of the main aisle made a loud popping sound. Mick watched the back of Denny Gallagher's head as he addressed the crowd with his mouth entirely too close to the grill of the mic.

"Hello your honors," Denny's voice crackled and popped with some distortion as he addressed the board.

Kenny Forrester stood and made his way down the aisle to corral his ward like a goatherd rounding the lost sheep. But Denny managed to make his point succinctly before Kenny could reach him.

"Buses I tell you," he blurted. "You gotta sink buses a couple hundred feet out beyond where the waves break and fill them with sand or cement."

The chairman stood and shot Kenny a reprimanding look as if he should have had his lamb tied to a post to avoid the disruption of his rogue comment.

"This is not a public hearing," the Chairman bellowed. "That's next month. This is a regular meeting of the Land Management and Zoning Board. We're only open to testimony presented by the recognized opposing parties."

Kenny reached the front of the room. But instead of ushering the elder Gallagher, he also spoke into the mic.

"Well, maybe you should listen to him," he said. "Just because he's old, don't mean he don't know what he's talking about."

Kian Taomessina stood a few rows back and spoke without the benefit of a mic.

"They're right," he said. "I read the case study on this. There are four known locations, in Australia, Belize, North Carolina and South Carolina where this approach has been taken, with two locations demonstrating positive results, one inconclusive and the site in Belize showing continued erosion, although there are many factors associated with that site."

At Kian's statement, the chairman banged a gavel against the table and told him, Kenny and Denny to come back at the open hearing the next month. The room grumbled with terse commentary shouted across the room. The First Selectman continued to bang the table until he reestablished authoritative control of the chamber.

"This meeting is not an open forum," the Chairman said. "Please be quiet and step aside for the next invited speaker, Mr. Michael Maguire, of Matunuck."

At the announcement of his slot on the agenda, Mick rose to his feet and shuffled to the podium. Kenny gave him a nod as he returned to his seat next to Denny and Kian. The silence in the room surrounded him like thick fog.

He delivered his speech in many ways as rousing as Shelly's or Jack's. The sentiment in the room seemed relatively split to him. But, clearly, by the time Mick closed the meeting with the final speaking part, the residents in the room had shed their polite patience with the proceeding and chose to scoff, comment and jeer at him when they disagreed. As distracting as it was to make his points under attack, the support he received from the group of residents clustered by his side of the room gave him confidence to finish strong.

Despite the boos and snide remarks, he also received cheers and supportive comments, with some residents swiping at each other. In response to the aggressive behavior, the First Selectman reprimanded several audience-members for their outbursts.

"It doesn't have to be buses," Denny shouted at one point. "It could be a truck of some sort or a train car or one of those big square metal containers you see on cargo ships."

As the chairman clacked his gavel again, Mick concluded his pitch.

The board huddled for a few minutes. The crowd buzzed. Several council members leaned awkwardly toward each other, speaking in hushed whispers. The chairman called Jack to the head table and asked him questions in a loud enough voice for Mick to hear from his front row seat.

"The proposal has an addendum that offers a scaled-back emergency plan?" he asked.

"Yes," Jack replied. "A thirty-day immediate alleviation of risk to the beach road as well as the Blackberry Beach Gap through movement of existing stones, placement of new concrete blocks and some limited pouring of cement to hold the makeshift barriers in place. It should hold back a hurricane-force surge for the time being while we set up to excavate behind the temporary wall and build the more permanent structure."

The chairman called for a vote on the emergency provision of the proposal, which passed. He also announced the date of the follow-up public hearing on the broader plan to build the more extensive versions of the walls at Mary Carpenter's and Blackberry Beaches. He thanked the crowd for attending. The board members filed out of the room into a back chamber behind the head dais.

Mick strained to eye Shelly across the room through the dispersing crowd. She stood with Ted Callahan and a lawyer for the town. A reporter thrust a portable recorder into her face and peppered her with questions. She answered sheepishly for a few minutes until Ted caught up with her, raised a hand to the reporter and ushered her out the door. Mick watched the back of her head bob up the stairs toward the outside hallway. As she moved out of sight, he saw her turn and look back at him. Her eyes didn't belie overt scorn, nor disdain, but neither did they exude the warmth and acceptance that he had come to expect and appreciate.

"Nice job partner," Bo said with a loud smack on the back. "A real showman. You were taking fire out there and still going. Reminds me of when I first started in dive bars and skeevy clubs and they used to throw beer bottles and shot glasses at me."

Shelly's blond hair slipped past the door frame on the far side of the room as the meeting space emptied. Mick thanked Bo for his positive feedback. The lawyers for the environmental organization shook his hand and thanked him before filing out. Matunuck residents, some of whom he had seen in passing - a few of whom were parents of his students - glared at him. Others gave him thumbs up signs.

The tall, handsome Jack Valerian pulled away from his legal team and approached Mick with a wide smile. He looked like a professional athlete; his face carved, his hair perfectly coiffed and dark with shiny brown streaks from the light of the overhead fluorescents.

"Mickey?" he yelped, accelerating and flinging his arms open for a hug. "I thought you moved to California and disappeared off the face of the earth."

"Last I knew, you ran off to Maine with some girl," Mick countered.

"I guess we both left town for similar reasons," Jack said.

Mick introduced his old friend to Bo. Bo gripped his hand and shook fervently before excusing himself to speak with the state and federal lawyers as they gathered their papers in preparation to leave.

"Man, I haven't seen you in twenty years," Jack beamed. "How's that daughter of yours? What are you doing here in South Kingstown? You moved back?"

"It didn't work out with Danielle," Mick explained. "I left it all behind; the music industry career, the fast-paced executive world. I cashed out my investments, basically bankrupted myself and moved back. I'm teaching music at the elementary school and writing songs for artists like Bo."

Jack gave an account of having followed one girl to Boston and another to Maine, whom he eventually divorced.

"She got the house and the kid," Jack said. "I kept the business and the Porsche. We get along. I live near her up there in Maine. We see each other. It's worked out fine, I guess."

As he reminisced with Jack, Mick noticed Bo engaging in an in-depth conversation with Jack's assistant. They pulled out maps and reports and appeared to point and debate several aspects of the plans.

184

"I haven't been back to Matunuck in so long," Jack said, erasing his smile and continuing in a more somber voice. "I heard about your mother. She was the heart and soul of Blackberry Beach. She and my mom really enjoyed hanging out together. I'm so sorry."

"It's been a tough couple of years," Mick agreed. "My dad's not doing great either."

Jack noticed Bo continuing to occupy the attention of members of the state's legal team and paused to wonder what discussion topic could interest them so intensely.

"I wish I didn't have to drive back up to Maine tonight," Jack said. "We're dredging a channel in Portsmouth and building a retaining wall next to the Ferry Terminal and the Duck Brook inlet."

Mick noticed Ted Callahan at the door between the meeting room and the hallway. Behind him in the marble foyer, a crowd of reporters surrounded Shelly and the lawyer for the town. Ted pointed at Mick and curled his finger, beckoning him to join him at the door.

Mick exchanged contact information with Jack and excused himself.

"It's great to see you," Mick said with another shoulder hug. "Keep in touch."

"Looks like I'll be dropping by over the next couple weeks," Jack said. "And then, if they approve the bigger wall, I'll be down quite a bit to oversee the operation."

Mick nodded, his enthusiasm dampened by the contrast between Jack's mission to build the wall and his opposition to it.

He greeted Ted in the doorway between the meeting room and the hall. He could see Shelly across the marble floor, facing a reporter and camera man by the water bubbler.

"I ran the contracts by Mr. Rutledge," Ted said in a hushed tone as the boisterous musician laughed heartily across the room and smacked the state lawyers in the back.

"Did you get the clauses you wanted?" Mick asked.

"It's not about what I want," Ted replied. "It's what's in your best interest. But yes, he accepted all my redlines. He should really have legal representation. I'm stunned that someone in his position is managing his

185

business on his own. For someone to reach such a pinnacle of success, he's crazy to have fired his legal representation."

Mick thanked the affable attorney, who handed him a folder and asked him to sign the document. Across the hall, Mick could hear Shelly reiterate her talking points from the meeting. Her thin voice echoed across the marble floor and walls. When asked if she disagreed with Mick's statement, she simply replied that she stood by her own opinions and that she didn't think he saw the big picture.

"He's all signed off, so once you sign this, our business is concluded," Ted whispered. "With this beach erosion suit heating up, I'm going to be tied up with the Homeowners' Association. And, it would be bad form to have outstanding business with you."

Mick nodded in agreement, etching his signature at the bottom of all four copies of the contract. Soon after Ted collapsed the folder and tucked it away, Bo stormed out the door with his arms around two of the state attorneys. The two town lawyers followed closely behind the trio.

"Come on Mick," he echoed his voice across the shiny open foyer. "We're hitting a whiskey bar on Waterman Street, wherever the heck that is."

Mick shook his head. Ted stepped back to let the entourage through the door. Jack followed behind and shook hands with Ted.

"Long time, Mr. Callahan," he said. "Say 'Hi' to Vivian for me."

"What's all this?" Mick asked, pointing to Bo's sudden friendliness with the crew of state lawyers and environmental engineers.

"I don't know," Jack replied. "Something about a plan to buy up houses in Matunuck?"

Mick shook his head and held his brow in his hand.

"I'm not a lawyer," Jack continued. "But I think he's trying to get them to claim Eminent Domain."

"Yo, Mick," Bo called from the glass doors to the parking lot. "You coming?"

Mick scrunched his face and looked for another friendly face who might be able to lend him a ride back to Matunuck.

"Sorry, man," Jack said, picking up on his hesitation. "I won't get home until after midnight and have to be at the site by five."

Ted sighed. He watched the last reporter finish interviewing Shelly. The light atop the camera dimmed and she stood, awkwardly looking at Ted to provide her ride home.

"I'll tell you what," Ted said to Mick, also sensing his reluctance to spend a late night out with Bo at a bar. "Meet me out front. I'll swing around."

As Ted left out the back door with Shelly, Mick and Jack embraced and promised to stay in touch. Jack exited the building behind Ted and Shelly. Mick flashed back to their annual beloved trip to the Rocky Point Amusement Park as kids with Ronnie, Marty and Ronnie's father, Mr. Benjamin. They spent the day sprinting from the Cyclone rollercoaster to the House of Horrors, the Musik Express and the Salt Water Log Flume. Mick recalled fresh lobster and clam chowder in the massive dining hall, followed by numerous turns on their favorite ride, the bumper cars. That special member of their group that succeeded at everything he did, Jack had a knack for crushing his friends while adeptly maneuvering his car away from danger at each turn.

"Such was the life of the king," Mick thought, wondering if they'd really stay in touch.

As the reporters gathered by the back entrance to the parking lot, Mick wandered the halls toward the front door. He spotted Ted's SUV in a parallel parking spot outside the main entrance to the town hall and trotted across the grass to enter the back seat.

"Hey Ted; Shelly," Mick said as he snapped his seatbelt. "Thanks for the ride."

Ted nodded in the rearview mirror. Shelly stared ahead without making a sound. They wound through the streets of Peacedale in relative silence. Ted adjusted the radio and settled on the XM 50s channel. Mick thought of his own father, who, thirty years earlier, used to tune into similar programming on the A.M. dial.

"Nice to see old Jack Valerian," Ted made small talk. "He looks about as fit and handsome as ever."

187

Mick agreed and observed that Jack hadn't been back to South County in more than a decade.

"Some people leave and just don't come back," Ted replied. "Viv and Bella may never leave. But not everyone falls in love with Matunuck like us."

At that, Mick thought he heard a gurgle of sarcasm from Shelly's passenger seat. He paused to see if she'd speak. But, in the reflection of the windshield, he could only make out the cold forward stare of her eyes. They settled into another long bout of silence along the Post Road from the hospital to the library before Mick decided to engage Shelly.

"You did a good job on your speech tonight," Mick said.

"Thank you," Shelly replied after a sigh and a lengthy pause.

The engine revved as Ted curled into the entrance of the Matunuck Beach Road.

"Hey, look," Ted interjected as he piloted the vehicle. "You both said your peace. There's nothing wrong with that. You don't have to debate each other. You can move on."

Mick didn't respond, scanning his mind for a way to reconnect with his neighbor.

"Do you really want the ocean to obliterate all those properties?" Shelly asked him, turning and peering at him between the seats.

"I sure don't want the beach to disappear forever."

"But it's fine if people's houses disappear?"

"You live on the complete opposite side of town."

"What does that have to do with it?" Shelly asked.

"Your place is set back. It's safe no matter what."

"I care about other people," Shelly raised her voice.

"I care about Matunuck," Mick raised his.

Ted tried to speak, but Shelly interrupted him before he could say anything to deescalate the dialog.

"You disappeared for twenty years," she snapped at him.

"Oh, we're back to that again?" Mick replied.

Ted cleared his throat. He subtly increased his driving speed and tried again to diffuse the tension.

"I thought you'd be able to share a ten-minute ride from Wakefield to Matunuck," he muttered.

"Apparently not," Shelly responded, folding her hands across her chest and returning to her blank stare out the front windshield.

Chapter 24

Ted swung his car across the circular cobblestone driveway to the inn. The wheels rumbled over the uneven surface and stopped under the overhang. Shelly and Mick exited the car and thanked Ted for the ride. A young man in his twenties in a button-down shirt, dark jeans and tennis shoes approached them holding a notepad.

"Ms. Newsome, Mr. Maguire," he called to them as they separated toward their respective homes. "I'm a reporter for the Narragansett Times. I just had a couple questions for you both."

Shelly rolled her eyes and sighed. Mick ignored the reporter and kept walking toward his house.

"Please, I know the Providence Journal and television news already ambushed you in the meeting tonight," he continued. "I didn't expect to find you both here. I just wanted to speak with you about the erosion problem and remediation proposals."

Neither Shelly, nor Mick reacted, but the reporter persisted.

"Is there any chance the three of us could sit together and discuss your opposing viewpoints?" he asked. "I promise to be respectful. I'll only print what you're comfortable exposing to the public."

Mick stopped. Shelly glanced sideways at him.

"Everyone in Matunuck buzzes about the erosion issue," the reporter continued. "We have some of the same problems where I live in Scarborough. But, it's so much worse here. And you're both so passionate about it. I'd love to reflect your positions accurately and fairly."

Shelly nodded at Mick, who turned to face the reporter.

"We could do a sort of 'he said-she said', side-by-side piece," the brash, young reporter concluded his plea.

"I'll do it if you do," Shelly said to Mick. "We could sit in the restaurant. I'll have Marty bring us some shamrock ice cream pie."

Mick considered it. He checked his phone and glanced toward his house. He had no messages from Haley about his father and the house remained dark.

"Alright," he responded. "Let's do it."

They eased into the booth at the back of the restaurant furthest from the kitchen. Shelly took the far side. The reporter slid to the bend of the u-shaped booth and Mick sat with his back to the kitchen. Like a political debate, he and Shelly faced each other with the reporter positioned between them.

Late in the evening and close to closing time, the tables around them sat empty. The sky above the ocean turned purple and black. Stars dotted the overhead canvas like paint splatters. A waitress that Shelly didn't initially recognize stood with her back to them setting new plates and silverware on a table that had just cleared.

The waitress turned to address her patrons, causing Shelly to gasp in surprise.

"Hey Shells; Mick" the waitress said to them, turning to the reporter to introduce herself. "I'm Lindsay and I'll be taking care of you tonight."

Shelly stared at her sister and then craned her neck toward the kitchen.

"Looking for Marty?" she asked. "He's in the basement cleaning up for the night."

Shelly stared blankly at her sister.

"He needed the help," Lindsay started to explain.

The reporter picked up a menu and pointed out the ice cream pie. Mick did the same. Shelly continued to glare at her sister. Her initial shock gave way to suspicion. Her eyes tightened from wide with incredulity to narrow with doubt. A range of terse comments and questions crossed her mind, none of which she opted to share in public. She composed herself and chose her words tactfully.

"How long have you worked here?" Shelly asked in a sweet voice.

"First night," Lindsay replied. "He's been down a server for a couple weeks, and I needed the income."

"Don't you own this place?" the reporter asked.

"I own the inn," Shelly explained. "I co-own the restaurant with my business partner, Marty Fazzini, who makes most of the independent day-to-day decisions."

Lindsay leaned in and softened her expression.

"Jeremy got a judge to let him cancel the card," she lowered her voice, the bracelets up her arm jingling as she moved. "I'm gonna need the money. And this allows me to make it without being too far from the girls. They can sit on the deck and color. Or play in the sand. At night, I can run up and check on them on during my breaks. It's perfect for me."

Shelly chose not to make a production and also ordered the special shamrock ice cream pie. Lindsay retreated to the kitchen. The reporter watched her, confused by the exchange, but didn't ask about the unusual dialog between them.

"Christopher Holden," the reporter said. "You can call me Topher."

They shook hands. Topher placed his notepad on the table and clicked his pen to extend the ball point. He wrote the date across the top of a clean page and took a breath.

"Quite a meeting tonight?" he threw out the first softball.

Shelly nodded and Mick agreed.

"I find it ironic that you've become the spokespeople for the two intensely opposing sides of the debate and yet, you share a ride to and from the meeting and live next door to each other."

"We didn't arrive together," Mick clarified. "We just came back together."

"Neither of us has a car," Shelly added.

"I see," Topher said. "How interesting. Has the controversy and contention of this debate caused a strain on you as neighbors? You seem to get along very well, even though you have such different viewpoints about this very emotional beach erosion issue that has some people at each other's throats."

Shelly shrugged. She lifted her eyes from the table to Mick's.

"We get along really well," Mick said, meeting Shelly's eyes. "Don't we?"

"Sure," Shelly nodded as Topher jotted his notes. "I guess."

"Let's get into the issues," Topher continued. "Ms. Newsome, you contend that the town, in conjunction with the state, should tap into state and federal emergency funds to build a sizeable steal, rock and cement seawall across the stretch of what is known as Mary Carpenter's Beach, including in front of the twenty-five homes that sit south of the Matunuck Beach Road between the street and the stretch called Deep Hole?"

"Uh, yes," Shelly replied. "That's right."

"Some call that an extreme solution and, as Mr. Maguire argued tonight, could irrevocably damage the beach as has happened in front of the Matunuck Trailer Park at the bend of the Matunuck Beach Road. What do you say to the critics of your position?"

At Topher's aggressive line of questioning, Shelly stiffened her posture. She raised her eyes to his, and her jaw tightened.

"You see this hotel?" she asked.

Topher glanced at the ceiling and out the window to the beach.

"It's beautiful," he replied.

"I spent a year building it. It hasn't even been open six months yet," she continued. "The property was owned by my grandmother. She had a house that stood a couple hundred feet closer to the water. It was there for a hundred years. I grew up in that house. In many ways, I felt my Grandmother's spirit in that house. I loved that place. Whenever I felt lonely, or scared or just sad, I could sit in the third-floor master bedroom, with its dinghy old carpet and dark-paneled walls and look out at the ocean and feel her with me."

The reporter furiously wrote in his notepad. Mick sat, quietly transfixed.

"In the last hurricane, Constance," Shelly finished her story. "The ocean surged and carved out all the sand under that beautiful old house. We tried like crazy to save it. Mick was there. But, despite all our efforts, there was nothing we could do to stop it. The ocean just swallowed it and destroyed it. The house my grandmother grew up in; gone. I wouldn't wish that on my worst enemy, never mind the amazing people of Matunuck. There are houses down by Deep Hole that have been there since the 1930's. These are peoples' homes; their memories; their family legacies. I love the beach. But I care more about all those people."

Lindsay brought three plates of pie. Shelly's demeanor shifted from strong and confident. She slumped back into her seat and relaxed her posture.

"Mr. Maguire, you made an impassioned argument that the beach in Matunuck represents the soul of the community," Topher read through notes he jotted during the meeting earlier that night. "You talked about how the seawall at the trailer park resulted in the destruction of the Blackberry Beach clubhouse. It sounds to me like the warmth and peace that Ms. Newsome found in her grandmother's house was similar to the comforting emotions you experienced at Blackberry Beach. I find it interesting that your motivations seem similar, even though your positions are diametrically opposed. How do you rationalize the dichotomy that a seawall could potentially destroy the beach, while the absence of erosion remediation would likely mean the destruction of property sometime in the next twenty years, ten years, maybe even as soon as the next five years?"

"I feel for the people of Matunuck," Mick replied. "I really do. I don't want anyone's property to be damaged. But the beach belongs to all of us. In essence it's all of our property. It's what makes Matunuck special. We call it God's Country here, and I believe it truly is like a small slice of heaven. Homes can be moved. There are still empty lots that could be given to the most at-risk homeowners. The beach represents the heart and soul of the community. And, every local business, from the pub to the market and the inn, all rely on Matunuck continuing to be a tourist destination - or at least a hopping summer beach community – to survive. Yes, building a big wall might protect some properties. But only for a short time. And, ultimately, it will irrevocably damage the community. That's why I'm siding with the conservationists and the retreat strategy, which has proven to work in other similar places."

Mick's phone buzzed as Topher jotted more notes. Shelly played with her pie while eyeing her sister in the kitchen. She watched Marty interact with her, analyzing his smile and supportive body language. Mick fell silent as he read a long text.

Shelly noticed the touch. It happened quickly with a fleeting subtlety. Nobody else would have given it a second thought. As Lindsay walked past Marty with two hands full of dirty plates, he brushed his hand across the small of her back. It may have meant nothing. But Shelly noted the maneuver in the corner of her mind and filed it away for her eventual interrogation of her business partner.

Topher flipped through his pad and changed his line of questioning.

"I also wanted to ask about your association with Bo Rutledge," he said. "It was quite a surprise to see him at the meeting tonight. Many people in the room were wondering if he would speak. They're intrigued by his presence and want to know his position on this issue. Will he serve as a celebrity spokesperson for your cause?"

Mick, distracted by his phone, didn't answer right away. Topher paused as Mick scrolled through Haley's message.

"I'm so sorry," he finally responded. "I have to go."

Shelly looked into Mick's eyes as if trying to read his mind.

"It's my cousin," he explained. "My dad's in the hospital."

Chapter 25

Three slices of melted green pie sat barely touched on the table by the booth. Mick hopped to his feet and scrolled through Haley's follow-up text messages. Topher closed his notepad and slipped past Mick at the end of the booth, giving him time to convene with Shelly, who leaned in to read over his shoulder.

"Is he alright?" she asked.

"He started throwing up," Mick paraphrased from Haley's texts. "He couldn't hold anything down. He had a fever and chills."

"Has this happened before?" Shelly asked.

"He's been nauseous plenty of times," Mick replied. "He's had fevers. His medicine helps regulate him."

"Maybe when he threw up," Shelly surmised.

"He couldn't hold down the medicine," Mick completed her thought.

Topher edged toward the door, eventually thanking Mick and Shelly and excusing himself. He offered to call as a follow-up to refine some of their answers and finish up with a few outstanding questions.

"Best of luck to your father," he said with a genuine smile before exiting the restaurant into the lobby to the parking lot.

Marty and Lindsay emerged from the kitchen and took notice of Mick's stressed expression. Lindsay looked to Shelly for context. Marty understood right away.

"Your father?" he asked.

"I have to call my brother and sister," Mick replied.

"How're you going to get there?" Marty asked. "I'd drive you, but I only have the Harley."

Mick looked up from his phone as if realizing for the first time he had no means of transportation. Shelly gazed out the window at the parking lot as if expecting a magic carriage to form from a pumpkin.

"I guess you could…" Marty started to suggest they ride tandem on his bike.

"Take the BMW," Lindsay interrupted him. "I can't leave the girls, but we're closing up and I don't need it tonight."

Shelly darted her head at her sister in wild surprise at her selflessness.

"Is he cleared to drive it?" Shelly asked.

"Since Jeremy cancelled the credit card, I'm not sure I'm even allowed to drive it," Lindsay quipped, pulling out the keys from the pocket of her black apron. "To be honest, I was supposed to return it last week."

With a roll of her eyes, Shelly took the keys from her sister's hand.

"Come on. I'll drive," she nudged Mick before turning to her sister. "Thanks Lindsay. That was really nice of you."

Shelly sped down the Matunuck Beach Road toward South County Hospital. Mick explained the situation to his brother and sister by phone. Shelly swerved across the short exit ramp onto the busy Post Road. Despite each sibling living an hour away, they both agreed to meet him at the emergency room.

Mick flashed back to the scene two years earlier when he and Shelly drove to Providence the day his mother passed away from her raging battle with cancer and his father passed out from his brain ailment.

"You didn't have to..." Mick started to tell her.

"Of course, I did," she replied, switching lanes and nearly cutting off an SUV attempting to pull a u-turn into the southbound lane toward Wakefield.

A squat, cement building, built in the fifties, South County Hospital lacked the amenities of the larger Providence hospitals.

Haley sat in the tiny waiting room with her purse drooping from her shoulder and a giant iced coffee in her hands. Dressed in an East Greenwich Avengers sweatshirt and black yoga pants, she crossed to greet Mick with a hug at the sliding door.

"I did everything I could," she launched into her update before Mick even had a chance to sit next to her. "I made his favorite chicken casserole and it must not have sat well with his stomach. I stirred the bubbles out of a glass of Coke and had him sip it slowly. I gave him plain white toast and saltines. I should have just made simple chicken fingers. Lord knows, my kids would have preferred that. I'm so sorry."

Mick assured his cousin that his father's nausea had nothing to do with her cooking.

"He gets sick sometimes," Mick explained. "You just caught him on a bad night."

"I told the ER doctor about your dad's brain tumor, but you may need to provide more information about what medicine he's on," Haley said.

Mick walked to the window for the administrator and quietly explained the details around Gordie's condition and the medicine he took to keep his symptoms in check.

Shelly sat quietly on a sofa with Mick's empty seat between her and Haley. Haley gave her a nod.

"We have to stop meeting in hospitals like this," she said with a half-smile, referring to the last time they sat together in an emergency room, soon after Gordie's first bout of lightheadedness nearly two years earlier.

A clamor by the sliding door caught their attention. They heard a familiar voice gasping for air and mumbling in the vestibule between doors. They watched Larraine Lang, with Theresa following closely behind, bluster into the waiting room and headed straight to the check-in window.

"We're here for Gordie Maguire," Larraine said, without noticing Mick, Shelly or Haley, or even introducing herself to the administrator in the window. "Is he okay? Please say he's okay."

Theresa looked over her shoulder and recognized Gordie's son and niece.

"Thank you for calling us," she said to Haley, tapping her aunt on the shoulder.

"The whole ride here, he kept telling me to call you," Haley replied. "Call Larraine. Call Larraine. That's all he kept saying. He could barely stop moaning about his headache. But he made sure I had the password to his phone so I could look up your number and give you a call."

"Thank you so much, Haley," Larraine gushed, turning from the check-in window. "I'd just be so distraught if anything happened to him. He must be so scared all alone in there."

Mick shook his head and thrust his hands through his hair, rubbing the back of his neck and massaging his temples.

The administrator promised to send the doctor into the waiting room as soon as possible. Theresa ushered Larraine to one of the seats next to Shelly.

For the next half hour, Larraine filled the quiet of the room with busy chatter. She talked about how they'd had lunch together earlier in the day and then walked the beach looking for pretty shells and stones.

"He tried to teach me to tug the waves," she recounted. "Can you imagine that? At our age. I was too afraid to get pulled under by the current. I sat in the sand where the water's only an inch deep and watched him. I was afraid for him."

Mick shot a look at Theresa.

"I was right there," she whispered to him.

"He's crazy, your father," Larraine continued. "He just went right under the waves and spun around in the ditch. I thought he was going to drown. I kept telling him to get outta there. But, he's so stubborn, he just swatted his hand at me and told me he'd been swimming there for seventy years and knew the Matunuck waves like the back of his hand."

Haley nodded and smiled at Larraine's story.

"I hope it's not my fault he got sick," Larraine continued. "I shouldn't have let him spin around so much in the water."

"It's not your fault," Theresa said, leaning into Larraine's good ear. "That was like two o'clock. He was fine all afternoon. I told you in the car, it's not your fault."

Larraine mumbled quietly to herself about her desire to take care of Gordie.

"How long have you..." Haley started to ask.

"Almost a month now," Larraine replied. "But we see each other almost every day. We have lunch together. We walk on the beach. He makes me the best dinners. He's a great cook. Oh, I hope he's okay. Please God, spare him."

Mick stood and walked away from the incessant chatter-bug, looking out the plate glass window for his siblings.

"He's just nauseous," Mick said, over his shoulder toward Larraine's vicinity. "He'll be fine."

The next forty-five minutes passed excruciatingly slowly as Larraine continued to fill the air with running commentary about how happy she and Gordie had been watching their television programs together and sitting on the love seat in Mick's house. Every ten minutes she walked to the check-in window to inquire about Gordie's condition. After ten o'clock, she grew tired and asked Theresa to check with the administrator, wondering aloud what was taking so long.

"He's probably dehydrated," Theresa surmised. "They probably have him on a saline drip with some medication for the nausea and the headache. It could be a couple hours. Why don't you let me take you home? They'll call as soon as they hear from the doctor."

"No way," Larraine protested. "I'm not going anywhere until I know my Gordo's okay."

Dana arrived first, followed by Conrad a few minutes later. Mick explained the situation to them, and they all sat quietly in the lobby awaiting an update from the doctor. Even Larraine ran out of words as the clock neared eleven.

A tall, silver-haired physician pushed aside the double doors to the emergency room and strode into the middle of the waiting area. Larraine sprung to her feet with surprising agility for her downtrodden demeanor and accosted the doctor before he could open his mouth to speak.

"Is he okay?" she asked. "Please, how's he doing?"

Mick stood and walked to Larraine's side. Dana and Conrad filled in behind him.

"Are you his wife?" the doctor asked.

"No," Larraine answered. "But. I'm the girlfriend and we're very close."

Mick stepped forward and identified himself as the son, the Health Proxy and the Power of Attorney. With that, the doctor addressed him with his summary.

"He's stabilized and comfortable," he said. "He was dehydrated from the vomiting and had a bad migraine. We gave him two bags of saline, something for the headache and something else to combat the nausea. He's asleep now. Between his age and his condition, we're going to keep him overnight for observation."

Mick thanked the doctor. Larraine asked if she could stay with him in the room, but Theresa talked her out of that idea. The doctor turned to leave the waiting room, but stopped himself.

"He's quite sunburned," the doctor observed from the papers in his folder. "Was he out in the sun for an extended period of time?"

"He burns like bacon," Conrad replied from just behind Mick's shoulder.

"We spent the day at the beach," Larraine added. "We probably should have been drinking more water."

"Yes, definitely," the doctor agreed.

"That's my fault," Theresa spoke up from behind the crowd. "I should have known better. I'm so sorry."

The doctor wished everyone a good night and invited them to return at the start of visiting hours the next morning at ten o'clock.

"We'll be here at eight," Larraine blurted.

Haley left to rejoin her sleeping family. Theresa ushered Larraine out soon after Haley. Conrad expressed hunger and Mick suggested the pub in Matunuck. Shelly passed on the invite to eat with the Maguire siblings and asked if Conrad would drive Mick home.

They rode in a caravan down the Post Road to the beach. Shelly turned right toward the inn as Conrad and Dana stayed straight toward the pub. Mick watched the tail lights to Lindsay's rented BMW disappear down Cards Pond Road.

The pub cast a glow across the bottom of the Matunuck Beach Road, illuminating the section at risk of plummeting down the dune into the ocean.

They heard live music and loud voices coming from the back porch. As they entered the dark building and Mick's eyes adjusted to the dim lighting, he focused on a familiar brown-haired woman knocking back a frothy Guinness from a tall, thin glass at the bar. Mick ambled to her side and straddled the stool next to her and her boyfriend.

"Hello Melodie," he said with his arms crossed.

Melodie's eyes bulged at the sight of her father next to her at the bar.

"Dad?" she shrieked. "Jeez. What are you doing out so late?"

Kyle took notice of the exchange and glanced curiously their way.

"Did you know…" Mick started to tell Kyle about Melodie's real age, stopping at her horrified expression.

Kyle set a beer glass aside and turned to give Mick his attention.

"Uh, did you know," Mick repeated. "This is my beautiful daughter Melodie?"

Kyle winked and turned to fill a beer for a patron on the far side of the bar.

Conrad and Dana each greeted Melodie with hugs and smirks.

"Thanks Dad," Melodie whispered. "Uh, Kian and I were just leaving, weren't we?"

Kian nodded, shook hands with Mick and finished his soda.

"Designated driver tonight," he proclaimed to Mick with his arms extended outward as if to demonstrate his sobriety.

Mick gave him a quick shoulder hug and watched them exit the pub.

"Let's get some wings and sit out by the beach," Dana suggested. "I want to talk about Dad. I'll meet you out there after I go to the bathroom."

As Dana crossed the bar, Conrad found a table in the far corner of the back deck.

"She's done a ton of research," Mick's younger brother explained, as they waited for their baby sister to return. "She makes a good case for the operation."

Mick shrugged in discomfort.

"Just listen to her," Conrad continued. "She only wants what's best for him."

Kyle hurriedly slid a tray of wings in the center of the table and moved through the crowd to address another customer at the register seeking to pay their tab.

"How long has he had these problems?" Dana asked before she even sat in her seat. "You keep telling us he's doing great. But, he's not. That much is obvious."

"Honestly," Mick replied, feeling blood rush to his neck. "He's been doing fine. We walk in the mornings. He takes his medicine, some of which are designed to block the growth of the tumor. He eats well. Most of the time you wouldn't even know he was sick."

"Except for the headaches and the dizziness," Conrad interjected.

"And the vomiting and passing out," Dana added.

"It's not every day," Mick said.

"Even if it's every other day or once a week," Dana snapped, "That's not a good quality of life. You're his guardian, we thought you were taking better care of him than that."

"I have been," Mick raised his voice.

"But you haven't been honest with us," Conrad said.

"I have too," Mick defended himself. "I've told you everything."

"Oh, like the little dizziness spell he experienced in the water swimming with you a couple weeks ago?" Dana asked. "He told Larraine, who blabbed to Theresa, who told me. So, you're not really telling us everything."

"Alright, so I overlooked that one."

"What else have you kept from us?" Dana asked. "How can we trust you? This is our father we're talking about. And you have a big responsibility as his Power of Attorney."

"He needs the surgery," Conrad said, bluntly. "Dana's talked to Doctor Clark. It's not too late for certain procedures."

"We could have had them try to remove the tumor two years ago," Dana added. "But he didn't want to do it and you supported him. That was probably a stupid idea."

Mick turned to hide his anger. The heat in his throat rose to his cheeks. He could feel the flush in his face.

"I have to balance what I personally think is best for him with his wishes," Mick said. "The surgery had less than a fifty percent success rate."

"It had a ninety percent survivability," Dana countered him.

"But less than fifty that he'd come out unscathed."

"We've lost two years that we could have spent fighting this," Dana's voice cracked as she argued her point.

"And in those two years," Mick retorted. "His tumor has not grown significantly. He's lived well, swam in the ocean countless times and met someone that he really digs. I don't know if it's the salt air or just the magic of Matunuck…"

"It's not magic," Dana cut him off. "He's been lucky. Glioblastomas kill most people in months, even weeks. Doctor Clark is amazed at how long he's survived."

"But it's not too late to get him treatment," Conrad said, looking at his sister. "Tell him."

"Full on removal's not possible," Dana explained.

"It never was a viable option," Mick agreed. "He was inoperable right from the day we found out about it."

"I know," Dana continued. "He hid it from us for months and that window closed. But advances in just the past ten years have enabled surgeons to map the brain in much greater detail. They can use dye to differentiate the healthy tissue from the tumor. They use three-dimensional models to plan the delivery of the radiation through focused proton beams and new techniques such as something called gamma or cyber knife to make sure they only get the cancer cells."

The bright orange chicken wings sat on the table uneaten, as the conversation intensified. Their somber expressions contrasted with the joyous crowd and raucous music around them.

"I thought the window was closed for some of that," Mick asked. "I tried to get him to agree. I'd have needed his physician to testify that his mental condition was compromised. I probably would have had to go to court to fight him and have him declared mentally unfit if he chose to take it that far."

"What's done is done," Conrad interjected.

But Dana didn't take the bait and continued her verbal barrage of her older brother.

"Then you should've gone to court and fought for him," she yelled, causing a few revelers leaning against the railing by their table to look her way. "You have a fiduciary responsibility here. There's still time to go forward with systemic therapies that can deliver chemo and other critical medicines directly into the tumor to give him a fighting chance."

"He won't..." Mick started to respond.

"Then you have to make him," Dana cut him off. "You have to convince him. We may not eliminate the tumor. He may not live ten years. But he'll live much longer than if we do nothing."

Mick looked away. His entire face burned. Blood pulsed through the veins in his neck and pounded his temples. Tension flooded his eyes and brow. He watched the ocean waves curl in the spotlight from the bar.

"Mick," Dana lowered her voice. "If you don't support this; if you don't agree to do whatever it takes to get him into the program..."

Dana paused. Conrad dropped his eyes to his lap. The cold plate of wings sat uneaten.

"If you don't do what you need to do," Dana continued. "I will."

Mick leaned back in his chair and strained his facial muscles to contain his smirk.

"What does that mean?" he asked.

With a sad pause, Dana looked away and wiped a tear from her eye.

"I've already talked to Lizzy Gingrich," she said. "Her firm specializes in Probate and Power of Attorney cases."

"What are you going to do?" Mick asked. "Sue me?"

"No," Dana answered, her voice hushing. "But I can file a motion to contest your status. You could be charged criminally for dereliction of your duty."

Mick stared daggers at her, wondering where she gathered the gall to stand up to him in such a bold and confrontational way. Always the little sister, she had looked up to him throughout their childhood.

"Seriously," Mick scoffed. "Criminal charges?"

"Alright," Dana leaned back as she responded. "Probably not. Obviously, we wouldn't go that far. I'm just upset about this. And you're not listening to reason here. We have to do something now before it's too late."

Mick glanced at Conrad, always his ally in life and in family matters.

"Sorry dude," Conrad said. "I'm with her on this one. It's two against one. You gotta do what's right."

"Or we just might have to take over," Dana interjected. "And do it *for* you."

Chapter 26

Shelly awoke to the sound of birds chirping outside the small window to her cottage. She heard the waves rumble and the wind ruffle the beach grass.

She looked out over the flattened cornfields by Roy Carpenter's Beach. The sun nearly blinded her as it reflected off the paved driveway between her place and Mick's house.

She thought she heard voices outside the inn and wondered if she'd have a more active breakfast crowd than usual for an October morning. The voices persisted and she assumed a big party stopped for a family brunch on one of the nicest autumn mornings of the season.

She grabbed her phone from the night stand and read a news article about yet another fast-moving hurricane forming off the coast of the Bahamas and threatening the tip of Florida.

She scrolled through her contact list and clicked her sister's number, sending her a text to thank her for loaning them the BMW the previous night.

"I left the keys with the front desk," she explained.

She next called Marty Fazzini, but received his voice mail.

"Seriously? My sister? Lindsay?" she left a short message. "I hope you know what you're getting into with that one. Hopefully in a month, I won't be saying 'I told you so'."

Shelly smiled as she considered ending the message but a new thought popped into her head and she added to her comments.

"I don't know," she continued. "She's been unusually nice lately. Maybe she's settling in and turning a corner. Maybe the job at the restaurant's giving her a better sense of ..."

The voicemail beeped, indicating the end of the message duration.

"... responsibility," she said to herself just past the obnoxious digital tone.

She tossed the phone and slid out of bed. With a stretch of her arms, she threw a robe over her sleeveless pajama top and walked a few feet to her galley kitchen to fix herself a bowl of cereal. The sound of the commotion outside the inn grew in volume and she wondered what kind of large gathering could create such a clamor. She moved toward the front door to check out the scene when her cell phone rang. She immediately thought of Mick and Gordie and trotted to the bedroom to pick it up.

"Good morning Shelly," said Ted Callahan. "I hope this is a good time to chat."

Caught off guard, Shelly covered her chest with her robe and sat on the bed.

"Hi Mr. Callahan," she said. "What's up?"

"Did you see the article in the Pro Jo this morning?" he asked.

Shelly shook her head and explained that she doesn't get the paper delivered, but that the inn receives fifteen copies and she usually reads it on the porch after the breakfast rush.

"They painted you as a driving force behind the movement to build the seawall," he said. "There's a big picture of you on the cover of the South County section. I'll text it to you."

Shelly's stomach lurched with jittery nerves at the thought of being featured so prominently in the predominant Rhode Island newspaper.

"Also, on another note," Ted continued. "I've set up an arbitration session with your sister's attorney."

"Is there a new development?" Shelly asked.

"Apparently, there's a bit of a discrepancy that they're looking to exploit."

"What discrepancy?"

"Well, the ownership of your property is based on the original land survey map from 1955 that establishes the boundaries of your grandmother's property."

"Ok," Shelly shook her head wondering where he was going with the history lesson and shuddering for some sort of bombshell news.

"Those property lines were drawn after the hurricane of 1954 flooded the Robinson Street Post Office in Wakefield."

"What does this have to do with my grandmother's property?" Shelly asked.

"Apparently, the 1955 land survey document was a recreation of an earlier record from 1919 that was destroyed in the flood."

"Ok," Shelly exhibited her impatience with a tremble to her voice. "And so…"

"In the 1919 document, which Silas Pavinuzzi has produced from an old anthology, he's making a case that the property on which your detached cottage sits is actually a separate parcel from your grandmother's property."

"A separate parcel?"

"That's right," Ted continued. "Apparently, it was owned by your great uncle William."

"My grandmother's brother," Shelly acknowledged. "He died of Parkinson's in the fifties."

"That's right," Ted continued. "Soon after the hurricane, they redrew the property lines. And when they did, they merged his property with hers to create one combined plot."

Shelly twirled a strand of hair as impatience overwhelmed her.

"Does she have a case or not?" she asked.

"They're making a case that the inheritance of your grandmother's land should be constrained only to the property lines established by the 1919 survey and that she should be entitled to half or all of the smaller plot upon which the guest house sits as well as the adjacent parcel you sold off."

Shelly froze and flopped backward onto the bed.

"So, she wants the cottage?" she asked with a loud sigh. "And Mick's property?"

"More likely," Ted replied. "She'd want the cash equivalent."

Shelly sighed and laid back on the bed.

"Then we'll have to fight her in court," she snarled.

"We can do that, but you should understand your options."

"We either win or we lose," Shelly said. "What other outcome could there be? And what are the odds we lose?"

"When you go to court, you always lose."

Shelly held her breath, interpreting Ted's comment in her mind.

"Let's say, she sues for the full value of the cottage, about a hundred fifty and Mick's land, which is worth about a quarter million," Ted explained. "You might win and not have to pay her, but you'd still incur legal fees, which could be extensive. You lose; you owe her the money and still have legal fees on top of the award, including the possibly of a ruling directing you to cover her fees as well. Maybe you get a partial win of a lesser award. You pay what you owe to Lindsay and still incur the legal fees. In every scenario, you've got significant fees to pay, never mind the decision on the entitlement."

"How much would the fees come to?" Shelly asked.

"It depends how long the case lasts," Ted replied. "My guess is that Pavinuzzi will drag it out to milk the clock as long as possible."

"So, I'm screwed," Shelly said, fighting the pit in her stomach that pushed tears to her eyes.

"I'll keep my costs low, but I'll need staff involvement and we'll rack up some fees that I'll have to pass on," Ted replied. "But, as a rule, any time you end up in litigation, only the lawyers make out."

"I don't even have that kind of money," Shelly said, her voice, hoarse with worry and cracking. "Is there any alternative?"

"Of course," Ted said. "We negotiate."

"That's why you scheduled the arbitration meeting?"

"We should approach it strategically," Ted explained. "We make an offer just attractive enough that your sister decides to take it rather than face the risk of a protracted litigation, which she could lose. I'll paint a horror picture of the rigorous defense we intend to make if she takes it to court to scare her into playing ball."

Shelly sat upright and listened closely to her attorney's guidance.

"What offer?" she asked.

"She'll want a six-figure payout," Ted surmised. "Say two hundred or so. We offer something like fifty or seventy-five grand, cash. We cut them a check right then and there at the meeting. I wouldn't even charge you for that. She pays Pavinuzzi a lot less than she would if we go to trial. You both walk away and the case is resolved. We build in language that she revokes any future claims to the combined property. We could even build in a clause barring her from ever attempting to reserve a room at your inn either under her own name or any other alias."

"I have a line of credit," Shelly said. "I could do fifty, but not seventy-five."

"I'd love to just make this go away," Ted replied. "I think fifty just might do it, if my theory of their strategy is right."

"It would really hurt to max out the line of credit," Shelly continued. "But, it's way better than two hundred, which, I don't even know how I'd get my hands on."

"The way I see it, if she pushes for two," Ted concluded. "It means their strategy is to threaten a fight over Mick's place with a fall back to liquidate the guest house and take the full profit of a buck fifty. We'd counter with an offer to split the difference."

Shelly flopped back on her bed and stared at the ceiling.

"She wouldn't sink that low," she said. "The is our grandmother's land. I'd be out of a place to live. She wouldn't take it that far."

Ted cleared his throat and didn't immediately respond. Shelly exhaled forcibly.

"Make the offer," she instructed her attorney. "Give her the fifty grand."

Mick awoke to the sound of loud knocking on his door. He'd stayed up late the night before, unable to sleep. His creative juices kicked in and a new song flowed from his head to his Word Doc. Around three in the morning, he e-mailed a full set of lyrics for a new song idea to his star-studded recording partner.

As the morning sun flared through his window, he eyed the flaming red numbers on his clock alarm, which read a few minutes before nine.

The knocking persisted. Mick checked his phone for an emergency alert about his father's condition. The doctor had assured him that Gordie had stabilized, but Mick well knew, that status could change in a heartbeat. He had only one text, from Haley, who told him she couldn't drive him to the hospital because her husband had to work and one of her kids had a stomach ache.

Mick threw on a t-shirt and descended the stairs as the fervent knocking continued. Without Gordie, the stillness of the house unnerved him. He'd grown accustomed to having as energetic and effusive a roommate as his father had turned out to be. The rapping on the door scattered the quiet. It echoed off the tile flooring and filled the open two-story foyer.

As Mick eyed the front door, the distinctive blurred shadow of a dark cowboy hat protruding from the head of his houseguest clued him to his early morning visitor.

"I got your e-mail about the new song idea," Bo exclaimed as he barreled into Mick's foyer. "Erosion? Really?"

"Morning Bo," Mick muttered.

"You want to record a song about beach erosion?" Bo asked. "It sure struck me as weird at first. I been trying to refine your melody to string the stanzas together. You really think this can work?"

"It's an analogy," Mick answered him. "It's about a lot more than just beach erosion. It's more about what causes erosion?"

"You mean the tides? The ocean?"

"Friction," Mick answered his own question. "It's about the unstoppable erosion of the body and the unfortunate decline of the mind. It's about erosion of precious relationships between people, and how they fade a little bit at a time, with each moment of disagreement and discord."

Bo suggested they pull out their guitars and try some possible chord progressions for the new song.

"Now?" Mick asked. "I need to head up to the hospital."

"But we need to develop this tune if we want to make it work," Bo countered him. "Listen, I patched up my relationship with my agent. I'm back with good old Fred. And he really likes your lyrics. He's thinking we could name the whole album 'Erosion' and make your song the first release. I don't totally get it, but he's into it and he knows good lyrics much better than I do. Plus, I came all the way out here to work with you."

Bo started to hum the melody Mick sent. He warbled Mick's tightly constructed rhyming scheme and set it to the moody tune.

"The dust and the must of a love gone bust," he sang as he tapped his thighs like a snare drum. *"The decay and the rust and explosion of lust. The corrosion, the implosion and erosion of trust."*

Bo repeated the lyrics a few times, adjusting the tune with each separate rendition.

"Where's your pop at?" he mused from the center of the empty kitchen, as if suddenly bursting through his last bit of attention span for the moment. "I was looking forward to them grits cakes again."

"He won't be making Johnny Cakes this morning," Mick explained, going on to describe the events of the previous night from the point they parted the meeting to the update by the doctor that they'd keep Gordie under their care through the night.

"Visiting hours open at ten. I've got a sub covering my classes. I was hoping to get there right on time," Mick said. "But I don't have a ride."

"Dayamn, I hope he's okay," Bo said. "I'll drive you there. We could hash out the new lyrics to the Erosion song along the way."

Mick thanked him and offered to whip up his own batch of Johnny Cakes. But Bo preferred to get on the road and start working through the harmonies for the chorus to their new song.

"Oh, by the way," Bo changed the subject again, as if remembering a critical detail he wanted to share, but lost track of in the talk of song lyrics and breakfast foods. "What's going down at the inn this morning?"

Shelly hung up with Ted and flung her phone against her pillow. She kicked off her slippers, trading them for running shoes and changed into a bright yellow t-shirt with beige cargo shorts. The voices outside her door intensified and she thought she heard some sort of chanting.

As she neared her door, a loud voice, amplified by a bullhorn seemed to prod a crowd into shouting something in rhythm she couldn't quite make out. But as she opened her door and the wave of sound entered the opening, she could clearly make out the Pink Floyd line; 'tear down the wall'.

Outside her inn, occupying her cobblestone drive-up, stood about two dozen people holding signs and chanting protest slogans against the seawall plan. Several people held signs with red circles and slashes through pictures of rock walls. Others held up the front cover of the Providence Journal, South County section, with red circles slashed through Shelly's picture.

Nervously, the inn owner lowered her head and walked through the crowd toward the front door to her business.

As she expected, the protesters recognized her and chanted a chorus of boos. She worried that someone might shove her or throw something at her. She recognized a couple of the members of the crowd from town. Fortunately, the group remained peaceful, albeit agitated and considerably disruptive to her business.

"Slow morning," Marty said to her as she entered the restaurant. "The few reservations we had cancelled. One lady told Lindsay she'd never eat here again."

Shelly closed her eyes and skulked toward the stairs to her second story office. She stopped and turned to her head chef as if to speak to him about something important.

"She's a good hire," Marty assured her. "She said she wants to make good. She seems like a decent person to me. I'm sure she'll do a fine job. Don't worry about it. I trust her."

Shelly withdrew the comment from the front of her mind and climbed the stairs. From the top step, she gazed out the window at the gathering crowd, which had grown even from the few minutes prior when she walked through it.

The phrase 'tear down the wall' permeated the tall glass window and echoed through the inn's lobby. In the distance, Shelly caught sight of her neighbor, Mick Maguire, emerging from his house and observing the commotion in the parking lot to her business.

A protester noticed him and cheered with her arms in the air. Mick shrugged and looked from side-to-side as if expecting them to target their enthusiasm at someone else, such as Bo, who stood behind him.

Shelly watched as the protesters surrounded Mick and pat him on the back in appreciation of his comments at the town meeting.

Mick looked up at the inn. He briefly made eye contact with Shelly before she closed the drapes and continued up the stairs.

Chapter 27

Mick extricated himself from the crowd outside the inn. Bo, having tipped his hat and quickly ducked into his truck, avoided recognition from the crowds that largely fixated on Mick as the local celebrity voice of their cause.

He and Bo skid in the sand as they sped away from Mick's house toward the hospital. Bo continued to hum the melody set to Mick's new lyrics.

"Quite a conundrum you got here," Bo commented. "This beach erosion problem's real interesting."

"It's sad," Mick replied. "It's splitting the community. Some people want the wall. Some people want the beach to remain untouched. My buddy Ronnie says he's going to sell his family's home because of the taxes he thinks he's going to have to pay either way."

"The problem ain't what to do," Bo said. "It's how to pay for it."

Mick looked at him, perplexed at his outside perspective.

"How so?" he asked.

"Man, anything can be done with the right money and investors," he said. "But everyone's hung up on the cost of building walls, the cost of adding new sand, the cost of protecting them birds. It ain't the right costs to think about."

"And what costs should we be thinking about?" Mick asked.

"The cost of buying up them houses," Bo replied. "I got the cash. I called in a few friends. I already contacted the owner of that big mansion with the funny tower and made an irresistible offer."

"You're going to try and go through with that plan of yours?" Mick asked.

"Let's just say, I got an ace or two up my sleeve," Bo laughed as he rolled down the windows, accelerated onto the Post Road and cranked the country music channel on his satellite radio. "They won't know what hit 'em."

Mick watched the wind stand up all the hairs on his arm as Bo weaved in and out of the lanes around the slower cars. Bo's dashboard display indicated an incoming call from a Rhode Island number. The radio automatically muted and the speaker picked up.

"This is Bo," said the driver of the vehicle.

"Hello, again, Mr. Rutledge," said the voice on the other end of the line. "It's Topher Holden from the Narragansett Times. I had some follow-up questions from our call earlier this morning."

Mick looked at Bo, who winked and shrugged his shoulders.

"I got my buddy Mick Maguire here in the car with me," he disclosed to the reporter.

"Oh, great," Topher replied. "I actually had questions for both of you. You're all making this so much easier for me."

Mick sat straighter in his seat. He listened closely to the voice streaming through the multiple speakers embedding into the dashboard, in the door by his feet and on the sides of the passenger headrest next to his ears.

"First, is your father okay?" Topher asked.

"He's fine, thanks," Mick replied.

"I didn't call you last night," said the young reporter. "Out of respect, I didn't want to bother you."

Mick thanked him as Bo exited the Post Road toward the hospital.

"Unfortunately, I got scooped by the Providence Journal," Topher said. "Did you see the big feature article on you and Ms. Newsome on the cover of the South County section?"

"I didn't see it, but I heard about it," Mick replied. "They're protesting at the inn right now."

"I know," Topher said. "I'm here right now. I just spoke with Ms. Newsome."

Mick shuddered at the thought of a twenty-foot seawall blocking the view of the ocean through the Blackberry Beach Gap. Since he could remember, the gap allowed clear visibility across the ocean to Block Island. In fact, due to the elevation and angle of visibility, the gap in the dunes created an illusion that Block Island was about ten miles closer than it actually was. Mick always enjoyed that vista as he exited the Post Road and accelerated up the Matunuck Beach Road.

"I guess I wanted to get your reaction to the decisions made in executive session after the meeting," Topher asked.

Mick looked at Bo, who pulled into a parking space far from other cars and cut the engine.

"What executive session?" Mick asked.

"I didn't know about it either," Topher replied. "I was so caught up in getting an exclusive with you and Ms. Newsome, I didn't realize the council members went into a closed private meeting. Then they met again early this morning in an emergency session."

"What did they decide?" Mick asked.

"Apparently, they cut a deal," Topher said. "It'll have to get final approval at the next meeting. But I heard from an anonymous source that they're going to give in to the environmentalists on not extending the wall to Deep Hole. They agreed to end it just past the pub in exchange for a free pass to seal off the Blackberry Beach Gap."

Mick froze in his seat at the news. Visions of a concrete barrier across the top of his beloved beach filled his head. He pictured the view from the roof of the Vanilla Bean completely cut off by a gaudy steel and concrete wall of ugliness.

"They can't do that," said Mick. "What about the injunctions? The petitions? The lawsuits?"

"Lifted, ignored and dropped, "Topher quipped. "Everybody gets something. The town drops in big blocks to protect the vulnerable part of the beach road by the pub. The homes at Mary Carpenter's get protection from the next storm surge. The pub gets relief from the battering waves of the ocean with the revetment wall. The environmentalists keep the eastern side of the beach clear of an ugly seawall and the homeowners by Deep Hole keep their beachfront property. They're calling it 'The Great Compromise' and a win-win-win-win for pretty much all the involved parties."

"What did Shelly have to say about that?" Mick asked.

"She's a source," Topher said. "You'll just have to read her quotes in my article tomorrow."

217

Mick slumped in his seat like a child. The plush custom leather seemed to swallow him.

"Would you like to make a statement about the agreement between the town, the state, the homeowners' associations and the environmentalist groups?"

Mick looked out the window at two hawks circling a small salt pond adjacent to the hospital parking lot.

"Nah," Mick replied. "I've got nothing to say about it."

To Mick's surprise, Topher didn't press him for a quote. Instead, he turned his attention to the beefy musician in the driver's seat.

"Mr. Rutledge," he said. "There are reports of a bid you've made on a property along the Matunuck Beach Road. Can you comment on your intentions to invest in the area?"

"Nah, man," Bo replied. "I ain't got no comment on that."

"There's speculation that you plan to buy out some of the houses along the shore by Deep Hole," he continued his line of questioning. "In fact, several residents have indicated that you or someone representing you has contacted them to ask about acquiring their homes in a significant bid over market price. Can you confirm your interest in these beach-front properties?"

"Don't know what you're talking about man," Bo responded.

"I see," Topher said, apparently pausing to jot notes in his notebook. "Last question."

As Topher peppered, Bo, Mick stared at him in disbelief.

"Is this why you haven't been available to rehearse?" he whispered.

"According to someone close to the situation," Topher continued, oblivious of Mick's quiet query. "There has been new talk of invoking Eminent Domain to force the homeowners closest to the pub to vacate their homes and designate them for demolition."

"Why would the state do that?" Mick asked.

"To clear room above the high tide mark, create a new public access point, reestablish an attractive beachfront and bring more tourists back to Matunuck." Topher explained.

"You'd have to ask the state's attorneys about all that," Bo deflected the question. "I'm just a simple country singer. I don't know nothing about real estate, east coach beaches or Elegant Domain."

"Do you deny that you've offered millions in donations to the State Beach Resource Management Emergency Fund to pay for the Blackberry Beach seawall in exchange for favorable access and/or a small section of private beach granted to the hotel you hope to purchase across the street from the pub?"

Bo held his finger over the 'End' button on the dashboard console as he answered Topher's final query.

"Even if I did pressure the state to invoke Eminent Domain," Bo said. "It would be for a good cause in creating a big, open and profitable beach."

"Legal analysts don't even believe Eminent Domain applies to this situation," Topher said. "How do you respond to those that see this as more of a payoff than a valid legal maneuver?"

"I don't know where you get off, man," he said. "I ain't involved in no legal dealings or nothin'. And that's a big 'no comment' from me. Thank you."

At that, Bo ended the call. Mick exhaled, absorbing all the information he gathered from the extraordinary line of questioning and revealing conversation he witnessed.

"You knew about all this?" he asked Bo.

"Some, not all," Bo replied. "Maybe more than I let on."

"You're paying for them to build a wall across Blackberry Beach?"

Bo softened and turned to face Mick.

"Look man," he started. "I know you love that little piece of land. But if we can get the legal team to come through on the Eminent Domain, we can build a new, even better Blackberry Beach, down a little further next to the pub."

Mick stared at his music partner. A bead of sweat from the heat of the morning formed along the base of his hairline.

"We can take out a half-dozen; maybe a dozen houses and bring in all new sand. Maybe twenty or thirty tons a year. We can bulldoze the rocks and put up a beautiful clubhouse; way better than that crappy wooden one you described to me. It would bring in plenty of business for the pub and the pizza place. Even Shelly would make out with more traffic to her hotel. Everyone wins here."

Bo removed his hat and placed it on the dashboard. His wavy hair framed his face.

"But we'd have to put up the wall along the top of Blackberry Beach in order to make everyone else happy."

"Can they use natural materials instead of steel and concrete?" Mick asked, dejection dulling his voice.

"Don't ask me," Bo replied. "I don't know nothing about building a seawall. But I understand the homeowners from across the street from the ice cream place made that a big deal in the negotiation. They said they didn't trust the effectiveness of a natural wall. And, the state had to give in on that point."

A curious thought sprang into Mick's mind.

"How did you know all this?" he asked. "Last I knew, you took a bunch of the lawyers out to dinner."

"We were on our way," Bo explained. "When they all got called back in. I asked if I could listen to the proceedings. They were reluctant at first, but I offered to make a few sizeable investments that might give them negotiating power, and they found a way to squeeze me in and give me a seat at the table."

Chapter 28

Bo accompanied Mick into the hospital lobby. Dana read a magazine with her two daughters. Mick approached slowly. They didn't hug. Instead, the two girls grabbed each of Mick's legs. Neither girl recognized Bo, politely saying "hi" to him before returning to their phones and their social media apps by their mother's side.

Bo removed his hat and took a seat. His discomfort showed on his face and in his slumped posture. They all sat in awkward silence. Bo checked his watch and scrolled through his e-mails.

Dana remained quiet, her pursed lips squeezed together, demonstrating her residual tension from the previous evening.

"Aren't you going to go see Grampa Gordie?" Dana's youngest daughter asked.

"Oh, I uh, assumed he wasn't available since…"

"We already saw him," the older daughter said.

Mick looked at Dana, who slowly raised her eyes from her magazine.

"I'm waiting for Doctor Clark," she said.

Mick looked at Bo, who shifted his weight from one side of the polyester seat cushion to the other.

"You can probably go back to the inn," Mick said to him. "My brother'll be here soon. He'll give me a ride back."

Bo nodded and offered his best wishes to Dana before standing and digging into his pants pocket for the key fob to his truck.

"Much obliged," he said, as he donned his hat.

"Radley can't make it," Dana said, softly. "He's excavating a big glacial sand deposit on his construction site. He already missed time yesterday and they need to stay on their production schedule."

Bo froze and gave Mick a look, wondering if he should stay or go.

"It's fine," Dana said. "I'll give you a ride."

Bo thanked her again and gave Mick a shoulder bump as he exited the lobby. Mick turned toward the guest sign-in desk.

"The crazy train's in there," Dana cautioned him.

Mick looked at her perplexed.

"Larraine," she clarified her snide remark. "She's actually kind of sweet in how devoted she is to him."

"He's been pretty lonely," Mick acknowledged. "He needed someone to focus on him and his happiness. It's better that than him sitting around drinking beer by himself every night."

"I can see she's been good that way," Dana conceded. "She's just a little bit looney sometimes."

Mick nodded in agreement before signing the register and asking the nurse to show him to his father's room.

The ten-square-foot space featured a bed and a chair. Larraine sat on the cheerfully upholstered chair, which she pulled up to the side of the bed. She hunched herself over the railing to hold Gordie's hand, resembling a pastor giving last rights to a dying patient.

Theresa stood impassively in the corner, leaning against the wall. Her head slumped forward and her knees looked ready to buckle as if she had stood on guard for some considerable time.

Gordie, looking tired and gaunt, flashed an enthusiastic smile and reached for his son as he entered the room.

"Get over here, you," he said.

Larraine picked up her head and sat back in the chair enough for Mick to rest his cheek against his father's chest.

"How're you feeling?" he asked.

"Terrific," Gordie answered. "Never better. I'm ready to pull out all these wires and tubes and ride some waves."

Mick chuckled as Larraine groaned.

"I'm telling you," she urged him. "You have to take it easy."

Gordie ignored his paramour's caution and addressed his son.

"How's the beach?" he asked. "Hurricane Cecilia's picking up speed down in South Carolina. It could hit."

"Oh Gordo," Larraine protested. "Don't say that. Let it go out to sea. Who needs another hurricane?"

Mick filled in his father on the latest drama regarding the seawall and Bo's offers to buy out the homeowners along the Deep Hole shoreline.

Gordie listened and asked clarifying questions. Mick marveled at his father's lucidity after a night in the emergency room.

"Did Kian show up?" Gordie asked. "I gave him an earful about the sunken bus theory. He said he'd research it. I asked him to take your uncle Denny to the meeting. Did they make their case?"

Mick laughed and confirmed to his father that his uncle Denny had definitely made an impression at the committee meeting.

Theresa convinced Larraine to accompany her to the café for some lunch, leaving Gordie and Mick alone in the room. Mick took the seat, immediately noticing the warmth of the cushion where Larraine had sat for the past hour.

"They let them in early," Gordie chuckled. "They showed up two hours ago. Rainey just kept begging to come see me until they finally gave in."

Mick laughed, imagining the poor receptionist tasked with trying to hold back Larraine Lang from the man she loved.

"She's a great girl," Gordie continued. "I'm glad I found her."

"I know how lonely it's been for you since Mom died."

A cloud crossed Gordie's eyes at mention of his beloved deceased wife.

"I felt like I wasn't faithful to her," Gordie lowered his voice.

"No, hey Dad," Mick scrambled to assemble awkward words of encouragement. "Nobody thinks that. It's 'til death do you part'."

"No, I mean in how I lived my life without her," Gordie clarified. "Before Larraine."

Mick squinted to understand.

"When she got sick, she promised me she'd live her life with a smile on her face and cherish every day, no matter how hard she had to fight just to survive her disease," Gordie's eyes reddened. "And she fought with every ounce of strength she had. And I'm sure she wanted to give up. But she never complained. And she smiled every day until the very end."

"You've fought your butt off too," Mick tried to console his father.

"But not like her," Gordie said, drying his eye with the back of his sunburnt hand. "She told me I should move on; enjoy the rest of my life;

find someone new. With her last few painful breaths, she only cared about me living a good and happy life."

"And you have," said Mick.

"I wasn't faithful to her dying wishes," Gordie shook his head, a tear dripping from his eye. "I nearly gave up. I lost the will to live. I didn't want the treatments. I figured I only had a few weeks to suffer through, so why not just give in."

"But you've lasted way longer than anyone expected," Mick said. "And you're still going strong."

"Other than the occasional nausea, seizures and black outs," Gordie laughed. "But the point is that Larraine helped me see the good in life again. She's helped me rediscover my zest for life."

Mick folded his hands into his lap. The tense conversation with his siblings from the previous night spun through his consciousness. He had practiced the combination of words while staring at his ceiling all night. And yet, in his moment of truth, he still couldn't will himself to deliver the message.

Clips of phrases like *"…as your Power of Attorney…"*, *"… my responsibility to make the hard decisions on your behalf…"* and *"… my call not yours…"* rolled around in his brain.

Gordie looked at him straight through the eyes. His deep blue irises reminded him of the calmest Matunuck beach day with the slow rollers ambling to shore against the cloudless azure sky.

"I'm going to take you off the hook kiddo," he said in a soft, assuring voice, with a steely stare that only an understanding father could deliver to his son of more than forty years. "I'm going to do whatever it takes to stay alive. If it means radiation, I'll do it. They want to drill holes in me, bring it on. I was afraid of the negative consequences if the surgery didn't go well. Now I'm more concerned about the downside if I don't."

Mick stared at his father, unsure of what to say.

"It's my call," Gordie concluded. "I thought doing nothing would put off the problem. I thought I could just worry about it later. But sometimes you have to take action – no matter the risk."

Mick felt tears seep from his eyes. Gordie reached for him and pulled their faces together. Mick felt himself hunch over the bed rail in much the same position as Larraine had.

"You're a good kid and you honored my wishes, even if you or your siblings didn't agree with them. It couldn't have been easy for you. I can't ask for any more respect from you than that."

"What made you change your mind?" Mick asked, knowing the answer as soon as the words left his mouth.

"It's like I told you a month or two ago on the beach that day," Gordie replied. "Life is simple. If you love something, or someone, you do whatever it takes. There's nothing more important. There's nothing more worth fighting for – maybe even dying for."

Dana entered the room with Doctor Clark. Mick made eye contact and gave her a knowing nod. With the power of unspoken non-verbal sibling communication, Dana understood the situation.

"Doctor Clark believes there's a solid window to target the tumor with the thermal imaging scan and insert the medicine capsule directly into the center of the mass," Dana announced.

"We can do it right here in South County to keep you close to home," the doctor added. "We'll need you to rest and avoid any strenuous activities. Drink plenty of fluids and keep steady vitals such as blood pressure, heart rate and hydration. We can schedule you for one week from today. We'll need several hours for prep. The procedure will take a couple hours and then you'll have another six to eight hours of recovery time. It seems like a lot, but you'll be comfortable and pain free from start to finish. All told, you'll be out of commission for about twenty-four hours."

Gordie looked at Mick, then Dana, then the doctor.

"Fine with me," he said. "Whatever it takes."

Chapter 29

Shelly awoke to a dark morning sky. Melancholy, grey clouds curled into themselves like used cotton balls. They blotted the sun and coated the potato fields in a charcoal aura. She checked the weather channel for a hurricane update. The attractive on-air meteorologist charted the progression of the sizeable storm from Category Two at the tip of Florida, to Three in Georgia and Four along the outer banks of North Carolina.

Most models predicted a turn to the east and a near miss of the New England coastline. But a few outliers showed Hurricane Cecilia clipping the tail end of Long Island and brushing the southern Rhode Island beaches from Watch Hill past Matunuck to Point Judith.

Dressed in jeans and a polyester blouse, she trudged across the cobblestone to the nearly empty inn to start her busy day. She had inventory to reorder, laundry to wash and advertisements to place. As she climbed the stairs toward her small office, she spied her sister in the main hallway walking toward her.

"Morning" she uttered with minimal enthusiasm.

"I hope your friend's father's okay," Lindsay responded.

"I think so," Shelly replied, glancing over her shoulder as if she could peer through the walls of the inn, and through Mick's window to check on him.

Shelly tried to put the legal matters out of her head and give more effort in conversing with her sister.

"How're your girls liking the inn?" she asked.

"It's not the Ritz, but it beats the Sunrise Motel," Lindsay responded with her typical sarcasm and a subtle curl of her lip. "They call it home and it keeps them in school."

Shelly changed her line of conversation to the business matter at the top of her mind.

"I put Jeremy's card through until the end of the month and it didn't get rejected," she said.

"You won't get another month out of it though," Lindsay deadpanned. "That's why I'm working. I may need a family discount. I can pay a little less than half the nightly rate."

"Why don't you just look for an apartment or something?" Shelly asked.

"There's nothing available," Lindsay replied. "And even if I did, it wouldn't be much cheaper. And I wouldn't have the kind of flexible working arrangement I have here. When you have two kids to take care of, they become your only focus. You gotta understand, a mother will do whatever it takes for her kids."

Shelly noticed Lindsay's black apron and understood she was on her way to work a shift in the restaurant.

"Are you moving in on Marty?" Shelly lowered her voice.

"No," Lindsay squawked. "He's a nice guy and pretty good looking. I mean, maybe at some point. But, not until I get my own life in order."

Shelly rolled her eyes and turned down the hall toward her office. Lindsay followed her, entering the messy hub closely behind her.

"It's not like that," she explained. "Nothing's happened. He's my boss. I wouldn't go there. Truth is, I used to cook with mom just like you did, and I'd love to run my own place just like you someday. And when I do, maybe I'll be up for a new relationship."

Lindsay leaned against the doorjamb and played with the string to her apron.

"What about you, missy?" she asked. "Your neighbor's pretty cute, and seems to have the same crush on you that you have on him."

"I don't think so," Shelly said. "I've known him for two years. We've lived next door to each other for six or seven months. We held hands briefly. But since then, he's been preoccupied with his music and his jobs."

"Blah, blah, blah," Lindsay teased her sister.

"Seriously," Shelly pushed back. "We're great friends. I've never had a guy friend – or any friend – quite like him. There may have been a spark a few weeks ago when we held hands briefly. But I think we're too far past that. I don't want to lose what we've got and won't risk pushing it with him."

227

"I don't know," Lindsay shook her head. "If you like him, you should just go for it."

As Lindsay addressed her, Shelly observed a text from Ted Callahan confirming the date of their next arbitration hearing at the office of Lindsay's lawyer, Sal Pavinuzzi.

"As for me, and your head chef, Martin," Lindsay concluded. "I've got my two girls to care for. That's my only concern."

A second text from Ted Callahan popped onto Shelly's screen, causing the aggravation from the previous morning to rush back into her consciousness.

"Their ask is 300K," Ted wrote. "Probably expecting us to counter at 150 and settle for 200. This changes the equation. Let's talk."

Shelly slid the phone face down onto the desk. Her meager smile diminished, converting to extreme expressionlessness.

"That and your ridiculous legal maneuvers," Shelly snapped.

Lindsay stood at attention, straightening from her casual posture against the side of the doorway.

"Look, I don't want to cause problems," Lindsay responded to her sister's snark with composed calmness. "When I turned down the inheritance, I was happily engaged. We were moving into his parents' lake house together. I got half the money from Mom and Dad and I didn't need Gramma's house. You were lost at the time. You dropped out of college. You were flipping burgers for minimum wage. You needed it more than I did. Honestly, I just had to get away after Mom and Dad died and Gramma got so sick. I couldn't take it all. Jeremey gave me an escape. I had no clue he'd be such a jerk."

Shelly shuffled her paperwork, vibing apathy and disdain.

"I'm not a gold digger or a trouble-maker," she concluded. "I'm just desperate. I tried to send you a letter and ask for what I needed, but you pushed back. I'll be completely broke in less than thirty days, unless I pull off a miracle. And this is the only way I can provide for my girls. We need a place to live and just a little bit of financial security. I'll get something out of him eventually. But until I do, I have to keep them in school and put food on their table."

"You could have just asked," Shelly said.

"I did," Lindsay replied.

"You sent a certified letter from your attorney demanding an ownership stake in the property. That's hardly an ask."

"It's all I know Shells," Lindsay said. "I follow my attorney's lead. I've been struggling with Jeremy so long, communicating through attorneys and intermediaries, arguing in courts and lawyers' offices. I only know how to fight for what I need."

Shelly picked up the phone and dialed one of her suppliers. She slid a folder across her desk and picked up a notepad and pen.

"You have to do what you have to do," Shelly said over her shoulder, as if dismissing her from her presence. "And so do I."

She clacked her keyboard to log in, as the line on the other end of the phone rang in her ear. She added one last comment as Lindsay took the hint and retreated toward the hallway.

"I guess I'll see you in court."

Mick Maguire strode quickly down Cards Pond Road toward the Matunuck Beach Road. He and Bo had intensely rehearsed their songs early in the morning. His fingers hurt from picking the same riffs on his guitar multiple times from six in the morning through eight. They played in the basement as opposed to the more echoey third floor music studio to avoid waking Gordie.

"We gotta speed up 'River Mist' more," Bo said toward the end of their session. "And we gotta slow 'Blanket on the Beach' and give it more twang. My fan base likes mid-tempo songs; toe tappers. Not slow dancers for the prom and not head bangers from some seedy New York night club."

"I'm not one to question you," Mick expressed his growing unease with Bo's chaotic feedback. "But I thought you wanted to cross over to rock and pop. Mainstream audiences like the extremes. They want their fast songs to rock and their slow songs to ooze."

"Yes and no," Bo replied. "I need to cross over to gain new fans. But I can't alienate the ones I already got. It's a fine line."

As Mick pushed back, Bo held firm.

229

"You may know music and lyrics and all," Bo scolded him. "But I know the industry, the fans and the demographics. You gotta trust my instincts here. And we gotta do it my way to get it on my album."

The revised pacing of his two songs felt awkward to Mick as they flowed through his mind. He hummed them to himself along his walk to school. He first played them in his head Bo's way. Frustrated with their lack of distinction, he replayed them at his own tempo.

"Are these even really country songs?" he thought to himself.

Mick stepped quickly down the beach road in fear of a potential downpour on his way to the little round Matunuck Elementary School building. His aunt Trudy texted him to let him know she had arrived at his house with a tray of freshly baked muffins.

"He's awake and alert," she reported to him. "Larraine and Theresa just showed up. They want to take a walk on the beach."

Mick replied that a walk would be fine as long as they kept it to a half hour and returned if the sun peaked through the clouds.

"NO SUNBURNS," he typed in all obnoxious capital letters.

As he entered the school building, he felt the subtle stares from his fellow teachers. Their eyes lingered on him as they passed him in the doorways or approached him from the opposite ends of the hallways. Even the students seemed to gawk at him with some whispering and giggling as he brushed by them outside his classroom.

He decided to skip his typical stopover in the teachers' lounge, and headed straight for the comfort and isolation of his classroom.

The bell blared from the grate in the ceiling, and the door swung open. It crashed against the rubber stopper and vibrated for a moment as Ricky Dolman burst into the room.

"My dad's really mad at you," he said, pointing and laughing in front of the other kids who filed in behind him.

Mick ignored the taunts of his student, but Ricky persisted.

"He says you don't know what you're talking about and that you're not a real Matunuck person."

Mick stared at the boy and shook his head to subtly signal his impatience with the verbal barrage, but Ricky didn't take the hint.

"He was saying all sorts of swear words about you," he continued.

"That's enough of that," Mick said.

Another girl in the class added to the commentary, indicating that her parents were mad at him as well.

Petey Forrester raised his hand, amid the growing chatter in the room, as other students repeated sentiments they heard in their homes.

"Yes, Petey," Mick called on his friend's son, hoping to change the subject and launch into the day's musical lesson plan.

"How come you got a broken heart?" Petey asked.

"A broken heart?" Mick repeated the question.

"My dad said you got a broken heart when Black Barry died," Petey explained. "Who's Black Barry?"

Mick briefly lowered his head into his hands with his elbows supporting the ten pounds of his skull.

"We're not here to talk about the beach erosion problem," Mick announce to the class.

But, with so many parents airing their opinions about him, he'd lost his authoritative advantage over the class. The pitchy voices continued to air their grievances about his publicly exhibited opinions regarding the Matunuck beach erosion problem. He quickly felt the room slipping out of his control.

"Ok," he raised his voice above the din, while launching one of his playlists on his phone. "Everyone grab a drumstick or mallet from the bin. Who wants to beat along with some AC/DC?"

The verbal tongue-lashing continued on his way home as Haley gave him a ride to his house through the drizzling rain.

"How could you sell out like that?" she berated him.

"Sell out how?" Mick asked.

"How could you trade the wall that those poor residents down by Deep Hole need to protect their property and then allow them to build that monstrosity on top of where our Blackberry Beach Club used to be. It's just so sad and hurtful."

231

Mick struggled to unpack Haley's complaint. He felt the heat of nerves rise from his stomach, the culmination of the day's disappointed looks and stares.

"You think I cut those deals?" Mick asked. "You think I have any ability at all to make these decisions?"

Haley shrugged as she turned onto Cards Pond Road.

"Like, I single-handedly negotiated with the state," Mick continued, raising his voice as he gained momentum. "I filed all the legal briefs and galvanized all the protesters to rally at the inn. I raised the money to build this ugly, piece-of-crap seawall, and then told the town council what to do and how to vote?"

"Well, I guess not," Haley conceded.

"I made one statement at a town meeting," Mick vented as Haley turned up his driveway. "I had an opinion. The environmentalists asked me to make a short speech. It just happened to be the last one of the night. And everyone in town was there, after a long, emotional night of arguing over what to do. And the reporters were there, and they decided to quote me and Shelly. And they splashed her picture on the front page."

"You were on page two," Haley interjected. "She's a lot cuter than you so..."

"I'm pissed off that I even said anything at all," Mick continued as Haley eased up to the side of his mailbox. "I don't believe in big rock seawalls. So, sue me. I guess I better not say that or someone will. I just didn't want a steel and cement wall where our beach used to be."

"Me neither," Haley agreed with him. "I just wish they'd do what Kyle wants to do, which is to harden up the area where the road is about to fall apart and protect the pub and then add natural clay, dirt, sand and shrubbery to either side of the wall to help protect all the houses. I don't want a steel and concrete barricade at Blackberry any more than you do."

Mick felt his nerves settle with the common ground he had with his cousin.

"But that's the costliest option," Mick said. "Those natural materials are much more expensive than the rocks and the steep girders and the poured cement."

Haley could see Bo's oversized vehicle parked a hundred feet ahead of them at the inn with its vanity New York plate, which read 'BoRut'.

"What about him?" she asked. "Can't you call in a favor and see if he'll get involved? I understand he didn't even say a word at the meeting. I don't understand why he won't take this on as his cause."

Mick kept his knowledge of Bo's plans to himself. He wondered if the shrewd celebrity would succeed in clearing enough houses to form an extended beach on the eastern side of the Mary Carpenter's Beach. He also tried to anticipate how the town or the state would pull off an Eminent Domain play within the emotionally charged Matunuck community.

"It's going to be interesting," he thought to himself. "And I'm not going to get involved moving forward."

He thanked Haley and opened the passenger-side door to return to his house.

"Nobody's happy about the compromise," Haley reiterated to him as he hoisted himself from his seat. "They want natural materials in front of those houses and a new natural dune constructed at the Blackberry Beach Gap. Nobody wants a steel and cement wall."

Mick shrugged and nodded. He withheld his comments, in his new resolve to stay out of the debate.

"Nobody's happy," Haley reiterated as he thanked her again and wished her a good night.

Chapter 30

Mick crossed the covered front porch and entered the house. He dropped his keys into the porcelain dish on the table by the door and crossed to the kitchen.

He had grown accustomed to returning from the school day to a bright home with multiple lights on and the sound of the television echoing through the two-story foyer. He grabbed a bottle of water from the fridge and slid two slices of cinnamon toast into the toaster as a snack.

The blue flickering light from the television room permeated the kitchen. He peered through the gap in the wall to greet his father.

But the white-haired septuagenarian wasn't there. Instead, what looked like a bundle of unfolded laundry rested in a rounded pattern like a giant crescent roll.

Mick recognized the curly hair of his father's girlfriend, Larraine Lang. She sprawled with a foot on the ground, and another curled under a pillow. One of her arms draped against the back of the couch while the other flailed outward as if seeking a high five from an unseen companion.

Her head lay crooked across a round pillow set angled against the armrest of the couch. Drool dripped from her mouth and her snoring competed with the volume of the television for dominance in the house. Mick checked Gordie's bedroom but didn't see his father anywhere. Through an open kitchen window, he heard voices.

"Yes, he's a great guy," he heard the soft voice of his daughter from the back deck. "We're still going strong."

"So, what's the problem?" Mick heard Gordie ask her.

"All of a sudden, we're in different places in our lives," she said. "He's graduating and I have two more years. He's got a job. He's starting to make money now."

"Well, that's hardly a problem."

"When our lease runs out," Melanie said. "He wants us to sign on a long-term apartment in a smaller place for just the two of us."

Mick peered out the window at the back of his father's white-haired head facing his twenty-year-old daughter. His toast popped, startling him. Engrossed in their conversation, neither Gordie, nor Melanie heard the rattle of the toaster.

"I'm just not sure that makes sense for me," Melanie continued. "I haven't told him, but I've applied for an internship next summer in Maryland at the Chesapeake Watershed Foundation. It could lead to a work-study semester. I could be gone for six or seven months. And, I can't guarantee that I'll stay here in Matunuck or even Rhode Island after I graduate. I haven't told him any of this. God, I haven't even told my dad yet."

Conscious not to eavesdrop – or at least not to get caught – Mick opened the fridge to retrieve the butter for his toast.

"You have to follow your heart," he heard Gordie say. "And you can't be afraid to take a risk."

Mick smiled at the thought of his father giving grandfatherly advice to his daughter, a phenomenon he obstructed for nearly twenty years by living in California for so long and neglecting to return to visit.

"Something I've learned very recently," Gordie continued. "You can't stand still. You can't just stay where you are. And, if you don't let yourself move forward, life passes you by."

Mick recalled his father giving him almost the exact same advice twenty years earlier when, as an impending nineteen-year-old father, he moved to California to follow his then baby-mama, Danielle, out to Los Angeles to live in an apartment near her parents.

"Go live your life," Gordie told him. "You can't cling to the past too tightly. Embrace new adventures. We'll always be here for you whenever you need us."

Mick grabbed the cinnamon sugar from the spice rack and dusted his toast.

"I have a little secret I can let you in on," Gordie said to Melodie. "I've been with Larraine for about a month now. It's been quite a rollercoaster ride with my headaches and blackouts. I can't even tell you how many times I've thrown up and not told Mickey about it."

Mick rolled his eyes at his father's admission, leaning on the kitchen sink to listen to the private conversation.

"I'd like to be with her on an even more full-time basis," he continued. "I'd like to get to a point where we could live together."

Melodie leaned back in her chair and reacted with a combination of shock and amusement.

"Grampa Gordie," she yelped. "You dog. After just a month?"

"When you know, you know," he replied. "If you think about it, you've got another eighty years left. So, a month for you is just a blip. I don't have eighty months. I probably don't have eighty weeks. I'm thinking in terms closer to eighty days at a time. So, a month is a pretty significant percentage of the days I have left. I want to make every minute count. And, I want to spend as much of the time I have left with her. Of course, I love you, Mick, Conrad, Dana and all the aunts and cousins. But it's different when you have one special person dedicated to you."

Melanie nodded in agreement. As she did, the front door of the house slammed against the side of the porch. The screen door slapped the doorjamb and the loud voice of Kenny Forrester echoed across the tiled kitchen floor onto the deck.

Mick jolted from his hunched position by the window as Gordie and Melodie both flinched at the commotion.

"Nice job Maguire," Kenny shouted through the kitchen from the foyer, his distinctive pronunciation of his surname sounding more like 'Maguiah'.

Mick stood at attention and dropped his toast to the floor, splaying bits of buttery cinnamon across the blue and beige tiled pattern.

"They're gonna build a big old wall right across the Blackberry Beach Gap," he continued to fill the modest kitchen with the considerable volume of his voice. "It's gonna be like twenty feet tall. You won't be able to see over it, maybe even from the roof of the Bean. This is a disaster."

Mick heard the sliding glass door slide. Gordie and Melodie entered the house as Kenny opened the fridge and grabbed a Coke.

"How is this 'disastah' my fault?" Mick asked, mimicking Kenny's radical Rhode Island accent.

"You make a big speech at town hall. You've got a seat at the negotiating table..."

"I wasn't at any negotiation table," Mick corrected him. "Why does everybody think that?"

"The paper called you an 'insider'." Kenny said, stressing the word 'insidah' with his pronounced accent. "You let them politicians cut some bogus deal to bring in cranes and bulldozers, steel beams and ugly boulders to ruin one of the nicest places in town."

"How did I have anything to do with any of that?" Mick asked.

"I don't know," Kenny beamed. "But, you're an easy mark to blame."

Gordie took a seat at the kitchen table while Melodie gave her father a hug.

"Did you bring up the plan to sink buses?" Gordie asked. "Did you, Kian and Denny make that point at the meeting?"

"Yes, Dad," Mick answered him. "Uncle Den made quite a spectacle, but I don't think the board was interested in a thirty-year-old conspiracy theory."

"They did it in Australia," said Gordie.

Following a knock at the door, Mick heard the youthful voice of Kian Taomessina from the other side of the foyer.

"Hey Mr. Maguire," he said. "I'm done with work for the day. Mel said she was going to drop by and say hi and that I could pick her up here."

At the sound of Kian's voice, Mick's mind wandered to the conversation between his father and his daughter that he overheard. He pictured Melodie wrestling with conflicting emotions of wanting to stay locally; wanting to be with the young man she loved; and wanting to spread her wings to explore the big world before her. He replayed his father's advice, admiring his insight and appreciating the trust Melodie had in him.

He thought of the nearly twenty years he spent in virtual exile, visiting only sporadically, and the myriad of similar conversations he could have had with his father had he stayed closer. A wave of regret washed over him. He could feel the tension rise in his neck. A sudden pit grew in his stomach, stemming from the comment his father made about potentially having only eighty days left in his life. His mind conjured an image of his ailing mother, in her wheelchair with her gaunt, bald head flopped forward, exhausted from the radiation and the drugs of her fight with cancer.

"I can't put him through that," Mick thought to himself. *"Screw my brother and sister. I have to talk him out of this surgery."*

Kenny gulped a mouthful of soda and let out a small belch. Melodie crossed the kitchen to greet her boyfriend with a kiss. On the couch, Larraine squirmed, twisted, flipped to her other side and continued to snore.

"Did you see the big crane?" Kian asked as he entered the kitchen. "They're already lowering cement blocks in front of the part of the road closest to the water."

"That's Jack Valerian's company," Kenny said. "I saw him down there this morning. He says they paid him a boatload to protect the road before the hurricane."

Mick snapped out of his reverie at the image of a five-story crane lifting two-ton cement blocks into place along the top of the high tide line by the old Mary Carpenter's Beach.

"Is he doing the Beach Gap too?" he asked.

"That's the plan," Kenny replied. "First priority's to protect the Matunuck Beach Road. Then, he'll move the crane over to the edge of the trailer park and start lifting the blocks in place there next. He figured he'd get to the gap in another day or two."

"Tell them again about the buses and how they can keep more sand closer to the shore to help combat beach erosion," Gordie interjected. "Tell them what you researched, Kian."

Kian launched into a detailed description of the differences between the gradual incline of the west coast shoreline and the more extreme angle and contour of the Rhode Island coastline. He talked about ocean currents and the impact of glaciers during the ice age. He eventually circled to the ebb and flow of sand with the outward currents in the winter and the inward flow in the spring and summer. He lost the room and, in the process shut down the conversation.

"The problem with this upcoming hurricane," Kian added. "Is the convergence with the Autumn Harvest Full Moon, which also happens to be a rare supermoon. Not only will it appear really big and glowing in the sky, but it'll affect a much stronger tidal pull. If we get any kind of storm surge, we could potentially see close to a hundred-year flooding."

"I guess that's why Jackie's rushing to build the temporary walls," Kenny said.

"What we really need is money for good quality sand and lots of it," Mick railed. "When I was in California, they spent hundreds of millions of dollars on sand deposits at all the major LA beaches. They trucked it in. They brought in bulldozers and rollers. They built huge artificial dunes out of organic material. And the beaches are all enormous out there."

"Well, we gotta do something about this," Kenny concluded. "They're gonna rip up that whole swampy marsh area next to the Vanilla Bean. They'll have to fill it in with concrete to support he wall. It's gonna look like crap."

Another light knock on the door reverberated through the foyer into the kitchen.

"Hello," said Theresa Abbott, Larraine's faithful caregiver. "I'm back from getting her car checked out. How's she doing the afternoon?"

At the sound of Theresa's voice, Larraine stirred and elevated from the couch.

"Do I have to go now?" she asked, grogginess dulling her voice as her eyes strained to focus. "Gordo and I are having such a nice time together."

Mick, Melodie and Kenny all looked at each other, pausing briefly and then breaking out in laughter.

"What?" Larraine asked, her hair matted against the side of her face.

"I'm serious," Kenny leaned in toward Mick's ear. "We have to do something - tonight."

Mick invited the group to stay for diner. He grilled a dozen kielbasa sausages under the oversized umbrella on his back deck. The wide vinyl octagonal cover shielded him from the still-strong but setting autumn sun. Kian, Melodie, Gordie, Larraine, Theresa and Kenny passed a salad around the oval glass table. Mick placed bottles of water, Coke, Sprite and root beer in the center, along with a loaf of French bread, which he sliced into one-inch rounds.

Kenny continued to complain about the unsightly rock wall planned for the location where the old Blackberry Beach clubhouse used to stand.

"If only them dumb plovers coulda nested in the marsh by the Blackberry Beach Gap instead of the Green Hill side of Cards Pond, they'd have to shut down the whole plan," Kenny mused. "The federal protections granted to them little guys at Cards Pond's iron clad. Nobody does anything in that area if it might impact the plovers."

"Maybe they still can," Mick blurted.

"I thought of that," Kenny replied. "But they're all in the cat tail grass on the far side of the pond and it's very hard to get there."

"You can't touch them," Kian cautioned. "It's a federal offense."

"If you get caught," Kenny shot back. "Nothing's illegal until you get caught doing it."

"Plus, you have to be very careful with them," Kian said.

"I know, I know," Kenny replied. "We did field work with them in college twenty years ago. You can't separate the babies from the mothers or they'll reject them and leave them on their own to get eaten by snakes."

Melodie scrunched her face at the thought of baby plovers being squeezed to death by oversized water snakes.

"You gotta trap the parents right by their nest so they can always see and hear their babies the whole time," Kenny explained. "Then, you slide a pallet under the nest with the cage right there next to them and lift the whole bundle with a fork lift. I got the cage, the pallet and a forklift at the shop. But, there's no way to get the truck in the right position over on the Green Hill side. It's too swampy and there's no roads anywhere near the edge of the pond"

240

Mick downed a sip of root beer and wiped his mouth.

"There might be another way," he said.

Everyone at the table stopped and gawked at him.

"Shelly showed me a rogue nest in a small grove of cat tails by the inn," he continued. "It's right next to her parking lot."

"You think we could get a forklift in there?" Kenny asked.

Mick took a last sip of his root beer.

"I think so."

Chapter 31

The morning after grilling kielbasas for Gordie, Melodie and his other host of dinner guests, Mick and Gordie strode along the Matunuck shore. The grey October morning sky belied the rumbling hurricane that had reached Washington DC and slowly inched up the eastern seaboard. Previous predictions of an early turn to the east gave way to more dire warnings of significant impact to the northeastern United States.

In reaction to the surging weather, the waves in Matunuck supersized from the unseasonably calm of the past few weeks.

Many of the cottages at Roy Carpenter's Beach already had sheets of plywood covering their exposed windows. The shoreline emptied of the usual dogwalkers and photograph-seekers, providing Mick and Gordie with a solitary walkabout without a single other soul on the beach. It felt like a golden carpet laid before their feet.

They stopped and stood with their backs to the Willow Dell pavilion. With cold mist in their faces, they watched a series of perfectly symmetrical ten-foot swelling mounds roll to shore and crash loudly against the sand and pebbles beyond the ditch.

"I sure would like one last swim in hurricane-sized Matunuck waves," Gordie mused. "Especially now before they get choppy. There's no better surf than these big round waves."

Mick stood shoulder-to-shoulder with his father and admired the might of the Atlantic Ocean with him.

"You'll be back in there soon enough," Mick said as a gust of wind battered his cheeks.

"I'm not naive, Mickey," he replied. "I know the risks and the odds. I know my life'll most likely change. It's already transformed more than I ever expected or wanted. Heck, it nearly came apart at the seams when your mother died."

"You don't have to do this," Mick whispered as if sheltering his words from unseen eavesdroppers.

Gordie laughed and walked eastward toward the town beach.

"I know," he replied. "I go back and forth on it myself."

"It's only a couple days away, but we can still delay it," Mick continued in his muted voice. "We can think about it a little longer."

"Lord knows, I'm going stir crazy in the house," Gordie started to agree. "I can't lift anything. I can't do yardwork. I have to stay out of the sun. I can only take a half hour walk with you before school."

Mick pushed a tuft of hair displaced by the wind into place as he observed the raw power of the sea clash with the girth of the trailer park wall. High above the tallest trailer, he could see the bright red and yellow lattice of the crane that lifted the cement blocks into place by the pub.

"You know what I'm going to do when I get out of the procedure?" Gordie asked, oblivious to the impressive feat of human engineering taking place a couple hundred yards away. "I'm going to take Larraine dancing. It's how we met. And it'd be my biggest regret if anything happened in the surgery. I'd just want to dance with her one last time."

They approached the seawall by the trailer park where Blackberry Beach once provided a sense of community to hundreds of Matunuck families. The engine of the crane rumbled and hummed. They occasionally heard the crash of cement against cement as another block dropped gingerly into place.

Mick guided his father through the soft sand to the top of the low ridge of the Blackberry Beach Gap. They looked down over the marshy area between the town beach parking lot, the Vanilla Bean and the Matunuck Beach Road.

As he imagined, the scene bustled with action. Several state vehicles parked haphazardly along the shoulder. A crew of orange-vested environmentalists waded into the muck to observe the newly discovered treasure nestled between a thicket of cat tail grasses.

Officer Pat O'Hannon, stood next to his police car, giving a statement to what looked like a news reporter. On closer view, Mick recognized Narragansett Times Staff Writer, Topher Holden, who, acting on an anonymous tip, first discovered the surprising family of Piping Plovers living in the small, marshy grove next to the Blackberry Beach Gap.

"You're going to get caught," Gordie nudged him. "You must've left tire tracks in the mud."

"We carried the pallet into the swamp by hand," Mick replied.

"You probably left foot prints."

"Kenny raked them out and then doused them with water," Mick countered him. "Plus, it poured rain last night. There's no trace."

"Jeez Al Pasty. You're an ecoterrorist," Gordie said, with a chuckle. "The feds'll analyze the sand from the tire tracks of the forklift and connect it all to Kenny, who's the only one in Matunuck with that kind of machinery."

Mick laughed at Gordie's attempts to naysay the previous night's covert activity in the pouring rain.

"He just happens to do contract work for the town in the spring," Mick said. "He has his own street sweeper. He swept away any trace from here all the way back to the inn's parking lot."

"I still think you guys are crazy," Gordie continued. "With Kenny's educational background in Oceanographic Landscape Management and Ornithology, he's an obvious suspect."

"They're not supposed to know we put them there," Mick said. "They're supposed to believe they nested there on their own."

"I don't know," Gordie shook his head in genuine concern for his son. "We're talking about a federal agency."

"Right," Mick laughed. "Government employees."

Gordie shook his head in mock disgust. His grin belied the respect and admiration he likely felt toward his son's act of social defiance.

"See," Mick laughed as he pointed out the arrival of Kenny's grey truck and the appearance of his bald head as he shook hands with Pat, Topher and the foreman of the federal environmental crew. "They called him in. They're tapping into his expertise to help evaluate the situation. He's part of their team."

Along their walk back to the house, Mick refreshed his local news feed looking for any mention of the discovery of endangered plovers just north of the Blackberry Beach Gap.

Gordie stopped, as usual, at the spot where they had released his wife's ashes into the ocean. Unlike his typical pattern, where his face turned red, his nose stuffed and his eyes formulated tears, he stood with his chest forward and inhaled the blustery salt air.

"She's up there in Heaven," he said. "She's smiling down at me. We're at peace with each other."

Mick watched a particularly sizeable wave slam itself to the shore and splash white foam into the air. He recalled his father's concern about not being faithful to her wish that he live his best possible life, even without her.

"I've talked to her," Gordie continued. "You know; to myself. She gives me strength and guidance. Most of all, she makes me feel like I'm going to be okay. I told you about how she wanted me to carry on with my life."

Mick could feel the conversation flowing toward the big ask. Armed with his knowledge of the private conversation on his deck with Melodie, he anticipated his father's request.

"You want to live with her?" Mick proactively brought it up. "And you want to make sure it's okay with me?"

"I'd like to ask her before I go in," Gordie nodded. "That way, if anything goes wrong…"

Gordie stopped in mid-sentence.

"If anything goes wrong," Mick completed his thought, "She'd know."

Gordie nodded. They took one last look at the big waves and finished their walk toward the inn.

"Look, if you really want her to move in," Mick said as they climbed the dunes toward the cobblestone driveway. "I can maneuver some furniture around; make some space. It's a decent-sized house. I'd be happy to accommodate her. Whatever makes you happy, Dad."

Gordie stopped. He seemed to lose his breath. He hunched with his head toward his knees. Mick worriedly slung an arm around his father's back, only to realize his reaction had nothing to do with distress. As soon as Mick reached for him, the white-haired seventy-something arched his back and threw his head upward. His belly laughter bounced off each stone in the driveway, and his face reddened. He wiped tears from his eyes as he continued to bellow in amusement.

Mick stopped walking and folded his arms across his chest.

"You thought I wanted *her* to move into *your* house?" he asked. "Oh, that'd be rich."

Mick threw his arms outward in confusion.

"I was going to move out," Gordie chortled. "And live in her place."

Gordie giggled softly as he entered the house. Mick climbed the stairs to dress for school. As he sat on the bed to tie his shoes, he refreshed the browser on his phone. He noticed a new post. The Narragansett Times article, with Topher Holden's byline, appeared at the top of the paper's web site. He grabbed his briefcase and said goodbye to Gordie, cautioning him to behave and avoid any strenuous activity.

He sat on the swinging bench and read Topher's article, which detailed how the federal environmentalists couldn't initially determine whether the birds had arrived on their own or through 'human intervention'. He clicked on a video file and watched Topher conduct a recorded interview only minutes earlier.

When asked how the unexpected discovery might affect plans to build the Blackberry seawall, the head federal environmentalist indicated a likeliness that the wall would have to be stalled. But his answer didn't completely satisfy Mick.

"We'll take a few days to determine whether to leave them here and declare this area part of the federally protected habitat," he said, with Topher casting a microphone to his mouth. "Or, whether we can move them back to where they belong."

"And you've ruled out human influence?" Topher asked.

"We don't see evidence of any tampering," the official replied. "The family of plovers appear to function cohesively. Had they been moved, and the parents separated from the babies, the mother would likely have rejected them. That doesn't appear to have happened, and we can't be sure how long they've been here. We see this as potentially an unexpected migratory pattern that we may want to take some time to study."

"But, to be clear," Topher rephrased a close iteration of his original question. "You believe this may impact the construction of the seawall?"

"Well," the official hedged. "The process of establishing a federal protected watershed is long and complex. We're dealing with an intricate combination of local and state politicians, political lobbyists, environmentalists and some influential civilians. There are risks to the community and some considerable financial concerns."

"So, no guarantees?" Topher tried to pin him down.

"With politics in Rhode Island," he replied. "Anything goes."

Shelly watched from her office as grey and black clouds swirled above Block Island. The sable dunes of the island's distinctive cliff faded to black as ferocious rain poured over the ocean.

As she stacked her papers into a folder and clicked out of her e-mail, Lindsay rounded the corner to her office. Shelly made brief eye contact before looking away.

"We shouldn't interact before the meeting today," Shelly said. "In fact, we should probably minimize all our interactions wherever possible."

Shelly noticed Lindsay's attire, including black yoga pants with a pale blue MATUNUCK t-shirt. Her apron hung from her neck, obscuring the 'A' and 'C' in the word 'MATUNUCK'.

"Is that what you're wearing to the meeting?" she asked, looking at her sister's face more closely than during her first glance.

She noticed puffiness under her sister's eyes and redness around her pupils. Her cheek shined in the dim fluorescent light.

"Is everything alright?" Shelly asked.

Lindsay stepped forward revealing more overt telltale signs of having cried. She wiped a drop from the side of her nose and cleared her throat.

"I called it off," she said. "I had no idea how far he had gone in demanding so much from you. He never gave me numbers, he just talked about full and partial interest. I told him I trusted him to do what he thought was best."

Shelly stared at her, straining to understand what she meant.

"When I saw what he was asking for," Lindsay said with a tear running down her cheek. "I told Mr. Pavinuzzi to cancel the meeting."

In the distance, the rumbling of thunder over the agitated ocean rattled the windows of the inn.

"I'm going to find another way to make ends meet."

Shelly sat back in her chair. Her shoulders slumped as if anvils had slipped past her arms and fallen to the ground beside her.

"You're not going to file a case?" she asked.

"No," Lindsay replied, tears dripping from her eyes. "You have to understand, Jeremy's a lawyer. His father's a lawyer. His mother's a lawyer. Both his brothers and his sister are lawyers. I was always helplessly outnumbered, outgunned and totally outmaneuvered. I had to hire a pit bull to go after them. And even so, we're up against a brick wall with the whole Williams legal machine."

"Why didn't you just talk to me?" Shelly asked.

"Mr. Pavinuzzi explicitly told me not to," she replied. "He told me not to trust anyone. He cautioned me against giving away any possible legal advantage I might have. I guess I just got used to following his advice without questioning him. I've been doing it with the Williams family so long, I just fell into letting Mr. Pavinuzzi make my decisions for me. Kind of like how I let Jeremy jerk me around while we were married."

"But you could trust me."

"Did you know I put him through college and law school?" Lindsay asked as if recalling the grueling ordeal of her contentious marriage. "That was Mom and Dad's money he used. And he didn't even need it. His parents could have paid. But he took my money without even thinking about it. And, the idiot I am, I just forked it right over to him. He said the pre-nup would protect both of our assets. But, in our twelve years together, we spent all the Newsome money first and then his parent's money after mine ran out."

Shelly gasped at Lindsay's admission and held her hand to her mouth.

"I've been fighting them so long," Lindsay concluded. "It's all I know."

Shelly pushed her papers aside, nervously not knowing what to do with her hands.

"What are you going to do now?" she asked.

"Beats me," she said, a defeated laugh seeping between her pursed lips. "I know I can't stay here. That's not fair to you. I know trying to take the guest house away from you was wrong and I'm sorry I even considered it. I'll just stay as long as I can keep using Jeremy's card and then try to find a cheap place, maybe up in Central Falls or Olneyville or South Providence."

Shelly opted to withhold sharing with her sister about the recent notification she received disputing the charges to Jeremy's card and declining any future expenses.

"You can stay until you figure it out," she said, walking around her desk to hug her sister. "We'll figure it out together."

The rain stayed out at sea, creating a scenic shadow of darkness a few miles out. The shaded veil over the swirling water contrasted with the clear, cool air along the break of the giant waves at the shoreline. Shelly rocked in her chair on the porch of the inn. The rooms sat nearly all vacant, aside from Lindsay's. The restaurant remained lifeless and shuttered. She leaned forward in her chair and peered through her telescope. She watched the massive waves collide against the mile-long Point Judith seawall on the far side of East Matunuck. Every few seconds, a massive array of salty foam exploded into the air like an all-white burst of fireworks.

Still a day or two away, squalls from Hurricane Cecilia raced through the spokes of her porch rails and spooked her wind chimes into a frantic jumble of dissonant ringing and clanking.

She felt a buzz in the pocket of her hooded sweatshirt.

"Meeting cancelled today," Ted Callahan texted her. "Not sure their angle now. Will call you later."

She closed her hand around the phone. It felt like one of those long, smooth rocks she used to skip across the pond with her sister.

She felt the need to express her relief, and realized she didn't have anyone nearby to confide in. She recalled her high school days, riding around Wakefield with Kyle Dolman. She thought of the disastrous relationship she had with her old boyfriend from a few years back. She looked over her shoulder at the parking lot, realizing Marty's motorcycle wasn't in its usual spot. She didn't have a friend to talk to, and it made her sad.

With a sigh, she clicked Mick's contact record.

"Whatcha up to?" she typed. "Had some news to share."

Mick sat at the workstation in his music studio. On one monitor, he had a control panel that assisted with the digitization and construct of his musical output. On the other, he posted his lyrics in a Word document. A third monitor displayed a browser with multiple open tabs. He toggled between the front cover of the on-line edition of the Providence Journal and a few other sites. In giant type, the ProJo headline article referenced Hurricane Cecilia and the rising odds of it striking Rhode Island. Every few minutes Mick refreshed the page in anticipation of an update on the Matunuck seawall situation, including the discovery of endangered Piping Plovers near the now infamous Blackberry Beach Gap. He maneuvered to another tab featuring an obscure Wikipedia entry on Bo Rutledge and his early upbringing at an upstate New York boarding school.

Mick strummed his guitar to the tracks that played out of his speakers and worked through phrasing and emphasis on how his lyrics would dance with his melody. He played with the distortion and tempo settings to try and conform to Bo's latest directions. After intensely trying to make the new ideas work, he undid the changes and set the songs back to their original formats.

He reviewed one of the latest e-mails from Bo regarding their collaborative songs.

"Made more changes to River Mist," he wrote. "Blanket on the Beach ain't doing it for me neither. Need major rewrite. Want to bring in an expert industry lyrics fixer to make it more country, and less beachie."

With a twitch of his finger on the refresh button, a new headline flashed across his screen.

'Bo Rutledge Rebuffed by Beach Residents.'

He scrolled down the page reading about how the country music star and multi-million dollar want-to-be real estate investor had made dozens of offers to homeowners across the Matunuck shoreline, only to receive a block of negative reactions. The article quoted several residents who vowed never to let go of their beloved properties no matter the ostentatious offer.

His phone buzzed and the computer dinged at the same time.

"On my way to the airport," Bo texted him. "Will drop by for a bit. Need to make an amendment to the contract. Bringing my old agent Fred back into play. Got a few?"

Mick descended the stairs to the kitchen. Gordie and Larraine hunched over the dinner table sorting little colorful puzzle pieces. Gordie flipped them all to face upwards, while Larraine separated the flat edge pieces from the interior ones. Theresa held an electronic thermometer to Gordie's ear and awaited the beep.

"His blood pressure's nice and low," she reported to Mick. "His heart rate's just right. Temperature's normal. All his readings are great."

"I haven't lifted a finger all morning," Gordie added. "You happy?"

The thermometer beeped and Theresa commented on Gordie's freakishly healthy vital signs.

Mick thanked Theresa and grabbed a bottle of orange juice from the refrigerator. As he did, he spied Bo through the foyer window crossing the lawn. His boots made a loud, rhythmic knock on the wood flooring, followed by five quick raps on the front door.

"Come on in," Mick offered as he opened the door.

"Nah, Man," Bo replied, with his ten-gallon hat held respectfully at his side. "I gotta catch my flight up at this T.F. Green airport. I just wanted to give you the addendum to the contract."

Mick closed the door behind him and joined Bo on the porch. A light rain pattered the wraparound roof.

"Dang homeowners," Bo complained. "Every last one of them turned down a million each to sell. Some of them houses were worth less than half of that."

"I'm not surprised," Mick said. "You have to understand how much the people of Matunuck love it here. You can't put a price on that."

"And then, they find them little plover birds next to the ice cream shop," Bo continued. "And now, the state ain't so sure about this deal with the homeowners and environmentalists to clear out beachfront property through Eminent Domain. Politics in this state are impossible."

"I guess money doesn't buy everything," Mick quipped.

"That's what people who ain't got it say," Bo retorted.

The burly country singer pulled a manilla envelope from under his armpit.

"Check out the addendum," Bo said. "It's all legalese; just basic industry boilerplate stuff. I had my lawyer review it and propose a few tweaks."

"It's already been reviewed," Mick said. "The original contract's been signed by both of us."

"I hear ya," said Bo, shifting his weight between his heavily booted feet. "But I done signed it prematurely. I had a little temporary blow out with my agent, who also happens to be my lawyer. And, it appears there's a couple items in there that ain't acceptable to us."

Mick took the manilla envelope from Bo and hesitated. The dollar signs associated with licensing his lyrics to a major recording artist danced in his mind.

"You can have your lawyer check it all out," Bo said. "It's standard stuff that any songwriter would agree to when cutting a deal with an established superstar such as myself."

The rain intensified. Bo looked over his shoulder as if assessing the distance back to his truck. Mick exhaled and handed the manilla envelope back to him.

"Ain't you gonna even read it?" Bo asked.

"No," Mick replied. "I don't think so."

"That's a big mistake," Bo raised his voice, causing his southern twang to disappear. "It's not every day that a well-established country music star such as myself picks a local indie songwriter as a partner. I met with you as a favor to your old boss and liked you – took a chance on you. Don't make me regret it."

"I'm sorry," Mick said. "I had my lawyer review the original contract a month ago, and I like it the way it is."

"Don't cross me," Bo snapped. "I'm well connected in this industry."

Mick flinched. His confidence bent, but didn't break. A gust of salty air rushed across the porch between them like a mischievous ghost. He felt dampness across his cheeks and thought of his original lyrics to his song about the Ocean's mist.

"Are you even from the south?" Mick asked him. "If you ask me - and I did some internet research on this - I think you grew up in the middle of Nowhere, New York. And I doubt your fans know you're a Yankee, do they?"

At that, Bo pointed a finger into Mick's face as if to berate him. Instead, he flipped his hat onto his head and walked slowly through the pouring rain back to his truck.

"Y'all just cost yerself a whole lotta money," he said, before slamming the door and peeling off down the driveway.

Chapter 32

The Matunuck sky turned dark as midnight. Mick could see the rain only a few miles out to sea like a black curtain hanging from a low ceiling.

He noticed Shelly's text and felt a flutter across his stomach at the thought that she had something she wanted to share with him. He tried to recall the last meaningful conversation he had with her, flipping back several weeks to their lunch at the pub after catching crabs together at Deep Hole.

He poked his head into the foyer and grabbed his hooded rain jacket, letting Gordie know he'd be gone for a while. The wind caught the screen door as he reached to close it. With the gust, he ended up slamming it with greater force than expected, eliciting another "Jeez Al Patsy" out of Gordie from the television room.

As Mick crossed the cobblestone and rounded the corner of the inn, he spotted Shelly in her rocking chair on the porch. She sat with her arms folded across her stomach. Her pale, grey sweatshirt gave the appearance of a lighthouse in a storm. She didn't notice him at first, appearing lost in thought and transfixed by the rabid waves. She twisted at the sound of his work boot striking the first wooden step.

"Hey," Mick said.

"Hey," she responded, her smile arching like a morning sunrise.

"I got your text."

"Thanks for coming over."

"It's been a while," Mick said, taking the second of the three.

"Yes, it has."

"You had some news to share with me?" Mick asked, slowly taking the third step and clutching the railing as the wind filled his hood and blew it off the top of his head.

"Lindsay dropped her bid for the cottage," Shelly said.

Mick pushed his head to one side.

"What do you mean?" he asked.

254

"She's not going to challenge me in court to try and take my house away from me."

"She was going to sue you?" Mick asked.

"Didn't I tell you?"

"First I heard of it," Mick said, finally stepping all the way to the top of the staircase. "Jeez. That's terrible."

"She was going to try and fleece me for a quarter million dollars."

"Wow, what a…"

"She's broke and desperate for the money," Shelly quickly clarified. "Her husband isn't contesting custody. But in return, he's enforcing their pre-nup and cutting her off from all his money."

"What's she going to do?" Mick asked. "I hope she can take care of her two kids."

Shelly didn't reply at first, instead, gazing at the ocean.

"I don't know."

"I think the contract with Bo is going to crash and burn," Mick changed gears and shared his latest news.

"I'm sorry," Shelly said. "He was kind of a jerk, anyway. You're probably better off."

"Probably," Mick agreed with her. "Less financially stable. But, maybe a bit happier. Definitely relieved."

Mick took a step closer and leaned against the railing.

"I'm going to record the songs myself," Mick said. "I'll start small. I'll play around the state, build up a social presence, maybe make it as an indie artist."

"Has Marty said anything to you about Lindsay?" Shelly asked, suddenly switching subjects again.

"No, why?"

"I don't know," she answered. "Maybe it's nothing."

"My dad's going to get the surgery," Mick changed direction yet again.

"That's great," she replied. "I hope it goes well."

Mick turned to lean forward against the railing. The wind whipped his hair. The rain moved toward the shore, reaching no more than a mile out.

"I hope it's the right decision," he muttered almost to himself. "I take him in for prep tomorrow. But I'm still thinking of telling him to call it off."

"Why?" Shelly asked.

"I don't know," Mick replied. "I guess I'm just afraid of the unknown."

Shelly moved next to him. She leaned against the railing, only a few feet away from him.

"You're very stubborn sometimes," she said.

Mick tried to read her face to determine if she was teasing or not.

"How so?" he asked.

"With the wall," she replied, immediately wishing she didn't bring that subject into their dialog. "With your siblings. With your dad. You cling to the past. Even in your songs, they're all about your sadness and regret. They're always about some girl you used to love in the distant past and then lost."

"You didn't hear the one I sang at the inn last month," Mick countered her. "Kenny specifically asked you to listen to it. It was a rare happy one for me. But you took off."

"What? When was that?" she asked.

"The night Marty served the swordfish with capers," Mick answered her. "I tried out a fun, upbeat beach tune that night. I thought you'd like it, but apparently, you didn't."

Shelly racked her mind to recall the evening Mick referenced, finally conjuring the image of him leaving the inn through the back door to play at the pub instead of at her inn.

"That was the night my sister showed up," she said. "And, you took off pretty quickly as I recall."

The rain started to bounce off the roof of the porch. Mick looked over his shoulder toward his house.

"I went there hoping to see you."

"And you left without even saying a word."

"You were obviously not interested."

"Oh, you can read my mind now?"

Mick pictured his father, alone at the house, holding his ailing head in his hands and stumbling across the living room. He pictured him stumbling over the glass coffee table and crashing through it. An image of him face-down, bloody in a pile of cracked glass sent a shudder down his spine.

"I just came here," he started to respond to Shelly. "I don't even know why I came here."

Shelly searched her mind for something to say that might change the tenor of their dialog. She wondered what he wanted from her. Sympathy? Support? Or the hard truth of friendship?

"I gotta go," Mick said, after a moment of silence between them. He turned back down the three steps.

"What are you going to do about your father?" Shelly asked.

"I don't know," he replied. "I know he'd hate to be incapacitated. He's got a good gig going with this woman he's dating. I'd hate to screw that up."

"He's his own man," Shelly counseled him.

"I know, but I've got the Power of Attorney," Mick replied, with rain dousing his hair. "It's my call."

In a moment of what Shelly perceived as the candid friendship she believed they had together, she decided to share her deepest impression with her neighbor.

"It may not be my place," she said. "I tried to stay out of it, but I really care about you and your father."

Mick smiled and nodded in appreciation.

"But don't let that Power of Attorney get to your head," she advised him.

"Come again?" Mick asked.

"It's just," she continued, pausing before expelling her criticism from her chest. "It's just that, sometimes, you can be a stubborn ass."

Mick took a step back. He flared his eyes and nodded in surprise.

"Thanks alot," he said with another glance toward his house. "Listen, I'm getting soaked. I'll talk to you later."

Mick took three strides toward his home, stopped and turned.

"My dad's going in for a very dangerous operation," he snapped at her. "There's a chance he won't survive. There's a hurricane coming, and, oh by the way, the last time a big hurricane hit, I lost my mom. So, excuse me if I wrestle with my conscience about what to do here."

Shelly's stomach dropped at his reaction. She instantly regretted the entire conversation. She wished she hadn't even texted him. She had only wanted someone to talk through her elation about Lindsay's decision not to sue her. She didn't bargain for a confrontation with the one person in town who made her feel the most comfortable and unguarded.

"I'm sorry," she said. "I was just trying to be a good friend."

"I've got plenty of friends," Mick snarled, turning away again and calling back to her over his shoulder as the rain suddenly teamed, filing the widening gap between them. "And none of them think I'm an ass."

As Mick returned, the roar of the weather obscured Shelly's call from the porch of the inn.

"Mick, Mickey," she yelled against the din of the rain. "Mick, come back. I'm sorry."

As Mick walked across the flooded cobblestone, he found himself pushing forward through the wind. He couldn't hear the music at first. The house looked dark except for a dull yellow hue from the television room. It flickered inconsistently, alternating between yellow and orange.

As he reached the porch, he heard the sound. Music from the fifties played, fairly loudly. He opened the door quietly. Shadows crossed the wavering candlelight. A slow song by the Temptations reverberated through the foyer. Mick padded into the kitchen and eased his head past the edge of the square window between the two rooms.

Lost in the moment, Mick watched his father dance cheek-to-cheek with Larraine. Their hands clasped tightly, wavering, extended chin-high in the air. Their eyes closed while their bodies swayed in rhythm to the music.

Mick scrolled through the calendar on his phone. He checked the time of the appointment with Doctor Clark at South County Hospital. He sent reminders to his siblings before setting his alarm and quietly slipping up the stairs to his bedroom for the night.

Chapter 33

On the morning of the surgery prep appointment, Mick awoke well before his alarm had the chance to jolt him from his bed. He checked his phone and reviewed an e-mail from the hospital. The message informed him that the hospital staff would assess the safety of conducting his appointment based on the trajectory of the impending hurricane and the likelihood of a significant weather event in the area. Mick started his computer and scrolled to the Weather Channel to check the latest update.

Usually giddy at the prospect of a hurricane strike, Mick exhaled in relief to learn that Cecilia had mercifully turned eastward and floated far enough out to sea to minimize the impact on the area.

While South County could expect moderate winds and excessive rain, the significant threat to the Rhode Island coast was largely averted with the fortuitous path of the behemoth weather pattern.

The only dire warning had to do with potential flooding of the beaches due to the surge and the timing of the Harvest Moon, sometime around noon and again at midnight. Soon after Mick finished investigating the weather update, the hospital sent a follow-up e-mail confirming the surgery prep appointment, immediately followed by the scheduled procedure to insert the medicine capsule directly into Gordie's head.

Mick donned his noise cancelling headphones and played back the music he had written for Bo. He decided to add a song about a hurricane and jotted some new lyrics on a scratch pad. He heard Shelly's voice in his mind about his tendency to dwell on failed relationships and the pain of sorrow and loss. He decided to write a song solely about happiness. A jumble of lyrics swirled in his head like the hurricane that spun out to sea.

He hummed a melody and strung together a line he hoped to work into a new tune.

"Smooth stones and giant swells. Soft sand and beautiful shells."

He jotted the line in the middle of the page. At the top of the document, he wrote a single word that served as the overarching inspiration for his new song.

"MATUNUCK."

Mick looked at his phone. He couldn't understand what he was seeing at first. After eight straight hours of writing and recording music through the night, he quickly realized that his alarm must have been beeping for several minutes. He removed his noise-cancelling headphones and turned off the buzzer before heading down the stairs. After letting Gordie sleep in on the dreary October morning, Mick gently nudged him in his bed. He sung a quick little ditty that his father used to sing to him before school as a kid.

"It's time to get up, it's time to get up. It's time to get up in the morning. It's time to get up, it's time to get up. It's time to get up in the morn."

Gordie opened his eyes a crack and smiled.

"I'm ready," he said.

Gordie asked for a king's breakfast including Johnny Cakes, bacon, eggs and home fries. But Mick reminded him that he couldn't eat before the surgery for risk of vomiting while under anesthesia.

"I don't need stinking anesthesia," Gordie teased. "That's for wimps."

The headlights of Dana's car illuminated the gloom of the morning. They flashed through the house and glinted off the chrome of the kitchen appliances.

"Can we swing by the inn parking lot and check out the surf?" Gordie asked.

Mick helped Gordie into his rain jacket and nodded.

"Larraine will be there?"

Mick nodded again.

"Make sure she goes home to get some rest," he said. "I already told Theresa. I'm going to be out of commission for twenty-four hours. No sense hanging out at the hospital the whole time. They'll alert everyone when I'm back to normal."

Mick and Gordie both held their breath. The phrase 'back to normal' lingered in the air until it burst with the sound of Dana's horn beeping.

"Alright already," Gordie mumbled. "Get off our backs, you Communist, will you? We're coming."

Mick helped Gordie into the front seat before sliding into the back. Dana swung the vehicle around to the side of the inn. The ferocious waves rose to a height they had only seen a few times in the past.

"They remind me of the ones that took down the Blackberry Beach Club," Gordie observed. "They're scary - chilling actually - and yet beautiful to behold. You hope they don't cause any problems for the community and yet, you can't take your eyes off of them."

Mick thought he saw Shelly in one of the windows. But the figure he thought he saw disappeared just before his peripheral vision could come into focus. Instead, the gold curtain above the main staircase flapped a few times before coming to a rest.

Dana drove slowly along the Post Road in the driving rain, hitting the occasional deep puddle that caused the car to jolt. Conrad followed in his pick-up truck, not too closely, behind Dana. She pulled under the main overhang. Mick helped Gordie to a wheelchair while Dana and Conrad parked.

"I don't need this," Gordie protested, "That's for old, sick people. I'm perfectly capable of walking."

As Gordie guided himself into the lobby of the surgery wing, Conrad leaned in and whispered to his brother.

"Still as much of a stubborn ass as ever."

Larraine and Theresa waited in the sitting room. When Gordie and Larraine saw each other, they lurched forward and hugged as if they'd never see each other again. Larraine broke into tears, causing Gordie's face to redden and his eyes to puff. Doctor Clark greeted them in the lobby and went over a few details. Both Gordie and Mick signed some last-minute paperwork. A nurse took his temperature and blood pressure, giving an impressed expression at his readings.

"Well, this is it," Gordie said as the nurse forced him to sit in the wheelchair based on 'hospital policy'. "No matter what. Know that I love you all very much, each and every one of you. You're my family. It's a great family. And, no matter what happens, we'll always be with each other."

Of the siblings, Dana cried first. She wiped her face with a tissue and blew her nose. Tears streamed down Mick's face. He used the back of his sleeve to clear his eyes. Conrad held out the longest. As his eyes started to puff, he turned to shield the view of the droplets gliding down the side of his nose.

The nurse wheeled Gordie backwards into the secured surgery area. The double doors started to swing closed. In the last moments where they could see his face, he smiled and said one final, indelible word.

"Peace."

Chapter 34

Dana suggested Captain Jack's off the Succotash Road exit for lunch. Conrad declined, explaining that he had to return to his job site to oversee the operation of loading their dump trucks and preparing them to haul hundreds of tons of sand, rock and dirt from their construction site to a refinery up in the Hartford area.

"I've got one of my quad-axle steel dump trucks acting up on me," Conrad said. "It's our oldest truck in the fleet. It's on its last legs and we just filled it with ten tons of sand. I don't want my guys driving it, especially in this weather."

Dana and Mick begged him to stay long enough to enjoy some fresh fish and chips at the well-known seafood restaurant. But Conrad reiterated the urgency of his work.

"To be honest, the hopper's so badly rusted, if the sand gets too wet, I'm not completely sure it won't just split apart and lose its entire payload," Mick elaborated. "We're donating it all to the city. We wanted money for it. They wanted us to pay them to take to off their hands. I have just enough time to get up there, make the dump and get back in time tomorrow for when Dad wakes up."

Mick tried one more angle to sway his brother.

"Did you see those waves?" he asked.

Conrad wavered.

"I bet you'd be bummed out if Dana and I swam in them and you didn't."

Mick's younger brother laughed and smacked him on the back.

"Tempting," he said. "But I gotta go."

Conrad drove ahead of Dana on the Post Road until Dana veered left to the exit for Succotash Road, one isolated peninsula over from their beloved Matunuck. As they made their way along the narrow two-lane street toward the iconic seafood haunt, Captain Jack's, they had to swerve into the middle of the road to avoid several deep and wide puddles along the shoulder.

As they eased past the water tower and community tennis courts, they noticed an unusually busy stream of cars coming from the opposite direction. They glanced at each other in surprise with a shrug. Moments later, they saw the police lights and a barricade across the road.

"Sorry, detour," said a stern police officer in a bright yellow rain jacket. "The water level by the marina is so high, it's almost up to the top of the bridge. The Governor's issued evacuation orders for East Matunuck, Matunuck, Green Hill and Charlestown. There are amenities available at S.K. High or in the URI field house. You'll have to turn around."

Dana joined a small line of cars heading north back toward the Post Road. She swung around the ramp to the southbound lane and beelined for the Matunuck Beach Road. Unlike the scene along the Succotash Road area, the Matunuck Beach Road seemed dormant. In fact, they didn't run into a single other car.

With the limited visibility from the rain, they couldn't see Block Island through the Blackberry Beach Gap. But the extreme churn from the ocean looked like it could top the dunes and flood Mary Carpenter's village at any point. Without communicating, Mick and Dana agreed to drive down to the Pub to check out whether or not the plucky Matunuck Beach Road would survive the super high tide.

As they rounded the bend, they observed the crane, tucked neatly behind the trailer park. It's boom and jib folded neatly above the cab. A hundred feet further along the road, they inspected the work Jack Valerian's company performed to protect the pavement with a temporary revetment. Cement blocks, three-deep cascaded from four feet above the road to the water level, stepping like an Incan pyramid. Sloppily poured cement held the blocks together along with iron rods drilled diagonally through the structure.

Dana pulled to the side of the road and they sat atop the tallest blocks to watch the giant waves take their best repeated shots at dashing the human handiwork.

They walked to the pub, which was still open, despite the Atlantic Ocean's onslaught against the flimsy-looking pressure treated beams of the extended porch.

265

They tried to find a seat, but had to squeeze into the far corner of the bar due to the immense crowd that gathered to eat, drink and cheer on the defiant configuration of weathered lumber in its battle with the sea.

Mick spotted his daughter at the far end of the bar with Kian and flung his arms outward.

"What do you live here?" he asked.

She blushed, even though she couldn't hear him through the din of the joyous crowd.

Pat O'Hannon entered the building in his full police uniform. He walked straight to the bar and conducted a serious conversation with Kyle Dolman. Mick watched Kyle shake his head repeatedly in disagreement. Mick understood the conversation, as did the rest of the bar, which started booing. Kyle rung a bell above the lighted rack of shot glasses to catch the attention of his patrons.

"Apparently, we've been shut down and ordered to vacate the premises," he announced. "I'm legally obligated to ask you all to leave. Although, none of us left when Katrina hit, did we?"

The patrons shouted all "no" and toasted Pat with their beers. Pat laughed and crossed the floor to embrace a tall, handsome man with wavy hair that Mick immediately recognized as his childhood best friend Jack Valerian. He sat in a dark corner with Kenny Forrester, Marty Fazzini and Aaron "Ronnie" Benjamin.

He excused himself from Dana, who decided to cross the bar to join Melodie and Kian, and slid through the packed house to join Pat and the reunited Kings of Matunuck.

They all smacked hands, hooted and hugged each other.

"What are you doing here?" Mick asked Jack. "I thought you went back up to Maine."

"My crane operator's stuck on the other side of the Succotash Bridge," Jack explained. "He's literally a mile away, but can't get here. I had to collapse the jib and move it behind the trailer park wall to avoid it getting swept out to sea."

Mick laughed at Jack for driving three hours for a twenty-minute task.

"Sucks to be the boss sometimes," he said. "They wouldn't let me take care of the Blackberry side until Kenny, here, and his crew of URI Ornithology students moved the family of endangered Piping Plovers back to the Green Hill side of the pond. And they dragged their feet on it until this morning."

Mick gave Kenny an impish grin.

"So, we couldn't get in there to do the work they hired us to do," Jack continued. "We bulldozed some dirt and clay in there. But that was the best we could do. I just hope it holds up."

Pat turned to Mick and Kenny, staring at them for a moment.

"Take a picture," Kenny quipped. "Lasts longer."

"Take a pit-chuh," Pat imitated him. "Lasts longuh."

A passerby pat Mick on the back and told him he heard him at the pub a month earlier and enjoyed his music. Pat continued to stare at them.

"You're welcome," he said.

"For what?" Kenny asked. "I just bought the last round."

"Next time you decide to commit a federal offense and then sweep the evidence off the street, check to make sure there aren't any local ice cream shops with security cameras facing the street."

"Holy shhh..." Kenny started to yelp.

"It's fine," he said. "I took care of it. Apparently, they uh, turned off the cameras after Labor Day."

"Man, thank you so much," Mick said.

"Just no more trouble out of you two, okay?" Pat scolded them. "You made your point. You delayed the wall. I'm kinda glad you did. But, we could all get in trouble, including me."

Mick and Kenny nodded in compliance and clutched him across the back in appreciation.

"How're your sisters doing?" Jack asked, his face lighting up.

"All married," he replied, causing Jack's eyes to lose their flare.

As Mick, Jack, Pat and the Kings caught up with each other, Joycie Dolman gave Mick a tap on the shoulder.

"A bunch of people have been asking if you'd play," she said. "They want to hear the song about the girl on the blanket at the beach."

Mick told her he didn't have his guitar, but Joycie offered him their house guitar.

"We keep an acoustic in the closet just in case," she explained. "A pub with live music's always more fun."

Mick agreed, smacking hands with Jack and asking him to stick around. He climbed the short stage and propped himself onto a barstool. Joycie handed him the guitar and flicked the spotlight. The crowd cheered and huddled closely around him. He could hear his daughter whooping from the bar.

After tuning the instrument, he launched into his first song. The crowd bopped and moved to the beat, singing loudly along with him as he repeated the refrain numerous times. He peppered in some cover tunes of popular rock and roll bands such as the Rolling Stones, Bon Jovi, Steely Dan, the Steve Miller Band and his favorite, the E-Street Band. Then he slowed the rhythm and pulled out his own original.

"This one's a tribute to all of you," he pandered to the crowd, goosing their excitement. "It's to everyone that loves this town, this beach and this bar."

The crowd erupted in cheers as he strummed the intro chords to his song 'The Ocean's Mist'. The reception to the down-tempo tune overwhelmed him as dozens of patrons crowded around him. They slung their arms together and swayed in unison to the soft, soulful melody.

As Mick closed the song, to wild applause, Kyle rang the bell.

"I think we have our official Matunuck theme song," he announced, to renewed applause.

A loud clap of thunder rocked the building. Mick could feel it shake. The deck continued to rattle and vibrate, but hold strong against the relentless Matunuck surf.

Mick thanked the crowd and returned to his table. He introduced Jack to his daughter and her boyfriend. Pat excused himself, leaving the bar to make his rounds through the town and check up on residents in the most vulnerable low-lying wetland areas.

"Kind of takes your mind off what's going on at the hospital," Dana said. "Larraine texted me that he's out of prep and moving to the operating table."

"Still there?" Mick asked.

"All day," she replied. "Poor Theresa, stuck in the lobby with her."

Mick and Dana shared a hearty laugh, causing the rest of the table to laugh with them, despite not knowing the joke.

"They start the operation in an hour," Dana explained. "They're running behind schedule. We may not hear anything for a while. There's nothing we can do tonight. We won't know anything until tomorrow morning."

He and Dana shared a large plate of clam cakes with Kenny, Marty, Aaron and Jack. Melodie and Kian ordered fried clams and French fries. Mick complimented Jack on the job his crew did to protect the Matunuck Beach Road.

"I know everyone's all up in arms about this wall," Jack said. "You especially."

"I just don't want to see it over on the Blackberry side," Mick clarified. "It's absolutely necessary where you built the temporary wall to prop up the road."

"I agree," said Jack. "I'm going to put up an amazingly beautiful and functional wall here by the pub. You'll be able to walk along the top of it. It will be wide and strong. It's just the reality of where we are with this side of the beach."

Mick nodded in agreement.

"They hired me to build the Blackberry side as well. And, I'll make it as nice as I can," Jack continued. "But, to be honest. I'd rather put in a natural revetment on that side. I proposed a combination of a dirt and clay base with some small boulders buried beneath five or six feet of organic mesh sandbags and a twenty-ton dump of fine sand with a tasteful slatted retainer fence. I committed to annual maintenance and replenishment, for a fair retainer fee. But the Town and Feds didn't go for it. If they were going to use their emergency money, they wanted a capital expense and not an operating cost. They wanted permanence in a one-shot deal."

Kenny leaned back in his chair, downed a gulp of beer and made a fateful suggestion.

"Then let's do it ourselves," he said. "I've got some sand at the shop. It ain't twenty tons, but maybe a half a ton. It's something. I got a small backhoe and my own bulldozer. We could push in more dirt, cover it with sand. Maybe it wouldn't look too bad?"

Jack laughed and clanked his beer with Kenny's.

"I wish," Marty said. "You heard Pat. He'll shut us down."

"You seen them waves today?" Kenny asked. "And that high tide? It ain't gonna hold. We gotta do something."

"A half ton of sand won't hold up," Jack said. "The ocean would suck that out to sea in a heartbeat.

Mick's mind kicked into hyperactivity. He formulated a plan that would take some delicate diplomacy with his brother. He leaned in to the table, speaking in a hushed tone. They leaned in with him, as if he were a quarterback leading a huddle before a critical third down.

"A half ton of sand won't cut it?" he repeated. "How about ten?"

Chapter 35

They filed out of the pub and walked the Matunuck Beach Road along the cement barrier that Jack Valerian's company constructed. Spray from the tidal surf battered the concrete and flailed over the wall. The cold, salty water doused them as the rain showered their heads.

Ronnie Benjamin hurried to his house to prepare for his segment of the plan. Marty called Pat O'Hannon, inviting him to Ronnie's blow-out poker night with him, Ronnie, Kian and Melodie. Kenny and Jack drove to the garage where Kenny stored his backhoe, bulldozer, street sweeper and fleet of trucks.

As the group scattered to perform their assignments, Mick, with his sister by his side, made the call to his brother.

"Are you crazy?" Conrad scoffed at the suggestion that he 'donate' a truckload of sand to the cause. "The old rig's dying. And the loader can barely handle the trip across town to donate it to the city, never mind a half hour up to Rhode Island."

"It's a quick hop up the highway," Mick suggested. "You've been complaining about how you can't find anywhere to get rid of the sand. Just drive slow. But get here quick."

"If the back splits open, we'd have material spewing out all over Route 95," Conrad answered. "I'm telling you, this baby's seen her last days. I couldn't even sell her to an auction house."

Mick tried to sway him, but Conrad cut off his older brother in mid-sentence.

"I'm all for saving Matunuck and fighting this ugly wall," he said. "But it's done. We'd be breaking all sorts of laws. And we can't possibly build a big enough sand dune to make a difference. They'd probably just clear it away and do what they want."

"It's not about building the ultimate wall. It's about demonstrating what a natural approach could look like," Mick replied. "Everyone's got skin in the game here. Kenny's contributing a half ton of sand. Jack's taking a big risk by using the crane to pull loose rocks from the crumbled part of the trailer park wall. Ronnie and Marty are going to cheat and let Pat win in poker to keep him distracted from his rounds. We're all pitching in."

"I'm fine with donating the sand," Conrad countered. "I just can't get it there."

"If this wall even remotely holds out," Mick pleaded. "Maybe they'll see that a natural solution can work."

"And if not..."

"C'mon, it'll be fun," Mick said, throwing a Hail Mary. "Have you seen the waves down here? When we're done, we'll all swim together. It'll be like old times."

"And then they'll lock us up," Conrad added.

"When did that ever stop you before?" Mick asked. "Plus, if you come down here tonight, you'll be closer to Dad in case anything goes wrong."

"Sorry," Conrad said. "I can't."

"But everyone's doing their part," Mick gave it one last argument. "Your piece is the biggest and most important. Without the sand, we can't make it work."

"You should have called me before you set the plan," Conrad replied. "Sorry. It's a hard pass."

Mick clicked the phone and slid it into his jeans. Dana looked at him with sympathetic eyes.

"I told you," she said. "He's an adult now."

Mick watched the water push the high tide mark toward the top of the gap behind the trailer park. It rode along the edge of the seawall and stopped only a dozen feet from the top of the meager sand dune.

"It's going to give out," Mick observed. "Tonight."

They walked along the back of the trailer park and stood at the top of the mound, where the parking lot to the Blackberry Beach clubhouse used to sit. The Ocean looked like it could rise by another few feet and just steamroll them into the swamp below.

Kenny and Jack rounded the corner. His yellow bulldozer churned through the sand and gravel pathway behind the trailers and pushed a sizeable load of dirt forward. Kenny waved his arms for Mick and Dana to clear out. They continued forward toward the parking lot of the town beach.

Jack hopped off the back of Kenny's heavy machinery and jumped into the crane. As Kenny circled the dune, precariously close to the lapping waves that rode up the beach, he found a spot of higher ground and used his digger to loosen up a large pile of stones and dirt.

The jib of the crane slowly articulated from the rig and extended over the short stretch of beach still unscathed by the storm surge. Kenny called out to Mick to confirm whether Conrad would arrive within the hour with the load of sand that they needed. Mick nodded sheepishly as Dana nudged him with her elbow.

Mick received a text from Ronnie about the progress of the poker distraction.

"Pat's here," he wrote. "Every time he looks away, we turn down the volume of his radio and stop the clock for a few minutes at a time. He's already won a couple hands and getting pretty excited. Will let you know if we lose him."

Mick replied with a smiling emoji.

"If something bad happens, let us know," Ronnie replied. "He could get in a lot of trouble."

"Will do," Mick wrote back. "We all could."

Kenny dislodged more dirt and maneuvered it into place along the top of the dune at the Blackberry Beach Gap. He used his scooper to pat it firm. The driving rain over the ocean lit up with each streak of lightning, far out to sea.

Not overly windy, the crane extended above the seawall and rose to an impressive height. Mick held his hand over his eyes in an attempt to watch it unfurl. But the rain battered his face, causing him to look away. Jack locked the crane into place and manually secured the block hooks around a loose boulder at the bottom of the wall. A relatively simple lift and move, he maneuvered the half ton chunk of basalt about ten feet into the air, swung it about thirty feet to the north and slowly lowered it in place atop the dirt and clay that Kenny laid in place.

"What's Conrad's ETA?" Kenny shouted from the cab of the bulldozer. "We only have so much time to get this done. A couple hours, tops."

Mick shrugged again.

"Check with him," Kenny called through the rain and the sound of the rumbling motor from Jack's crane.

Dana gave Mick a stern look, imploring him to come clean.

"You're gonna get everyone in trouble," she said. "And for what? All their efforts probably won't even stop the tide from breaking through."

Mick rubbed the back of his neck. He opened his mouth to speak, but couldn't find any words to express the jumble of thoughts and feelings swirling his mind like the storm system that churned two hundred miles south of Block Island.

"Plus," Dana continued. "What if something happens to Dad while we're out here?"

Between dropping him off in the late morning and staying with him through the mid-afternoon in the hospital, and then hanging out at the pub throughout the early evening and then finally engaging in their covert operation as the sun dropped below the horizon, they seemed to run on some sort of detached autopilot. Mick and Dana acted on adrenaline and instinct as if in denial of the grave danger facing their sole surviving parent.

"Larraine and what's-her-face are there," Mick rationalized. "The staff said they could stay two hours past visiting hours at ten. If anything happens tonight during the actual surgery, they'll let us know right away. The hospital's ten minutes up the Post Road."

"I guess there's nothing we can do sitting in the waiting room," Dana reasoned, checking the battery status on her mobile. "And we both have our phones with us."

"He'll be asleep all night until tomorrow morning," Mick continued. "And frankly, I need to keep myself busy. Let's see how much we can accomplish with the rocks and dirt we have."

"Fine," Dana relented, as the mist from the light precipitation dotted her face. "The cottages in the village are all empty now that the summer's over. I don't see any lights on. But we should go make sure, especially since you've got Pat distracted. If this dune gives out, it'd be a disaster down there."

Mick agreed with his sister and decided they should check the forty-seven homes to make sure all the summer homes were dormant as expected. As they walked back through the access path toward the Matunuck Beach Road, they heard the rumble of another engine.

They spied a massive quad-axle steel dump truck rolling past the Vanilla Bean. Upon seeing his siblings in the glow of his headlight, Conrad pulled the cord and let loose the jarring wail of his horn. He stopped along the side of the marsh. Mick helped Dana into the cab and followed behind her. Their clothes dripped all over the front seat.

"What made you change your mind?" Mick asked.

"I couldn't bear to think you guys would swim in the big waves without me," he replied.

Jack moved a third rock into place and started recoiling the jib of the crane. After some complex maneuvering, Conrad managed to position the dump truck to back gingerly along the sand access path, past the dormant crane and right up to the area of the Blackberry Beach Gap. Kenny stood on top of the largest rock, waving his gloved hands to Conrad, beckoning him to keep moving backward. But before he quite reached the spot where he could effectively dump his payload, his massive drive wheels started to spin in the gushy mud by the side of the trailer park entrance.

"Come on," Kenny shouted, not realizing the problem. "Another ten or twenty feet."

Conrad shifted and tried to move backward and forward, but between the weight of the truck and the softness of the surface below him, his wheels sunk deeper into the muck.

They all surrounded the vehicle and brainstormed ideas. Mick desperately suggested they push, which elicited laughter from Kenny, Jack and Conrad. Kenny offered to swing his bulldozer around and give the rig a shove. But Jack came up with the final idea

"Dump out half the sand on the eastern side of the dune and push it into place with the bulldozer," he called to Kenny through the rain and occasional blusters of wind. "We'll detach the hopper from the cab, secure it to four joist cables and I'll lift it over to the far side with the crane."

"We'll make two big deposits on either side and I'll use the dozer to fill it into the middle," Kenny agreed.

Conrad raised the front of the payload, spilling a massive pile of sand out the back. Kenny drove the bulldozer all the way around, through the entrance to the town beach and out across the road to the back side of the trailer park. Conrad detached the cab from the back of the dump truck and helped Mick, Dana and Jack secure the four joist chains from the corners of the free-standing hopper to the crane's main block.

As Kenny busily handled his task, Jack slowly raised the sand-filled ten-gauge steel hopper into the air. Sand spilled into the wind like grains in an hourglass. Mick and Dana stood far back and watched as the lightning from over the ocean illuminated the silver hunk of heavy machinery. Jack adeptly lowered it in place, just above the high tide mark. He pulled different levers in the cab of the crane, causing the front of the hopper to rise while the bottom remained close to the ground. The maneuver resulted in a massive pour of sand into a pile on the far side of the dunes.

Jack's activity concluded just as Kenny arrived to push the sand pile into place on top of the base of dirt, clay and rock they had previously erected.

Mick texted Ronnie to ask about the poker game.

"Winding down," he replied. "How's it going there?"

"Almost done," Mick wrote. "Can you buy us more time?"

A long pause made Mick nervous as he watched Jack lift the dump truck hopper back into the air.

"Pat's hungry," Aaron said. "Marty's going to whip up some chocolate chip cookies. Might get you a half hour?"

Mick waved to Kenny and pointed to his wrist to give him the heads up that they needed to clear out. Kenny held up both hands to indicate he required ten minutes to finish constructing the dune. He watched Jack in the cab of the crane, pulling levers frantically. He heard Conrad swear as one of the chains pulled loose from the iron hook affixed to the Gusset Pocket of the hopper.

The giant tub wavered in the air. The crane buckled. Jack looked calm, but flared eyes at Conrad, who swore into the wind at the realization of the situation.

"Oh no," Mick tried to sympathize with his brother. "Your truck."

"I'm not worried about that," he said. "I was going to junk it anyway. I can write off the loss."

Mick and Dana looked at him, confused.

"It's evidence," he completed his thought, waving a piece of scrap metal he found along the base of the trailer park wall.

Conrad ran out to the beach to catch Jack's attention. He waved his arms and pointed toward the ocean. As he did, he used the metal to pry the license plate off the back of the hopper.

Jack looked at him perplexed, before picking up his meaning and giving a thumbs up sign. Instead of trying to bring the hopper back, over the dunes, he swung it toward the raging water. He gently lowered it on top of a wave and let it slide along the back of the swell into the water, just beyond the infamous Matunuck ditch. They watched it float outward with the waning tide. As it disappeared from sight, it filled with seawater and sank like a shipwreck. Four boom cables fell from the sky, ejected from the top of the jib by Jack with a flip of a switch. Kenny rode the bulldozer back to the trailer park entrance. Jack withdrew the rig and returned the crane to its dormant state.

Mick checked his phone and alerted the crew that high tide had passed and that the ocean should continue to recede.

"I just hope the ocean takes my hopper far enough out that nobody finds it," Conrad said. "They better not be able to trace it back to me."

"If that happens," Kenny said. "We'll all cop and share the blame."

"Might I remind you all," Dana said. "For one, we just might have saved Matunuck tonight. And for two, Jack has a contract to build a wall here. That's all he did tonight."

"Not much of one," Jack shouted over the scream of the wind.

Mick flinched at the feel of his phone vibrating in his pocket.

"Can't hold him off any longer," Ronnie texted. "Leaving now."

They all looked at each other. Conrad jumped into the cab and spun his wheels to escape. Kenny pulled up in front of him and gave him a shove out of his rut.

"I'm going to try and make it to Cards Pond Road and park in the lot for the theater before Pat gets to the Beach Road from Washington Ave."

Kenny jumped in the cab of his bulldozer and tried to follow behind Conrad. But at only a few miles an hour, he decided to turn back. Instead, he rolled his machine right into a grove of cherry blossoms and lowered his bucket and ripper below the top of the growth.

They heard Pat's car and watched it pass the Vanilla Bean toward the entrance to the newly enhanced Blackberry Beach Gap. Dana, Mick, Kenny and Jack crawled in the mud under the long track wheels of the crane.

The police car pulled into the sandy accessway. The headlights illuminated the gravel in front of the crane. They heard the door slam. They could just make out Pat's rubber boots and the trail of his flashlight as he shined it on their makeshift natural berm. They huddled closely and froze as Pat spotlighted the ocean. He inspected the holes where Jack had removed the three boulders. He stepped right up to the track wheels and shined his light into the cab of the crane. He placed his hand on the hood of the still-warm engine.

Time seemed to stop. Mick, Dana and Jack froze. Rainwater dripped from the undercarriage of the crane onto their heads. Their hands sunk deeper into the muck. Pat returned to his car and opened the door. They heard him laugh to himself, as he cranked the vehicle into reverse and drove away.

Chapter 36

Shelly stayed up late watching television and listening to the rain dance on her roof. She checked her phone for a message from Mick. She wondered how his father's operation went. She also hoped to apologize for insulting him. Mostly, she just wanted to hear his voice.

She blamed herself for pushing him away, for holding his hand that day on the beach; for liking him in a romantic sense. She thought of her two other major personal entanglements over the past dozen years; first the showdown with Joycie in high school over Kyle, and then the jerk she lived with a couple years before meeting Mick.

The sound of the rain filled her bedroom with white noise. And yet, it felt eerily quiet to her. She muted the television and started a new text to Mick.

"Thinking about you," she typed, without sending at first. "Hoping your father's okay."

She stared at her words, pondering each choice. Should she write out full sentences? Should it be "thinking of you" or "thinking of you tonight"? Should the last line end in "okay", "alright" or "well"?

Before she clicked 'Send', she heard pounding on her door. Loud claps of thunder vibrated her roof and windows. But the simple knock on her door gave her the biggest jolt of nerves down her spine.

"Coming," she shouted, as a second, more urgent set of rapping echoed through her kitchen.

"Can we come in?" Lindsay asked. "They're terrified of the lightning. We're surrounded by windows up in that third-floor bedroom. None of us can sleep with the flashes and the pounding of the thunder."

Shelly withheld the urge to laugh at her sister for fearing the distant rumble of thunder over the ocean and the faint traces of heat lightning past Block Island. She invited them into the cottage.

"It's late," she said. "You're wet. Let me throw your clothes in the dryer."

Lindsay thanked her sister and gave her a tentative and awkward hug. The two girls hugged each leg and thanked their 'Auntie'.

Shelly hung their rain coats and offered them Golden Oreo cookies from her sparse cupboard.

Lindsay apologized for the late-night intrusion, but Shelly assured her she was just watching random television and didn't mind.

"You and the girls can take the bedroom," Shelly insisted. "I'm fine on the couch."

The two girls brushed their teeth and hopped onto Shelly's bed. Lindsay tucked them in and promised to join them shortly.

"I want you to know," Lindsay said. "I've started looking. It may take some time to find a place I can afford, but I'm going to pull it together and get out of your hair."

Her bracelets jingled as she glanced through the bedroom door, leaned in and whispered.

"Pavinuzzi has an angle with Jeremy," she said. "He found a flaw and thinks he can exploit a loophole. I'll keep you posted."

Shelly left a nightlight in the corner of her bedroom and stood her phone against her clock alarm playing soft Disney soundtrack songs to dull the sound of the storm.

Lindsay squeezed between her daughters under the covers and thanked Shelly for her hospitality.

As soon as Shelly closed the door, she regretted leaving her phone. She had yet to push the text to Mick that she wanted to send.

She lay on her couch, staring out the window at the mad surf. The rain subsided. A window opened in the clouds along the horizon. She could see the bottom edge of the orange Harvest Moon somewhere in the sky between Block Island and Orient Point, New York.

Restless, she continued to miss her friendship with Mick. Out her family room window, she strained to see if she could spot a light in Mick's window. But his entire house seemed as dark as the overhead sky. She opened her front door and gauged the temperature. She threw on a pair of shoes and a rain jacket. The hood slumped over her eyes until she cast it backwards to hang limply between her shoulder blades. She brushed her straight blond hair behind her ears.

A bigger piece of the moon revealed itself from behind the clouds, casting a faint orange glow across the cobblestone driveway.

Shelly imagined herself moving out of the cottage. She pictured herself living somewhere other than Matunuck. She wondered if living next door to Mick placed them too close to each other, leading to their status as good friends instead of anything more than that.

The waves, still ferocious, seemed to dull slightly with the passing of the tide from flowing to ebbing. Less choppy, they rolled more smoothly than earlier in the evening. The increasing orange glow from the moon highlighted the giant dimples between the swells. Shelly decided to stand in the cold, wet sand and watch the waves crash to the shore for a while.

In the distance, she heard voices. She looked as far as she could, but the darkness and the distance betrayed her senses. She retreated to the porch of her inn and engaged her telescope. With some focus and another increase in the intensity of the moonlight, she made out the form of five bodies frolicking in the water.

Still enormous, the five daredevils floated over each wave like cars on a rollercoaster. She zoomed in and recognized Mick, Dana, Conrad, Kenny and another man that looked familiar to her, but whom she couldn't quite place.

As she zoomed back out, the left side of the frame caught her eye. She saw the natural sand dune, sloped and misshapen. Compared to the diagrams of massive seawalls from the town meeting, it looked like as if a bunch of children had tried to recreate the state's grand plans with a giant plastic shovel and pail. The bright, new sand shined like a movie screen, reflecting the orange moonlight. Shelly set aside the telescope. The moon peeked to half way beyond the break of the clouds.

She felt her bare feet squish in the soft sand. A gust of rogue rain washed over her. It coated her hair and wet the top of her shirt that stuck up from the inside the rain jacket.

As she neared Roy Carpenter's Beach, she saw one of the swimmers ride a twelve-foot wave and crash to the beach. The other four bobbed over the rolling surf like seagulls or buoys.

"Mick," Shelly thought as she walked the beach in his direction.

Though the lightning over Block Island had subsided for at least the past thirty minutes and the rain finally stopped with the parting of the clouds, she still considered them crazy for venturing into the dark ocean, even with the spotlights atop the crane lighting the area.

The mammoth wave crashed Mick to the sand and spit him past the high tide mark to the base of their makeshift sand dune. He sat, wet, bloodied and sore with the lapping of the next wave riding up his legs and into his face. He watched his siblings and best friends laugh and cheer as they played in the surf like teenagers.

"Come on Mickey," shouted Conrad as he took a similar tumble from the top of a gargantuan swell.

Conrad slid across the pebbles not far from Mick. He groaned from the pain while simultaneously laughing from the thrill. He army crawled through the aftermath of a second wave to Mick's side.

"Some crazy night, huh?" he asked. "Definitely goes down in our Matunuck book of stories to tell our grandkids."

Mick didn't respond. He looked to the west. He could barely trace the spire of the inn on the horizon. A light flickered in one of the windows.

"Mickers," Kenny called from fifteen feet in the air as he soared over a wave. "Come on back in. These are the biggest waves in the past ten years."

"What is it?" Conrad asked quietly, as Dana, Kenny and Jack yelped in ecstasy from just beyond the break of the waves.

"I'd love to keep swimming with you guys," Mick said. "But something's missing."

Conrad looked west with Mick.

"Or someone?"

Noticing them sitting by their lobsided sand dune, Dana, Kenny and Jack emerged from the water, hobbling and sprinting to escape the undertow.

"Are you coming back in?" Dana asked.

"Nah, I'm calling it a night," Mick replied. "I have to do something."

Mick rubbed a towel across his dripping hair. He thanked Dana for having driven them to his house to pick up bathing suits and towels.

"I always have mine in the car," Dana said. "Because you never know."

Kenny decided to drive the bulldozer back to the garage. Jack said he had a hotel room awaiting him in Wakefield.

"I'm freezing," he said. "I can't believe you losers convinced me to do this."

"Uh, you were the first one in, Jackie," said Mick.

"No, not the swimming," he replied. "I'm from Maine. This is nothing. I can't believe we built this freaking sand dune – in just a couple hours."

"It looks like crap," Conrad observed. "Definitely the amateur hour here."

"It's not about building *THE* wall," Mick said. "It was about building *A* wall and showing what could be."

"Good," Kenny added. "Cause if the ocean rose another couple a feet, you know this little mound a sand and mud ain't gonna do nothing to protect them cottages."

"It's symbolic," Mick said. "We're just trying to make a point and build up a little publicity."

As Kenny disappeared past the Vanilla Bean in his bulldozer, Jack gave Mick, Conrad and Dana hugs and thanked them for another memorable Matunuck night.

"I'm going to have to come down here more often," he said.

"The king is back," Mick yelled to him as he climbed the sand dune toward the main road.

Dana glanced up and down the Matunuck Beach Road. She saw Jack walk to his car in front of the pub and speed down the road behind Kenny. Mick stood alone on the beach with his brother and sister. The moon peeked past halfway beyond the clouds.

"We better get out of here too," she said. "It's way past midnight. I'll drive you both back to the house."

As Dana made the suggestion, Mick noticed the figure walking between Willow Dell and the town beach. Conrad and Dana exchanged knowing glances.

"We'll just meet you back there," said Dana.

"It's unlocked," Mick replied.

"Good luck," Conrad winked at him. "With whatever it is you need to do."

Mick nodded, hugged both siblings and thanked them for a great night before parting with them and heading back toward the western side of the beach.

The moon peeked three quarters out of the clouds enabling Mick to make out Shelly's sleek, slender body. He put on his t-shirt and flung the towel around his shoulders. Goosebumps exploded from the pores in his arms. They approached each other just as the moon broke free from the clouds and shrouded them in golden light from above.

"You did this?" she asked, nodding her head at the mound of sand that stretched from the town beach parking lot to the side of the trailer park wall.

"I don't know what you're talking about," Mick replied with a sly smile. "It was here when I got here."

"I see," she giggled. "You could've gotten yourself killed swimming in these huge waves after midnight."

"I know the Matunuck surf like the back of my hand," Mick replied noting a gash and string of dried blood across one of his knuckles. "What are you doing out so late?"

"I couldn't sleep," she answered. "How's your dad?"

"No word," he said. "We thought we might have heard from Doctor Clark by now. I'm sure he's fine. I guess we'll just have to wait to find out tomorrow morning to make sure nothing went wrong overnight."

Mick paused. The moonlight tangled its golden fingers in Shelly's thin, blond hair.

"I have a solution for you," Mick said with a sheepish grin.

"About what?" she asked.

"You should give her the guest house."

"Who? Lindsay?"

"She needs a zip code to keep her kids in school. And they need the stability of a home."

"I was actually thinking about that," Shelly said, the glow of the moon casting an aura around her head and illuminating her face in soft backlight. "I've lived here my whole life. I mean, literally here. On the beach. And I love it. But maybe I'm growing stagnant. Maybe I've been too complacent. I thought I was happy. But, maybe there's something else out there for me. Maybe it's time I moved on and tried living somewhere else."

"No way," Mick said. "You belong here, in Matunuck."

"Well then, where would I live?" Shelly asked. "I'm not sure I could squeeze into the guest house with Lindsay and both her kids for too long. And, I want to help them out."

"You should move north,"

"Blackberry Hill?" she asked. "I couldn't afford to pay Lindsay the six figures she almost sued me for. I sure don't have a million plus for a place up there. Or do you mean the other side of the Post Road? It's definitely a little more affordable, but I couldn't imagine having to drive to the beach."

"No," Mick laughed at her, drawing closer. "Just by a couple hundred feet."

Shelly didn't follow him at first. Then the light in her eyes twinkled as his meaning dawned on her.

"My dad's moving out," Mick elaborated. "Once he fully recovers, he's going to live with Larraine. It'll be lonely without him by myself in that big empty house."

"So, you're looking for a roommate?" Shelly asked, angling her face and leaning into him.

"Well," Mick hedged, shifting the weight between his feet before exhaling and taking a deep breath. "Absolutely."

As Mick moved toward her, a pang struck Shelly in the stomach. She placed her hand on his chest and lightly pushed him away.

"It's a great offer," she said, imagining herself as Mick's houseguest. "And the answer's 'Yes'."

Mick looked at her curiously.

"But...?" he asked.

"But I think we should just be friends."

Chapter 37

The bell rang at three fifteen on June 21st, the official first evening of summer. Mick wished his students a great break as they bolted out of the room.

Ricky Dolman handed him a 'Thank You' card with a hundred-dollar gift certificate to the pub. Petey gave him a hug and told him this was the year he was finally going to beat him in whiffle ball. Several other students dropped cards and gift certificates onto his desk. Most of the flimsy pieces of paper entitled him to a free ice cream cone at the Vanilla Bean.

Haley offered him a ride home, but he decided to stretch his legs and enjoy the perfect Matunuck weather. As he turned up the Matunuck Beach Road, he traced the contour of the long straight street past the Vanilla Bean, across the marsh and up the back incline of the gorgeous natural berm that Jack Valerian's landscape engineering firm built with town, state and federal funds across the Blackberry Beach Gap.

As he neared Cards Pond Road, a small, compact car pulled to the side of the shoulder next to him. Kian Taomessina popped his head out the window and offered him a ride. But Mick declined, opting to soak the sun and gain the exercise.

"You're going to meet us at the grill for dinner tonight though, right?"

"Definitely," Mick confirmed. "It'll be my last chance to see my daughter for the next six months."

Kian gave a thumbs up.

"How are you doing?" Mick asked, leaning into the opened passenger side window.

"If we can't make it through a long-distance relationship during her internship and work-study semester," Kian said. "Then I guess we just don't belong together. The only alternative is for me to quit my job and go to Maryland with her."

"And that's asking a lot at this point," Mick agreed. "You're what, twenty-two? You've got a good job."

"And I love it here," he said. "I go back and forth. Part of me wants to quit and follow her there. And part of me feels like I need to let her go and hope she comes back to me. I honestly don't know what I'm going to do."

"You can't quit," Mick said. "You just got that grant to study the effect of that mysterious truck with no license plate or identifiable registration information buried out past the sandbar in front of Blackberry Beach."

"An unsolved mystery for sure," Kian agreed. "Kind of like with Mel and me. I guess our little love story will just have to remain unfinished for a little while as well."

"I guess so," Mick acknowledged.

Mick wished the young man the best of luck and promised to see him at the grill later that evening.

Kian sped off to the beach while Mick turned west toward the driveway to the inn. He entered his house. The screen door slammed. Shelly greeted him from the kitchen and reminded him of their dinner at the grill.

"I know," he replied. "I remember."

"I was thinking we'd walk there instead of taking the car," she said. "It's a nice night and the ocean is so calm."

"Like a pond," Mick agreed, "And the beach is nice and wide today."

Mick headed up to his studio to edit his tenth and final song for the indie album he hoped to release by Labor Day. At the top of his Word document with all his lyrics, he looked at the dreary album title; 'EROSION'. He highlighted the seven letters and replaced the downbeat sentiment with a new, more upbeat and positive album title; 'MATUNUCK'.

After an hour and a half, Shelly poked her head though the doorjamb and pointed at her watch. They strode past Lindsay's guest cottage and entered the inn. Marty carted two plates of swordfish with gorgonzola and capers across the aisle to Kyle and Joycie Dolman. They smiled and waved to him. He wished them a happy anniversary.

Shelly asked if Marty had seen Lindsay, and he told her she'd be at the grill all night as she expected a busy dinner crowd beyond the extended Maguire family.

They slipped off their shoes and walked barefoot in the waning sun. The dunes along Roy Carpenter's beach looked the same as they had seven months earlier around the time Hurricane Cecilia grazed the Rhode Island coast. They still resembled wedding cakes with their sculpted layering and their tall, rigid steepness. The damaged homes along the front row of the village had long since been removed. The remaining houses looked relatively unscathed from the long winter.

They passed Willow Dell and ambled up the incline by the town beach. They met Jack Valerian in the parking lot with his daughter after a long day of relaxing in the sun and swimming in the placid surf.

Shelly gave him a hug. Mick smacked hands with him and scolded him for not telling him he was in town.

"I know, man," Jack said. "First I was so busy with the project. Then, I owed this little princess a lot of quality time. We're going to be down a lot more this summer. I'm going to rent a house next to Benji's place on Washington. I'll roast you in whiffle ball. I promise."

Shelly and Jack's daughter wandered toward the marsh to take a closer look at the man-made berm atop of the infamous Blackberry Beach Gap. Shelly complimented Jack on how beautiful it came out.

Out of earshot, Jack slung an arm around Mick's shoulder and whispered privately to him.

"You never explained how that night worked out," he said.

Mick smirked and looked over his shoulder.

"I was there on the beach with her," he explained. "The moon was out. I had just asked her to move in with me."

"Even though you weren't even dating or anything at that point?" Jack clarified.

"Yes, that's right."

"Bold and risky move."

"She seemed into it," Mick continued. "I thought for sure she wanted to kiss me. She seemed like she was moving toward me. I leaned in to kiss her and then she stopped me."

"Rejected?" Jack asked.

"I guess," Mick replied. "She put her hand on my chest and told me she just wanted to be friends."

"Ouch," Jack replied. "So, what did you do next?"

Mick noticed Shelly and Jack's daughter returning from viewing the natural barrier that his company constructed. Jack stood at attention and removed his hand from Mick's back. Shelly looked at them with vague awareness of their conversation's subject matter.

Before Shelly reached full earshot, Mick whispered to his friend a quick answer.

"I played the stubborn ass card," he said. "I'll call and explain later."

Mick and Shelly took the bamboo tunnel between the town beach and the Vanilla Bean parking lot. They rounded the bend by Community Road and spotted the orange, red and green neon sign above the building that used to be known as Bozzutto's Tuni Grill.

Instead, the name of the place now read; 'Gordie Maguire's Beachside Grill'. The sign, which hung from the stylish new arched wooden roof recently added to the structure, cast a multi-colored glow across the parking lot. The blur of color resembled an Irish flag.

"It chokes me up every time I see that sign and think that you and Lindsay named your new place in honor of my dad," Mick commented.

"That was all Lindsay," Shelly said. "It was mostly her money that she got from Jeremy in the palimony suit. I'm just a silent partner. She wanted to reflect the spirit of Matunuck."

They entered the busy restaurant. Melodie threw her arms around her father and thanked him for attending her sendoff. Kian shook both sets of hands and led them to a table with Trudy, Haley, Miles and their two kids. Conrad, with his wife and two kids sat with Dana and her family at the next table. Mick's cousin, Bethanne, took the orders and served the meals.

Mick excused himself and rounded the corner back into the smaller section of the building with the grill. Lindsay frantically sliced vegetables for the salad and darted into the back room to refill the lettuce bin. She gave him a smile before disappearing through the back door. Her chef's apron flew behind her as she vanished from sight.

"I wanted to offer my compliments to the chef," Mick called to the hunched, white-haired fry-cook.

A bit more frail, with a slight hunch, Gordie Maguire turned, spatula in hand, and gave his son a wave.

"Assistant Chef anyway," Gordie replied. "Give my regards to the guest of honor. Tell her I'll be out to give her a big hug and a kiss after I finish grilling up all these dinner orders."

Mick gave him a thumbs-up sign and told him to give his best to Larraine. Gordie grilled his signature steak sandwiches and big round juicy burgers for the packed house before joining the family to wish Melodie a safe trip.

Soon after, they visited the side window at the Vanilla Bean for ice cream cones before watching Kian drive Melodie up the Matunuck Beach Road toward the airport for her flight to Maryland.

Mick and Shelly returned along the beach. The golden sun drifted toward the horizon, calling to mind the night when they met up under the Harvest Moon.

Shelly slipped her hand into Mick's, as she had the afternoon, two and a half years earlier, when Gordie ceremoniously poured his wife's ashes into the sea.

"It all happened right here," Mick commented. "My mom. My dad. That crazy night we got caught in Hurricane Constance."

"The night under the Harvest Moon after Hurricane Cecilia," Shelly added with a nudge to the ribs. "Thank God you're such a stubborn ass and didn't listen to me."

"Thank God, you kissed me back instead of smacking me," Mick replied.

Shelly tugged Mick by the hand.

"Come on Mickey," she said. "Let's get back."

"What's the hurry?" he asked.

"It's the first night of the summer," she said. "I just want to celebrate."

"Shamrock ice cream pie at the inn?" Mick asked.

"It's been at least twelve hours since I woke up in your arms," she cooed. "I'm ready to go back again."

Hand-in-hand, they trotted into the setting sun from the town beach, to Willow Dell, to Roy Carpenter's and eventually disappearing over the dunes by the inn, back to their shared home.

The End

If you loved EROSION, consider other works by Greg McLaughlin available at select bookstores and on Amazon.com including:

MATUNUCK: *Romantic Comedy & Family Drama* – A Prequel to EROSION, MATUNUCK tells the story of how Mick Maguire returns to the sleepy beach community of his childhood after eighteen long years. He arrives to care for his ailing parents and sell the family beach house, eliminating the Maguire family from Matunuck. A tale of love, loss, romance and forgiveness, Mick makes a last-minute effort to reconnect with old friends and reconcile with his family before it's too late. Available at **Wakefield Books**; *Wakefield, RI*, **Rarities Books & Bindery**; *Wakefield, RI* or at http://amazon.com/dp/B08NX2WNNM/

THE TRIPLE DATE: *Romantic Comedy* - Rival marketing directors compete for the same job while their teenaged children begin dating each other and their single parents start a poorly hidden affair. Along the way they fight their own attraction to each other as only one of them can possibly earn the big promotion. http://amazon.com/dp/1720272468/

BROKEN ENGLISH: *Social-Political Drama* - A husband and father is forcibly deported by immigration agents and must survive the streets of a foreign country without any money, a job, a place to live or even a working understanding of the language. Meanwhile his wife and teenaged children battle the U.S. legal system to secure his return. http://amazon.com/dp/1092225536/

THE SECOND COMING: *Spiritual Thriller* - When a charismatic, mysterious figure arrives in Manhattan, people take sides as to whether this potential new Messiah could be a divine revolutionary sent to change the world for the better, or a menace and threat to society that must be destroyed. Would there be peace? Or would there be further violence and conflict? Would a possible second coming unite our world or tear it apart? http://amazon.com/dp/1723767581/

UNDER THE AURORA: *Crime Thriller* - A mentally-ill, suicidal homeless man witnesses a horrific human trafficking crime and has to evade corrupt cops, a deadly human trafficking ring and vengeful gang-leaders while escaping the streets of Seattle with the homeless woman he loves. http://lnkd.in/e_i9Asz

THE B TEAM: *Romantic Comedy & Sports Drama* - All Braden Shaw wants to do is play ball. Why can't the parents and coaches understand that? A romantic comedy, social satire and feel-good family sports story all wrapped in one. http://amazon.com/dp/B08KJHVZJ1/

THE THIRD PARTY: *Political Thriller* - "Don't vote for PARTY, POLICY, or PERSONALITY," says Gov. Clinton Groverton, Independent Candidate for the Office of the President. "Vote for LEADERSHIP." The problem; for more than fifty years, no independent Presidential candidate has won even a single state. As charismatic, smart and principled as he is, can Groverton compete with the two entrenched, cut-throat parties in his unlikely bid for the most powerful job in the world? http://amazon.com/dp/1728714788/

THE CURVE IN THE ROAD: *Supernatural Thriller* – Cooper Jackman can't forget. His hyperactive memory recalls every image of every moment of his life. It includes minute details such as the score of a ball game on a specific date. It also forces him to relive his worst memories such as the accident that disabled the love of his life as if having happened that moment. Can Cooper use power to save? Can he escape it as a curse? https://www.amazon.com/dp/1790661978/

HEADLOCK: *Personal Memoir* - A non-fiction account of how I found the motivation in my late 40's to lose 80 pounds in one year by running 1,000 miles, lifting weights, doing 10,000 pushups and working out with college NCAA wrestling teams to prepare for and compete in the USA Wrestling Senior National Championship. http://amazon.com/dp/1728773687/

Made in the USA
Middletown, DE
09 July 2021

43864071R00169